INDIAN COUNTRY

By Philip Caputo

A RUMOR OF WAR
HORN OF AFRICA
DELCORSO'S GALLERY
INDIAN COUNTRY

PHILIP CAPUTO

INDIAN COUNTRY

BANTAM BOOKS

TORONTO • NEW YORK • LONDON • SYDNEY • AUCKLAND

INDIAN COUNTRY
A Bantam Book / June 1987

Grateful acknowledgment is made for permission to reprint the following excerpts:
Poems by Lloyd Frank Merrell from WHEN PINE WAS KING by Lewis Reimann,
copyright © 1952 by Lewis Reimann. Reissued under 1981 copyright © by Avery Color
Studios, AuTrain, Michigan 49806. Indian Chants are modified versions from
CHIPPEWA CUSTOMS, reprinted by the Minnesota Historical Society Press,
copyright © 1979. "THE RED-HEADED STRANGER" by Carl Stutz and Edith
Lindeman, copyright © 1953, 1962 PINE RIDGE MUSIC CORPORATION, copyright
© Renewed 1981 CBS CATALOGUE PARTNERSHIP. All Rights Controlled &
Administered by CBS ROBBINS CATALOG INC. All Rights Reserved. International
Copyright Secured. Used by Permission. "MY FATHERS HOUSE" copyright ©
Bruce Springsteen ASCAP. "GOODNIGHT SAIGON" by Billy Joel, copyright ©
1981, 1982 JOEL SONGS. All Rights Controlled & Administered by BLACKWOOD
MUSIC INC. All Rights Reserved. International Copyright Secured. Used by
Permission.

Library of Congress Catloging-in-Publication Data

Caputo, Philip.
   Indian country.

   I. Title.
PS3553.A625I5   1987   813'.54   86-26606
ISBN 0-553-05187-3

Published simultaneously in the United States and Canada

Bantam Books are published by Bantam Books, Inc. Its trademark, consisting
of the words "Bantam Books" and the portrayal of a rooster, is Registered
in U.S. Patent and Trademark Office and in other countries. Marca Registrada.
Bantam Books, Inc., 666 Fifth Avenue, New York, New York 10103.

PRINTED IN THE UNITED STATES OF AMERICA
MV   0 9 8 7 6 5 4 3 2 1

This book is for
BILL HAWK

With special thanks to
Linda Grey, for her invaluable
insights and suggestions; Aaron
Priest, for his patience and faith;
and to Jim Harrison and Thomas
Sanchez, for their help and friendship

Indian country (in'dē ən kun'trē) *n.* [*U.S. mil. slang*] 1. term used by American soldiers during Vietnam conflict (1961–75) to designate territory under enemy control or any terrain considered hostile and dangerous   2. [*fig.*] a place, condition or circumstance that is alien and dangerous

God of the Sea, I beg you, punish Ulysses for this. Visit him with storm and shipwreck and sorceries. Let him wander many years before he reaches home, and when he gets there let him find himself forgotten, unwanted, a stranger.

—H O M E R,
The Odyssey

INDIAN
COUNTRY

ONE
WABUNNOONG´
(EAST)

1

The motion of the earth no longer seemed synchronous with the movements of the clock. The time was not yet four on a mid-April afternoon; there should have been plenty of daylight left, yet dusk was falling in the Huron Mountains, the wilderness where the two young men had been hiking since late morning. A horizon two thousand feet high hid the sun, lowering over Lake Superior, and the pine branches overhead dimmed a sky that would have appeared bright to anyone outside the forest. The false twilight deepened as the minutes ticked toward evening; the dense trees, swiftly turning from green to black, intensified the shadows cast by the highest hills until the ravines and valleys appeared buried under drifts of powdered coal. The impression of an advancing darkness was strongest alongside the river the two young men were following, the Windigo, a fast trout stream swollen by spring floods. Thick stands of bog spruce grew down to the river's edge, their reflections muddying its clarity so that channels only two or three feet deep looked twice that, the pools beneath the overhanging banks fathomless. In the deep shade, gloomy as a midnight swamp, it seemed to Christian Starkmann as though the elements of nature had, for some secret and malevolent reason of their own, conspired to force night to fall before its time. Starkmann was no stranger to the wilds; but he had never been in them during any season other than the summer, the lush and drowsy summer, when, at this northern latitude, the light did not begin to die until nine o'clock. The forest wore an alien mask now, and its premature blackening quickened a dread in him, of what he didn't know.

He paused for a moment and relieved his aching shoulders by bending forward, shifting the full weight of his pack onto his back. He was very tall, with strong, wiry legs, but his torso was like an overtrained marathoner's: somewhere between lean and consumptive, poorly designed for carrying heavy burdens.

"Not much farther," said his friend, a stocky Ojibwa known as Bonny George, a shortened version of his cumbersome name, Boniface George St. Germaine. "Half an hour on the outside."

"I hope so. You have to get used to this. I don't."

"You mean they don't make you carry fifty-pound packs in divinity school?"

"They make us read Scripture and sing 'A Mighty Fortress Is Our God.' "

"How are you going to get used to carrying the weight of sin? The weight of your own sins and those of your flock?"

"Lutheran ministers don't hear confessions. And they don't hump heavy packs for miles unless they're missionaries, and the Mormons have pretty well cornered the missionary market."

Starkmann enjoyed the sound of their voices, which seemed to hold back the threat of the ever-increasing darkness.

"Don't whine," said Bonny George. "In the old days, Indian trappers used to carry a hundred and fifty pounds of hides on their backs. That's how we used to measure distance. Ningo'anse' biwin, meaning 'from one resting place to the next.' The distance a man could hump that weight before he had to stop, maybe half a mile."

"Save the history lessons for later. Let's go. I don't want to pitch camp by flashlight."

"You'll thank me for this tomorrow, you yellow-haired honkie. The rainbows in there are big as salmon, I swear."

Bonny George hooked his thumbs under the straps of his olive-drab Duluth bag and smiled. He had a beautiful smile, as engaging and uncomplicated as a child's, his black eyes laughing in the copper disc of his face. Then he turned and started up the trail with his quick, springy stride. Starkmann followed, tightening the bellyband of his pack to ease the pull on his shoulders. On a street in town, he would have appeared the more impressive and graceful of the two: six feet five inches tall, a human spire crowned by blond hair so pale it was almost white. But in the woods, he felt bony and awkward compared to his friend, whose compact physique and agile movements reminded him of a bobcat or wolverine. Starkmann's feet, which had carried him effortlessly down football fields and varnished basketball courts, stumbled in the twilight on half-buried rocks and tripped over the tree roots that twisted across the trail like petrified snakes. The low branches snatched at the canteen buckled to his belt, caught on the rod case tied to his pack, and slapped his face, each slap telling him that the forest bore him some malice. How strange it looked in this season, with the hardwood branches bearing only a hint of green, the trunks bruised by the winter, whose battering had ended only two weeks ago, when the last snowdrifts melted and the rivers sent the last floes of ice spinning into Lake Superior.

The earth still held buried memories of winter: a cold that lay just beneath the surface, a cold that the air, chilled by the loss of light, seemed to draw upward through the thin crust of sandy pine loam. Starkmann could see his breath as they climbed out of the spruce bog and up a granite ridge. Ahead of him, steam rose off Bonny George's sweat-spotted shirt.

The walking was easier on the crest of the ridge. The granite, troweled smooth by receding glaciers and two hundred centuries of floods and weather, lay on the forest floor like a slab of pavement from a lost city, its gray stained by moss and lichens. Below, the river butted noisily into a line of boulders that barred the water's headlong rush for the lake, miles downstream. Bonny George turned off the trail and onto a deer run, weaving downhill through tangled tag-alders to the riverbank. Without a second's hesitation he jumped onto the nearest boulder, then sprang to the next and the next, until he was on the other side. Starkmann, who'd never felt clumsier, stood poised at the water's edge, looking down into the river. It sent up a misty spray as it crashed against the natural barrier, then sluiced through the channels between the boulders before tumbling down a series of slick granite steps into the deep waters of the spruce forest. He judged the distance to the first rock to be four feet; with his long legs he could have made it in a single stride, but the river's white leap and lunge made him dizzy. The channel widened before his eyes, magnified by his anxiety into a chasm. He saw himself swept under by the freezing current, search teams dragging for his blue, lifeless body.

"He who hesitates is lost," Bonny George shouted above the roar. "On the other hand, look before you leap."

Starkmann took his eyes from the moving water, stretched his legs across the gap, and balanced himself atop the boulder. He hopped onto the next, and the one after that, then, pulled to one side by his shifting pack, slipped on the fourth. He saved himself from falling in by desperately embracing the rock, though his left leg got wet up to the knee, the cold so intense it was as if a vise had been clamped on his calf.

"Jesus!" he hollered, jerking his leg out. "Jee*sus!*"

"Your Jesus can't help you now, preacher's son. C'mon."

He stood, and in three more jumps reached the far side, where he emptied his boot and rubbed the circulation back into his numbed foot.

"All I've got to say is that those fish had better be as big as salmon."

"I caught a six-pound rainbow in there last year. Almost no one fishes this stretch of river. Too far into the bush. It's damn near virgin."

"Virginity admits to no degrees," Starkmann said, trying to sound flip and funny to conceal his uneasy feeling, strengthened by the near fall into the river, that the wilderness possessed an active hostility.

He laced up his boot and followed Bonny George through another thicket of tag-alders, then up a sandy bluff atop which hemlock towered more than a hundred feet and strands of grandfather lichen hung like tinsel from the branches of balsam fir. The Indian led the way onto an ancient logging road—a track so faint it would have been invisible if this had been summer—and walked along it to a clearing where the ruins of a two-story log cabin stood in a stubble of berry bushes and bracken fern. Windowless, with a low doorway on ground level and another above, a bare pole leaning from a squat lookout tower on the roof, and the chinking between the logs long since crumbled to dust, it was as forlorn a building as Starkmann had ever seen.

"This is it?" he asked, disappointed. He had expected palisades, blockhouses, rusty cannons pointing toward the forests, where, he imagined, painted war-parties once crouched, signaling with birdcalls before the dawn attack. "This is your great discovery?"

"This is it." Bonny George dropped his Duluth bag. "I didn't discover it. Grandpa did, years ago. Remember his camp?"

"Sure," Starkmann answered, picturing the brown and black dome of Louis St. Germaine's wigwam and the canvas tarp that sheltered the old man's fire-scorched cooking pots.

"It's only three, four miles from here."

Starkmann's eyes followed the Indian's finger, pointing eastward, then returned to the decayed cabin.

"You said a fort. An honest-to-God frontier fort."

"You forget. I'm an Indian, a maker of myths, a dreamer of dreams. I exaggerated."

"What about the trout as big as salmon?"

"That's no exaggeration. I don't tell fish stories. C'mere. Look at this."

He removed a flashlight from his Duluth bag and, ducking under the lower doorway, crawled inside. Starkmann went in behind him after shedding his pack, the release from its weight making him feel light as a balloon. Both young men had to crawl under a ceiling only three or four feet high. The flashlight played over rough-hewn logs and sagging beams dripping with cobwebs. Some small animal darted through a chink in the wall with a scratching of clawed feet.

"There it is." The light shone on a name and date carved into a crossbeam:

EDWARD CADOTTE
APRIL 1847

"Imagine that. He was here a hundred and twenty-two years ago this month."

"Who was he?" The worn carving made Starkmann uncomfortable. In that musty, cryptlike space, he wasn't sure if it was an inscription Edward Cadotte had made to leave some trace of himself behind or a grave-marker.

"A trapper probably. Grandpa told me this place was a kind of warehouse built by the American Fur Company—you know, Astor's outfit. The trappers would store their skins here, and when they had enough, they would pack them up and portage them down to L'Anse."

Bonny George crawled outside.

"I love finding old stuff like this," he said. "If I go to college when I get out, maybe I'll study archaeology. Spend my life digging up ruins and relics. My name will be in *National Geographic*."

He hoisted himself easily onto the upper floor—it was close enough to the ground to allow a man of Starkmann's height to see inside without standing on tiptoe—and planted himself in the middle of a small room, his black hair shining in the dim light that angled through a hole in the roof where a trapdoor had once led to the lookout tower.

"I figure the furs were stored below and the trappers stayed up here. What was good enough for them is good enough for us. Pretty cozy, hey?" His thick, pulp-cutter's hands gestured with the enthusiasm of a real estate agent showing a new apartment. "No tent to pitch and high enough off the ground to keep our food out of reach of old Mr. Bear. Old Mr. Bear just got out of hibernation last month and he is hun-*gree* this time of year."

Starkmann's eyes were level with his friend's ankles.

"If I can see inside flat-footed, so can Mr. Bear."

"But Mr. Bear won't be able to get his fat, furry ass through this narrow doorway. He can look but he can't touch."

They brought their packs inside and spread out their foam pads and sleeping bags. The plank floor was surprisingly solid in view of its age. Darkness had fallen by the time Bonny George fired up the propane backpacker's stove, its flame a blue circle under the frying pan in which pork and beans bubbled. He seasoned them with chopped onion, whistling to himself. While he tended to supper, Starkmann sat and looked through the doorway at the firs above the river and at the tops of the hemlock, silvered by a rising moon. The eerie yodel of a loon floated on the breeze from some distant lake or pond, and a fox, drawn by the smell of the beans, rustled in the underbrush at the edge of the clearing. Starkmann kept his ears pricked for the snorting and thrashing of a bear. Only black bears lived in these woods. Benign animals compared to grizzlies, they could be dangerous at this time of year, edgy, half-starved, and not shy about barging into a remote camp or cabin for food, the sows ready to defend their newborn cubs with an implacable, maternal fury. Now, as he gazed at the inky wall of the woods, Starkmann's imagination began to transform bushes and tree stumps into bears; he could see them, the piggish red eyes, the enormous necks and power-ful haunches under mats of midnight fur; and this image temporarily became the object of the dread that knocked and thumped against the walls of his heart. He could not understand the cause of this lurking terror; he was nineteen, a full-grown man.

His unfamiliarity with the woods in this season, the raw, bleak appearance that made them look wilder than they did in the summer, did not satisfy him as an explanation. His father might have ascribed the emotion to original sin: Once man had lived at peace in the natural world; then came the catastrophic bite of the apple, and man was cast into a darkness bristling with dangers. Starkmann, though, was a modern young man, with a rational as opposed to a spiritual temperament, despite his divinity school studies. He believed that just about everything was scientifically explainable, and whenever he encountered or experienced anything that defied analysis, he became upset and confused.

"The beans are done. The finest from Bonny George's Injun kitchen."

Starkmann left off his reflections to tend to the more basic demands of his empty stomach. He rummaged in his pack for his mess kit, and pulled out the mountaineer's pressure lamp he'd bought in the camping department of Mage's Sporting Goods in Chicago. A peg in a rafter made a hook from which to hang the lamp. He lit it, and its hiss and steady flame cheered him considerably. The light gave a mahogany cast to the weathered walls and burnished the coppery brown of Bonny George's skin. He thought, as he waited for the scalding beans to cool, that the scene might have been an illustration out of a frontier novel: the lamp glow on the hand-hewn logs, the tattered Duluth bag with its leather straps, the two woodsmen eating their supper, and all around them the mystery of the wilderness.

The pork and beans congealed into comforting lumps in their stomachs. Bonny George put on a pot of coffee for the next morning.

"We'll fill our canteens tomorrow," he said, washing out the frying pan with the last water in his saddle canteen. Starkmann was relieved; he'd been worried he would have to go down to the river in the dark to clean up.

The washing done, the two young men got their equipment ready. They did not want to waste any time with preparations in the morning; their plan was to be on the river at first light, the best hour for fishing. It pleased Starkmann to see all his gear neatly laid out: his faded fishing vest with its attached mesh creel and its many pockets bulging with fly boxes and spare leaders, clippers, hooks, and various odds and ends; his rubber waders, patched here and there; his landing net; and his prize possession, the varnished split-cane rod his father had given him the year before as a reward for his agreeing to give divinity school a try.

"No wonder your back was aching," the Indian said, looking skeptically at all the paraphernalia. "Are you expecting to have your picture taken by *Field and Stream*?"

His kit was much simpler: a short spinning rod, more practical on Michigan's brushy streams than Starkmann's whippy fly rod; a worm can, and a jar of dough balls—salmon eggs wrapped in cheese-cloth. He had a pair of rubber wading boots but no waders, which were too bulky to pack into the bush. Bonny George usually fished from the banks, making short sidearm casts into the current or dabbing in the pools with a weighted line. If he did have to wade, a strong constitution and an innate stoicism allowed him to withstand the icy shock of northern rivers.

He whistled as he tied a hook to his line, then tested the knot by tugging on the hook with two fingers of one hand, the rod held in the other. Looking at him, Starkmann felt a sudden rush of love, as strong as any he would have felt for a brother. He wanted to embrace Bonny George's shoulders; his arm, almost of its own will, began to reach out, a movement he checked immediately. He was the son of a Missouri synod minister, after all, possessed of an emotional reticence that prohibited extravagant displays of feeling. There was also a certain fear in this reluctance to express what was in his heart, a fear that he would lose control, say something best left unsaid, or do something sloppy and awkward, like break into tears. For as the love rushed through him, the fact he had kept buried all day under layers of make-believe, pretending that this was just another of their fishing trips and that everything would go on as it always had, the inescapable fact rose into his consciousness. He tried to keep his mind occupied by selecting the flies he would use the next day, his fingers sorting through the assortment of bucktails and streamers, dry flies and nymphs.

"Don't tell me you're going to go purist on me again." Bonny George unlaced his boots and zipped open his sleeping bag. "Why do you think I brought along five dozen nightcrawlers and a jar of salmon roe?"

"I'll try artificials. If they don't work, I'll switch."

"I don't believe you. Look, we're deep in the boondocks, far from the prying eyes of civilization. The snobs from Trout Unlimited won't see you if you tie a worm to your hook." He crawled into his sleeping bag and lay with his hands folded behind his head. "I swear there are times you make me glad I was born a backwoods blanket-ass. There's nothing morally wrong with using bait."

Starkmann laughed, even as he wondered how Bonny George could joke and talk about trivialities at a time like this.

He continued to sort through his flies, pretending to be absorbed in their selection, but he was thinking about the day he and his friend had met, almost ten years ago.

It had been in early June, Starkmann remembered, when school was over and his father had taken him, for the first time, on his annual fishing trip to Michigan. They'd left Oak Park before dawn, Christian feeling sleepy, but also excited and relieved to escape a household overpopulated with females—his mother and three sisters. It made him feel grown up to ride in the front seat instead of in the back with Stephanie and Jennifer, the two younger girls. In the early afternoon, with Chicago and its suburban girdle three hundred miles behind, they crossed the Wisconsin-Michigan line into the Upper Peninsula. After driving northward another hour, they turned off the blacktop onto a gravel road that, his father said, led to the cabin of the Indian who guided for him each year. Christian was eager to meet a real Indian, but his eagerness turned to apprehension after they bounced down the signless road for a long time without seeing a house, a town, or a human being. The forests appeared to the nine-year-old as wild as those he'd seen in the movie *The Last of the Mohicans*. He pictured half-naked savages, bows and tomahawks at the ready, keeping themselves out of sight as they glided through the pines. He looked at his father, whose clean-shaven jaw, set at its confident angle, reassured him somewhat; nevertheless, he was compelled to ask if Indians still scalped white people.

"No, they don't, son," Lucius said. Christian could tell, by the cool tone his father used when upset, that he was in for a sermon or a scolding. "I want you to forget those lies you've seen in the movies. Indians are not savages, and these Indians up here—they're called Ojibwa—never fought a war with white people. Of course, that didn't . . ."

"What're they called, Daddy?"

"Ah-jib-away. You shouldn't interrupt grown-ups. It isn't polite."

"Yes, Daddy."

"I was saying that it didn't do them much good not to fight the whites, because they lost their land, the same as the Sioux and Cheyenne. Do you understand me, son?"

"Sort of," Christian replied, though it occurred to him that his question had not been answered.

"That's good. And I also want you to understand that Louis is a fine man. He has never been anything but honest in his dealings with me. He doesn't drink and doesn't smoke."

"Like you."

"That's right. One more thing. His grandson is living with him. The boy's the same age as you, but he's been a troublemaker ever since he lost his parents. A terrible thing, both of them gone within six months of each other. George has got a chip on his shoulder because of that, but if he starts any trouble with you, don't get into it."

Christian's heart dropped. He'd looked forward to spending two weeks alone with his father in the woods. Until this moment, he hadn't known another boy would be with them. He had a difficult time making friends with other children; now he would be expected to buddy up to some Indian orphan who, he'd gathered, was also a bully.

His spirits took another dip when they left the gravel road for a dusty two-track, and came upon a shack set in a clearing—Louis's house, his father announced. Accustomed to the solid, genteel homes in Oak Park, Christian could not imagine the place as fit for human habitation. Sheets of tarpaper fastened by flimsy wooden strips covered the walls and roof. The porch leaned to one side, giving the shanty the appearance of a face with its jaw knocked askew. Out in the brush that excused itself as a yard, a rusted automobile lay on its back, its tires and moving parts cannibalized so that it resembled a carcass picked over by vultures. A blue pickup truck was parked beside the shack, a vehicle so old and battered it seemed incapable of motion. The whole tumbledown place had an air of impermanence, and was somehow sinister, what with the overgrown clearing and the dark green woods beyond.

"Daddy, we're not staying *here,* are we?"

"Be polite, Christian. Louis is very poor. This is his home."

"Please tell me we're not staying here."

"We'll be staying at a lodge about ten miles from here. It has showers, electricity, everything you're used to," Lucius said, unfolding his long body out of the car. "I'll tell Louis we're here."

Relieved by this news, Christian remained inside and watched as Louis emerged from the shack to shake hands with his father. He was dark-skinned and gray-haired, and looked short beside Lucius's six feet four inches. Christian guessed his father had been right in telling him that the movies lied about Indians. Louis was not dressed like a movie Indian, but in a denim shirt, high-topped boots, and a pair of old-fashioned overalls held up by suspenders. He did not wear his hair in braids, Indian-style. It was cut short, like a white man's. Louis, in fact, was almost disappointingly ordinary in appearance.

Christian relaxed and looked around while the two men talked. Only then did he notice that three more ramshackle structures stood in the clearing; one was an outhouse—cripes, they didn't even have toilets—and the other two were low, windowless log buildings with flat roofs. A dark-haired boy, filthy and barefoot, was playing beside one of the log buildings. He had to be George, the orphan-bully, although he was awful small to be a bully and troublemaker. Christian was sure he would tower over him as much as his father towered over Louis.

"Son, c'mon over here. I want you to meet Mr. St. Germaine."

Overcome with shyness, the boy hesitated.

"Did you hear me, Christian?"

It was a command, not a question. He got out and walked over to the two adults. "How're you, young fella?" Louis asked, shaking his hand. He had an unwashed smell that made Christian draw closer to his father's scent of soap and shaving lotion.

"I'm fine, Mr. German."

"It's Saint Germaine," he corrected with a laugh. "So you're gonna fish with your old man this year. Couldn't of picked a better year. Never seen so many brookies, hey."

Christian said nothing, fascinated that Louis did not speak like Chingachgook and Magua in *The Last of the Mohicans*. He spoke like anyone else, except for the *hey* at the end of his sentences. (Christian would later learn that this was a characteristic manner of speech in the north woods.) But the old man's face was certainly an Indian's, with its long, hooked nose, creased skin the color of a baseball glove, and deep-set black eyes, the most piercing eyes that had ever looked into Christian's. They gave him the creeps. Their dark light seemed to burn right through him. He was glad when Louis transferred his gaze to his father, and invited them inside to make plans.

They sat at a wooden table in a combination kitchen, dining room, and living room. While the two men studied a map and discussed their fishing strategy, Christian's eyes roved about. An old-fashioned oven squatted in a corner beside a sink with a hand-operated pump. Some kind of wooden radio, like the kind Christian had seen in his grandmother's attic, shared another corner with a bundle of cane-poles and fishing rods. But the objects that caught his attention were a hide drum—a real tom-tom!—a couple of rattles, and a stack of what appeared to be yellowed, rolled-up newspapers.

Louis must have noticed him staring because he interrupted the talk with Lucius to ask, "You wonderin' what those are, young fella?"

Christian made no response, unsure if it would be impolite to admit that he was.

"Cat got your tongue?"

He shook his head.

"The boy don't say much, Lucius."

"He takes after his mother."

"Well, if you are wonderin' what those are, they're scrolls, made outa birchbark."

Christian squirmed under the Indian's penetrating glance.

"Might say they're the same thing to me like the Bible is to your old man."

"You mean you're a minister?"

"Sort of."

The boy could not imagine the old man dressed in a suit and tie, like his father, speaking from a pulpit.

"But I'm a little bit more than a preacher. A doctor too. Sort of."

"I don't think Christian understands all that."

"Bet you don't either," said Louis with a grin that deepened the creases in his face.

"Maybe not. We are here to fish, not to talk religion," Lucius replied in the clear, definite voice with which he delivered sermons at his church, Grace Lutheran.

"That's right, and I'll guarantee you'll limit out every day. Never seen so many brookies." Then, facing Christian, Louis asked if he wanted a Coke—he must be thirsty after that long drive.

The boy looked to his father to see if it was all right to accept. Lucius nodded his approval, and Christian said yes, he would like a Coke. The old man opened a wooden box with the word *Jefferson* stamped on it. The hourglass bottles of Coke were inside, atop blocks of ice.

"Thank you, Mr. St. Germaine."

"You're welcome, young fella."

"Louis," said his father, "you ought to get a generator. Then you could have a refrigerator instead of an icebox."

"Generator would be one more thing to worry about."

"Then how do you listen to the radio?"

"Don't. Now we gonna get this fishing trip planned or what?"

The two men resumed their discussion while Christian drank his Coke. Soon after he finished, he had to pee. He didn't know what to do. Would it be impolite to go without permission? But if he asked, he would be interrupting the grown-ups, which also would be impolite. Two or three times he tried to call his father's attention to his dilemma by wiggling and grimacing, but Lucius was too absorbed to notice. Christian felt a flicker of anger; he needed his father's approval to do almost everything, even go to the bathroom. Finally, unable to stand it any longer, he raised his hand as if he were at school and blurted out, "I've got to go, Daddy."

"Go ahead, then, Chris."

Having forgotten about the outhouse, he anxiously searched for the bathroom.

"It's outside," Louis reminded him, laughing. "You're in the boondocks, young fella."

Having never gone into one before, he approached the outhouse warily. As he opened the door, his nose assaulted by the stench, George called out to him:

"Gotta go number one or number two?"

Christian did not say anything.

"If you gotta go number two, watch them spiders, hey. Bite you on the butt."

Christian could not hold it another second, and spiders or no spiders, ran inside to relieve himself. When he came out, George was standing in front of him, his feet, hands, and knees covered in dirt, his face round as a dinner plate.

"Get bit?"

"I only had to go number one."

"Sometimes they'll bite your dork. The big ones, hey, jump right up and bite your dork."

Christian started back toward the cabin, but George blocked his way, smiling in a way that might or might not have been friendly—Christian couldn't tell.

"My name's Boniface. Boniface George, but just about everybody calls me Bonny George. What's yours?"

"Chris."

"Wanna see my road, Chris? I'm buildin' a road, hey."

He went along because he knew his father would consider it the correct thing to do. Bonny George—cripes they had funny names up here—seemed friendly enough, not at all a bully or troublemaker.

He was building his road with a toy grader, a miniature replica of the kind Christian had seen on the highways. It was a really nice, expensive toy, an extravagance considering the squalor in which Bonny George lived. The Indian boy squatted in the dirt and, making engine noises in his throat, plowed a smooth path with the grader's blade. A strong but pleasant odor leaked through the chinks of the log house beside them. It was, Bonny George explained, a smokehouse where his *mishomis*—which meant "grandfather" in Ojibwa talk—cured venison and bear steaks.

"He's gotta do that cuz he don't got no 'lectricity for a fridge. This place is for the shits, ain't it?"

Christian, whose parents insisted on proper use of the language and forbade profanity in any form, was as startled by the four-letter word as he was by Bonny George's bad grammar.

"Uh . . . where do you go to school, George?"

"Don't. Grandpa took me out. He teaches me."

"I didn't know he was a teacher, too."

"He ain't, 'xactly. He teaches me how to talk his talk, and his religion. He says I can go back to reg'lar school, when I've learned all that."

"Boy, I wish I didn't have to go to school."

"You'd wish it if you have to live here. Ain't this place for the shits, hey?"

"It's okay. It's just fine. I mean, it's your home, where you live."

"It's where I live, but it ain't home. You shoulda seen my home. My pa built it hisself. Had runnin' water, 'lectricity, a TV even." Bonny George pushed the grader along with a growl. "Pa made him good money, but Grandpa don't make hardly nothin', a few bucks from guidin' and trappin' an' whatever sick people can give him when they come here to get better."

"Is he a doctor? He told me he's a doctor, sort of, and a minister too."

"A what?"

"A preacher."

"I guess so." Bonny George's voice burst into another mechanical roar as he added another foot to his road. "But he don't make no money. When I grow up, I'm gonna drive me one of these, hey. My pa useta drive one of these and made him some good money."

"What's your pa do now?" Christian asked before he could catch the slip of the tongue.

"Nothin'. He's dead."

Christian wanted to run and hide, he felt so ashamed of himself. He was sure he'd hurt the other boy's feelings, but when Bonny George looked up at him, his eyes were dry.

"A tree falled on him."

"A *tree?*"

"When he weren't drivin' one of these, Pa cut trees down— whatcha call a lumberjack—and one day he was cuttin' down a big old tree and it falled the wrong way, right on top of him. Splat!" His hand slapped the earth. "Squashed him like a bug, hey."

Christian said nothing, trying to picture a man squashed like a bug. He couldn't do it. He couldn't, for that matter, picture anyone dead. Suddenly, the Indian boy's imitations of an engine rose to an hysterical pitch. Instead of methodically pushing the grader, he began to wheel it crazily across the dirt patch, making hairpin turns while he screeched to mimic the sound of squealing tires. Then he flipped the grader over, his voice an eruption of noises—shattering glass and crunching metal—his small hands tossing dirt to suggest an explosion or collision.

"That's how Ma got kilt," he said, breathing hard from the outburst. "Know what my ma was?" Bonny George rose to his feet, his eyes wild now. "Know what she was?"

Christian shook his head.

"A blanket-ass. That's what Grandpa says. A fuckin' drunk blanket-ass. Got herself drunk after Pa got kilt an' tipped her car over in a ditch."

His ears burning from the obscenity, shocked that anyone could speak of his mother in such language, and frightened by the unexpected change that had come over the other boy, Christian turned to walk back to the cabin. Bonny George grabbed him by the shirt sleeve.

"Betcha don't know what a blanket-ass is. Betcha a nickel."

"Let go of my shirt."

"It's a fucked-up Indian. Most Indians is blanket-asses, Grandpa says, but he ain't no blanket-ass and I ain't neither. I'm a real Indian."

Christian pulled away hard, ripping his shirt.

"Now look what you made me do!"

"Did not!"

"Did so!"

"You done it yourself, hey."

Christian looked at his torn sleeve and began to cry, not because he was afraid of the crazy-eyed Indian but because he feared his father would think he'd been fighting and give him a scolding. Embarrassed by his tears, he ran toward the car, intending to lock himself inside. The next thing he knew, he'd been tackled from behind and was down on his stomach, Bonny George sitting on him and punching him in the back of his head.

"I'm pretty tough!"

"You're crazy!" Christian sobbed, covering his skull with his hands against the blows.

"Take that back! You take that back!"

Christian rose to his hands and knees and threw off his adversary. He popped his fist straight into the other boy's nose, drawing blood and a howl of pain that brought the two men running from the cabin. Lucius Starkmann took hold of his son's arm and shook him.

"What's going on, Christian? Just what's going on?"

"He started it! He hit me first."

"What did I tell you about fighting? What did I tell you?"

"But he started it, Daddy."

"I don't care who started it. What did I tell you about staying out of trouble, Christian? What?"

"Take it easy on the young fella," Louis said calmly. "Any money says George started it." Christian, expecting that Bonny George would get a spanking or tongue-lashing, was amazed when Louis looked at his grandson's bloody nose and grinned. "Well now, George, it's just like I told you it is, ain't it? Everything comes around back to you. You give plenty of kids bloody noses—now you got one. Get inside, clean yourself up, and get to work on the tackle. We got fishin' to do."

"And you get in the car and wait there," Christian's father ordered.

The boy shot a hate-filled glance at Bonny George and shuffled to the car, feeling a terrible injustice had been done to him. A short time later, Lucius climbed in and started down the road to the lodge. Father and son did not speak for several minutes, Christian sulking in the seat.

"You know, I've got half a mind to turn around and take you back home," Lucius said to break the silence. "Do you want that?"

The boy shrugged.

"Yes or no."

"No."

"Then I expect, I *demand* that you behave yourself the rest of the trip."

Christian sat silently, wishing his father would speak to him as Louis had to Bonny George. The old man's voice had been firm but somehow gentle and warm. He had let his grandson know that he'd done wrong but hadn't made him feel ashamed of it.

"What does the Bible say about fighting, son?"

"I don't know."

"What does your name mean? What does it mean to be a Christian?"

"A Christian believes in Jesus."

"And what does Jesus have to say about fighting? I taught it to you myself. Matthew, Five, thirty-nine."

Staring out the window at the pines and maples, the boy tried to remember the passage.

"*Resist not evil,*" Lucius prompted. "Now give me the rest."

"Resist not evil, but who . . . who shall . . . I can't remember, Daddy."

"*Whosoever shall smite thee on thy right cheek, turn to him the other also.* Turn the other cheek." He fixed on his son a look of unappealable judgment. "That, Christian, is what you failed to do this afternoon."

The boy hunched down, feeling he'd done worse than offend his father: he'd violated an ordinance of heaven itself.

But the next morning, when Louis and his grandson stopped at the lodge to begin the day's fishing, he was inclined to doubt the efficacy of turning the other cheek. The bloody nose had humbled Bonny George. He seemed to respect Christian and to be genuinely sorry for getting him into trouble.

"Hope your old man didn't give you a whuppin'. Sure sounded like he was goin' to. Did he whup you?"

Christian gestured vaguely to leave the question open and, in that way, to hold on to Bonny George's sympathy.

"My grandpa don't whup and yell at me. It's the only thing I like about livin' with him. He don't whup me and holler at me, like Pa done, because he says that if I do somethin' bad, somethin' bad will happen to me just naturally."

Over the course of the next few days, the two boys became fast friends and had a fine time, tramping through the woods with the two men, fishing the secret holes Louis led them to. The deep, cold waters were loaded with brook trout. Christian yelped in delight when he caught his first one, a beautiful fourteen-incher with an orange belly and gray-black flanks speckled with rose. His father shook his hand and patted him on the back, which was as much outward affection as Lucius would allow himself; but Christian felt in that handclasp and congratulatory pat the warmth of a full embrace, as he saw in his father's smile forgiveness of his trespass.

Bonny George was impressed with his catch.

"Fourteen inches, hey. That's big for a brookie."

In a flourish of magnanimity, Christian offered his trophy to the Indian, who was too proud to accept.

"I'm gonna catch me a bigger one," he vowed.

He made good on the promise two days later: a sixteen-incher.

Their rivalry continued throughout the rest of the trip, but Christian was never able to better Bonny George's prize. The idyll ended all too soon. Christian felt downhearted the day he and his father left for home. When they returned to Oak Park, where the orderly lawns held no promise of adventure, he missed his new friend and the big wild woods.

The friendship begun that summer was renewed the next, and now, Starkmann reflected as he studied his flies, it had lasted an even decade. He supposed they made an odd pair, but the adventures they had shared in the vast forests, where they had to rely on each other, had drawn him closer to the Indian than to his classmates in high school and college.

Bonny George knew the woods as well as Louis, perhaps better. Lucius, in the meantime, had stopped affording himself the pleasure of his yearly fishing trip. A social crusader most of his life, he had been captured by the civil-rights and anti-war movements; when he wasn't attending to his pastoral duties he walked in freedom marches, made speeches at demonstrations, and dashed off indignant letters to the newspapers.

So the boys had the woods and the summers to themselves. As soon as school was out, Christian would ride the train to Marquette, where Bonny George would meet him in a rattletrap, war-surplus jeep the two had bought together for under a hundred dollars.

They would spend about a month together, sometimes camping out and moving from place to place like angling gypsies, sometimes staying at Louis's cabin, helping him to keep the place from ruin when they weren't fishing. They would roam the woods by day, and entertain each other at night with talk about sports and girls—occasionally boasting of sexual conquests they never made. Or they would scare each other with ghost stories and speculations about killer bears. Now and then, Bonny George related some of the tribal lore he'd learned from Louis, or told a folktale from the ancient Norsemen and Greeks; his granfather's instructions had awakened in him a fascination with all mythology, which he read voraciously, becoming a backwoods autodiktat, a font of obscure legends and fables.

One year, they stayed a few days at the Louis's remote camp. It was on a small lake in the Huron Mountains, far off the trails worn down by backpackers and berry pickers. The camp was tidy compared to Louis's shack, the wigwam's frame of bent ironwood in good repair, the canvas roof and walls taut and waterproof, the cooking gear as orderly as anything you'd find in a well-kept kitchen, the firewood stacked just so under a plastic sheet. At the far end was a smaller wigwam, the cramped sweat-lodge where, Bonny George said, his grandfather took purification baths by pouring water over heated rocks.

"That's what he does out here when he ain't runnin' traps. Takes sweat baths and starves himself. He has visions, you know—all that traditional stuff."

Bonny George was attending the white county high school and, Christian had gathered from his tone of voice, had grown skeptical about the beliefs Louis had taught him in his childhood. Christian had little knowledge of the old man's pagan creed, but found in the camp an atmosphere of tranquillity that made him feel the way he was supposed to feel in church but never did: at peace with himself, in touch with some greater force or power. He remarked on this one night around the campfire, and wondered aloud if he was just imagining things.

"Grandpa would say it doesn't make any difference," Bonny George said, stirring the embers with a stick. "The way he sees things, if you imagine something or dream something, it's just as real as those trees over there."

"I don't get it."

"I don't neither. I don't get half the stuff he says sometimes. The old man's worried about me. He thinks going to that high school is turning me into an apple. That's the next worst thing to a blanket-ass. Red on the outside, white on the inside. But I know what you mean about this place. I always like it here. It's like there's something here, some kinda . . . well, I don't know. Something." He paused as the wind raised a flame from the coals. "Harmony—that's it. That's what the old man calls it. That's what life is all about, he says, finding harmony, but I'll be damned if I know what he means."

Harmony, Starkmann thought, emerging from his reverie. He could use a little harmony right now, as his thoughts turned from the past to the future.

It was difficult to imagine what the next summer would be like without Bonny George, and the next summer, and the summer after that. *Don't go. You don't have to go,* Starkmann said to himself, squinting with a jewel-appraiser's eye at the white wing and scarlet hackle of a Marabou streamer. He would have been less troubled if his friend were going to prison—a fixed term, a certain date of release. *Don't go.* He placed the Marabou in the box with his other wet flies, arranged in tidy, colorful rows. *Don't go!* The words roared in his brain and forced their way into his throat. He wanted to climb to the lookout tower above and shout them at the top of his lungs, over and over, until their echoes filled the woods. But his inner censor checked him again.

He snapped the fly box shut and said, "You ready to turn in?"

"What does it look like?"

Starkmann snuffed the lamp and slipped into the sleeping bag. The darkness seemed absolute at first, for the moon held low to the horizon. Gradually, as his eyes adjusted, he could discern the trapdoor overhead and, outside, the conical outlines of the balsam firs. Lying awake with his mind racing, he tried to distract himself by conjuring fantasies of a giant trout bending his rod, the fish leaping, its colors bright in the early sun—an attempt to expel from this valedictory trip its sense of mourning and departure by reviving the anticipation that had always quickened him when a day's fishing lay ahead. There had been, in that happy expectancy, a great deal more than the mere hope of filling his creel or capturing a trophy: The magic of standing in a wild river at dawn, the scent of pine in the air, had become the magic of his youth distilled into its purest form. With the forest so hushed and still that it, too, seemed to expect something wonderful to happen; with the river's unknown reaches awaiting his discovery and its hidden beauties eager to reveal themselves to his questing eyes, he felt as though all the world and all the future were spread before him, endless and ever new. Now his hope had become tinged with apprehension, his sense of infinite possibilities circumscribed by a knowledge that things ended after all, some forever. It wasn't a knowledge he'd acquired until last month, when he'd received Bonny George's letter. He'd read it over twice, and suddenly, everything had changed. He could no longer read a newspaper or watch the evening news without a sense of doom. The grainy images of death he saw on the front pages or on the TV screen, the headlines and mournful statistics, assumed a new, appalling significance. His friend might not have a future, and that possibility, a probability for all Starkmann knew, somehow diminished his own future.

"All right. Out with it. Speak."

The Indian's voice startled him.

"Out with what?"

"Don't kid me. I've known you too long. You haven't even tried to sleep. You've been thinking deep thoughts."

"We agreed that we wouldn't talk about it this trip."

"If not talking about it is going to give you insomnia, then let's talk, hey. I want to have fun tomorrow. I don't want some gloomy-guts for a fishing partner."

"How can you be so damned casual about it? Like you're going to summer camp or something."

Starkmann unzipped his sleeping bag and sat up, shivering at the touch of the night air. He sat with his arms around his upraised knees and stared out the door at the moon, now high above the scraggy rim of the pine ridge across the river. "You've still got time."

"I passed my physical. On Tuesday they're going to shove me onto a bus."

"That still gives you a couple, three days. You could be across before they missed you."

"I thought about it, Chris. I even had my spot all picked out, a sharp curve in the tracks where the trains usually slow down. All I'd have to do is hop a freight, and in no time I'd be across the Soo Locks and in Ontario. But like I told you in my letter, the more I thought about it, the more I realized I'd have to *stay* in Canada because everybody starts looking for you when you do that. The FBI. The CIA. The IRS. The National Rifle Association. You name it. And those guys are all tight with the Mounties. They get the Mounties after you. The Mounties always get their man, right? So there I'd be, way up in Canada, waiting for Sergeant Preston of the Yukon to nab me and haul my blanket-ass back across the border and turn me over to the FBI, and bang, into the slams. No, thanks."

"There are guys right now living in Montreal and Toronto. They've got jobs, apartments, girlfriends, and no Mounties banging on the door."

"*White* guys. Protective coloration, you know? The only place I'd blend in would be a reservation, and I'd have to be enrolled, same as on this side. You can bet the locals wouldn't be excited about harboring a fugitive. They'd probably turn me over. Go directly to jail again. I'd go nuts behind bars."

"Know what you're doing? You're thinking up every excuse you can not to try it."

Bonny George turned onto his side, propping his head with his palm.

"All right. I'll tell you the real reason. The only family I've got left is here. My grandpa is about it. I couldn't imagine myself taking a step like that, turning my back on him for good, never getting to see him again. One thing he taught me about was imagination. He told me that if you can't imagine something happening, then it can't happen. And I just couldn't imagine myself crossing that border for the rest of my life."

A loon warbled away off somewhere, the only sound except for the unbroken murmur of the river. Starkmann sat without speaking, tapping his teeth with a thumbnail. Go to war, go to jail, or go into exile—it seemed to him that his friend should have had more options than those. This was America, the land of options and choices, hundreds of them, arrayed like snack foods and breakfast cereals on a supermarket shelf. Yet, even in America, a man's fundamental nature imposed limits on the courses of action he could take. Bonny George's pride and dignity would prohibit him from using most of the ploys clever young men had invented in the past few years to keep themselves out of uniform. He could not feign the mincing walk and lisping speech of a homosexual, or roll his eyes and drool in fits of make-believe madness, or, more drastically, lop off a finger and pretend it had been an accidental injury.

Nevertheless there had to be an alternative he would find acceptable, and Starkmann, staring at the moon boxed by the doorway, his thumbnail clicking against his teeth, tried to think of one. He felt embarrassed by his divinity-school deferment, somehow less of a man for not having to face the hard decision that had confronted his friend. He saw himself as a coddled, protected, middle-class white kid, and a fraud to boot: He'd enrolled at Illinois Lutheran College, his father's alma mater, only because it had been Lucius Starkmann's wish. His father. What would his father say to Bonny George? That was a rhetorical question; he knew what his father would say because the Reverend Starkmann had already said it, in a letter Christian had received just before leaving for this trip on spring break.

He thought about his father's words, and the longer he thought about them, the more he sensed the man's presence entering the derelict cabin. It filtered through the cracks in the walls and through the moonlit door until Starkmann could almost see him, tall and gaunt, with a body that was all acute angles, with narrowed eyes and lips pursed into a down-turned crescent above his jaw, as if he were perpetually facing into a severe wind.

In appearance, Lucius was the photographic image of his grandfather, a circuit-riding preacher from whom he'd also inherited a zeal for difficult causes, the more difficult the better. The grandfather, when he hadn't been spreading the gospel to pioneer German farmers marooned on the bleak grass seas of western Illinois, gave fiery speeches on behalf of abolition and made his house a way station on the Underground Railway during the Civil War. Lucius had cut his teeth on tales of runaway slaves hiding in the cellar and, long before civil rights had become popular, had got his head cracked by a brick when he tried to help a black family move into Cicero, an all-white suburb of Chicago. Six years ago he'd marched to Washington with Martin Luther King, Jr.; a year later, he'd ridden a freedom bus with students half his age into Mississippi, where he'd suffered the blows of police billy clubs and electric cattle prods with the exaltation of a Christian martyr under a Roman lash.

But it was war that outraged him the most, war in general, the war in Vietnam in particular. To him, war was the gravest injustice, the unpardonable crime. His hatred of it arose from what had happened to his father in World War I: Leaving a pregnant wife behind, he'd gone overseas a jaunty doughboy and returned horribly disfigured from a mustard-gas attack in the Argonne. He had spent the rest of his short life railing against the colossal butchery he'd seen in the trenches, the idiocy of generals, the monstrous indifference of governments that had wasted an entire generation of young men. He died, an embittered man of forty-one, the year Germany invaded Poland.

Lucius, then twenty-one, blamed his father's death on the world's insane rush into another war that promised to be bloodier and vaster than its predecessor. The invasion had destroyed his father's will to live. Lucius became a conscientious objector, which, in those patriotic years, was the next worse thing to a traitor. His German surname had led to talk that he was a Nazi sympathizer, an absurd accusation in view of his populist beliefs and a family history that dated back almost to the founding of the Republic. The charges clung to him nonetheless. To prove their falsity, his politics moved leftward in the postwar years. He was vocal in his protests against the Korean War, vocal enough to earn a subpoena from Senator Joseph McCarthy's witch-hunting committee in the early 1950's. That, in turn, caused his expulsion from his post in the small Republican Illinois town where he had been an assistant pastor. Branding him a Communist sympathizer, the congregation had petitioned his superior to dismiss him. Lucius moved himself and his family (there were only two children then, Christian and his older sister, Anne) to Oak Park, a monied but somewhat liberal community where he hoped to find an atmosphere more congenial to his views. Such was the case for a number of years; but in 1966, when he raised his voice against the Vietnam War from the pulpit of his church, a few of his more red-white-and-blue listeners appealed to the Lutheran Council to transfer him. They argued that he had no more business preaching politics than a politician did preaching religion. Lucius countered with a long letter to the Council, reminding them of the Lutheran belief that civil obedience did not always merit salvation in God's eyes. If a law or a government is unjust, he argued, it is the Christian's duty to disobey it, a duty that falls heaviest on the shoulders of a clergyman. The war in Vietnam was not only unjust but illegal; therefore he had no choice but to call for his congregation's resistance.

This time he won. He hung on to his post. To show he meant what he'd said, he gave a sermon suggesting that it was the moral duty of young Americans to break the draft laws and burn their registration cards. Two years later, enlisted in Senator Eugene McCarthy's crusade, he campaigned tirelessly, organizing precinct workers, ringing doorbells, giving political speeches that were part sermon, sermons that were part political speech. When McCarthy failed to win the nomination, Lucius Starkmann flung himself into the chaotic street demonstrations outside the convention center in Chicago. Amidst tear-gas clouds lit by the nervous blue flashes of the squad cars, his unyielding jaw set against the mass charges of police and National Guardsmen, he stood on the barricades with the righteousness of a believer assured of salvation.

His battles had hardened him, and made him famous. His notoriety had been provincial at first, confined to Chicago and its environs, where the newspapers described him as "the controversial pacifist minister from Oak Park." In the spring of 1968 his prominence in the McCarthy campaign anointed him with the oil of national celebrity: an appearance on the network news. Christian, who was away at school at the time, would have missed the event if he hadn't taken a study break and gone to the lounge for a Coke just as the news came on. A classmate called him over to the TV: "Chris, look at this. It's your dad. He's on Walter Cronkite!"

And there he was, on a podium beneath the rust-red wings of the Picasso statue in the Civic Center Plaza, haranguing a rally, a mixed bag of dreamy flower children and affluent liberals who held aloft blue and black signs that read: McCARTHY IN '68. Starkmann's first impression was one of disbelief: That wasn't his father on the screen but someone playing his father. His second impression was one of cold. Lucius Starkmann was a harsh-looking man in the flesh, but the camera somehow magnified this quality. His wavy hair, now gone white, flowed with the frigid grace of the wind-sculpted drifts that piled up on the Lake Michigan shore in January; his face resembled an ice carving, and his eyes were the blue of a polar sea. Only his gestures revealed the passion that lay under the frozen exterior like a volcano under a glacier. He pointed his finger at the crowd, shook his fist, and rapped his palm against the podium with a fervor more suited to a backwoods revivalist than a suburban minister, with—and Starkmann was embarrassed to notice this—a hint of the mad quakings of a soapbox fanatic in Bughouse Square. The heated movements looked especially odd because the voice to which they were intended to add effect, the voice Christian and his sisters knew so well, was as cold as the rest of him. It was a voice that flailed the audience indiscriminately, as if all were guilty. It flung into their faces words hard as hailstones, and froze in their tracks the secretaries, office workers, and stockbrokers strolling by on their lunch hour. Starkmann could see them on the fringes of the rally, stopping suddenly to listen; and the keenness in his father's voice seemed to pierce the dense garment of their complacency, a keenness that chastened, scourged, burned like a blast of arctic wind.

That same severity had been in the letter Lucius had sent in response to the one Christian had written describing Bonny George's situation and asking for advice. In his precise script, the elder Starkmann answered that it was the obligation of all young Americans to refuse service. The draft absolved no one of personal responsibility; one *chose* to be drafted over the alternatives, unpleasant to be sure but alternatives nonetheless. To allow oneself to be inducted was, therefore, the moral equivalent of volunteering. He went on and on and, toward the end, quoted Tolstoy, something to the effect that the Napoleonic Wars would have never been fought if a hundred thousand Frenchmen had not been willing to follow Bonaparte into battle. "And the filthy, unjust war we are now waging, to our everlasting shame," Lucius concluded, "would end tomorrow if every young man of military age simply said, 'No, I won't go.' It would end in an hour if every man now fighting there laid down his rifle and refused to fight any longer. At the very least, those men would, by so doing, save their souls from the judgment that, I assure you, will come for their participation in an act of prolonged mass-murder. I don't know what Boniface's decision will be, though I know what it ought to be. Whatever, it will be *his* decision. He is a human being with free will, not some dumb organism whose destiny can be determined by an indifferent, irresponsible government. If he answers his draft notice, that is, if he *consents* to take up arms for a nation that once visited upon his people barbarisms as awful as those it is now inflicting upon the Vietnamese, it will be an act I shall find difficult to understand and impossible to condone."

In his dormitory room, Starkmann read and reread the letter several times, searching for a fissure between its rigid lines through which he might feel the warmth of some sympathy for Bonny George's predicament. But its gelid surface was seamless, like a lake frozen solid. He could not fathom how his father could demand of Bonny George, whom he had known for so long, the same martyrly sacrifice he had always demanded of himself. It evidenced an adherence to principles so pure as to be monstrous. And his logic! Of course Napoleon would not have conquered anything if a hundred thousand Frenchmen had not been willing to shoulder muskets in his name; nevertheless they had. Of course this war would end immediately if every soldier laid down his rifle; nevertheless they did not, for whatever reasons—perhaps for as many reasons as there were soldiers. Starkmann realized in that moment that his father was a living example of how extremes grow to resemble one another. The man had a warrior's soul. If he had been a general, he would have been like Patton; brave, brilliant, single-minded, and utterly intolerant. Starkmann tore the letter in half and dropped the pieces into the wastebasket. As he looked out the window at the quadrangle, he thought, with a sincerity he found shocking, *I hate him.*

"That noise is driving me nuts," said Bonny George. "You sound like a woodpecker."

Awakened from his memories, Starkmann stopped tapping his teeth and folded his hands, prayer-fashion, under his chin.

"I was just thinking."

"Take it easy with all this deep thinking. It's me, not you, who's going in."

Starkmann drew himself down into his sleeping bag.

"It doesn't seem right somehow," he said. "Day after tomorrow, I go back to campus and you go into the army."

"We can trade places."

"You'd hate divinity school a lot more than I do."

"How is the great white father by the way?"

"He's the same as ever," Starkmann answered, stifling an impulse to shout *I hate him!* "Maybe he's gotten a little more famous."

"Yeah. I saw his picture in the *Free Press* a few months back. Showed it to my old *mishomis.* 'Hey,' I said, 'that's Christian's dad right there in the *Detroit Free Press*. The Reverend, the guy you used to guide for.' "

"What'd he say?"

"Nothin'. Just shrugged. You know he always liked your old man, but I think him being a minister always made Grandpa a little nervous."

"Why? He's some kind of minister himself."

"The Indian kind. Minister, doctor, psychiatrist, fortuneteller, and magician all rolled into one. Anyhow, I once heard him say that the missionary's cross did more to ruin the Indian way of life than the army's guns and the trader's whiskey."

" 'Christ's cross has saved us from the pagan's circle.' "

"Who said that? It sure don't sound like you."

"Saint Augustine."

The Indian rolled onto his back and clapped his hands once.

"My oh my, this ignorant blanket-ass is getting an education tonight! What do I know about Saint Augustine? I cut wood pulp for a living."

Starkmann was about to say something when the sound rose out of the blackness north of the river. He did not pause an instant to wonder what it was but, reacting instinctively, tore at the zipper of his sleeping bag to free himself and sprang into a crouch, his hand on his knife. Goose bumps prickled from his scalp to his feet when the sound came again, beginning as a moan, then rising to a wail as steady as a siren, then abruptly dipping an octave before it broke up into a series of yips and barks. Its operatic notes were still echoing when it was answered by another call, and another and another, each cry merging into the echo of the one preceding until there was hardly a second of silence, just one loud, unending howl. Starkmann had heard coyotes and wild dogs before, but this chorusing had a range and a resonance beyond any dog or coyote.

"Listen to them," Bonny George said, a statement Starkmann thought unnecessary. "Wolves. Just listen to them."

The Indian crawled out of his sleeping bag but, instead of crouching as if he expected an attack at any moment, leaped out the door onto the ground.

"Chris!" he called. "C'mon out here and look at this!"

Wolves. Starkmann stayed put, his eyes searching for the flash of jaws that he knew were powerful enough to hamstring a moose.

"C'mon, Chris. Ain't nothing going to hurt you out here."

Embarrassed by his display of nerves, he straightened up and dropped into the clearing. The cold outside the cabin surprised him, the bite in the air more like early November than April; but it was a night of such splendor that he ignored the chill and the wild yowling in the woods. Directly overhead the Milky Way was as distinct as a highway across the sky. The constellations shone brilliantly, except to the north, where they were blurred by the white sheets of the Aurora. Now shimmering like translucent curtains drawn over the windows of heaven, the northern lights suddenly streaked across a million miles of space to burst in silent explosions. Fountains of light, pale greens, reds, and yellows, showered the stars and geysered up to the center of the sky, where they pooled to form a multicolored sphere, a kind of mock sun that gave light but no heat, pulsing, flaring, and casting beams in all directions, horizon to horizon. Below, the wolves howled with midnight madness and the two young men stood in speechless awe. Even after the spectacle ended, the Aurora fading again to a faint shimmer, they stood as silent and transfixed as the first human beings ever to behold the wonder of creation. Starkmann felt the diminishment that is not self-depreciation but humility; for what was he and what was Bonny George? Flickers of consciousness imprisoned in lumps of dust; above them a sky ablaze with the Aurora, around them a wilderness where wolves sang savage arias to a frozen moon.

"Magic and power." Bonny George spoke almost in a whisper. "Wawasaye. The northern lights. Grandpa says that when the northern lights dance, the power of the bear is at its highest, and the bear guards the secrets of how to cure diseases. Wawasaye. Just look at them, Chris. Are they unbelievable or what? God, am I going to miss this."

He tossed back his head, so that the moon highlighted his face, and, cupping his hands over his mouth, almost perfectly mimicked the howling in the forest. A wolf answered. The Indian responded in turn, his Adam's apple throbbing as he dropped the long wail down to a lower register and punctuated the call with staccato barks.

"Where'd you learn how to do that?" Starkmann asked, impressed by the accuracy of the imitation.

"I didn't learn how. I've always known how because the Indian and the wolf are brothers." He smiled, but it was difficult to tell if he was joking or not. "God told the wolf and the first Indian: 'Whatever happens to one of you will also happen to the other.' Grandpa taught me that."

Starkmann shoved his hands in his pockets and hunched his shoulders against the cold.

"You almost sound like you believe it."

"If you believe that Christ's cross saved you from the pagan's circle—whatever that means—then I believe that God made the wolf and the Indian brothers. Why not? 'Axe time, sword time, ere the world falls, wind time, *wolf* time, ever shall brother his brother slay.' "

"What the hell is that?" Starkmann shuddered slightly and suppressed a nervous laugh; he had the odd feeling he'd heard those words before on another night in another northern forest.

"It's this prophecy a witch gives to Odin predicting the end of the world. The Twilight of the Gods. There's war all over the world. Brothers killing brothers. Fathers kill their sons. Sons kill their fathers. And it all comes down when this giant wolf leaps up and swallows the moon and the sun in his slobbering jaws. Get the picture? When white people came over here, they brought all that baggage with them, and they wiped out the wolves because they were afraid of them, not just because wolves raided livestock. Get it?"

"Sure," Starkmann said, just to be agreeable. He wanted to return to the warm chrysalis of his sleeping bag.

"The wolf was killed because white people were afraid of him. The Indian was killed for the same reason." He wasn't looking at Starkmann, but at the gauzy light that shaded the northern stars. "That's why wolf and me are brothers. That's why I can talk to him, and him to me. Listen."

He threw his head back once more and howled, stretching the sound into a high, thin keening. In a few moments a wolf sent its response, and Starkmann felt another shudder deep inside himself. Somehow, though he'd never seen a wolf except in the picture books of his childhood, he could envision the animals, standing out there among the tall trees, gray-furred and bushy-tailed, their jaws pointed toward the sky.

"I'll translate the conversation. The very first howl we heard was a directional call. Wolf was trying to locate his brothers. Those short barks were a hunting call, wolf telling his brother that he was onto something—a big buck, I'd guess. Wolf is strong, but he can't handle a big buck alone. He needs help. That call I just gave is a kind of lost call. Wolf's brother telling him he can't find the pack."

Starkmann did not say anything. There was enough mystery in this night to make him a little irrational and incline him to believe that Bonny George could indeed converse with wolves.

His friend now regarded him with a wry grin.

"So, you see, if you can talk to them, you don't have to be afraid of them. Damn if you weren't a sight, Chris. All hunkered down with your knife, hey."

"Look, that was the last sound I expected to hear. I thought there were hardly any left in Michigan."

"Hardly any *are* left. Maybe three, four packs on the whole

Upper Peninsula. The pack we just heard are probably immigrants. I'll bet they crossed the ice from Canada or Isle Royale this winter. They do that sometimes. That border doesn't mean a damn to them. There's one difference between me and wolf. Wolf comes and goes as he pleases, hey. Doesn't know if he's in Canada or the U.S. of A., and doesn't care."

He gave a bitter laugh and turned his eyes again to the northern lights, which had undergone another transformation: Now they hung in long, staggered shafts, like the pipes of a celestial organ.

"I'm going to miss this," Bonny George said again, his voice catching a little. "I'm going to miss the hell out of it."

2

They woke before sunrise, drank their coffee, and set off with the morning star glimmering in a purple sky. But for a couple of quarreling ravens, the forest would have been utterly still. Bonny George's fishing spot, where the trout grew as big as salmon, lay more than a mile upstream. To save time the two young men walked to it cross-country instead of following the twisting course of the river. Their trail was a run that deer had blazed across a crescent-shaped neck of land formed by one of the river's long bends. Starkmann lumbered in his chest waders; he felt as stiff and graceless as the Tin Man in *The Wizard of Oz* and found himself continually turning around to free his landing net, tied to a D-ring on the back of his vest, from the grasp of the pine branches. Less encumbered, Bonny George bounded along, holding his rod with the tip pointed behind, a green canvas creel slung over his shoulder. In a quarter of an hour they heard the river again, flinging itself over a waterfall, but they did not see it until after they'd labored over a bluff, their breath misting in the sharp air of this interim season that was neither winter nor spring.

The falls were more a spillway than a proper falls. The river cascaded down through a crevasse between two boulders into a shallow pool, where it cut vees around sharp rocks and swirled in pinwheeling eddies, then went over a low granite ledge that extended ruler-straight from bank to bank, in the strands of falling water like the teeth of a comb. Downstream, shadowed by leaning hemlock, the river widened itself into another pool, larger than the first. A winter-thinned doe was drinking on the far side of the pool. Starkmann and Bonny George would not have seen her in the early-morning twilight if, just as they reached the bottom of the bluff, she hadn't raised her head and flashed the white blaze on her throat. They watched her for a minute or two as she dipped her head to lap the water, her spindly forelegs spread wide, then lifted her nose to sniff the air for danger. Her thirst quenched, she turned and moved off into the forest with the uncertain gait of a newborn fawn. The months yarded up had been hard on her; what with the wolves, it seemed a miracle she'd survived the night, Starkmann thought. As he watched the deer, he saw, out of the corner of his eye, expanding rings in the middle of the pool. A second later a furious boil broke its quiet surface, and a silvery back arched out of the water almost as a porpoise arches. Then it was gone, the biggest trout he'd ever seen. He stared openmouthed for several seconds, half-convinced the fish had been an apparition.

"What did I tell you, unbeliever?"

Starkmann had nothing to say.

"Why do you think I spooled fifteen-pound test onto this old spinning reel? Preacher's son, if you hook into one of those beasts with that fancy swizzle stick, you're going to need the help of Jee*sus*."

"I've got a few heavy leaders."

"Those'll help you more than Jee*sus*."

They walked softly down to the bank to rig up, the river roaring in their ears. Three mallards swimming in slow water beside a grassy bank skittered and rose with a startling beat of wings, the drake's head an arrow of iridescent green. Starkmann watched them soar over the hemlocks, then looked at the river, pale-brown from the decayed cedar in the soil but achingly clear. As he studied the riffles and back-currents, his eyes scanning downstream to the pool where the doe had watered and the giant rainbow had rolled, the old eagerness and expectation flowed into him. He rubbed the ferrule of his rod against the side of his nose, lubricating it with the oil in his skin so it wouldn't stick, then jointed the two lengths of split bamboo. His hands shook slightly when he threaded the line through the guides and tied to the leader his most natural-looking fly, a Muddler Minnow.

He waded into the stream while Bonny George, stalking like a hunter, crept along the bank to the downstream end of the pool. The current pulled the waders tight around Starkmann's legs. He could feel the cold even through the rubber and his woolen socks, and took each step cautiously, aware that the loose shale and slick rocks beneath his feet could betray him at any moment. Behind him, the water crashing through the crevasse flung icy droplets against the back of his neck. The hint of danger, the possibility that he might slip and fall without warning, heightened his excitement, and there were no thoughts in his mind about Bonny George's going into the army, about his father, about any of it. He edged into the middle of the river, shuffling as an old man shuffles down a hospital corridor, and turned to face directly downstream, spreading his legs to brace himself against the current. The ledge was perhaps thirty feet in front of him, the pool just beneath it. Bonny George stood on a tabletop rock beside the bank at the far end, casting a doughball upstream and letting it drift back toward him.

Starkmann stripped line from his reel and, holding it in long loops, snapped the rod for the back cast. The loops peeled from his fingers and flew through the guides until the line was out straight behind him; then he flicked his wrist on the forward cast. The fly shot out over the ledge and landed with a soft splash. He was pleased with the cast—a good fifty feet. Fly fishing, for all its impracticality, delighted him: the whip of the rod, the swish of the line through the air, the thought-killing concentration required.

Though he had a slow-sinking line, the force of the current held the Muddler too near the surface. He mended, moving the fly into a whirling eddy that would carry it closer to the bottom. He could almost see the great trout, holding under the banks and submerged logs, jut-jawed and heavy-bodied, the females swollen with roe. They were, Bonny George had told him, lake-bred trout, driven upstream on spring spawning runs by a biological imperative so tyrannical it would not allow them to rest until they reached the pools in which they had been born. There they gave birth to another generation, then returned to Superior. The fry, those that survived, would follow when they were big enough, and fatten to maturity in the lake until, the memory of their birthplace imprinted on their tiny brains, the same compulsion drove them to make the same journey: river to lake to river, an unending circuit.

Starkmann watched his line angling down. When the fly had sunk as far as it could, he started to retrieve it with short, quick strips, his lungs held breathless in anticipation of a strike. The sun came up, its light setting fire to the river. He gloried in this moment of advent, the redolence of pine as heady as a drug. His next cast dropped the fly a foot or two to the side of the first presentation. He concentrated, trying to make his mind one with the trout's, to picture where it lay and what kind of action would persuade it to seize the artificial. You cannot teach Zen to an angler because he already knows it—Starkmann had read or heard that somewhere. He slowed his retrieve, twitching the rod tip to make the Muddler appear like a crippled minnow, but the big trout did not get to be big because they were stupid. He tried another cast. Off in the distance, ravens screeched their discovery of carrion. The sun climbed, painting itself gold. Its brighter light uncovered details invisible in the predawn twilight: hidden snags, pebble-strewn trenches, and, at the near end of the pool, the top of a log slanting into the brown depths like the mast of a sunken ship. A tug on the end of Starkmann's line made his throat go tight. He flicked the rod tip to set the hook, but missed the strike. The possibility that it had been a small fish consoled him only a little.

Bonny George let out a whoop. His rod was a pulsing bow, the taut line cutting zigzags through the still water. Not without envy, Starkmann watched him work the fish until it was on the surface, thrashing.

"Small one, Chris. Must be a local."

He meant a rainbow native to the river as compared to the migratory trout.

When he'd pumped the fish into landing range, Bonny George knelt on one knee, the rod held high above him, and with a movement almost too quick to be seen, snatched it from the river, his thumb and forefinger hooked over its eyes.

"Not so small after all. Close to two pounds, I'd say." His grin a crescent moon under his hooked nose, he stood and held the still-flopping fish in the air.

"Mr. Sportsman, this bait-tossing blanket-ass just caught your lunch for you."

"Thanks, noble savage." Despite the quip Starkmann was snapping a mental photograph of the scene as a kind of keepsake: Bonny George, his round head resting neckless on the shelf of his shoulders; the backdrop of tall pines reflected in the pool, and the fish with its shining belly, its lateral stripe pale-rose in the light of the new sun. Far off, the ravens' cries continued to trouble the morning stillness. A lone bird, drawn by their calls, glided overhead on its dreadful wings.

After fishing the pool half an hour more without producing another strike, they abandoned it in favor of some others downstream, also lairs of monster rainbows. When that strategy proved ineffective, Bonny George became defensive and inclined to make excuses, as if he were a guide and Starkmann his customer.

At midmorning, their stomachs growling, they took a break in a meadow where a spring bubbled out of moss-haired rocks and the sun fell warm on their backs. Starkmann peeled off his damp waders and socks. One of the patches was peeling back at the edges. He hung the socks to dry on a tag-alder branch, then took two tins of pickled herring and a foil-wrapped packet of crackers from the back pocket of his vest. The two young men made finger sandwiches of herring and crackers and ate ravenously, washing breakfast down with spring water so cold it was just this side of ice. While Bonny George gutted his trout and studied its entrails for clues as to which bait would be best, Starkmann lounged in the grass, his legs pleasantly tired from fighting the river. A kingfisher made a smudge of blue and white against the spruce that fenced the meadow. The grass felt good on his naked feet, the sensation taking him back to one of those long-ago summers when he walked barefoot in the woods with his father, who was then initiating him into the mysteries of fly-fishing. The remembrance weighted Starkmann's heart with a sense of loss, that strange and inevitable loss of connection between father and son. He could think of nothing they had in common any longer, nor see anything of Lucius in himself beyond his height, fair complexion, and pale-blue eyes.

The breach between them, opened three years ago when Lucius had behaved atrociously at Anne's wedding, had widened the next year, during Christian's senior year in high school. A few months before graduation, Christian announced that he would not enroll as a student of divinity. Mathematics and physics having been his best subjects, he wanted to pursue a scientific course. Besides, he was a disaster as a public speaker even in class. He could not imagine himself sermonizing to hundreds of people. Lucius, the fervent liberal in public but an autocrat in his domestic life, was upset by his son's declaration of independence. He had set up a trust fund to pay for divinity school; it had always been his hope and ambition to see his only son follow him into the ministry, he said, as if the church were a family firm. Off and on, the argument lasted for weeks, ending when Lucius offered a threat and a compromise: If Christian did not enroll as a student of the ministry, he would not see one cent of the trust fund; if, on the other hand, he tried divinity school for a year and found it was not for him, he would be free to take up whatever course he wished. Christian gave in, a surrender that forced upon him a recognition of how tightly he remained in his father's thrall, and gave rise to a secret desire to commit a liberating apostasy.

A tap on his shoulder brought him back to the present. Bonny George pointed to the blunt, brown head of a beaver, swimming downstream.

"If I was a traditionalist like Grandpa, I'd say that was a sign. Mr. Beaver is telling us where the fish are, hey." Bonny George stood, his enthusiasm restored. "Put your waders on and pack your trash. We're going."

"Where? The fish are here. They're just not biting."

"For a reason. They've got it too easy in these quiet pools what with all the spring runoff. Too much feed in the river. All they do is lie down there and wait for breakfast, lunch, and dinner to drift into their mouths. There's a big beaver dam downstream of here, with real fast water below it, real rainbow water. The fish have to work for their supper in there, snatch at whatever comes by before the river takes it away. We'll hike to it. Over that. There's a great view from the top." He pointed to a high ridge, glowering north of them. "A great view. Listen to me. I sound like a park ranger."

In the virgin woods on the ridge, they again found themselves in a premature twilight. The trees, spaced as in a park, stood straight and very tall. Far above, their branches wove a dense, quilled awning that allowed the sun to fall only through the places where it was rent, the angled shafts of light giving the woods the appearance of a picture-book enchanted forest. The earth smelled of dampness and shade. Toadstools clumped in the blue shadows, and a fungus that might have been a throwback to the life-forms of the world's beginning scaled the jagged stumps of trees felled by lightning, wind, or age. In places, half-concealed by underbrush, dark holes peered out from the face of the ridge—bear dens or wolf lairs, Starkmann imagined as he sidestepped up the slope, his waders dragging on his legs like a ball and chain. In front of him, Bonny George skirted a deadfall whose trunk, lying flat, reached as high as Starkmann's chest. Its roots flared out like the twisted spokes of a huge wheel. He wondered how old that tree had been when it had fallen, and tried to guess the age of the living trees, so high he had to crane his neck to see their tops, their trunks thicker at the base than cathedral columns. He was surprised to notice they were white pine, as surprised as he would have been to see buffalo grazing on a Kansas range. White pine had once covered the Upper Peninsula from end to end; then, during the logging boom that had begun in the last decade of the last century, they were cut down in a slaughter that had been to the north woods what the annihilation of the buffalo had been to the plains. Over a period of twenty years, the great trees fell by the hundreds of thousands to the logger's axe, and vast fires burned over the slashings until, it was said, most of the Peninsula resembled a battlefield. These trees had escaped somehow, and Starkmann remarked on this, holding his voice down, as if to speak loudly would offend whatever spirits guarded the place.

Bonny George paused for breath and explained that the ridge had been too steep and rugged for the horse-drawn skidders to haul the timber to the railheads.

"So the loggers left it alone. It's one of the last stands of virgin white pine left on the U.P., hey. Some of these trees started growing before Marquette and Joliet ever saw this place. Beautiful, isn't it?"

Starkmann wasn't sure if *beautiful* described it: *haunted* or *primeval* would have been more like it. The forest belonged to an older America, untouched and unowned. As he climbed through it, there were moments when he felt an odd awkwardness that had nothing to do with physical grace. It was more a fundamental disharmony between his own rhythms and the deepest rhythms of the woods; he was dancing out of step with the forest's silent music. At other moments, looking at the columnar trees and pillars of sunlight, he had the sensation that he had stumbled into a forbidden temple, which his heavy footsteps, his very presence, had profaned. Minute by minute, the dread he had felt the day before crept back into him. He could neither shake it off nor explain it, unless it was some half-formed racial memory: a century and a half ago, his ancestors had left their tame and tired Europe to pioneer in forests such as these; and they had suffered and died in them, falling to cold, to wild beasts, and to the red man's arrow.

The soil thinned near the crest of the ridge; the trees grew smaller. Soon there was no soil at all, just bare granite blocks. The only trees were jack pine, sprouting from the fissures in the granite, upon which lichens spread in reddish smears like dried blood on stone altars. A raven rose with a rubbery slap of its wings. A dozen more perched motionless in a nearby pine: black ornaments in a Christmas tree. As the two young men drew closer, the birds flew off, squawking protests against the intrusion.

"I knew they were running a buck," said Bonny George, abruptly veering off toward something he'd spotted out of the corner of his eye. Starkmann saw it a second later: an antlered head lying beside a stump like a trophy fallen from a wall. Little else remained: a few tufts of hair and meat speckling a large dark stain in the pine needles. The skeleton had been torn apart, ribs and leg bones crushed for their marrow, the fragments scattered like bits of broken china. Whatever the wolves had left had been disposed of by the ravens, the forest's garbage men. They had even pecked out the eyes.

"Some buck too." The Indian pointed with his spinning rod. "Look at that rack."

But Starkmann could not look at the antlers. The maggot-squirming cavities where the eyes had been fixed his gaze, hypnotized him, and persuaded him that living eyes were on his back.

"Hey, George. Let's get going."

"The way I figure it, the first wolf we heard ran him along the ridge line." Squatting on his haunches, Bonny George studied a paw print like a detective examining evidence. "Then the others came up and cut him off and cornered him here."

The hairs on the back of Starkmann's neck rose from the stare of the watching eyes. He started to turn to look behind him, but stopped himself, afraid of what he might see. *Wind-time, wolf-time.*

"Let's go. Let's get back to fishing."

"They don't always wait until their prey is dead, y'know. They'll bring down a moose or a big buck and it'll still be alive when they rip its belly open and tear the guts out. Sometimes a moose or a deer will actually *see* itself getting eaten."

"Let's go."

Atop the ridge, where they sat to rest on an outcropping, Starkmann no longer felt menaced by the invisible eyes. He was on the high ground, where a human being ought to be, a clear view all around him. Ten or twelve miles northward, the big lake showed as a blue haze reaching away from where the woods ended. In all other directions, there were only woods, rising and falling in varying shades of green until they bumped into the sky. Even Lake Superior did not mark their end; it was no more than a gigantic eye, glimmering in the face of a forest that greened southward across the Upper Peninsula into northern Wisconsin, west into Minnesota, east into Ontario, and north five hundred miles to Hudson's Bay. From this vantage point, the international border and the boundaries between the states seemed ridiculous fictions compared to the geographical reality. Michigan, Minnesota, Canada—it was all one forest, broken only by its lakes and rivers. It dawned on Starkmann then that he and Bonny George were not on a ridge at the northern edge of the United States but in the heart of a continent. And what a wild heart it still was, a heart the white man had ravaged but never completely conquered, home to the bear and the coyote, the wolf and the wildcat, Indian country.

Indian country. An idea—actually it was more a notion than a fully-rounded idea—began to tease Starkmann's brain. *Indian country.* Why hadn't he thought of it before? He popped to his feet in a state of uncharacteristic excitement.

"I just realized it, George! You don't have to go to Canada. You're as good as there already."

The Indian, lounging on the outcrop with crossed legs, looked up, a tight smile skewing a corner of his mouth.

"For a college man you can be pretty slow sometimes. I thought of it weeks ago."

"You don't have to leave your grandfather." Starkmann went on as if he hadn't heard. His arm described an arc over the boundless green. "Look at this. A man who knows this country and knows what he's doing could hide out up here indefinitely."

"Let's say I did it. Hid out in these woods where no one could find me. Come next winter, when it gets down to thirty or forty below, where are you going to be when I've got icicles hanging from my dork? Warming your hands between some coed's legs, that's where. Or don't divinity students do things like that?"

"I'm trying to help. We've got a problem. Problems have solutions. I'm giving you a solution."

"You're the one with the problem. You're starting to sound like a missionary, except instead of saving my red soul from the devil, you're going to save my red ass from the army. Why can't you lay off?"

Starkmann's emotional watchdog censored him from giving the answer he wanted to give.

"I guess because I think the war is wrong."

The Indian scrutinized him for several moments.

"Do you really think it's wrong?"

"What do you mean? Sure I do."

"Do you think it's wrong just because your old man does? What's wrong with it?"

"Are you trying to tell me it's right?"

"I don't think it's right or wrong. I think it just *is*, like a blizzard or one of those storms that come up on the lake in the fall."

"Then why did you write and tell me you were thinking of taking off to Canada?"

"Because I knew I'd miss all this. I like the way I live. I love it, hey. I love the fishing in the spring and summer, and the hunting in the fall, and checking traps with my grandpa in the winter. I even like going into the woods to cut pulp. When I knock off, everything seems fine. No matter what was bothering me, it stops bothering me after I've been in the woods. The woods make everything all right." Bonny George sat up and flung a stone over the lip of the ridge. He threw it so hard that, for an instant, it looked as if it would defy gravity and sail through space forever; then it dropped into the trees below. "But it wouldn't be the same if I had to keep on the lookout for the FBI, or the federal marshal, or whoever they get on your case. I can just see myself, hiding out in a cabin like I'm John Dillinger or someone."

Starkmann did not know what to say. He watched a squirrel dart up a jack pine. Far beneath him a patch of the river flashed through the trees.

"Besides, when Estelle Hicks sees me in uniform, she'll spread those white girl's thighs for me. She's a cheerleader now at U. of M., screwing the captain of the football team, I'll bet. But when she sees me with my medals—so long, football hero; hello, redskin lover boy."

Estelle Hicks had been his unrequited love in high school.

"She isn't going to sleep with you just because you've got a uniform. C'mon, George, this is serious."

"No, it isn't. You are." Bonny George got to his feet. "You wanted to get back to fishing. Let's go."

They followed an easy trail down the spine of the ridge toward the riverbed. Starkmann was frustrated, and a little annoyed with his friend's stubbornness. Or was it Indian fatalism? The war simply *was*, like a storm. Why, he wondered, did that make no sense on the one hand, while on the other it made more sense than anything he'd heard from his father? Lucius opposed the war, Bonny George accepted it as a fact of life, but what did he, Christian Starkmann, think? Distracted, he tripped over a root and stumbled forward like a dazed fighter before he caught his balance. But the near fall knocked a thought loose.

"Hey, George, you asked me what's wrong with the war. Do you want to know what I think is wrong with it? Not what my father thinks, but what I think?"

"Watch it!"

A low pine branch that had caught on the Indian's shirt whipped back and stung Starkmann in the chest. He shoved it aside.

"Do you want to know what's really wrong with this war?"

"I hope there's plenty rainbows in those rapids. We've got to do something to keep your mind occupied."

"What's wrong with it is that guys like you have to go and guys like me get out of it."

"Preacher's son, if your conscience is bothering you that much, we can do what I said last night. Trade places."

"I was stating a principle."

Bonny George stopped walking and stood looking at the ground, his hand braced on a tree.

"Listen, it's settled," he said tiredly. "I thought it out. I talked to Grandpa about it, and it's settled."

"What'd Louis say?"

"Nothin' at first." The Indian gave an embarrassed smile. "After I told him I wasn't sure what to do, he had to go off and meditate. So that's what he did, and when he came back, he said he'd had a vision, and the vision told me I should go. To Nam, I mean."

Starkmann paused, disbelieving what he'd just heard.

"A *vision?*"

Bonny George nodded.

"What kind of vision?" Starkmann laughed. "Christ, that's crazy."

"Grandpa can get pretty weird when he goes traditional. You don't know how weird. If you saw him when he gets like that, you wouldn't think he was the same guy. You only know half of him, the half he shows to white people."

"All right. He gets weird, but you can't go off and do something like this because he had a vision. You don't *believe* that stuff, do you?"

"Let's say I keep an open mind about it."

"George, that's . . . Look, is that all he said? That he had his vision?"

"No. He gave me a history lesson, a kind of pep talk, I guess, all about how the Ojibwa migrated from the Atlantic to the Great Lakes and then west of the Mississippi, and whipped everyone along the way. We whipped the Iroquois, and we whipped the Sioux. We even whipped the U.S. Army in the last Indian war."

"So what?"

"So, the Sioux didn't fight the last battle at Wounded Knee. The Ojibwa did. The Battle of Leech Lake, Minnesota, in the fall of 'ninety-eight. And the Ojibwa won that one. Killed eighteen troopers and their commanding officer, and sent the other ones running back to Fort Whalton."

"That isn't what I meant. I meant, what's all that tribal lore got to do with you?"

"We're not pacifists. We're not cowards. We don't run. That was pretty much Grandpa's message."

Starkmann flinched as if he'd been struck.

"What do you mean by that? What's that supposed to mean?"

Bonny George smiled and shook his head.

"That was my *mishomis* talking. Even the spics can't beat an Indian when it comes to macho. It's got nothing to do with you, Chris. Look at it this way: I have to go and you have to stay because that's the way things are. Can't you see that? It's just the way things are. Onward, Christian soldier. This is supposed to be a fishing trip."

He started off again. Starkmann followed, not entirely sure if his friend's assurances had been sincere. Coward. The word burned inside of him, burned. It would gall him if that was what Bonny George thought of him. Then, his mind suddenly turning in the opposite direction, he thought: what difference does it make what he thinks? Maybe he isn't brave enough *not* to go. I have to go and you have to stay because that's the way things are. Was that courage or resignation? And if he was going because his grandfather had received a message in a vision, he had to be half crazy. And so did Louis.

With these thoughts and questions spinning around inside his head, Starkmann walked on down the trail. A chipmunk sitting on a stump watched him with quick, nervous movements of its head while, far behind, the ravens shrieked over the scraps of their carrion feast.

3

The beaver dam had been constructed on the ruins of a man-made one, built by the CCC back in the thirties and later dynamited by an irate Finn who'd objected to the government's meddling with nature. Behind the barrier of logs, branches, and twigs, the beavers' domed lodges humped like the backs of enormous turtles out of water as wide and smooth as a pond. Downstream, wild with released pressure, the Windigo battered through a gorge, its froths and boils now disclosing, now concealing rocks against which the sturdiest canoe would have been smashed to splinters. Gentler rapids whitened the water below; riffles bubbled at the edges of glassy channels. This is where Starkmann and Bonny George started fishing, Starkmann inching out into the middle to give himself casting room. The current clutched his legs as if it existed for no other reason than to upend and drown him. Some distance away, Bonny George tossed his bait from a fallen hemlock that reached halfway across the river, like a broken bridge. His rod bent immediately, and he reeled in another small trout, smaller than the first, and slipped it into his creel. In less than ten minutes he'd caught two more, but released the last: The three fish in his creel would be more than enough for lunch.

All the while, Starkmann kept casting across the current, letting his fly tumble until the line came taut; then he would begin his retrieve. He was aware that he wasn't concentrating, but could not get his mind to focus. The sound of the river made him irritable; there was in its incessant boom an urgency and turbulence that aggravated the unrest within himself.

He snapped his rod for another cast but had too much line out; the back-cast snagged in a tree leaning over the bank. Instead of wading to shore to free it, he yanked the rod, which broke the leader and left the fly dangling on the monofilament strand. It looked like a hairy, legless spider. As he tied on a new one—he chose the Marabou streamer—Bonny George whooped again; another trout had snatched his bait. Envious and angry, Starkmann felt like throwing his rod at him. Wolves and Indians are brothers. Legendary bears guard the secrets to magic cures. Mystical visions. Why worry about a superstitious bush redskin's opinion of his physical courage? That wasn't fair, Starkmann chided himself. It was snobbery, and it did nothing to resolve the self-doubts awakened by his friend's remark. The question nagging Starkmann was: had he given in to his father's wish out of filial loyalty or because he knew that a divinity student's deferment and a cleric's collar guaranteed his safety? Maybe he *was* yellow, and, yes, his father as well. He remembered the shame that used to prick him in high school, when he entered his friends' houses and saw the mantelpiece photographs of their fathers in uniform, heroes in the one crusade the Reverend Starkmann had avoided. But how could the courage of a man who had braved so much opposition, who had withstood the blows of billy clubs and electric cattle prods, be suspect? For the first time, he wondered whether his father, ashamed of himself deep down, had accepted those blows as a form of self-punishment, or as a way of proving that he did not lack bravery after all. Starkmann did not know what to think, what to believe. His mind tumbled like the river, and the only firm moral bottom he could find was the principle he had enunciated. That men like Bonny George had no real choices, while men like himself could live their lives as they pleased, offended his sense of fairness. Possibly that explained his missionary obsession: helping his friend escape would justify his own evasion.

These were Christian Starkmann's thoughts when his fly vanished in a riffle, the rod bent almost into a U, and the line burned off the reel with such speed that it was down to the backing in seconds. The suddenness and power of the strike arrested his heart and instantly blew every thought out of his head. The fish was running downstream, toward the deadfall where Bonny George stood, gesturing and shouting encouragement. The trout would snag the leader in the submerged branches if it did not strip the reel first. Starkmann tightened the drag, lifted the rod against the fish's strength, and stopped its run within a yard of the deadfall.

"I can see it!" Bonny George hollered, looking down. "It's right under me. It's a beast, Chris, a beast!"

Now, the panic of the strike and the first run over, Starkmann began methodically to work the fish back toward him, the line and the thin, bowed length of bamboo quivering with tension. Through them he felt every move the trout made, each shake of its head and fan of its tail; and out of this telegraphy he formed a picture of it, swimming with the fly streaming from a corner of its jaw. It came slowly, fighting every inch of the way. Half the lost line had been retrieved when the fish streaked off on its second run, angling across the river, the reel screeching; then, as if it knew a bow in the line would create slack and make it easier to spit the hook, the fish turned sharply again and ran upstream. It ran against the river as swiftly as it had run with it. Starkmann, turning to face the fish, almost falling as he turned in the swift water, could not believe the trout's strength. He watched his line peeling away from him into the gorge, where the rapids pounded like surf on a rocky coast.

It was a frightening sight, all that white fury booming straight at him; the fear itself compelled him to wade toward the dangerous water. He pretended that this risky maneuver was justified by the fish's size and power: To gain line on it, he had to chase it on foot. He waded easily for the first few yards, where the water was shallow; then it reached past his knees. When he was waist-deep, his movements became those of a man walking through quicksand. He regained a few yards of line. The water rose higher, breaking against his chest. His muscles stiffened from the freezing spray splashing over the top of his waders. He wasn't worried about them flooding from the top because he'd cinched his waist belt tightly; but he knew he could not pursue the fish any farther. He was already at the mouth of the gorge, its rock-sided throat boiling in front of him.

The movements of the trout, signaled through the rod and line, told Starkmann that the fish had tired and was holding behind a boulder, where it had found refuge from the current. With his tackle held out high in front of him, he tried to budge it. The line went limp. He wound up the slack, praying the hook had not pulled. In a moment, he was tight to the fish again. It jumped the moment after, its leap like an outdoor artist's fantasy, the head pointed at the sky, the thick body arched, the tail clearing the water, droplets flying as the trout shook in midair, then flung itself back into the river. Its speckled colors had been dazzling, its size startling. It was not just the biggest trout he'd ever seen; it was bigger than anything he'd ever imagined. And now it was making another run downstream. To keep his rod pointed at it, Starkmann pivoted. The current knocked him off balance. He took a couple of sidesteps to regain his foothold. The bottom, ground into powder by the river's endless milling, crumbled sickeningly beneath him and, in an instant, vanished altogether. He was swept away, his legs thrashing in a deep channel he hadn't seen through the water's roil. Still holding his rod in one hand, he desperately stroked with the other for a shoal a few yards away. A strong eddy spun him around as if he were nothing more than a floating branch, and carried him into a rapid at the channel's edge. The rapid struck his face with the force of a blow, tore the rod from his hand, and slammed him into a rock that shredded the frayed patch in his waders. Water poured in through the hole, numbing his leg from the calf down. He clawed for a handhold on the rock, but the river ripped his fingers loose and shot him back into the channel, his landing net dragging behind, the flooded boot pulling him down. Snatches of things flickered before his half-blinded eyes: a patch of sky, white spume, a burst of the forest's green. Where was Bonny George? He screamed his friend's name, swallowed water, and choked just before he careened headfirst into another rock. There was an instant of color-spotted blackness. What he saw next was the syrupy brown of the channel's depths, and mist hazing a steep ledge beside him. He reached to grab hold of the ledge but the current snatched his hand away. His legs kicked hard for the surface, the coldness of the water shooting bolts of pain through his head. He caught a short breath before the weight in his boot again sucked him down. He could no longer hear the river's thunder. It was quiet, so quiet. He liked the silence. The ache in his skull wasn't as sharp. Ahead, through an amber fog, sunken branches reached out for him like skeletal fingers. He knew he should be afraid of them, but he wasn't. The silence lulled him. He felt drowsy, quit struggling, and let himself drift in the soundless, ceaseless flow.

A violent pull in his midsection jerked him back to the surface. The booming filled his ears once more, and he saw the sky. He was floating on his back in still water while Bonny George pulled him by the arms toward the bank. He drew in a breath and gagged.

The Indian beached him like a boat, rolled him over, and straddled him. His friend's strong hands pressed down on his back, then relaxed, then pressed down again. Water in his lungs siphoned through his throat and gurgled out of his mouth. He coughed, then breathed free, aware as he breathed of how cold he was, cold all over except for a spot above his right eye, warmed by blood.

Bonny George got off him and helped him sit up. He was a little dizzy, his vision slightly blurred. He sat trembling with his arms folded and his knees drawn in to his chest.

"Are you all right?" Bonny George asked.

"Cold."

"You were headed right for that deadfall I'd been standing on. River's dredged the bottom under it. Must be more'n ten feet deep and full of branches."

"I'm cold."

"You would have got caught in those branches like a whitefish in a gill net, and then I reckon you would have been as cold as a man can get."

"I'm really cold now."

"You would have seen your Jesus, preacher's son."

"Freezing."

"Get those waders and your clothes off."

Starkmann, hunched down and shuddering, was revolted by the idea. He didn't move.

"This is a medicine man's grandson talking to you. You'll get hypothermia if you keep your clothes on." Bonny George was also drenched, his hair matted to his forehead. He reached into his trouser pocket and took out an aluminum cylinder of waterproof matches. "Good thing I always carry these in the boondocks. I'll get a fire going. C'mon, get those clothes off."

Starkmann sat and shivered. He shivered so hard he thought he was going to shake himself apart.

"All right, I'll give you a hand."

Bonny George undid the waist belt and tugged and pulled the waders off. They lay on the ground like molted skin. What looked like a gallon of water had spilled out of the hole where the patch had been.

"Are you going to do the rest, or do I have to undress you like a baby?"

Starkmann got slowly to his feet, took off his trousers, and unbuttoned his shirt with a quaking of wrinkled fingers. His knees shook from another kind of cold: The reaction to his close call set in as he remembered the weird attractiveness of the river's depths, its womblike silence, the ease with which he'd surrendered himself to the power of its endless tide. He wondered how long he had been under. It had seemed like hours, though he knew that could not have been possible. He touched the cut over his eye. It wasn't deep. The blood had clotted, but the bump on his forehead was tender, big as a golf ball.

"We'll fix that with the first-aid kit at camp." Bonny George tore a sheet of bark from a birch tree, cut it into strips with his pocket knife, and laid the strips on the ground for tinder. "Meantime, you'd best move around. Get the blood pumping. Find me some squaw wood. I'll pick up some logs."

The Indian loped off upstream, toward the beaver-slashed woods near the dam.

When he'd gathered enough kindling, Starkmann piled it atop the strips of birchbark. Bonny George reappeared a short time later, carrying an armload of beaver-gnawed logs. He then jury-rigged a rack by placing four forked sticks in a square around the firewood and laying two more sticks lengthwise in the forks. After the Indian had stripped, both young men draped their clothes over the rack. The bark took to the match like paper; soon a big fire was crackling. Starkmann huddled close to it.

"The greatest wonder that ever came to the Indian was fire—that's what Grandpa says."

And to Starkmann the fire did seem a wonder at that moment, a sacred magic.

"Soon as our clothes are dry we'll hoof back to camp." The Indian poked one of the logs. "I'll tell you, I've heard some guys *say* they'd do anything to catch a big fish, but you're the first one I've ever seen do it."

"It was some fish."

"Lost your fancy swizzle stick. That fish was so big, she's probably gonna pull it all the way to Lake Superior if she hasn't thrown the hook."

"How big do you think?"

"Fifteen pounds if she was an ounce, a big steelhead female that hadn't roed out yet, but she wasn't worth drowning for. What the hell were you thinking of, chasing her into that white water?"

"I guess I wasn't thinking, period."

"Didn't you hear me hollering at you to get your skinny white butt back downstream? Next thing I know, your skinny white butt *is* coming downstream, fifty miles an hour. You don't want to take chances with this old cannibal, hey."

"This what?"

"Cannibal. That's what Windigo means in Ojibway. It's an evil spirit that gets into people and drives 'em so insane they eat other people."

A spasm of cold shivered up Starkmann's spine, and, turning his back to the fire, he looked at the river. It had seemed evil, alive with lethal intent when it was sweeping him away, the malevolent force he had dreaded; but that, he realized, was nonsense. The river was flowing now no differently from the way it had before he'd fallen in, no differently from the way it would have had he drowned in it, flowing as it had ever since its birth in the waters of melting glaciers twenty thousand years ago. Neither evil nor good, the river simply *was*.

"How long do you think I was under?" he asked.

"I don't know. Not long. A few seconds maybe."

"It seemed a lot longer. Even now, when I think about it, it seems like I was down there for hours. It was like a dream. You know how dreams seem to go on and on all night, but I read somewhere they don't last more than a few moments."

"I don't know about that," Bonny George said with a shrug of his square shoulders. "I'm a pulp cutter, hey. My grandpa's the dream expert. All the *Mide* masters are heavy into dreams."

"I wonder what makes them seem to take a long time when they don't."

"What are we talking about dreams for? Got enough to deal with in the real world. What we have here is one white-ass and one blanket-ass, both buck-ass naked with one fishing pole between them and no fish for lunch."

"What happened to the ones you caught?"

"I lost my creel when I went in after you."

There was something in the flat simplicity of the statement that moved Starkmann and made him wish he had not been born with such a reserved nature. Absently, he watched three black ducks skimming over the river toward the pond above the dam. What was the form, the protocol for thanking a man who has saved your life?

"How did you . . . ?"

"I don't know," Bonny George answered before he could finish the sentence. "I saw you go under, and I dove off the log and somehow got a hold of your belt. Next thing I knew I was on my feet in the shallows, dragging you to the bank."

Starkmann sat silent for a minute or two, wondering, had the situation been reversed, if he would have had the same courage. He liked to think he would have, but wasn't sure. Without a word he turned and offered his hand.

"Oh, hell, Chris. It wasn't a favor."

"Dammit, George," Starkmann said, holding his hand out.

The Indian shrugged shyly and extended his hand, and when Starkmann clasped it and saw the smile curving under the Roman nose, his inhibitions broke down for once, and he hooked an arm around the thick neck and pressed Bonny George's face to his chest and held it there without embarrassment.

"Dammit, George. Dammit."

"Take it easy," Bonny George said, wrestling free of the embrace. "This looks real weird, two naked guys hugging in the woods."

Starkmann laughed with release and looked into the cheerful fire. He could still feel the warmth on his chest, where it had been touched by his friend's face, and it struck him that he could not imagine their lives following separate paths. It seemed impossible. No, it *was* impossible. In that instant he made a decision. Actually, he wasn't sure if he could call it a decision, since that word implied careful thought, a weighing of pros and cons. This had come in the manner of an inspiration. All of a sudden it was *there*, inside him, the clear knowledge of what was required of him, required not by others but by himself. He did not have any choices, either. His nature dictated what he had to do: He had to share the risk. *Ich kann nicht anders.* The words on Martin Luther's monument. I can do no other. This necessity was so obvious that, he suspected, it had probably been there all along, staring him in the face. He simply hadn't seen it, or had refused to.

A giddiness made his head feel as if it were about to float off his shoulders—relief from his dread. He now recognized that he had unconsciously known, at least since yesterday, that he would come to this moment, and the dread had been the fear that always precedes a decision to do something irrevocable. Now that it was done (and as far as he was concerned it was as good as done, the act of signing his name a mere formality), he felt as light as the air itself.

He took a stick and poked one of the aspen logs, rolling it over in a puff of sparks and white ash.

"I was just thinking . . ."

"Yeah? You should've been thinking before you walked into that white water."

"I was thinking about what Louis said. That if you can't imagine something happening, it can't happen."

"How about that. My old *mishomis* getting inside the head of a preacher's son."

"I can't imagine your getting on that bus come Tuesday and me driving back to campus. I can't imagine that any more than you can imagine yourself going to Canada and never coming back."

Bonny George shook his head.

"That subject again. You just almost drowned and you're on that again. A kraut gets something into his square head and you can't blow it out with a nuclear device."

"Well, something's got into my kraut head and there's no getting it out."

Starkmann was not being deliberately oblique. What he was going to do was, for him, so daring, and would cause his father such pain, that he had to get used to the idea, live with it for a while before he could state it directly.

"Just what's got into your head?" Bonny George hesitated and Starkmann saw comprehension flood his eyes. "Wait a minute. . . . Hold on one goddamned minute."

"I think it's been in the back of my mind ever since you wrote and told me you'd decided not to go to Canada."

"That bang you took in the head did some serious damage. You think you owe me one, right? I plucked your white butt out of the river, so now you owe me something. Listen, you don't. You thanked me. You gave me a great big hug. You can kiss me if you want, but don't do anything dumb. You don't have to go."

"Yes, I do. And not because I feel I owe you anything. Because I can't imagine not going."

Agitated, the Indian stood and brushed the dirt and pieces of bark from his buttocks.

"I can't talk about this kind of thing buck-ass naked, my dork hanging out." He took his half-dried trousers off the rack and pulled them on. "You're not making any sense."

"It's your philosophy."

"Blanket-ass philosophy. Blanket-ass philosophy is for blanket-asses, not for honkies. C'mon, suit up. We'll hike back to camp. I'll make you some coffee, take care of that cut. You'll feel better."

"After we hike out of here tomorrow, we'll drive into Marquette . . ."

"They probably won't take you. They'll reject you on grounds of insanity." Bonny George lifted his face toward the sky. "O Lord, O Great Spirit, whatever you're called, help me to understand the paleface. They're crazy."

Laughing, Starkmann followed the trajectory of the Indian's gaze, and saw a raven lofting blackly out of a pine on the other side of the river. He aimed an imaginary shotgun at the bird, swinging his arms to lead it. It glided across the river and soared overhead, its broken shadow falling on the birch forest, Starkmann tracking its flight with the barrel of his make-believe gun.

"*Bang,*" he said with a grin. "*Bang-bang.*"

The raven cawed, and was answered by another, deeper in the forest.

BAWAJIGAYWIN

(VISION QUEST)

Migizi—eagle—a good sign, he thought in the ancient language. The eagle perched atop a dead pine, branchless as a pole.
Wawiekumig had been so absorbed in his study of the scroll, which
told the story of the bear's four breakthroughs, he had not heard the
eagle fly in nor seen its shadow cross the sun. Even when he had
lifted his eyes to rest them and looked straight at the bird, he had not
noticed it; motionless, wings folded tight along its body, feathers
bark-brown, it had at first appeared to be part of the tree, the tree's
top. Then it had turned its head and half-lifted its wings, folding
them again, and he had realized his mistake. It was a bald eagle, a
young one, its head not yet turned white. Its appearance augured the
success of the difficult endeavor he had begun today, for his clan was
the Bird clan and the eagle their do-dem; as the eagle sought the
upper reaches of the sky, so did the Bird people seek the upper
reaches of awareness and the eagle's all-encompassing vision. Migizi
was also his personal manito, guardian spirit. Sixty-nine years ago,
before he became Wawiekumig and was known only by his English
name, Louis, he had flown around the world with one, seeing the
world as the eagle does, whole and entire.

He had been thirteen then, on his first Bawajigaywin, and had
made this flight after fasting eight days and nights in the platform his
father had built high in a white pine. The experience of circling the
earth from far above had been a wonder, but also baffling. When his
father, whose tribal name was Tcianung, had come to check up
on him, he asked help interpreting what he had seen. "I've taught you

that the meanings of a man's dreams cannot be explained by anyone but himself," Tcianung, a first-degree Mide, had replied. "Meditate a while longer and tell me what you learn." *Man*—Louis had heard the word: a man's dreams, man, not boy. He understood that to gain the fullness of his manhood it was not enough merely to acquire a vision, but also to have the power to know its significance.

And so, remaining on the platform another day and night without food or water, he had pondered his dream, using reason at first. But reason could carry him only so far. Understanding escaped him. In the gray before dawn, weak and dizzy from his fast, he felt an energy enter him, beginning at his feet, then rapidly flowing through his entire body; and this energy force, which he would later learn was ahmunisoowin, revealed the dream's significance in a burst of insight.

As soon as it was manifest, he climbed down, returned home, and after restoring his strength with fried rabbit and maple water, told his father: "From now on, I shall be called Wawiekumig, Round Earth, and I wish to have a shirt with beadwork in the shape of an eagle. The eagle is to be my guardian in bad times, my guide in times of temptation. He has shown me my purpose in life: I wish to begin studies for the Mide."

Tcianung answered that the shirt would be easy—his mother was excellent at beadwork and would make him a fine one—but studies for the Mide, there was a problem. Few of the Mide masters were still alive, and those who were charged exorbitant fees: not pelts, rifles, and knives as in former times, but money, as much as a hundred dollars just to start. Tcianung, a trapper, did not earn enough to afford such a sum.

"Then I'll go to work," said Wawiekumig, filled with the sense of maturity Vision Quest had brought to him. "I'll earn it."

He hired on as cook's boy in a logging camp, where he scrubbed pots and pans, cut firewood for the stove, and learned the lumber-jacks' colorful English, along with a few other things about them he did not care to know. In a year he had saved enough for six months' instruction, which he took under Red Sky, a holy man who knew the Mide backward and forward. By the time he reached fifteen, Wawiekumig had been initiated into the first degree; but, as the instruction fees increased for each level, more than ten seasons passed before he could wear on his dancing bags the cross-pole symbol of the fourth degree.

Though young, he swiftly became known as a Man-Who-Knows-Everything, priest, prophet, and healer. He cured the sick in mind and body with the remedies he had learned; in a vision he had foretold of hard times, the times the white people called the Great Depression, and had instructed the tribal council to prepare for the worst; he had conducted funeral rites, guiding souls down the Wide Path to the West into the Village of the Dead and the Dzhibai Midewegun, the Ghost Lodge.

The Man-Who-Knows-Everything, a man with powers in this world and the invisible world, an important man on the Vieux Desert reservation until the Mide declined in influence. A man in whose presence others had to tread lightly, for if he knew good medicine, he also knew the bad, mudjimushkeeki; if he could guide one spirit safely into the Village of the Dead, he could, if he chose, cause another to wander forever through the swamps of the Afterworld. The Man-Who-Knows-Everything—Wawiekumig basked in his reputation, though he'd never abused his powers, knowing that to do so would offend the Mide manitos and bring upon him and his own family death, disease, and madness, knowing that he did not know everything, nor even a small part of it. The more he learned, the more he realized how much more there was to learn, the universe infinite in its mysteries. The higher he climbed the levels of spiritual enlightenment, the higher he realized he had to climb, just as migizi, soaring above the clouds, sees there is more sky above, and above that still more, leading to the border between the physical world and the truly real world, the world of dreams and of the manitos, who were themselves but faces of Kitchi-Manito, the Great Spirit, who is all, all that ever was, is, will be, or can be.

He is the only Man-Who-Knows-Everything, and He is not man, Wawiekumig said silently, watching the eagle. The slight turns of its head, the half-extensions of its wings as it adjusted its grip on the treetop were the only movements within his circle of vision. He had not heard it flapping overhead, nor seen its shadow pass the sun. Ten years ago he would have seen it right away; twenty years ago he would have heard the whisper of its glide; forty years ago he would have known it was coming before he saw or heard it. But he was in his eighty-second year now, his senses failing. The decline of his eyesight, his growing deafness did not trouble him; those were natural in a man so old. Of more concern was the diminishing of his ahmun-isoowin—his spiritual sight and hearing. Ahmunisoowin—the intuition of the imagination, the power to perceive truths beyond the reach of the senses and reason, to receive messages from the invisibles. He would need that power to the full for the ordeal ahead, one that could well kill a man of his age. This morning he had risen before dawn and left his cabin in the truck, following back roads until there were no roads, then continuing on foot, six, seven miles, his pack heavy on his shoulders, as heavy, he'd thought, as the Pack of Life had been upon the Bear's back. He walked without trails to guide him, knowing the way because he'd made the journey so often, each journey more difficult. He had begun to doubt his strength, but migizi, appearing at this moment, restored his confidence; this was a sign and not an accident or coincidence, for nothing happens without a reason.

Not one to ignore such a fortuitous omen, he rose, slowly and stiffly, ducked into his wigwam, and took a pinch of tobacco from his medicine bundle, an otter-skin bag that hung from the center of the roof. He went outside and, padding softly so as not to startle the bird, stood at the base of the tree, scattered the tobacco, then turned his eyes upward.

Migizi, greatest of all birds, he prayed, not to this eagle, this young one with head still brown, but to the power it represented. Migizi, you who sees all, who never kills but to eat, cares for your young, and mates for life, I call upon your sky-spirit-power to help me in my quest. You can carry this prayer. Each day you fly from the crack between night and day to speak to the Creator, reporting to him on the condition of us, the Ojibwa, the Anishinabe, the Original Men. You know who I am. You are do-dem of my clan. I flew with you around the world. You are my guardian and guide. I am Wawiekumig. You know that each year at this time, in the shining-leaf month, I come here to my sacred place to hold the Ghost Supper. It's a long way to come for an old man, but I've come and done things in the proper way. I have put down tobacco, made food offerings to the fire, set out food for the spirit of my dead kinsman, whom I have summoned to the feast and have asked to return to the Village of the Dead when the feast is done, all in the proper way. I have done this every year, according to the old customs, but this time, I've come for different purposes.

Wawiekumig, at the bottom of the tree, eyes held fast on the eagle, paused before reciting his purposes.

In recent seasons, I have sensed loss of faith, which is loss of imagination. I am losing my power to dream. I have fallen out of harmony somehow. I have come here to restore balance. There are things I desire to know that can only be known through dreams.

Is the world coming to an end?

It is I, Wawiekumig, who asks this.

A long time ago, when the Anishinabe strayed from the path of the Midewewin, and the Creator was going to destroy the world for .their offense, you, migizi, winged from the crack between light and darkness and went to him. You pled with him to spare the world so long as one human being beats the waterdrum in the proper way and uses tobacco as it was meant to be. Eagle, you *preserve the world*. You know better than I what has happened. Hardly anyone follows the Mide path any longer. On this reservation, all the old men, my Mide brethren, are dead. Skwekomik is dead. Eshkwaykeezhik is dead. Odinigun is dead. Endusogijig, Niskigwun, Budigons—all dead. I alone am left alive. On this reservation, where once I was called a Man-Who-Knows-Everything, respected and even feared, no one comes to me any longer for my medicine. No one asks my advice. No one seeks the truth. My own clansmen have turned their backs on my medicine. Some take to the peyote cult, some to Christianity, most to no religion at all except the religion of whiskey. On this reservation, I alone am left to sound the waterdrum. Now the years are falling on me heavier than blizzard snow. I am white with age. Who will sound the drum when I am gone? All the old men are dead.

Eagle, I don't know how things are elsewhere. I haven't been away from my home in a long time. If things elsewhere are as they are here, then I am afraid that soon there will be no one left anywhere to sound the waterdrum and the world will be destroyed.

Wawiekumig stood without moving, the climbing sun making him squint as he looked at the young eagle, feathers turning gold-brown in the morning light. Wawiekumig, motionless, searched deeper into his mind for his purposes.

All the old men are dead, he repeated. All my close kinsmen are dead. I have no successor. To whom shall I leave my scrolls and medicine-bundle? Shall I burn them? Who, when I die, will conduct the funeral rites so that my soul will journey without misfortune down the Path of the Dead and enter the Ghost Lodge?

It is I, Wawiekumig, who asks you this.

This is a bitter thing, migizi, to come to the end of my life with no one to whom I can leave my knowledge and medicine, no one who will guide my soul on its journey down the Wide Path to the West. I have great understanding. Four times I have been struck and killed by the white shell, four times more struck and reborn. But something has happened for which I have no understanding. I have never misused my powers, never sought to enrich myself, as some holy men have done, never practiced mudjimushkeeki, knowing that if I did evil to others evil would come to me, but that is what has happened anyway. I've had long life and health, but my close kinsmen are all dead, even the youngest, and now I am alone. Did I offend the Mide manitos in some way that this has happened to me?

Now Wawiekumig felt a choking in his throat—the old grief rising in him, its sharpness undulled by the years.

Eagle, he prayed, displaying strength by holding back his tears, I come here seeking to make contact. I seek to leap over the crack between the visible and the invisible. In the past I have summoned my kinsman-spirit here to the Ghost Supper, and have been content to perceive his invisible presence. This time, I wish to *see* him, to hear his voice, to speak to him. Maybe he knows the answers to my questions.

I am old and alone. The sorrow has never left me. The first year after his death, I carried a lock of his hair in his spirit-bundle and blackened my face to sign my mourning, according to the old customs. Eshkwaykeezhik and Niskigwun held the restoring ceremony for me at the end of the year. They wished to see me released from grief. We had a feast and then went to his grave and buried his spirit-bundle with him. I pretended my mourning was at an end, but it was not, is not. My heart is dead from grief. I wish to speak to my kinsman to heal loneliness, if only for a little time. This is what I will try to do. Aid me in my attempt, migizi.

It is I, Wawiekumig, who asks this, I, who flew around the world with you.

He slapped the side of the tree. Fly away, eagle. The bird held to its perch. Go on, fly away, carry my prayers with you. Wawiekumig slapped the trunk again and stomped his foot.

"Fly, migizi, *fly*," he said aloud, his voice causing the eagle to raise its wings. With a single strong stroke, it sailed off, talons drawn beneath its white-spotted tail.

The old man watched it until he could not see it any longer, only the sky, empty. He sat down at the door to his wigwam and resumed his studies of the bear, who carried the Pack of Life through four walls until he came to the place where he founded the first Midewegun, where the Original Men could go to speak to God.

TWO

NINGGABEUHNOONG´

(WEST)

4

Christian Starkmann woke to the first morning of his thirty-second autumn, startled into consciousness by the digital alarm, a mean electronic buzz. His eyes snapped open, the only part of him that moved. His body remained frozen in the position it had been in the foxhole: curled up tightly on its side, his head tucked into the hollow formed by his stomach and folded knees so that he looked like a bent spoon. With his face buried he could not see anything, but his mind's eye held an image of the napalm—gobs of jellied gasoline spreading through the jungle like a fiery marmalade—and this image persuaded his instincts that it was not yet safe to move. He might suffocate if he sat up; the napalm would suck the breath from his lungs. Of course nothing of the sort could possibly happen. He was home in bed beside his wife, not in the foxhole beside half-Pryce and Captain Hartwell. That is what his rational mind told him, but his instincts had mastery for the moment and held him rigid against his will.

He passed ten or fifteen seconds in this state before reason began to gain the upper hand. His body lost its rigor and slowly unfolded. He rolled onto his back, turned off the alarm and sat up. Every nerve in him was tautly drawn, his senses keen with an animal alertness, as if the alarm had warned him of some danger. What danger, he could not imagine; yet his ears pricked for a strange sound while his eyes probed the predawn murk for a movement or an unfamiliar shape. They studied the darkest corners of the room and took in the outlines of the two simple bureaus, the half-open closet door, and the west window, framing the silhouette of the ridge dividing his property from the Indian reservation. There seemed to be no threat, but he couldn't be sure. Inside the room the only light was the faint red luminescence of the numbers on the clock. Outside, despite the early-morning hour, the shades of midnight clung to the sky like an indelible stain, blotting the line between ridge and sky so that the two appeared to be one, except that the ridge was much darker. It looked to Starkmann like a black hole in space, as though some gravitational whirlpool had sucked all the light out of the world.

June stirred, turning onto her side. The whisper of the sheets was boosted into a loud rustling, as if by a hidden amplifier in his ear. Starkmann's heart, reacting reflexively to the sound—almost identical to the one a man makes when crawling through dense underbrush—knocked against the bottom of his throat. A prickling rushed with malarial heat into his face. For a few moments the autumn morning assumed the breathless oppression of a jungle afternoon, squeezing a flow of sweat from his forehead. He took several deep breaths to settle his nerves, then looked at June, sleeping her usual sound sleep. Her long, straight hair blackened the pillow, and her hips, curving under the blanket, seemed outthrust to him in invitation. He thought to make love to her, although he did not feel desire; the desire for desire, rather, a yearning to excite himself so he could enter her and find, in her wet heat, calm and forgetfulness of where he had gone last night. He leaned over to kiss her, but just as his lips were about to touch her face, he withdrew without willing to. He was under the command of some other will, one that forbade him to touch her this morning. He smelled of mud and sweat, of blood and fire. He was tainted by where he'd been, and unfit to love her. He always felt this way after awakening from the nightmare, but the familiarity of the sensation did not make it less disturbing, any more than the nightmare had been made routine by its constant recurrence.

He got out of bed and walked to the bathroom to shower. His muscles were stiff from lying cramped up in the foxhole for so long, or rather, from lying in bed as though he'd been in the foxhole. He flipped the switch to the bathroom light. There was a second's pause before the demand-generator kicked in and the light went on. Its brightness relaxed somewhat the grip the dream still had on him. How he hated the dream! It was always the same, and it always ended at the same point: the moment when the napalm burst in the woods, as blinding as an eruption on the sun, and he curled up in the hole, trying to breathe through nostrils scorched by the stench of burning gasoline and burning flesh.

He had not had any bad dreams for a long time; then, exactly one year ago today, this nightmare had occurred for the first time.

Since then, it had returned at random intervals. Sometimes it would strike for two or three days in a row. Sometimes it would vanish for a whole month, only to come back again. Because he never knew when the dream was going to happen, Starkmann had come to dread falling asleep. He would watch the hands of the clock sweeping toward bedtime with the emotions of a condemned man awaiting the hour of execution. Often he forced himself to stay awake for as long as possible. He'd made it for forty-eight hours once with some pharmaceutical help, and then collapsed—and, of course, had the dream. He did not know why this had begun to happen to him, but he was afraid it was going to drive him crazy. He was more afraid of going crazy than he was of anything else. He knew something about going crazy, more than he wanted to know.

He turned on the shower. The water hissed against the plastic curtain, like the shrapnel that had left tiny scars, the size of mosquito bites, on his back. He urinated and noticed that the linoleum had begun to come up around the base of the toilet. He made a mental note to fix it. It made him feel more in command of his life to at least take notice of such minor problems and promise himself to attend to them someday. When steam misted the cabinet mirror, he stripped off the green boxer shorts he slept in and dipped under the curtain rod. A man of ordinary height could have passed under it without touching a hair on his head. The hot water felt good. Starkmann bathed fastidiously, though he had washed the night before and was to spend most of today in the woods. He showered every morning, but made sure to do a thorough job this morning. The smells of the dream—the mud of the foxhole, Hartwell's and half-Pryce's blood, the dense, sickening stench of the napalm—clung to his skin like a foul plastic food wrapper. He wondered how this could be. If he had only been dreaming, why and how did those odors linger long after he'd awakened? Who had ever heard of such a thing? He worked up a heavy lather and scrubbed hard with a coarse cloth, reddening his skin. He felt like scouring his skin off entirely, scraping it down to the bone. Bone was pristine. Bone was odorless. Bone was more beautiful than flesh because it was far less corruptible. Flesh began to rot almost immediately after death, but anthropologists continued to dig up million-year-old human skulls and rib cages and femurs. Starkmann had seen the skulls in magazine and newspaper articles, grinning across the ages with the triumph of their survival.

A vague gray light was pressing through the window when he reentered the bedroom to dress. He moved carefully to avoid waking June, though she could probably sleep through an earthquake. He reset the alarm so she wouldn't be late for work. As he watched the luminous digits advance, he envied June her ability to sleep so well, and a wave of resentment passed through him. That she should be sleeping peacefully while he was in a state like this seemed unfair. It made him feel as isolated from her as he did from most everyone else. If she were also troubled by nightmares, they could talk about their dreams. She would understand what he was going through and would not, as she would now, suspect his sanity if he told her he suffered from a nightmare unlike ordinary bad dreams. It had smells. It was not a muddle of confusing images but clear and coherent, a reproduction of an actual event so faithful that it was more like a video-taped replay than a dream.

He put on his jeans and flannel shirt, then his wool socks and rubber boots. Just before going downstairs, he peeked in on the girls, asleep in the room across from his and June's. The room was tidy on Lisa's side, a mess on Christy's. The younger girl's carelessness upset Starkmann, who could not stand things being out of place. Also, Christy was his and June's together. He expected more of her, but his anger passed as the morning twilight fell on Christine's face, a child whose beauty inspired forgiveness for her shortcomings. He made a start to hug and kiss her goodbye, but checked himself and walked out of the room down to the kitchen.

His stomach too unsettled to eat anything, he brewed a cup of tea for breakfast and drank it standing at the counter. It was pleasant in the kitchen, the brightest room in the house. Starkmann had remodeled it himself when they moved in last year. He'd thought a new kitchen, with all the latest appliances, would make June happier with the house.

After finishing his tea, he went to the refrigerator and took out the sandwiches she'd made for him the night before. Then he got his thermos and put it and the sandwiches in the back flap of his cruiser's jacket, hanging from a nail on the back porch. The jacket was already heavy with the gear he carried in it: compass, angle-gauge, aluminum grid tags, waterproof matches, and jackknife.

Outside, dew beaded on the propane tank behind the porch and on the shingle roofs of the generator shed and the outhouse, a relic kept in use for those times when the well-pump went on the fritz. The air was brisk and tingling, a north-woods autumn morning. He drew in several deep breaths the way a thirsty man drinks, the good, sharp smells of the woods cleansing his nostrils. The birch and aspen in the meadow beyond the yard trembled yellow in the breeze, and the pine picketing the rim of the ridge stood distinct against a pearl-colored sky. On the other side of the vegetable garden, which June struggled to keep alive in the Upper Peninsula's Siberian climate,

Starkmann's yellow retriever was trying to flush a chipmunk from the woodpile. The dog poked her nose and paws into the crevasses between the split logs stacked beside the barn—now converted to a garage and tool shed—but the chipmunk had bunkered in.

"Hey, Butternut," Starkmann called, tossing his jacket into the cab of the company pickup. "Hey, girl."

The retriever looked up and trotted toward him. His heart rose at the sight of her coming across the yard, well-muscled, tawny as a lioness against the green shields of fern in the meadow. He squatted down and embraced the dog's strong neck, her haunches solid-feeling against him, steam blowing from her jaws.

"Want to hunt, don't you, girl? Woodcock and grouse, Butternut." He patted her shoulder. Her coat was smooth and shining. "We'll go soon. There's still too much cover, but how about we scout the edges on the Blackwash this weekend?"

Butternut was all restless anticipation, alive with nervous energy.

"Three more days and we'll get out there." Starkmann stood and looked out into the meadow, where he exercised her during the off-season. A woodcock cheeped somewhere in the bracken. "Yeah, Butternut."

After feeding the retriever, he walked around the yard to make sure everything was normal, a habit he had developed since the onset of the nightmare. The meadow on which the house stood, shaped into a wedge by the junction of two rivers, the Big and Little Fire-dogs, gave him a clear field of vision for about fifty yards in any direction before the woods started. The meadow offered little cover to possible intruders, except for the few stands of birch and aspen clumped amidst the low ferns. The woods, which belonged to Starkmann, forty acres of them, were mostly cedar swamp and second-growth pine, crowded and tangled, difficult to get through. The one likely avenue of approach to the house was the gravel road that led to the county blacktop a quarter-mile away. That was the only weak point; otherwise, nature had provided him with a good defensive position, the two rivers like a moat around three sides of his property, the cedar swamp covering the fourth, which faced the ridge. But he knew no defense was impregnable and that it was imprudent to feel too secure. After he left, June and the girls would be alone for an hour or two, until June went to work and the girls to school. Butternut was a good watchdog; she would bark at the approach of strangers, but no more than that, she was so friendly. And so Starkmann listened for the warning calls of jays and ravens, and studied the ground for strange footprints or tire tracks, scanned the treelines for things that did not belong there.

Satisfied that everything was all right, he entered the garage, where his tools hung in orderly rows from a pegboard above a bench into which he'd bolted the reloaders for his rifle and shotgun shells. There was a faint sulfurous odor from the powder bags stowed under the bench. He climbed into the company truck, a beige Ford with the words G.S.I.&T., TIMBERLANDS DIVISION painted on its door panels, and backed out cautiously to avoid scraping June's Wagoneer and the mini-tractor he used to cut summer grass and plow winter snows. He took it slow down the gravel road; its close-ribbed bumps could wrench the wheel from a man's hands at high speed. The truck rattled over the log-and-plank bridge spanning the Big Firedog. The river, which got its name from an old Ojibwa myth about a huge, red-eyed dog that led lost men out of the forest, was running under the bridge with a whispery, rushing sound that saddened Starkmann. It always saddened him, though he didn't know why. To keep his spirits up he thought about Butternut, and the way she looked, ready and strong, and he heard in his imagination the thunder of a grouse flushing from cover. In another week or so the trees would drop more of their leaves and give him good shooting in the birch and aspen edges on the Blackwash.

A doe was browsing beside the unmarked mailbox and the NO TRESPASSING sign at the junction of the road and the blacktop. Startled, she raised her head and stared at the truck with eyes like bright stones before she bounded into the woods, her tail a bobbing white triangle. Starkmann turned onto the pavement and headed toward Vieux Desert, eight miles away. He drove leaning back in the seat, an elbow out the window, steering easily around the bends of the road, which followed the contours of the land through stands of red pine and balsam. The grandfather lichen hanging from the balsam made the trees look like mournful old men. Then the blacktop climbed Hunter's Hill, a high hardwood ridge overlooking the town and the lake. At the top the truck's sideview mirrors flashed in the sunrise, glowing on the horizon like a distant forest fire. The hardwoods on the ridge—sugar maple whose leaves blazed red as the sun—slid down to where the town formed a bracelet of frame and shingle buildings around Vieux Desert Bay. Beyond the bay was the lake, its cold gray-green reaching toward Canada. He could see, along the west shore, the Coast Guard station with its tall lighthouse, the ruins of the sawmill, its timbers so blackened with age they looked burned, the abandoned fish house at the end of the trawler dock, and the yellow log cabins of Pedersen's resort. A spur of the ridge blocked the rest of the town from view, except for the smokestack of the old veneer mill, which rose above the tops of the trees at Raddison's Point.

He went on downhill and through the outskirts, past tired wood houses with old pickups in the dirt driveways, auto chassis jacked up on cinder blocks, wheel hubs rusting, and hand-lettered signs in the yards: WORK WANTED . . . CARPENTRY BLOCK BRICK PLUMBING ANYTHING . . . HOUSE FOR SALE.

By the time he reached the center of town, he was sitting straight up, both hands gripping the wheel tightly. He stopped at the corner by Williams' Fish Market, then turned onto Front Street, his eyes flicking back and forth to check the windows of the buildings. He glanced in the rearview mirror several times, although he didn't quite know what he was looking for or expected to see. It just seemed a good idea to be aware of what was going on around him. In any town or city, even a town as small as this, you could never be too careful. *Alert*, he thought, looking at the advertisements pasted in the window of the IGA, then at Jensen's Hardware, then at Myra's Gift Shop, where driftwood sculptures were sold to summer tourists. *Alert, alive.*

At this hour, the only place open was Swanson's Bar and Grill. It had been a saloon and brothel in the days of the logging boom; now it was famous throughout the county for its hearty early-morning breakfasts, dished out to pulp cutters and skidder drivers and others in the timber trade. Starkmann caught the smells of bacon and eggs and home fries blowing out of the kitchen exhaust fans into the street. They made him hungry, but when he looked at the dozen-odd trucks and jeeps angle-parked in front, he knew he could not go inside. He did not feel strong and confident enough this morning to face the sidelong, suspicious glances of Doris Swanson's regular customers. Nor could he bear Doris's false smile. Who could tell what she was really thinking behind that big, fraudulent grin of hers? Maybe he was being unfair. Doris had never accused him of anything to his face. No one in Vieux Desert had said or done anything cruel to him, certainly nothing as cruel as what had been done to him in California years ago by the man in the maroon Plymouth. The townspeople knew he'd been in the army, but not in the war. He hadn't mentioned a word about the war to anyone except June, and had sworn her to keep quiet about it. If they didn't know he'd been in it, then they could not possibly know he'd once been crazy. So why did people look at him mistrustfully? Had his secret marked him in some way that wasn't visible and yet was just as obvious as the scars on his back? He hoped this wasn't true. He did not want to be despised. All he wanted was to be left alone, doing no harm to anyone, having none done to him.

Starkmann decided to eat breakfast at Burger King later on, after he finished at the office and headed out for the sections he'd been cruising this week. He did not feel in enemy territory in Burger King, or in McDonald's, Wendy's, Kentucky Fried, Mr. Chicken, Mr. Donut, the Holiday Inn, Day's Inn, Quality Inn, or Best Western. Those places were neutral territory, where no one cared who you were or what you'd done.

Past Swanson's, he braked for Vieux Desert's only stoplight, at the intersection of Front Street and the East Bay Road. He checked the rearview mirror one last time; then, instead of turning left onto East Bay, which would have taken him directly to his office, he continued straight ahead, past the Methodist church at the edge of town and back into the woods. Eventually the road would join another, which would loop around and lead to the office from the opposite direction. The route took him some ten or twelve miles out of his way, but it was the one he followed every morning. He guessed he liked the drive, a beautiful one through acres of maple and beech. As he took the truck around the gentle curves, red and gold leaves fluttering past the windshield and the early sun falling through the branches in slender shafts, he began to relax again. He settled back in the seat and, drumming his fingers on the steering wheel, whistled an up-tempo version of "Taps."

From a distance, the office could have been mistaken for a sportsman's rustic retreat. The cedar-frame building stood on a land-scaped hill near the lakefront, and the only thing that told anyone it was a place of business was the sign at the entrance to the drive:

GREAT SUPERIOR IRON & TIMBER
TIMBERLANDS DIVISION
WESTERN DISTRICT

Starkmann parked in front and got out of the truck, his boots crunching in the sand the wind had blown in from the dunes. He could see them from the hill, their slopes greened by wild grass and littered with driftwood logs. The bleached logs looked like dinosaur bones and gave the dunes the appearance of a prehistoric graveyard. Beyond the mounded sand, the calm lake had the menacing serenity of power in repose. If an autumn gale blew up, the water would be whipped in no time into twenty-foot seas, swallowing shorelines in acre-size bites, snapping ore-freighters like matchsticks—and forget about recovering the bodies of the crew. The Ojibwa had a legend that Gitchee-Gumee never surrendered its dead, and Starkmann knew the legend was true, scientifically explainable. Superior was a constant thirty-four degrees below the thermocline, too frigid for bodies to decompose, bloat, and rise to the surface. They stayed there forever, down in the black cold.

Starkmann unlocked the front door. He was always the first to arrive. He liked it that way. When he was alone, the office belonged to him. He passed through the reception area, where Shirley Johnson, the secretary, answered phones and typed letters behind a partition of frosted glass. Starkmann's workplace was in the large room on the other side of the partition. It had a map table and rows of filing cabinets filled with charts and aerial photographs, a new computer for inventory, and topographical maps tacked to the pine-paneled walls. The two small side offices belonged to Ralph Harding, the district Lands Department manager, and Bill King, head of the Procurement Department. The door to each was bracketed by photographs of Great Superior's operations: stark black-and-whites showing mills grinding wood into milky pulp, open pits cratering the hills of the iron range, a skidder hauling hewn logs down a muddy skid-trail, ore cars unloading taconite into a freighter as long as a city block. Great Superior did not manufacture plastics or microcircuits or Teflon computer terminals. It made its money in the old-fashioned way, by tearing riches out of the earth.

Starkmann's title in the company was Assistant District Lands Manager. That sounded prestigious, but it only meant that he was a timber cruiser, his principal job to scout the woods in his area for harvestable trees.

He went to the aluminum urn next to the map table and put coffee on. This was one of the domestic chores—shoveling the sidewalk in winter was another—that had fallen to him because he arrived before everyone else. The urn resembled the kind used in mess halls—which reminded him of a lot of things he did not need to be reminded of. He plugged it in. Its light winked on, a single red eye.

He poured a cup, sat down at the map table, and shuffled aerial photographs of a section he'd finished cruising the day before. He had ten thousand acres to cover for the company's computer inventory by the end of the year. Soon, management in Detroit would press a few buttons and their computer would tell them how many cords of pulpwood and how many board feet of sawtimber could be yielded by the six hundred thousand acres of forest that Great Superior owned in three states. The age of electronics had come to the land of Paul Bunyan; an IBM had replaced Babe the Blue Ox. Starkmann shifted two aerials of a maple ridge under the stereoscope. He looked through the lenses, which gave depth to the photographs, relief and contour.

The ridge rose in an illusion of three-dimensional reality, as if he were looking down on it from the plane that had taken the photographs. He felt a little dizzy. I should have had breakfast, he said to himself. He wondered if he ought to eat one of the sandwiches he'd brought for lunch. No, he would go to Burger King for breakfast, saving the sandwiches for later.

He began to transfer information from the aerials onto the type-map he was making. A type-map showed the locations of different species of trees in a stand—a reduction, in Starkmann's opinion, of the enigma of a wilderness into the explicitness of a shopping-mall directory. Over here, on the higher elevations, we have upland hardwoods with a sawtimber density of eight. If you're looking for softer wood, shoppers, please descend a hundred feet to the lowland conifers department.

His long torso bent over the table, he drew in the type-lines carefully, letter-coding each: M for maple, P for jack and red pine, E for lowland hardwoods, A for aspen. He peered again through the stereoscope, then took his eyes from it to mark the contour elevations on the map. He wrote the numerals perfectly. Attention to detail was critical. One number could make a difference. Numbers on a map, he thought, and suddenly the lines and numbers blurred. Starkmann's head swam. His heart was banging against his ribs and chest. He lifted his eyes to regain his focus, but his head kept whirling until he was on the verge of throwing up. When he stood to go to the bathroom, he had the sensation that he was on the deck of a rolling ship. Microscopic bubbles popped and sparkled in front of his eyes. He didn't know if he was seeing spots or grains of dust flashing in the sunlight that sloped through the windows. He watched his hand reach through the iridescent swirl to open the toilet door. For a moment he thought his hand was going to miss the knob; his fingers would close on thin air. This proved some sort of delusion; his hand grasped the knob quite easily. He stumbled to the toilet, bent over and vomited, but there was nothing in his stomach but bile. It splashed in the bowl, black as a disgusting secret. When the contractions in his belly stopped, Starkmann stood over the commode with his hands braced against the wall. He was very frightened. Nothing like this had ever happened to him before. His heart kept whacking at his ribs, and he was afraid he was suffering a coronary. But that was impossible. He was only thirty-two. He sucked in air until his heartbeat slowed and the vertigo subsided. He went to the sink, rinsed out his mouth, then sprayed the room with the deodorizer Shirley Johnson kept in the medicine chest.

He walked back to the map table. Just before sitting down, to test his perceptions and coordination, he closed his eyes, spread his arms, and drew his forefingers toward each other, touching their tips. Perfect. Not a fraction off. But he was still frightened, and could not understand what had come over him. He tried to analyze the episode rationally. Maybe it had been hypoglycemia. June had told him about the illness. One of her cases, the wife of an unemployed iron miner, suffered from it. The woman got terrible dizzy spells, blackouts, and even hallucinations because of low blood sugar. That was probably the explanation: he had not eaten this morning and his blood-sugar level was way down. Maybe he should see a doctor about it. How reassuring it would be to hear such a diagnosis, because Starkmann suspected the attack had nothing to do with his blood-sugar level. It was some new and awful aftereffect of the dream, another sign that he was going to go crazy again.

When he heard two cars pull into the lot, he picked up his pencil and went back to work. He couldn't concentrate at all, but it was important that no one, especially Bill King, think anything was the matter with him. He was certain that King, the only man in town to know the truth about him, was looking for an excuse to get him fired.

King and Harding walked in, Harding's head cocked to one side so he could hear the other man with his good ear. They were talking about Detroit's chances of making the division playoffs this season. They interrupted the discussion when they saw Starkmann.

"Morning there, Chris," King said.

"Hey, Bill!" Starkmann answered, affecting a cheerful, eager-beaver tone of voice.

"Chilly for September. Bet we'll have the first snow in two weeks." King's smile rearranged the loose folds of his face, and he rubbed his hands to emphasize the coldness of the weather. He took one of the mugs beside the coffee urn and tapped the spigot. "Well, what's your opinion?"

"We get these early cold snaps sometimes. We'll probably have an Indian summer in October."

"I didn't mean the weather. I meant the Lions. What's your opinion about the Lions this year?"

Starkmann shrugged noncommitally. He did not follow football very closely. Although he'd liked playing the game, it bored him as a spectator sport.

"Well, the Lions didn't look so hot in that preseason game last week," King said. "They didn't show me anything."

His eyes, set deep and close, a mole's eyes, shifted toward Harding, who was stirring Carnation into his coffee. Harding was tall and rangy, though not as tall as Starkmann, while King looked the way a lumberjack was expected to look: of medium height, thick-chested, with shoulders as wide and straight as a windowsill.

"I think that they've got a shot this year," Harding said.

"Ralph, how the hell can you say they've got a shot, with the Vikings in the Central Division?"

"Chicago might be pretty good too," Starkmann cautiously offered, to make himself part of the conversation. He could hear his own voice, as if he were outside of himself.

"Chris, the Bears are Walter Payton and that's it. Payton is one of the greats, but he doesn't make a team. Chicago's the least of Detroit's problems. Now the Vikings and Tampa Bay—"

"I don't think Minnesota is as good as they seem," Harding interrupted, stressing his point with a movement of his blue-veined hands.

The door opened and Shirley Johnson came in. She was a fiftyish woman whose girdle made her walk pitched forward from the waist up, her haunches sticking out behind her like the rump of a stout bird. She looked at the three men, then at her watch.

"Goodness, I'm not late, am I?"

Shirley usually arrived before King and Harding.

"No," Harding said. "We're just early."

"Thank goodness." Shirley had never been late in her life.

She entered her frosted-glass cage. Starkmann could hear her opening desk drawers and shuffling papers. King was looking at the floor, as if pondering a weighty question.

"Tell you what, Ralph. Let's end this discussion with a bet. Let's put the moolah where the mouth is. Twenty-five bucks at two to one says the Lions don't make the playoffs this year."

"Fair enough." Harding shook the shorter man's hand ceremoniously. "Chris is witness."

They went into their offices.

It relieved Starkmann to be alone again. The whole time with Harding and King, he'd been frightened that the mysterious vertigo would attack him in front of them. He spun around on his stool to confront once again the orderly, charted world of his maps, but he'd lost his ambition for paperwork.

"Chris, c'mon in," Harding called. "Let's talk over what we're going to do today."

Inside Harding's office, more photographs relieved the monotony of the wooden walls. They were historical photographs, one showing a team of river-hogs assembled before a spring drive, another of lumberjacks in plaids and suspenders, standing with their double-bit axes beneath pine trees taller than radio towers. A citation from the Raddison County Jaycees hung on the wall above the bookcase that contained back issues of *The Northwoods Logger*, the magazines stacked to serve as bookends for a pricing manual, a book about forest management, and a saga about old-time timber cruisers, *Prospectors for Green Gold*. Starkmann sat in the chair in front of Harding's desk. The room was so cramped that he could not extend his long legs. He had to sit bolt upright, which made him feel like a suspect in a police station.

"Did I make a bad bet?" Harding asked, cocking his ear to one side.

"I don't know."

"C'mon, Chris. You were the ballplayer."

"A long time ago."

Starkmann avoided looking directly into the older man's eyes, a leaden gray under thin sandy brows. He trusted Harding as much as it was possible for him to trust anyone, but he could not look into his eyes. He looked at the photographs instead.

"What the hell," said Harding. "If I'm at the point where I can't lose twenty-five bucks, I might as well go have another heart attack. Fall face down into the mashed potatoes and call it quits. Anyhow, what've you got on tap for today?"

"More of the same. Computer inventory. Those forties west of here."

"How about that intensive inventory? How's that coming? Cruising for dollars."

Cruising for dollars meant an inventory of a certain species of tree. In this case, it meant hardwoods for a new sawmill Great Superior had proposed building on the site of the old veneer mill at Raddison's Point.

"I haven't been able to get on that for the past two weeks."

Out of the corner of his eye he could see Harding staring at him.

"Yeah, I know. Chris, you've got to get hustling."

"I'll get on it."

"How's it look so far?"

"Give it another twenty years and there'll be enough high-grade maple to keep a mill going."

"The company doesn't have twenty years."

"I know," Starkmann said quietly. Something was coming.

"This town doesn't have twenty years, either. We've got a full-bore depression in the U.P. The only thing that's gone up around here is the unemployment rate."

"I know that," Starkmann answered, annoyed at being told the obvious. "I can't make the trees grow any faster than they're supposed to."

"A lot of people are counting on that mill. To hear them talk in town, they think it's as good as built. They can already see the paychecks going into the bank. Hell, some of them have got the money spent." Harding paused, drumming the desk with his long fingers. "Our baby might have to go out the window. You know that, too, don't you?"

Starkmann slid down in the chair and folded his hands over his waist. He looked at his hands and joined his forefingers and thumbs, forming a small triangle. "Our baby" was the forest conservation plan that had been one of the Lands Department's victories over Procurement. Harding, with figures Starkmann had taken a year to compile, had persuaded the company to set aside fifty thousand acres of second-growth hardwoods in the district for controlled harvesting. Only the older trees, those within a few years of natural death, would be cut; the others would be left alone until they, too, reached maturity. Starkmann had worked hard on the plan; he'd walked over hundreds of miles in every sort of weather and put in many hours of overtime, studying maps and inventory sheets like a student cramming for an exam. The effort was worth it, because he believed in the project and the idea behind it: that a compromise between the laws of nature and those of the marketplace was not impossible. Selective cutting would preserve the forest for decades while, at the same time, yielding a modest but steady profit.

"The company is going to need about five million board feet per year to make the mill a going operation," Harding continued.

"Clear-cut, you mean. They might have to clear-cut," Starkmann said, thinking: if you've got thousands of acres of second growth with only one high-grade saw log per tree, you cut more trees, making up in volume what you lack in quality—a matter of fundamental economics.

Harding shrugged, as if to say it was out of his hands.

"All for bowling alleys."

"Not just bowling alleys. Racquetball courts, gymnasiums, roller rinks, dance floors, any damn thing that needs high-grade hardwood. But it's more than that. That new mill is hope for people in this town."

Starkmann studied the triangle he'd made with his thumbs and forefingers. He wanted to hear something other than what he was hearing. After all, the conservation plan had been Harding's idea. Now he sounded as if he were arguing against it. Maybe he was more of a good company-man than he'd seemed to be.

"What happens after the wipeout? The mill shuts down, same as the veneer mill did. Then everybody in town is back to where they are now. Drawing unemployment and jacklighting deer so they've got enough to eat for the winter."

"Look, I know how you—I mean the generation you're from—feel about things," Harding replied. "Save the whales. Stop killing baby seals. All that. And I'm not unsympathetic, hey. You know I'm not, but this is a timber and mining company, not the National Park Service."

Starkmann looked up, his eyes flicking around the room like those of a fugitive searching for an escape. "What you're telling me is that the intensive inventory is just going through the motions. The company's already decided to go ahead with the mill. All they need from me is the numbers to figure out if they have to clear-cut or not."

"I don't know what they've decided. I do know they're going to need your volume estimates by the end of the year, and that you're quite a bit behind schedule."

Harding gestured to the younger man to close the door. As soon as it was shut, Starkmann felt the vertigo coming over him again, and he gripped the arms of the chair like a frightened airline passenger. Not now, he said to himself. Please not now.

"Chris, I think you've done a damn good job, the seven years you've been with us. You're better than most of the cruisers I've worked with. Most of the stands you've cruised have cut out to within ten percent of your estimates, and we're usually happy with fifteen percent." Harding tried to fix his eyes on Starkmann's but failed. He started toying with the old cruiser's compass he used as a paperweight. It was a beautiful instrument, its face, almost as large as the face of a small alarm clock, set in oak and rimmed in brass. "But maybe we've laid on you a little more than you can handle. That computer inventory and the intensive—it's probably too much for one man."

"I can handle it okay," Starkmann said, thinking: Here it comes. "I can take care of it on my own."

"Well, look, it isn't just that you're running behind. It's your estimates. To some people, they look too conservative. Some people think we've got more high-grade out there than your estimates are showing."

"What people?"

"Bill for one. He knows you backed the plan as much as I did, maybe more. He kind of thinks that you're a little too attached to it. He thinks maybe that's why—Christ, how the hell can I say this? —maybe that's why you've been dragging your feet and coming in with such low numbers."

Starkmann said nothing. King. He should have known King was behind this. He clutched the arms of his chair, shifting his glance from the compass to the photograph óf the river-hogs—hard-looking men holding their pikes and peavies like knights with their lances—then back to the compass. He held his eyes on it because he'd read somewhere that dancers and figure skaters prevented dizziness when doing spins by making sure their eyes always returned to the same point.

"No one is saying that you've been deliberately dragging your feet or misreporting."

"What are they saying, then?"

"That maybe you're so committed to the plan that your heart isn't in this sawmill project. That you're not seeing what's out there because, well, you're just seeing what you want to see."

"What do you think?"

"I think you're probably right. If I didn't have doctor's orders to take it easy, I'd go out and hump the boondocks and prove it."

"Then why don't you talk to King?"

"I have, but it isn't just Bill. It's Furman."

Furman was the regional vice-president.

"I guess Bill mentioned some of his misgivings to Furman. Furman's bringing a man in from eastern district to run a check cruise and see if those numbers match up with yours."

"Is King trying to get me fired?" The words were out of Starkmann's mouth before he could stop them.

"*Fired?* Where the hell did you get that idea?"

"Is he or isn't he?"

Harding paused, surprised by the question.

"Bill thinks a lot of you."

"A lot of what?"

"What's the matter with you? He isn't trying to get you fired any more than I am. Look, you know as well as I do that all those guys in Procurement think the Lands Department is full of soft-headed environmentalists, but Bill *likes* you, for Chrissake."

"Maybe he's got you fooled, but he doesn't have me fooled."

Harding answered this comment with a knitting of his brows and a baffled silence that told Starkmann he had gone too far. His tongue had run ahead of his mind.

"All right. Maybe I've got him wrong," he said, trying to back out of the corner he'd put himself into.

"You *are* wrong." The older man took a breath and fiddled with the compass, standing it on end, then laying it flat. "Look. Furman is bringing another man in to back you up, but that doesn't mean he's questioning your competence. It's for damn sure no one is trying to get you fired. Get that idea out of your head."

"Suppose this guy comes up with different estimates? Suppose he tells them that there's enough high-grade out there to lay a bowling alley around the world?"

"Nothing will happen to your job, if that's what you mean. All right?"

"All right."

The dizziness had drained out of Starkmann. Now, as if through some process of emotional transfusion, anger was flowing into him. He knew he had to get out of the cell-like room before he lost his temper. He lost it rarely, but when he did he lost it all, flying into a rage so consuming it was like a transcendence into another state of being.

"I think it would also be a good idea if you dropped the computer inventory for a couple of weeks," Harding said, running his finger over the rim of the compass. "Get caught up on the intensive. All right?"

"All right."

"On your way out, check on LaChance's job. He says he's finishing early."

Starkmann gave a vague nod and pursed his lips.

"I know, he's a pain in the ass, but it's part of the job. Goes with the territory. If I know Sam, he's probably finishing early because he hasn't bothered to cut back in the corners, but be diplomatic with him. The company likes to maintain good relations with the natives, especially the chiefs," Harding said, but Starkmann wasn't listening.

5

He pulled out of the lot cautiously, but once on the road and out of sight of the office, he stepped hard on the gas, hoping the acceleration would purge his anger. He fishtailed around a couple of sharp bends, tires squealing, and did sixty miles an hour on the straightaway past the town dump, where ravens were landing and taking off like small black airplanes. When he entered the red-pine forest beyond the dump, he held his speed and had a weird urge to jerk the wheel and crash head-on into the biggest tree he could find.

That goddamned King! He was a subtle one, a real snake. Starkmann wished he could have found a way to explain to Harding that King despised him because King knew about his breakdown. Starkmann had discovered this one night several months ago, when he, June, and the girls were having dinner at Swanson's. King was in a nearby booth with two other men, talking about the killings that had taken place the previous day in Wilson's Crossing, a town about a hundred miles from Vieux Desert. The news had been in the papers, on the radio and television: A Vietnam veteran had shot his estranged wife to death with a rifle, then held his children hostage in his wife's house. Sheriff's police surrounded the place. After a standoff of several hours the veteran released the children. Once they were safely out of the way, he opened fire, but shot over the heads of the police. The deputies drove him out of the house with tear gas. He came running out the front door, firing his rifle into the air until a blast from a deputy's shotgun cut him in two. Later, a TV reporter had interviewed a friend of the dead man, and the friend said, "The cops didn't kill him. He just made them pull the trigger for him."

The comment had upset King. In the restaurant, Starkmann heard him say to his friends: "What a load of bull. The guy was a murderer. He killed his wife, and that reporter was trying to make us feel sorry for him." King's voice sounded very loud, as if he wanted to make sure Starkmann heard him. "It was probably dope. Those guys we sent over there weren't like we were back in WW Two, no sir. They were smoking dope on the front lines, even shooting heroin. You read about it in the papers damn near every day. Dope addicts. What happened doesn't surprise me. I'll bet the guy was out of his mind on dope. Almost all of those guys over there were nut cases. Me, I blame the government. They shouldn't have let any of those guys back into society until they were off the dope and back in their right minds. And the ones they couldn't get straightened out, they should have kept locked up, hey. Maybe then the kind of damned shame that happened yesterday wouldn't happen."

Starkmann could not eat. He wanted to cry, thinking about that tormented man in Wilson's Crossing. At the same time he wanted to tear King apart. Suddenly he jumped out of the booth, startling June and the girls. He startled himself. He hadn't meant to spring out of his seat like that; the movement had been as reflexive as the blinking of an eye. He stood for a moment or two, sick and sweating and afraid he'd given himself away. He didn't know what to do next. Then he walked into the men's room, to make it look as if he'd leaped up because he needed to go to the bathroom. He locked the door and rinsed his face in cold water. Just as he opened the door to leave, King walked in, smiling. Starkmann thought he was going to jump out of his skin; he recognized that smile, almost an exact duplicate of the smile of the man who had stopped to pick him up that day twelve years before when he'd been hitchhiking to San Francisco from Travis Air Force Base.

It had been a cool, sunny afternoon—Starkmann remembered that—and he'd changed into his civvies, as he'd been told to do by his sergeant. But he'd been unable to hide his military haircut. The short hair was what had given him away. Starkmann had been standing at the roadside for about half an hour when a maroon Plymouth pulled off the road and the driver opened the passenger door. Starkmann, lugging his AWOL bag, ran up to the car and started to climb in, tricked into a sense of safety by the man's friendly smile. "Just back from Nam?" he asked. Starkmann answered that he was. The man's expression changed in an instant to a snarl. Without a word of warning he jerked a portable fire extinguisher from under the dash and sprayed a cloud of carbon dioxide into Starkmann's face, then punched the gas pedal so that the door swung back and knocked Starkmann into a culvert, where he lay for several minutes, choking, his eyes on fire.

"Giving your better half a night off from the kitchen, Chris?" King asked. Starkmann tried to answer the question, but the words caught in his throat. The seeming innocence of the question, like the false smile, could not hide the expression in the tiny mole's-eyes, an expression full of knowledge that was also a judgment. The expression said, "I know you for what you are, and I hate you for it, and I'll make you pay for it." King knew! But how? Maybe he'd run into someone whom Starkmann had known in the war. Maybe, like the guy in California, he'd perceived the truth through some sort of sixth sense. But he *knew*. There was no doubt about it. That was why he had spoken in such a loud voice when talking to the men in the booth; it had been his way of telling Starkmann that he'd found him out.

"Hey, Chris. Are you all right?" King asked. "You look sick."

Starkmann nodded, and then, in desperate need of fresh air, bolted out of the bathroom and almost ran toward the front door, leaving an angrily puzzled June to pay the bill. Swanson's was a big place; it was a hundred feet from the men's room to the front door, and the whole way out, Starkmann could feel King's eyes boring into his back.

Now, driving the blacktop toward Marquette, he tried to put the memory of that night out of his mind. Ever since then, the new life he had built up here had been in jeopardy. King could wreck it at any time with just a few words—which was why, Starkmann figured, King had never said anything to anyone. Knowledge of a secret grants power only so long as the secret is not shared. King had kept quiet and bided his time, and was only now making his move. Given the choice, Starkmann would have preferred a quick, direct assault, like a blast of carbon dioxide in the face, to King's waiting game, his behind-the-back whisperings and cunning maneuvers. Starkmann wondered what he ought to do about this business, or if he ought to do anything.

The road crawled up a hill. From the top, he could see the lake and a flight of mallards, strung out over the water in a long, dark line, like a kite tail without a kite, their heads pointed southward, their cries an annunciation of winter. Maybe the best thing to do would be to get the inevitable over with, pull up stakes and leave for some other part of the country. Where? Montana possibly. Or Idaho. Would June go with him? He would have to give her some reason why they were moving. He could not tell her the entire truth. If she knew what King knew, then she also would despise him and would leave him. Perhaps she wouldn't. You just couldn't tell about women when it came to things like that, even a woman you'd been married to for nine years. Maybe he would head south instead of west, south to the humid marshlands that were the mallards' destination. June would like that. She hated the winters up here. They would go south, and live far up some isolated bayou where no one could ever find him. An idle fantasy. If he could not escape in a place as remote as the Upper Peninsula, he could not escape anywhere. Another Bill King would show up sooner or later.

As he neared Marquette, the woods grew thinner and more domesticated. Rustic signs began to appear at the roadside, announcing the names of secluded vacation cottages owned by part-time wilderness lovers from Detroit and Chicago. Some had names like The Birches or Whispering Pines, while others were called by Indian words to give them native mystique. He could not see the cottages, only the signs and the mailboxes and the gravel drives curving through the trees. After a few more miles the forests vanished altogether and were replaced by another kind of wilderness: the glass-and-plastic, Formica-topped, neon-lit glut that had become the standard outskirt of the American town. Starkmann passed a used-car lot, where shiny pennants snapped in Superior's breeze, and pulled into Burger King, the comic-strip letters of its sign playfully askew, as if they'd been drawn by a kindergartener.

He went inside and gave his order to the counter girl, who was wearing a yellow-and-burgundy uniform and a mechanically friendly smile. She called the order into the kitchen over a microphone, took his money, and rang up the sale on the computerized register. A few minutes later she handed him his breakfast, Burger King's "Good-Morning Special"—two fried eggs, two sausages, and two microwaved waffles served in a compartmentalized Styrofoam plate, coffee in a paper cup.

Starkmann sat down in the rearmost booth, his back to one wall, his shoulder to another, his eyes on the door. There were only half a dozen customers in the place, all transients, people from somewhere else on their way to somewhere else. None of them knew him, none wanted to know him. They had not even turned their heads when he'd walked past. His height and shock of pale hair drew attention in most places, but he was as invisible in this artificial wasteland as he was when cruising alone in the woods. He chewed one of the radiated waffles slowly and watched a middle-aged couple, the man in green double-knit trousers, the woman in a print dress, get up and slip their plates into the slot of the disposal bin, then walk outside to their car. In a few minutes they were replaced by another couple, so similar in shape and blank expression they might have been the first man and woman in different clothes. Starkmann had noticed this phenomenon before and guessed it accounted for his own invisibility: As soon as people entered the standardized, franchised world of the urban borders, they lost a measure of their distinguishing features. Like lizards or fish camouflaging themselves to blend in with their environment, they assumed the uniform appearance of their surroundings, their faces all merging into a common face. This Burger King looked like every other Burger King, and everyone in it looked like everyone else, which meant that no one looked like anyone in particular. That was why, Starkmann figured, he had never suffered a suspicious glance or hostile word in Burger King. He could have been on the FBI's most-wanted list, his photograph plastered on post office walls around the country, and not a soul would have noticed.

He forked an egg over the second waffle and finished eating while a busboy wiped with a quick, circling hand the table where the first couple had sat. Starkmann stood and dumped his trash, wishing he could have stayed in Burger King all day. He went outside to his truck and started down the highway. As he drove past Mr. Donut, Tastee-Freeze, and McDonald's, its arches humping like plastic rainbows the color of squeeze-bottle mustard, it occurred to him that, in these monotonous outskirts, he could escape society as completely as any hermit in the mountains. He could move from one town to the next, eating in fast-food restaurants, sleeping in chain motels, an Interstate nomad, a citizen of the fringes, unnoticed, unremembered, unknown.

6

He drove west toward Sam LaChance's logging site. The highway had once been a major Indian trail, and its four lanes still followed a route blazed by Ojibwa, Ottawa, and French *coureurs de bois* in the days of the fur trade. A Soo Line freight, bound for Sault Ste. Marie and Canada, clattered down the tracks on one side. On the other side the unpeopled Huron Mountains rose, their dark heights scowling as if to warn humanity to stay out. Starkmann looked at the mountains and listened to the clacking of the train, and felt the sadness he had felt earlier, when he'd crossed the Firedog River. Sorrow filled him, for no ostensible reason, and he had to beat back an urge to cry. Then the sadness passed, as quickly and unaccountably as it had come on.

After twenty miles he turned off the highway onto a dirt road. Rocky bluffs rose on either side, the ore-reddened rocks like stained gravestones. Below, a river danced over a gravel bar. The road ran parallel with the river for half a mile, then curved away, climbing out of a gloom of hemlock and spruce, up through jack-pine barrens and over ridges of red and sugar maple. A set of bulldozer treads the logging trucks dragged to smooth the road lay against an embankment like the shed skin of an armored reptile. The Ford bounced and banged for another two or three miles, and Starkmann cursed when his head cracked against the roof.

He shifted into four-wheel drive when he left the road for an even rougher skid-trail. Slashings lay everywhere, and the woods had the ruined look of a battlefield the day after the battle. He parked the truck beside a mound of rotting hemlock logs. As he climbed out he heard a chain-saw buzz somewhere up ahead. The saw fell silent, buzzed again, and again went silent. A tree cracked and crashed to the ground. Starkmann started up the trail, hopping to the side when a cable-skidder rolled out of the woods on its giant tires, dragging a bundle of eight-foot maple logs, choker chains rattling. The driver waved. He was a heavyset kid in black T-shirt and marine fatigue cap, one of Black Sam's grandsons. Starkmann waved back, then continued up the trail to a clearing, where he saw LaChance, high above the ground in the cab of the loader-slasher. The machine looked like a big robot, a monster from outer space, or a mechanical dinosaur, depending on the angle from which it was viewed. Black Sam was its master, pulling levers that manipulated a long steel arm with two claws at one end and hydraulic joints. It reached down, picked up half a ton of topped maple, loaded it into the slasher, which cut it into four- and eight-foot lengths, then grappled the logs and stacked them on their respective decks: saw log, veneer, tie cuts, pulp.

Starkmann's eyes went immediately to the decks. LaChance had a reputation for trying to dodge mill standards by tossing low-grade saw log in with the veneer, pulp in with the saw log, anything to skim an extra dollar or dime. Not that LaChance needed to cheat; he was rich by the standards of the Upper Peninsula, a minor land baron who owned several thousand acres that he was selling off in five-acre lots to sportsmen and outdoorsy types. He also held fifty-percent interest in the old veneer-mill property, which he and three partners, two of whom had since died, had bought cheap when the mill closed, and which he and the other surviving partner now planned to lease to Great Superior for a sum said to be considerable.

The loader's whine stopped, the great orange arm drooped, as if exhausted by its efforts, and Black Sam climbed down, as limber as a man half his age. Except for the yellow hard hat resting atop his head, he was dressed like a lumberjack of old in high-topped boots, whipcord trousers held up by wide suspenders, and a flannel shirt, checkered in green and black. His dimensions were likewise Bunyanesque. At six feet seven he was the only man in the county whom Starkmann did not have to look down on. But if their height nearly matched, their bulk did not. Starkmann looked like a sapling next to LaChance's solidly muscled two hundred and seventy pounds. With his enormous shoulders and chest, Black Sam gáve an impression of indestructible massiveness. His nickname derived from his coloring, Mediterranean olive darkened a shade or two by the Indian in his blood and by his beard, which, even when freshly shaven, formed a ring of coal dust from his left ear to where his right one should have been. A bear had bitten the ear off long ago and, with the same bite, had laid open one side of his face, a wound whose scar curved from his temple to just under his hooked Canuck nose. Sam's fight with the bear, a sow that had attacked him when he'd come between her and her cubs, had taken place more than thirty years before and had made him a hero of local legend. He'd killed her with a hunting knife, his only weapon. Besides chewing off his ear and shredding half his face, she'd broken six of his ribs and fractured his collarbone; but when all was said and done, the bear lay dead and Sam was still breathing.

"Morning, Mr. Starkmann," LaChance said, offering a hand. "How's it goin'?"

Starkmann warily surveyed the immensity of callused flesh in front of him before extending his own hand.

"Fine."

"How about June? Those two girls of yours. Okay?"

"Sure."

"So what brings you here? Hell, I know. We're finishin' early, so they sent you to have a look-see."

Starkmann nodded. Sam's eyes, like two dabs of tar stuck beneath his brow, sought the younger man's, which feinted left and slid off to the right, fixing on an imaginary point in the distance.

"Know what I always notice about you, Mr. Starkmann? You don't say much."

"No."

The reply had not been intended as a joke, but LaChance let out a belly laugh that crashed through the woods.

" 'No.' Ha! That's a good one, hey. I tell him he don't say much, and he says, 'no.' Reminds me of that joke about President Coolidge. President Calvin Coolidge. You hear that one?"

Starkmann shook his head.

"That Coolidge, he was another one who never say nothin'. One day these two newspaper fellas make a bet. One newspaper fella bets the other one twenty bucks that he can't make President Calvin Coolidge say more'n two words. Next day, the newspaper fella goes up to Coolidge and says to him: 'Mr. President, me and my friend made a bet I can't make you say more'n two words. And Coolidge looks at him and says, 'You lose.' "

Sam laughed again. Starkmann forced a smile.

"Anyhow, you wanna look around, look around. Have a look at those veneer logs. Bird's-eye maple, goddamn."

Starkmann walked over to the decks, his boots slipping in the reddish gumbo churned up by the machinery, his nostrils tingling from the tang of newly cut timber. The veneer looked good, the small maple hearts staring like rows of wooden eyes. But a glance at the saw-log deck told him that the sticks at the bottom were under minimum diameter. To make sure, he squatted down and drew his tape measure across the log ends. Remembering Harding's caution to be diplomatic, he gazed up at Sam without saying anything.

LaChance took off his hard hat and ran his square fingers through his hair, thin but with only a suggestion of gray in it.

"Somethin' the matter?"

"A few of these sticks are a little shy."

Dropping onto his haunches, LaChance squinted at the tape and feigned a surprised expression that might or might not have been intended to make light of his attempt to pass one thing off for another.

"I'll be damned," he said, standing and jamming his hat back on his head. "A little shy. Not many of 'em, though."

"Enough. Ten, maybe fifteen percent."

"So they're an inch under. What's that?"

"An inch is what it is. An inch makes it pulp."

Numbers. A whirlpool spun inside Starkmann's head. When he stood, the blood rushed from his brain and the line of the woods seemed to tilt to one side.

"Pulp. Now what use I got for pulp, goddamn? Pulp's break-even for me no matter what. Can't make no kinda money with pulp."

"They'll catch it at the mill, so you might as well redeck it now."

Starkmann spoke with exaggerated care, like a drunk trying to sound sober. He held on to one of the top logs, half convinced he was on the verge of fainting.

"Redeck 'em, shit . . . Hey, you all right?"

"Sure."

"All of a sudden you look pale as a ghost, Mr. Starkmann."

"Skipped breakfast this morning," he lied. "Got a little lightheaded is all."

"Hey, you gonna work in the woods, you don't skip breakfast. You gotta eat, Mr. Starkmann."

Starkmann, nodding in agreement with Sam's dietary wisdom, removed his hand from the log to test his balance. He was all right. The dizzy spell had come and gone.

"Anyhow," LaChance said, gesturing at the decks, "this inch business don't make no sense to me."

"Mills get picky in hard times."

"That's what don't make sense. Hard times, timber getting scarcer every year, and the mills get fussier and fussier. And what happens to us loggers? We got the government on our backs. Workman's compensation. Forty-eight cents of every dollar I make goes to workman's comp, and I can't pay that without losin' money if I don't sell sawtimber. Pulp ain't no good to me."

They'd begun walking the site, closer to the two fallers whose chain saws sounded like big model airplanes.

"And another thing don't make sense to me is you fellas. Now some loggers is sloppy, deckin' saw log with pulp and losin' money for themselves and for you. It makes sense to me you fellas make sure they don't do that." LaChance's accent, as it usually did when he got excited, had begun to slip into the cadences of French Canada. "But if maybe I think some timber right on the border and I make the judgment, okay, maybe it makes grade, maybe it don't, but it's better that I sell it for maybe a grade higher than what it is. Then I make money and you make money—hell, the mills make money too."

"Sam, saw log is saw log and pulp is pulp."

"I'll tell you, when your company builds that new mill, they ain't gonna be so fussy. They're gonna have to compete with that big floorin' mill down at Dollar Bay and they ain't gonna be able to compete if they go thumbin' their nose at good wood just because of an inch."

"That's if they build it."

"Whatchew mean, if? They're gonna build it, hey. If? Where do you get that, Mr. Starkmann?"

"Like you said, timber is getting scarcer every year."

"There's still plenty of it. Plenty of good sawtimber in these woods if everyone wasn't so goddamn fussy. The trouble with you, Mr. Starkmann, is you're one of them new college-boy cruisers. Old days, cruisers come up the hard way, out of the loggin' camps. Some of 'em was crew bosses, thirty men under 'em and tough men too. Now you fellas come along with your college degrees and your inches, and you see a knot in a tree and look at it for ten minutes, tryin' to figure out how come that tree got a knot in it."

Starkmann did not respond. He heard in LaChance's complaint an echo of the army lifers he'd listened to, those indolent master sergeants who, with faces like raw T-bones and beer bellies that hid the clasps of their cartridge belts, spent half their time mourning the death of the "old army" while cursing the new. He understood LaChance's point—contract loggers had huge equipment and labor costs—but his sympathies diminished when he looked at the stumps and saw that a lot of trees had not been cut to diameter limit. The lumberjacks, out of sheer laziness, had sawed too high up on the trunk, leaving good timber to rot in the ground. He debated whether he ought to say anything. The more discrepancies he mentioned, the longer he would have to stay here. The hell with it. He would point it out to Sam and get it over with.

"Don't you think your boys should be cutting a little closer to the ground?"

A short distance away, one of the fallers approached a red maple, a towering beauty without a stopper in it for the first fifty or sixty feet. The man, holding his chain saw in one gloved hand, looked up to check the lean of the tree.

"Now what's the matter?" asked Sam.

"A lot of these trees haven't been cut to limit."

The chain saw exploded, drowning the last half of the sentence in its noise. Bark splattered into the air as the saw snarled, its carbide teeth revolving at four thousand feet a minute, biting through the maple's scaly skin into its meat, chips a fine spray, like a gush of white blood. Then there was silence as the lumberjack paused to check the lean again.

"Didn't catch what you said, Mr. Starkmann."

"Here. Take a look," Starkmann said, stretching his tape across a stump.

The saw roared once more, angry and relentless. The whirling teeth bit deeper into the tree's flesh, flashing toward its heart. A mass of brown pulp spewed out from the cut, sap bubbling at the edges. The maple groaned, leaned a little farther in the direction of its natural slant, then gave out a shriek and toppled, the windy rush of its crashing branches like a last expulsion of breath.

"Sixteen inches," said Black Sam, reading the tape.

"Two inches off."

"There you go again with your inches, Mr. Starkmann."

"They make a difference."

"Yeah. Ask any woman."

Starkmann started to say something, then checked himself, drawing his lips into two tight straight lines. He shoved his tape into his jacket pocket and walked to the fallen maple, where he watched the lumberjack draw a logger's rule from the hewn base of the tree to the first branch.

"Whatchew got there, Armand?" asked LaChance.

"Sixty-seven feet," answered Armand, recording the length in his notebook.

"Pretty good. Watch how you cut, though. Couple them back there wasn't cut to limit."

Armand, dark and hook-nosed, a scaled-down version of Black Sam, gave Starkmann a quick glance.

"Okay. I'll watch it. But it's tough workin' in here. Too much brush. A tree here, a tree there, maybe another one yonder. Can't strip-cut no more. Just wander around, beatin' the bush and lookin' for somethin' worth cuttin'."

"Last roundup of sawtimber in this stand, Armand. This time next year, gonna be nothin' in here but pulp."

Armand shrugged as if to say "What can you do?" and yanked the pullcord. Swift as an executioner, he topped the maple just beneath the first branches, the chips gushing in a yellow-white spout.

"Mr. Starkmann, you care to measure this one to see if it's up to snuff?"

Starkmann said nothing. He should have left well enough alone.

"Armand, this fella is somethin' with a ruler."

"Yeah?" said Armand, shouldering his McCulloch.

"Measures everything down to the inch. He's somethin' to see."

"Okay, Sam."

"Just kidding you, Mr. Starkmann. Don't take things to heart."

"I'll have a look at the back corners and then get the hell out of here."

"Suits me. I got work to do."

Starkmann loped off, wondering if the last remark had been a simple statement of fact or a parting slap. As he climbed a low hill tiled with red leaves, both chain saws ripped the forest's silence, their roaring and sputtering achieving a kind of rhythm, like machine guns firing short bursts. The top of another tall maple shuddered, leaned over, and vanished. The tree struck the earth with a thud.

The morning had warmed and he'd begun to sweat under his jacket and heavy shirt. The air smelled of dying leaves, a pungency that reminded him of other leaves, tumbling in a chemically induced autumn, mahogany and mimosa and wild tamarind gassed to death by the spray planes. The herbicide squadron's motto had been *Only You Can Prevent Forests.*

At the bottom of the hill he found the bearing tree that marked one corner. An aluminum grid tag was nailed to its trunk. The first time he'd come upon the tree, two years before, he'd been running boundary lines with notes from the original 1850 survey and was confused when he'd chopped deep into the trunk and couldn't find the surveyor's blaze. Then, recalling that hardwoods grew wood on their sunny side, he'd moved around, cut into the bark on the shady side, and uncovered it, a mark made by a man more than one hundred and thirty years earlier. Finding the old blazes always excited him; it was like discovering evidence of a vanished civilization. Once he'd cut into a sugar maple and seen V-shaped slashes made by Indian maple-tappers long before the surveyors had mapped the woods.

A quick look around told him LaChance's crew had cut in the corner. He started off toward the opposite corner, keeping his direction by instinct. Seven years' experience in the woods had rid him of dependence on a compass. It comforted him to know he could never get lost, that he knew how to find bearing trees and follow them in a straight line until he came to a logging trail, a road or stream.

The other corner had been worked as well, which relieved him. He did not want to feel obliged to confront LaChance again. He cut across the forty at a diagonal, keeping clear of the fallers, and trudged toward his truck down the rutted skid-trail. Sam, back in the cab of the loader, leaned out of the window and yelled something, but Starkmann could not hear him over the growl of the saws.

7

He spent the rest of the morning walking through rolling hard-woods, broken here and there by aspen whose leaves quaked in the wind like thousands of nervous golden hands.

With his mind and feet he divided the forest's fenceless chaos into orderly segments: eleven paces to a chain, fifty-five to a talley; four talleys to a quarter-mile, the length of a forty-acre square. Every two chains, he dropped a plot, a stake with a plastic ribbon that would be used as a reference point for the check-cruiser whom Furman was sending in. At each plot he measured the density of growth with his angle-gauge, an instrument with an opening shaped like a truncated triangle in its middle; when he squinted through the aperture, the trees that fell within his field of vision were counted in his volume estimates, which he recorded on the tally sheets in his aluminum clipboard. Occasionally he paused to check the soundness of a tree, or measured it for grade with his cruiser's stick. Four fifths of a log-length clear of stoppers in four-foot cuttings was the requirement for top-grade sawtimber; two thirds in three-foot cuttings made it grade two; and half in two-foot cuttings, grade three. Starkmann reveled in his work because its technicalities demanded a concentration that would not allow him to think about anything else, like going crazy. At the same time, he questioned its commercial nature and felt uncomfortable about the way it forced him to look at the natural world. A forest's market value became its only value. The Indians' view was probably closer to his own: a view that saw mystery in some ancient pine or maple, not just so-many board feet of saw log or cords of pulp.

As he walked beneath the trees he recalled a poem he'd read, written by a man named Reverend Frank Merrell, a backwoods preacher in the boom days:

> I might have seen the pine tree
> Securely clasp the loam
> To poise a harp of emerald
> And crotch a squirrel-home.
> I might have seen her jewels
> At autumn's auction sale,
> But I was blind computing
> The lumber it would scale.

He hoped his job would not blind him to the magic and beauty of the wilderness; but even if it did, he would not quit to make his living at something else. He could never work anywhere except in the woods, the great woods that had seemed full of menace when he was younger but were now his sanctuary. The real menace lay outside, in what people were pleased to call civilization. He had known that to be true ever since his encounter with the stranger on the road between Travis and San Francisco. He remembered pulling himself out of the culvert, so frightened of being attacked again that he'd walked the rest of the way to the airport. Several motorists slowed and gestured offers for a ride, but he waved them off and kept walking, convinced he had returned to a land as alien and hostile as the one he had left.

From San Francisco he had flown home on leave. His parents, his sister Anne, and her husband, Ed, met him at O'Hare at midnight. His mother and sister kissed him. His father and brother-in-law shook his hand, but his father seemed embarrassed by him, as if he were greeting a son just released from prison. This struck Starkmann as an appropriate response, because he felt like an ex-convict or, closer to the truth, a fugitive.

His father did not speak during the drive from O'Hare to the house on Elmwood Avenue. To fill up the awkward silence, his mother and sister brought him up to date on family and neighborhood events: births, deaths, marriages, and other irrelevant information. They spoke to him as if he were still a student, home on spring break, and he hardly listened to them. He felt tired and numb. Only four days before, he had been in the heat and mud of brigade headquarters, surrounded by the threatening hills near the Cambodian border. Now he was in a car with his family, driving south on Mannheim Road toward Oak Park; and instead of jungle, he was looking at factories, motels, apartment buildings, houses, and automobiles. Everything should have been comfortably familiar, but it wasn't. All of it looked stranger than those hills on the far side of the earth. He grew uneasy. He was all right as long as they were moving, but whenever they stopped for a red light, he broke out in a nervous sweat, expecting something awful to happen at any moment. He did not like being a stationary target, and wished he had his rifle.

He wished even more to hear his father speak. Say something, Dad. Put your arms around me and say, "We're happy to have you home, son." Starkmann had seen a father and his soldier son embrace in tears at Travis, and had dreamed of coming home to a similarly emotional welcome. In his father's arms he would not feel afraid and in need of his rifle.

They pulled up to the house. The leaves of the big oak trees along the street took on an eerie color in the glare of the streetlights. The house, a mock-Tudor built in the 1920's, looked artificial, like a false front in a Hollywood back lot. When he stepped inside, Starkmann felt as if he were a guest, entering an unfamiliar house. The furniture, the pictures on the walls, the clean smells, all seemed foreign to him. His two younger sisters, Jennifer and Stephanie, had waited up for him. They hugged him and chattered in the way of high-school girls. He wanted a drink, but except for wine at dinner, his father did not allow alcohol in the house. There were only sodas. He got a Coke from the refrigerator and talked to his sisters for a while. Then his brother-in-law asked him what was really going on over there. Ed's face assumed a very grave expression, as if he were a minister of state who intended to use whatever information Starkmann gave him to make a critical foreign-policy decision. Ed sold tools for Black & Decker. Starkmann did not answer Ed's question. He would have found it easier to describe what was really going on on the dark side of the moon.

His father finally broke radio silence. "I think Chris is exhausted," Lucius said to his son-in-law, with whom he had entered into a tenuous truce, his disapproval of Ed having mellowed into a begrudging tolerance. To his son, Lucius said, "Your mother has your old room ready for you." Christian understood why his father wanted him out of sight. He tried to speak. He had something important to say to Lucius, but no words came when he looked into his father's eyes, staring at him as they had when he was a boy and had done something wrong.

He went up to his room. Everything was as he had left it a long time ago: his football and basketball trophies, his team photographs and high-school graduation picture, in which his face looked so astoundingly young that it did not seem to belong to him. Nothing in the room belonged to him. It was someone else's room. He got undressed and lay down but could not sleep, tired as he was. He was not used to sleeping at night. Night belonged to the enemy. He stayed awake until dawn. Only then did he feel safe enough to close his eyes.

It went like that for the next several nights. He would lie in bed, staring into the darkness and listening intently until first light. Then he would fall asleep. Nightmares troubled him. He dreamed that a squad of Viet Cong was hiding in the alley and waiting in ambush for his father, who was driving to church to preach his Sunday sermon. Christian could see the guerrillas crouched behind a barricade of garbage cans, but Lucius was unaware of the danger. When he drove past the alley, the Viet Cong opened fire, and Starkmann watched helplessly as bullets riddled the car and great gouts of blood spewed from his father's body.

After this and worse dreams had recurred several times, he went to a gun shop in Chicago and bought a weapon. He knew a weapon would help him sleep better. An M-1 carbine modified for sporting use was the one he chose. He sneaked it, along with a box of ammunition, into the house and hid it in his closet. That night, after loading the magazine, he got into bed with the carbine. Aware that his family would regard this as bizarre behavior if they saw him, he locked his bedroom door. He curled up under the covers, nuzzling the carbine's barrel with his cheek, his hand resting on the stock, and fell into a blessed, dreamless sleep.

After he had been home about ten days his mother thought it would be a good idea to hold a party for him. The Reverend Starkmann, who wanted to forget that the past year had ever happened, opposed the idea. Mrs. Starkmann won out in the end, a rare victory in confrontations with her husband.

The celebration was held on the back lawn, on a breezy afternoon in mid-July. His mother had invited everyone on both sides of the family, as well as neighbors and several of Starkmann's old high-school friends. There were fifty or sixty people altogether, standing around on the grass, sipping punch and eating snacks Mrs. Starkmann and her daughters had laid out on a long table. Christian watched the people from the window of his room. Although he recognized the faces, he felt that he did not know a soul. His father, who had joined the gathering for appearance's sake, stood a little apart, the sides of his hair, swept back by the breeze, white as the wings of an arctic tern. He managed to look coolly remote and ill-at-ease at the same time, exactly the way he'd looked at Anne's wedding reception four years earlier.

Christian pushed the memory of that unpleasant day out of his mind and left his room, intending to greet all the kind people who had come to welcome him home. He started downstairs, and then stopped so abruptly it was as if he'd bumped into an invisible wall. He could not face anyone. He felt ashamed of himself, too ashamed to look his friends and relatives in the eye and talk to them as if nothing had happened in the past year. This reaction, utterly unexpected, mystified him. He returned to his room, closed the door, and stood by the window, watching them all as they chatted amiably and sipped their punch from clear plastic cups. He knew all of them, loved ones and friends, but felt the worst loneliness of his life. He longed for his friends, D.J., Ramos, and Hutchinson, suddenly missing the quiet times he'd spent with them, sitting atop the bunker at dusk, sharing smoke and laughter before darkness cursed them. He missed the domesticity of the perimeter, that circle of wire, sandbags, and men, a great hoop of comradeship and safety in the jungle. He even missed the jungle, and realized that its foreign greenness had become more familiar to him than the green of the lawn below. He belonged there. The bush was his true home, and his nostalgia for it was so strong that, when he closed his eyes, his mind seemed to leave his body, entering another dimension in which it traveled backward in time. He was on the perimeter again. He could see, smell, and hear everything with incredible clarity. D.J., Ramos, and Hutchinson were walking alongside him toward their old bunker. He was the first one inside, and his loneliness vanished as soon as he stepped into its dimness and caught the odors of dried sweat and damp mud-caked clothes, the musk of brotherhood.

The sound of footsteps in the hall returned him to the here and now. He recognized the footsteps as his mother's. She knocked and said, "Chris? Aren't you ready yet? Everyone's waiting for you." Starkmann did not answer immediately, trying to adjust from his brief journey into the past. She knocked again and he opened the door.

Rosemary Starkmann was a tall, handsome woman, slim as a girl. Christian thought she looked very smart in her beige summer dress, her brown hair pulled back, accentuating her angular cheekbones. She asked if he was all right. He replied that he was—he would be down in a minute. "Everyone's waiting for you," she repeated, her eyes turning upward, a sign that she was annoyed. "I've gone to a lot of trouble, Chris." He apologized, but after she left, Starkmann remained in his room, screwing up his courage and wishing Lucius had been the one to come for him. He wanted to set things right with his father. Then he would feel truly welcome and be able to face all those people without shame. He wished for this even though he knew the Reverend Starkmann was too stubborn and reticent to make such a gesture.

After Starkmann had enlisted, his father had written him a long letter expressing his total shock and disappointment at what his son had done. He'd said he hoped Christian turned out to be a bad soldier because a man could not be a good soldier and a decent human being at the same time. A good soldier belonged to a different species, *homo furens*, half man and half beast. "I do not fear for your life or safety," he'd written, "but for what may happen to you inside. *Homo furens*, half man, half beast. That is what I fear you will become."

Starkmann had been a good soldier. Had that expelled him from the ranks of civilized humanity? Perhaps it had and perhaps that was why he felt too ashamed to face everyone. But he would have to face them. He could not disappoint his mother. And no actor about to walk onstage for the first time ever felt as frightened and sick as Starkmann did when he left his room and walked downstairs to greet the people on the lawn. He pulled off a credible performance, but the effort so exhausted him that he went to bed long before the last guest had left.

Two days later Jack Deeter, an old neighborhood acquaintance who had been at the party, invited him out for a night on the town. Starkmann declined at first, but changed his mind because he did not want anyone to think him peculiar. No one, not even his parents, knew he had been crazy (he had not been crazy long enough to warrant notification of his family). There was no reason to arouse suspicion with odd behavior. He was determined to behave normally. A soldier home from the wars was supposed to have a good time; that's what he would do.

The evening turned out to be dreadful. He discovered that Deeter, who was several years older, had invited him out only to impress him with how much money he was making as a real estate broker. They went to a number of discotheques, nightclubs, and bars on Rush Street, and at each one, Jack would pull out a wad of bills, making a great show when he tipped the waitresses and bartenders. They all knew him and treated him deferentially, while he swaggered about as if he were a show-business celebrity.

Starkmann was disgusted and tried to pick up girls to distract himself. He did not have any luck. The girls all looked beautiful and were reasonably intelligent, but he found he had nothing to say to them. He might as well have been an immigrant attempting to converse in a language he didn't know. At one discotheque a girl asked him to dance, but when Starkmann got onto the floor and the music started and bodies began to jerk and twitch in the flicker of strobe lights, he felt as if he were taking part in a weird rite of a tribe not his own. He left the girl on the dance floor and went back to the bar.

As the night wore on, the drumbeats of the music began to sound like artillery, the strobes' flashes to look like muzzle bursts, disclosing hostile faces, staring at him. Everyone was staring at him. He was sure of that. They were staring at him as if he were some sort of dangerous freak. His haircut had given him away again—his hair and, he guessed, something in his bearing or manner that told people what he was and where he had been. At times their stares grew so intense that he became as frightened of them as they seemed to be of him. He waited for something to happen. Something had to happen. Finally it did.

He and Deeter, after leaving a singles bar, were waiting at the corner of Wells and Division streets for a taxi. A car full of teenagers, slowing to turn at the intersection, suddenly veered toward the curb. One of the kids in the back rolled down a window, a white bag in his hand. As the car cruised by, he yelled, "Hey, fuzz-head, eat this!" and flung the bag at Starkmann. It arced through the air like a giant snowball, then struck him in the face, splattering him with hamburger scraps, greasy French fries, and gobs of milkshake. He tasted the milkshake. It was chocolate. He did not lose his temper. He was living in a dangerous land, where he was hated, and attacks were to be expected. His father had suffered the blows of billy clubs on civil rights marches with forbearance; surely he could withstand something as petty as this. Deeter, however, was enraged and all for getting a cab to chase the kids down. Starkmann did not want to take part in a punitive expedition. If, by some miracle, they caught up with the teenagers, there would be a fight, and he would have no choice but to kill them. He didn't want to kill anyone. He'd done his share of that. Besides, he wasn't angry. He was grateful it was over with, at least for tonight, and it had not been anywhere near as bad as what the man in California had done to him.

But he did not go out again after that night. There was no sense looking for trouble. He stayed in his room most of the time. His room had become his perimeter. He left it for family meals but hardly spoke to anyone at the dinner table. He acted as if he were a boarder, half-listening to his sisters' babble about their adolescent crises and problems and his father's discussion of his latest hopeless crusade. After dinner Starkmann would watch television, unless the news was on, in which case he would read whatever was handy. Then he would go up to his room, lock the door, and fall asleep with the carbine in his arms.

His leave ended in early August. As he could not take his carbine with him, he broke it down into its component parts, wrapped them in oiled cloth, and locked them away in a trunk in the attic. Relieved rather than sad, he packed and left for Fort Polk, Louisiana.

He returned in April of the following year, with an honorable discharge and the hope that things would be different. Of course they weren't. The house was just as strange, his father no less distant than before. After several weeks of idling about, he decided to go back to school and enrolled at the University of Illinois's Chicago campus.

It was by no means a radical campus, on the order of Berkeley or the University of Chicago, but there were a few demonstrations and enough anti-war sentiment to make him feel uncomfortable. Although he had let his hair grow and wore the shabby clothes then in fashion among students, he was constantly afraid that his classmates would see through his disguise and accuse him of being a war criminal, a child-killing, village-burning massacre-man—God knew what.

He could not bear sitting in the crowded lecture halls. He would not be at his desk longer than five minutes before he could sense someone behind him drawing a bead on his head. It came as a physical sensation, an unpleasant tingling in his scalp. At other times he worried about so many people jammed into so small a space, shoulder to shoulder, and imagined the horrible scene that would result if a bomb or shell pierced the roof. Often, he became so nervous about this possibility that he had to get up and leave in the middle of the lecture.

He dropped out before the semester ended.

Afterward, he made a few attempts to land a job, but a recession was on and work was difficult to find. At one plant, the personnel officer, after reviewing Starkmann's application, told him to roll up his sleeves. Starkmann asked why. He knew why, but he wanted to hear it from the man. Had he ever used heroin while he was overseas? the man asked; if he hadn't, he should have no objection to rolling up his sleeves. *This*, Starkmann thought, *is what blacks have to put up with all their lives.* He bent down, took off one of his shoes and his sock, and propped his bare foot on the desk.

"You didn't shoot it into your arms, where everybody could see the tracks," he said, shoving his foot toward the personnel officer's face. "You smoked it or shot it between your toes. There's my toes. Check 'em out."

The man ordered Starkmann to leave and, to make sure he did not cause any trouble, called a security guard to escort him out.

Starkmann went back to loafing about the house, snuggling up each night with the carbine. He disliked himself for his idleness. It was no way for a strong young man of twenty-one to spend his time. He thought he should find a job, any job, and move into his own apartment, but could not overcome his inertia. He felt he could not strike out on his own until he had resolved matters with his father. Either they would reconcile or have it out, once and for all.

Lucius was very busy with church affairs and the McGovern campaign, which was gearing up for the following year's national election. He was chairman of some quasi-political organization called "Clergymen for Peace in Asia," and spent a good deal of time away from home, attending meetings, rallies, and caucuses. If Starkmann was to catch him, he would have to catch him on the wing.

One night at dinner, exasperated with Christian's indifference and aimlessness, Lucius urged him to pick up where he'd left off and resume his studies for the ministry. Starkmann said he did not think that would be a good idea. Eyes like ice floes, his father asked him why. Starkmann looked at him, the man of unyielding principle, and a toxin that had been building in him for a long time suddenly spilled out.

"Because," he said, "I don't believe in any of those lies and bullshit you preach on Sundays. I never did."

He had not intended to say anything so brutal. The words had spoken themselves. He expected his father to rage at him, but Lucius only folded his napkin and went into his study, his injured silence a worse reproach than anything he could have said. Christian's mother was the one who became angry. He might be a grown man, Rosemary said, her fine lips trembling, but as long as he was under her roof, he was not to speak to his father like that again. Nor was he to use gutter language, especially in front of his sisters.

Starkmann apologized. Later, he climbed the stairs to his room and began to pack.

His father came up, looked at the clothes strewn on the bed, and asked his son what he was doing. It was the first time they had been alone together in years, and Christian sensed an opportunity that would be lost forever if it were not seized that moment. For all the distance that had grown between them, there remained memories of the times when they had been close: only memories, fragile as thread, and yet if they took up those threads now, perhaps they could, with patient weaving, repair their broken bond. Christian would say "I'm sorry for what I said, for the pain I've caused you, for everything." And his father would reply: "I'm sorry, too. I love you, Chris," and they would embrace. He imagined this scene so vividly it seemed inevitable; but when he tried to offer his apology, his tongue felt like a steel bar in his mouth. He glanced out the window, its panes fired by the sunset, and saw his face reflected in the blazing glass. He knew then that he was not entitled to his father's forgiveness, because of the wrong he had done him. He was not entitled to much of anything, for all the wrong he'd done. Any good or happiness that came his way from now on would be nothing more than blind luck, and he could not count on holding on to it for very long.

"I'm packing," he said, still staring at his image in the reddened window. "I'll be leaving in the morning."

"My son left a long time ago," the Reverend Starkmann replied. "He never came back." Then he walked out without another word.

Starkmann left home the next day, and drifted for the next several months. His plan was to live a marginal life, the only sort of life he deserved to live. The less he had, the less he stood to lose. He took on menial jobs when he needed the money, pumping gas in Shreveport, loading trucks in Houston, sweeping floors in Phoenix, washing dishes in San Diego.

There seemed to be turmoil almost everywhere he went—riots and demonstrations, the pop of tear-gas guns, the chants of angry crowds rising above the choirs of police sirens, the sounds of an America gone berserk. His country was not as he remembered it. It was pulling itself apart. Had it changed that much in the year or so he'd been gone, or had he? He didn't know. It didn't make any difference in the end: He could find no common ground with those who had not shared his experiences, and avoided those who had, afraid of the chance, however unlikely, of running into someone who knew he'd gone crazy and had been in a hospital bed when D.J., Hutch, and Ramos had been vaporized by a booby-trapped 250-pound bomb.

In the spring, after the snows melted in the passes of the Rockies, he left the West and thumbed eastward, back toward more familiar territory. When he crossed the Mississippi he turned north, heading for the Upper Peninsula, whose empty forests prickled across twenty thousand square miles. He was drawn to that borderland by its remoteness and desolation, and by something else, some nameless imperative.

*   *   *

It was midafternoon; the sun was angling sharply through the trees. Starkmann, breaking for lunch, sat on the soft earth with his back cradled in the hollow of a sugar maple. He ate his sandwiches slowly, immersed in his aloneness, which was very different from loneliness. After he'd finished eating he sipped the tepid coffee in his thermos and totaled up his tally sheets. He wanted his figures to look encouraging, but they resisted subjective interpretation. Two could not be anything other than two. He had seen some amazing things done with arithmetic during the war: five enemy dead magically became ten; ten, twenty; a hundred, a thousand. He was now under pressure to come up with another kind of numerical fantasy, but couldn't do it. There simply wasn't much high-grade sawtimber, not in these woods.

The rows and rows of numbers on the sheets reminded him of his conversation with Harding this morning and brought a coldness to his chest. He was now in a position to lose, a position he had got into willy-nilly, for he had come to the U.P. with the intention of living as minimally as he had on the road. He'd taken a shabby cottage in the woods, without a phone or running water, with only a rickety genera-tor for electricity. He had paid the paltry rent with odd jobs cutting pulp and firewood. A battered pickup that continually broke down was his only means of transportation. Two or three times a month he drove into Marquette for supplies, but fished and hunted for most of his food, living like an Indian or frontiersman. He guessed he was as happy as he could ever hope to be, which wasn't happy at all.

One winter evening he was again struck by the loneliness that had assailed him on the day of his welcome-home party. He had felt it once or twice on the road, and had come to call it The Loneliness because it was a unique sense of isolation, a sense of being adrift without landmarks, a compass, or a soul to guide him. He stepped onto the porch, the emotion choking him, and muttered, "I'm alone. I'm so alone." Then, to purge the blockage in his throat and the ache in his chest, he shouted the words into the woods, which flung their echo back at him. "I'm so alone. *Alone.*"

He met June in the spring of that year. She was waitressing in the Marquette bar and grill where he usually ate when he came into town. He'd noticed her the first time he'd stopped in at the place. It was difficult not to notice her: she stood five eleven in the sneakers she wore at work, and had black hair that reached down to the middle of her back. With her wide hips ("When God dished out asses," she

later told him, with typical bluntness, "I came back for seconds"), a
crooked front tooth, and the long, Gallic nose she'd inherited from
her French-Canadian father, she was far from beautiful, but Starkmann
could not take his eyes off her. He liked the sassy way she handled the
customers—a rough bunch of miners and woodsmen—and the movements of her ample buttocks beneath her tight uniform reminded him
of how long it had been since he'd touched a woman.

Each time he saw her he wanted to strike up a conversation, but
was inhibited by his natural shyness, a shyness intensified by his
reclusive life in the woods. He was relieved from the obligation of
making the first move when, on a slow day, she took the initiative and
started talking to him, asking him his name, where he was from, what
he was doing in the Upper Peninsula. Though her interest pleased
him, the questions made him ill at ease, because he did not like to
reveal much about himself—or anything at all, for that matter. June's
ability to draw answers from him disturbed him. That was not all he
found disturbing about her. Her eyes, almost as black as her hair,
looked at him as no other woman's ever had; they were not flirtatious
but carnal, challenging, and knowing. They seemed to strip him and
rove over every inch of his naked flesh, to probe into his heart and
mind and see his every thought and emotion.

He averted her glance by fixing his on a deer mount over the bar
while he asked a few particulars about herself. Her name was June
Josette Giroux, which, she said, was too Canuck to be true, though
she was Finnish on her mother's side. Giroux was her maiden name.
She was divorced, with a small daughter named Lisa. Hers had been
a shotgun marriage. A man ten years her senior, Jack Ripley, had
made her pregnant her last year in high school, then abandoned her
and their child two years later. All that had happened in Sault Ste.
Marie, her hometown, which she'd left shortly after her divorce to
come to Marquette.

"This town isn't much," she said, lighting a cigarette (she smoked
heavily in those days, before she'd become pregnant with Christine).
"But it's Manhattan compared to Sault Ste. Marie."

She'd been more or less driven out of there, she volunteered
without any prompting from Starkmann. She'd slept around in the
months following the end of her marriage, behavior that wasn't
tolerated in Sault Ste. Marie, where the guns of the sexual revolution
had been only a distant rumble on the horizon. Her neighbors
complained about the parade of men coming and going at odd hours,
and their gossip compelled her landlady to double her rent overnight,
an underhanded form of eviction. Though unrepentant, June got the
message, packed her suitcase, gathered up Lisa, and hopped a Grey-

hound to Marquette. She'd since "cleaned up her act," as she phrased it, and was now waitressing days while attending night school at Michigan A & M, the local college. In another few months she would have an associate's degree in sociology.

Starkmann listened to her confessional biography, stunned by her candor. He thought of his mother, that discreet, quiet woman, and could not fathom June's brash willingness to expose her life to a virtual stranger. With the feeling he knew more about her than he ought to know, or wanted to know, he paid his tab, told her he'd enjoyed the talk, and started for the door.

"I suppose I talked too much," she said, picking up on his distress. "I didn't bother you, did I?"

"No. I just don't think it's smart to tell everything about yourself to someone you hardly know."

"Maybe that means we ought to get to know each other better."

"Maybe."

"How's this for putting it on the line? You're the best-looking man I've seen walk in here. Or anywhere."

He stood by the door, flattered by her compliment, dumbfounded by her forwardness. She was daring him to act, and out of masculine ego, if for no other reason, he took her up on it.

"Okay. Let's go out sometime. You know, a movie or something."

"Your style needs a major overhaul, Chris. How about giving me a day and a time?"

"Next time I'm in town. Next Wednesday. Seven."

"Make it Tuesday or Thursday. I've got classes on Wednesday."

"Thursday's fine."

He left, afraid he was getting into something he'd do well to stay out of; but as he walked to his truck he began whistling and admitted to himself that he was looking forward to next Thursday. He could not recall the last time he'd looked forward to anything.

Their date went well. They saw a comedy at the Northland Theater, then had a few drinks at Vandy's, a popular bar on Third Street. Everyone there seemed to know her, and Starkmann both admired and envied the ease with which she handled herself in crowds, among whom he felt awkward and out of place. After several more dates he discovered a few things about her he did not admire. Her brassiness got out of hand sometimes, bordering on pugnacity. She also had a habit of using language he hadn't heard since he'd left the front lines. But she possessed a quality that pulled his attention away from these flaws, a magnetism that wasn't feminine but *female*— the magnetism of a woman, earthy and sensual, with a capacity to occupy his mind to the point that he could think of nothing but her.

He respected her courage, raising a child on her own, the strength it took to work hard all day and attend school at night; and the way she carried herself, with the jauntiness of a wounded but defiant soldier, captivated him. In time, a measure of her frankness rubbed off on him. He told her a little about the war, though he kept the worst to himself, secrets that would forever remain classified, even from her. Still, it was the first time he'd spoken about Vietnam to anyone, and he'd done so without fear or distrust.

Starkmann fell in love. He wasn't sure why, which troubled him because he didn't like mysteries. He remembered the moment it happened—or, rather, the moment when he realized he'd been in love all along. They'd been walking through Presque Isle Park, along Superior's shore. He stopped to kiss her, and when she lifted her face to meet his lips, he saw an expression of pain and sadness mingled with the challenge in her eyes. In that instant he knew the magic of encountering a kindred spirit. She, too, was lonely, an exile suffering from unseen wounds, those inflicted by her husband's desertion, and, as he'd learned in another of her confessionals, by her father, who'd left home when she was thirteen.

If this kinship of souls offered some explanation for his love, it did not help him understand why she was attracted to him. He had nothing to offer a woman. He was a semi-employed veteran with no prospects for the future. Finally, he gathered the nerve to ask what she saw in him. Loyalty, she answered. She didn't trust men. She expected them to run out, but her intuition, which she did trust, told her that he was not that kind. He was no deserter. He was constant, and whether he'd been raised with that virtue or had acquired it in some other way, maybe in the war, she'd sensed it in him from the beginning. Starkmann flushed at the reference to the war, for he regarded his crackup and hospital stay as a form of desertion. Nor did he consider himself all that steadfast, though he was gratified that she did and was determined to prove her right. They were married three months later, in the last weeks of autumn.

Marriage put an end to his marginal life. June was not about to join him in his backwoods shack. He moved into her apartment in Marquette. It was pleasant enough, spacious and well-lit, and they could look out the front windows to the dome of the county court-house and the twin bell-towers of Saint Peter's cathedral; but Starkmann had a difficult time readjusting to civilization, and a still more difficult time playing stepfather to Lisa—then, as now, a child in-clined to spells of self-pity. He could not hold on to a job for longer than a few weeks. He worked on the ore docks for a while and quit, at a sawmill, and quit that. Menial labor did not suit him. June, in the meantime, had received her degree and had landed a job as a state social worker. Her salary paid most of the bills, which made Starkmann unhappy with himself. He felt trapped.

At her urging, he decided to give school another try. He enrolled at A & M on the GI Bill. The campus was small, the students too poor and pragmatic to be concerned with politics, rallies, and events in a far-off country like Vietnam. Their indifference relieved Starkmann; he could move among them without fear of being noticed or asked about the war. The war was as good as over anyway. A cease-fire had been declared the year before—1973—and with the sputtering, uncertain end of the fighting had come a cooling of the passions it had aroused. The news was no longer full of reports of battles and body counts, of draft-card burnings and undergraduate mobs shouting *What do you want? Revolution! When do you want it? Now!* with the same rhythms and mindless enthusiasm of earlier student generations yelling football cheers.

In this quieter, saner atmosphere, Starkmann, after a semester casting about for a subject that held his interest, took up forestry. It was an odd departure for someone who had once studied religion, but it appealed to his scientific bent as well as to his love of the natural world. He was fascinated to learn how moss, lichens, and tundra plants pioneered life on rocky slopes exposed by melting glaciers; how lakes died, choking under mats of sphagnum and sedge, and how their deaths gave birth to forests, soil establishing itself on the mat, then shrubs and bog trees such as tamarack and spruce colonizing the humus, their debris building more soil until no trace of the lake remained, its grave marked by the tall firs of the climax forest.

Starkmann threw himself into his studies with a zeal he'd never known was in him. By taking extra courses and attending summer school, he earned his degree in under three years. He was hired by Great Superior soon afterward, thus adding steady, enjoyable employment to his list of acquisitions, which now included a daughter of his own. Christine had been born the year of his graduation. He changed diapers, helped bathe her, and took over her night feedings so June could sleep. Holding the infant in those hushed hours, he knew a happiness he'd never thought possible. He felt he had put the war behind him, locked his memories of it in the rearmost vault of his mind.

Now, as he sat in the woods, he was galled by the stupidity of that illusion. Though he was done with the war, it was not done with him. The war had started again on September 21, 1981, with the first occurrence of the nightmare. Its assaults afterward began to wear him down, to chip away at his peace of mind, waging a kind of guerrilla warfare on the life he had built for himself, June, and the girls. He grew edgy, roaring like an irate sergeant at his daughters for minor infractions, quarreling with June over petty matters. Once, in an after-dinner conversation, she'd brought up his father, asking why he had no communication with Lucius. Starkmann, his nerves frazzled by the previous night's troubled sleep, saw a white light, blinding as a flashbulb. He hollered that she was never to mention his father again and, with more strength than he realized he had, picked up the dining room table and flung it into a wall.

Mortified by his outburst, he ran out of the apartment and took a long walk to try to figure out what was happening to him. He hiked to the top of Ridge Avenue, then down to the park, and from there to the ore docks, where, in the gleam of deck lights, a freighter was taking on a load of iron. Looking at the great ship, his mind cleared by the chill October air, Starkmann convinced himself that he needed a change of scene. Town living did not suit him. Too confining, too many people. He had seen, on his drives to work, a house and forty acres of timber for sale outside of Vieux Desert. Maybe that was where he belonged. Maybe there, in his own house, on his own land, he would recapture his happiness and sleep without dreams of fire and death.

He returned home, buoyed by the conviction that he'd found both the source of his discontent and the way to end it. June was in the bedroom, crying—the first time he'd seen her in tears.

"I thought you'd left," she sobbed. "That's how Dad did it. Just walked out one night and never came back."

"June, that's . . ."

"Stupid and silly, I know. But that's what I thought."

"I don't know what got into me. I . . . oh, hell . . ."

He sat on the edge of the bed and held her.

"Don't you leave me," she said in a tone that was half plea, half threat. "Don't you ever leave me."

Starkmann's desire to buy the house matured into an obsession after the real estate agent showed him the property. The moment he set foot on it, he had a feeling of coming home, a feeling so powerful that, if he'd had a mystical bent of mind, he would have believed he'd lived there in a previous existence.

June was opposed to the whole idea of moving. She was not going to live in the boondocks—next door to an Indian reservation, no less—and drive thirty miles to and from work in all kinds of weather. He deployed various arguments to overcome her objections. The price was irresistible, forty thousand for all of it, only eight thousand down. Eight thousand! she countered. That would wipe out their savings and leave them with a mortgage of thirty-two thousand, and with interest rates what they were, their monthly payments would be, let's see, about four hundred a month, twice what the apartment cost. Starkmann reminded her that their combined income was almost twenty-five thousand a year, which made them aristocracy in this region of laid-off miners and gypsy loggers. They quarreled about it for a month. Starkmann won the dispute through a form of emotional bribery. He knew he had been unpleasant lately, he said, and, unwilling to tell her about the nightmare, ascribed his unhappiness to his dislike of living in town. The house would make him happy, restore him to his old self. He could fish on his own property, hunt in the meadow where grouse and woodcock nested. Reluctantly, June surrendered. They moved in after Thanksgiving.

Recalling that day, Starkmann berated himself for falling prey to another illusion. The change in his outer life had not effected change in his inner life. Moving into his own household had not kept the nightmare at bay; it did not respect geography, or his new status as a man of property. Maybe, he thought, ownership was the problem. Maybe he possessed too much. Maybe the bill for his unearned happiness was coming due. A flight of screeching ravens stirred him from these thoughts. He looked up at the birds, and saw by the sun that it was getting late, a reminder that he had work to do.

He picked up his instruments and started walking, deeper into the forest.

8

She left her office feeling good, not I'm sitting-on-top-of-the-world terrific, but pretty good, all things considered. Today had been one of her court days, and those usually sucked her down into the pits, but she had actually won a case today. The judge, who had continued it ten times over the past year, had finally issued a pay order to a man three years behind in his child-support payments. True, her client wasn't going to get anything near what she wanted or needed. The woman had five kids, for God's sake, and Erickson, the county state's attorney, hadn't even bothered to ask her what she thought would be a fair amount—which was typical of him; he just set the amount arbitrarily and scheduled the judge to issue the order, a lousy hundred bucks a month. Even after getting off so easy, the defendant, a tough-looking iron miner, had called June a bitch after they'd left the courtroom. Still, she had won. Not that June felt any sense of great triumph. She wasn't a lawyer for one thing. Her official title was Court Representative, Bureau of Child Support Enforcement, Michigan State Department of Public Assistance—a glorified welfare worker. For another thing, she knew the woman wasn't going to be much better off, because only half the money was going to go to her, the rest to the Department's public aid fund. So she would get fifty dollars a month to supplement her ADC, a lousy sixty dollars per kid per month, and here it was 1982, with inflation double-digiting and food costs out of sight in this godforsaken nowhere because food had to be imported from downstate, as if the Upper Peninsula were a Third World country, which, in a way, it was. Five kids. June had

had a hard time raising Lisa after Ripley had left them without a dime; she couldn't imagine what it would be like to have five on her hands. For God's sake, hadn't any of these women heard about the pill?

She felt warm in her wool dress and sweater as she walked to her car. It must have been seventy degrees, downright tropical for a northwoods October, with the wind out of the south, the sky clear, and Lake Superior as blue as photographs she'd seen of the Caribbean. The fine weather accounted for her good spirits as much as winning the case. Indian summer days like this one always made her upbeat and aroused in her a hope that this year, for a change, would bring a short and mild winter, a hope that had never been fulfilled. She forced herself not to think about the winter, which she dreaded in the way, she imagined, people in the Middle Ages must have dreaded plague. She would enjoy this unseasonably mild afternoon for what it was worth. When she got to the top of Ridge Avenue, where her Jeep Wagoneer was parked, she turned around and looked at the town, spread out below alongside the lake, and her heart sort of rose. Marquette was really a pretty town. The sandstone walls of the county courthouse were rust-red in the late-afternoon light, and its copper dome glowed like a miniature sun, except that it was streaked with green here and there. The domes of the archdiocesan church, where she occasionally attended Mass, gleamed just beyond, and there were the roofs of the houses and then some wooded hills, Mount Marquette the highest one, with a taillight park at the top where high-school and college kids steamed up car windows at night. It was such a fine, bright day that even the stacks of the state maximum-security prison, way off in the distance, looked cheerful as they leaked smoke into the pale northern sky.

She got into the wagon, aware now that she was being given the once-over by a couple of football types from A & M. They were standing across the street, two brainless young hunks in letter-sweaters who were looking her up and down. Their stares made her conscious of her size, which often caused her problems in court, where the judges, who almost always sided with the men, sided with them even more when she walked in, looking like an Amazon or whatever. June pulled away from the curb, carefully avoiding any eye contact with the two college boys. She knew she had a way of looking at men that was often misunderstood. Well, sort of misunderstood. She never intended any kind of provocation. She wasn't a flirt; she just had a look in her dark eyes that was there as unconsciously and naturally as the color is in a bird's wing. It was a look that told men "I love it." And June did. She'd loved it from the moment she'd done it the first time with Ripley, when she was sixteen, and it hadn't been the big disappointment it was supposed to be; it had been just as good as she'd imagined, but then, Ripley was a real star in that department. For all his other flaws, which were countless, he'd been some lover. He had seemed like everything she'd ever wanted back then. He was a lot more experienced, a lot older. Ten years older. Ten years, June thought as she turned onto Third Street. Jesus, Ripley was now forty-two. It was difficult to think of him as a middle-aged man. She wondered where he was. Wherever, he wasn't sleeping in any cold, empty bed—that was for sure. He had some bimbo to keep him warm, some too-young, too-confused female who'd believe his lies as *she* had, believe Ripley would stick around and love only her.

Near the bottom of Third, the after-work crowd had begun to gather in Vandy's for cocktails. June got a little pang, watching the people walking into the bar and hearing a snatch of music from the jukebox. She would not have minded a scotch or two to unwind and celebrate. She also would not have minded the company. Sandy Jackson, her best girlfriend, was probably inside, sipping a Bombay extra dry. June missed people a lot. There was something about a crowded, noisy bar that she liked, probably because it provided such a welcome contrast to the isolated silence of living in a backwoods, eight miles outside of a one-horse town like Vieux Desert. Marquette had only twenty-odd thousand people, nearly forty thousand if you counted the next-door mining towns of Ishpeming and Negaunee. Forty thousand people did not exactly make the place Chicago or New York, but at least you didn't see the same faces day after day, and at least you felt you were living in modern times, whereas in Vieux Desert you often had the feeling you'd been caught in a sci-fi time warp and had gone back to the Great Depression. All those derelict sawmills and dusty loggers' bars like Swanson's, half the men out of work. Once, she'd seen a photograph of the town taken in 1931, and except for the TV antennas on the roofs and the late-model cars on the streets, the place didn't look any different today. Nothing happened. Nothing changed. The biggest event in the eleven months she'd lived there was when Paul LeFevre, a commercial fisherman, tried to blow up a trawler owned by some Indians who'd docked overnight in the harbor. Vieux Desert. The forsaken quarter. The Frenchmen who had named it sure had it down right.

She tried to turn her thoughts in another direction. They were souring her mood and stirring up a resentment toward Chris. She loved him, she'd been a good and faithful wife to him these nine years, and she'd stand by him no matter what, but why had he stuck her and the girls out in the middle of nowhere? They lived like some pioneer family, except for the demand generator that supplied electricity and the well that gave them running water; and the couple of times the generator had gone on the bum, knocking out the wellpump, they'd had to light kerosene lamps and had gone to the bathroom in the old outhouse, which stank of lye and feces and was crawling with spiders. She worried a lot about the girls, marooned out there. They hardly saw their friends, and what if one of them got sick or hurt? The nearest doctor was here in Marquette, and if something happened during a bad blizzard with the road blocked . . . Jesus, she didn't even want to think about that!

It seemed to her they had been doing fine in Marquette. Then Chris got it into his thick German skull to move to Vieux Desert because he felt cooped up in an apartment. Okay, fair enough, but why a house *and* forty acres of useless swamp and scrub timber nearly ten miles outside of town? Chris had never answered that question to her satisfaction. All he said was that he'd bought the land precisely because it was useless; no one else would have it, so he would not have to worry about other people living too close to him. She answered that it didn't make a lot of sense to her, but he never elaborated. He wasn't much for talking. Sandy, who'd been a witness at their wedding, called him the reincarnation of Gary Cooper. *Yup. Nope.*

He was a strange one, all right, and the last year or so he'd become stranger, more quiet and self-contained, as though he were living inside an invisible telephone booth. A couple of weeks ago he'd come home from work and said that Bill King was trying to get him fired—the company was down on him about something. Naturally, the news had scared her: they'd never be able to keep up the mortgage on her salary alone; they'd have to sell out or lose everything, the way a lot of people these days were losing their property, what with the unemployment rate up here at nearly forty percent. She'd seen the foreclosure notices in the courthouses, and these awful leeches, profiting from other people's misfortunes, lining up on the courthouse steps for the foreclosure sales. She didn't want anything like that to happen, but when she asked Chris to explain what made him think King was trying to get him fired, he didn't say anything, naturally. The mystery man.

June had left Marquette behind, and was on the road to Vieux Desert—woods on both sides, the maple trees blazing. She could not have ordered a more beautiful afternoon. She guessed it was unfair, even selfish of her to criticize Chris for being what he was. After all, she'd known what she was getting into when she married him. He had been doing some kind of hermit number, living in a run-down deer camp all by himself, when they'd met. She remembered that day, nearly ten years before, when she was waitressing at Rex's Bar and Grille. He'd been coming into the place off and on for a few months, and the first time she'd seen him, she thought she was going to faint. June had always had a weakness for Nordic types—Ripley had been tall and blond—and Chris looked like the original model for them all. It had been an unusually warm day in March, she remembered. He came in wearing one of those sleeveless army undershirts beneath his windbreaker and when she saw his height—one of the few men in the world who made her feel petite—and those long, wiry muscles in his arms, his blue eyes, white-blond hair, and his yellow beard—he'd grown a beard, living out in the boondocks—her knees started to go out from under her. He looked like some Viking god. Most of all it was his eyes. They were the clearest she had ever seen, and yet they seemed to be hiding something; she sensed some kind of force or turbulence under all that cold, placid blue, the way you can look at a frozen river and sense the current, tumbling invisibly beneath the ice. When he looked at her as she came up to him to take his order, she felt as giddy as a schoolgirl having her first crush, a feeling that embarrassed her. After all, she wasn't a schoolgirl but a twenty-two-year-old divorcée with a child and a bitter marriage behind her.

Weeks and weeks passed. She tried her best to get his attention, but nothing seemed to work. Finally—it was just before Memorial Day weekend—she decided she wasn't going to let him walk out again without speaking to her. When Chris ordered his sandwich, she struck up a conversation with him, or tried to. He said very little, only that he was working as a part-time logger, and living somewhere in the boondocks, and that he came into town once a week to buy groceries. She had turned on her look, and there had been nothing unconscious or natural about it that time. It was entirely calculated. But it didn't have any effect. He started to leave. Self-conscious about her Canuck nose, her crooked tooth and big behind, obvious in the tight-fitting waitress uniform, she did not feel pretty or desirable, and decided she couldn't afford to be circumspect or coy. She didn't know how he was going to react to her boldness, whether he would be flattered, flustered, curious, or angry. Or maybe he would just laugh in her face and go out the front door. He didn't do that, thank God. He didn't appear to have any reaction at all. He looked at her with no expression in his wonderful eyes and said, "Okay, let's go to the movies." That was all, as though he were asking for another cup of coffee.

But he showed up the following week and took her to the

Northland. They had a few more dates in the weeks that followed, and he was always prompt and polite, just as steady as he could be, and she liked that after her erratic father and no-show ex-husband. Sometimes, though, he seemed too considerate. She began to wonder why, after they'd been seeing each other for two months, he hadn't put the Big Move on her. For God's sake, he knew she was no sweet young virgin. Maybe she wasn't good-looking enough for him, too much on the hefty side, although her height carried her weight pretty well. Possibly he had some sort of moral objection to sleeping with a woman outside of marriage; he'd told her he had once studied to be a minister. But he'd also told her that he'd been in Nam, and mentioned something about the little whores who took on the GIs in Saigon. He must have been one of their customers once or twice at least. It could have been he was indifferent about women. He seemed indifferent about most everything. Nothing excited him in any way. He hardly ever laughed or smiled. She would have written him off as a handsome bore if she hadn't had an instinct that a lot was going on inside him. There was a tension in his indifference, as if, every minute, he was struggling to contain powerful emotions that could not be controlled if they were ever released. He was all wrapped up in himself—not in the egotistical sense but literally: wrapped up, tied in knots, imprisoned, June suspected, by something inside himself that needed to get out, and this whatever-it-was gave him an air of elusiveness and mystery that compelled her. She'd intuited that the war had something to do with it; she'd read in the papers that the war had weirded-out a lot of guys. Something terrible had happened to him, she was certain; he'd suffered some awful loss, and being a woman, she flattered herself into thinking that she could heal his pain. But the first time she asked him about the war, he got nervous and really clammed up, didn't say a word all night but stared off into space, his mind somewhere else.

One evening they went walking through the park. As usual, she was doing most of the talking. Suddenly, as in an old-fashioned romantic movie, he took her by the waist and kissed her passionately. He started to say something—her intuition told her he wanted to say he loved her—but the words never came. Frustrated by his reticence, she became determined to force him to express his feelings, one way or another.

The next afternoon, he came into town as she was getting off work and asked her to his place for dinner. He would cook. He said he'd become a good bachelor cook. It sounded a little peculiar, inviting a girl to dinner in a backwoods deer camp, but she agreed. Maybe this would be her chance to get him to speak his mind.

Leaving Lisa with Sandy, she went out with Chris in his beat-up truck, which threatened to fall apart any second. Ten miles outside of town he turned off the pavement and got onto a dirt road that went straight into the darkening woods. The whole enterprise began to seem pretty dubious to June. Though she'd been born and raised in the Upper Peninsula, and had learned from her father to hunt and fish, she had always lived in one town or another. The woods scared her. So did Chris. She'd read, in those stories about war veterans, how some of them were closet berserkos, quiet and pleasant one minute, full of rape and mayhem the next.

Her heart plummeted when they finally got to his place. It looked like one of those shanties Indians lived in, a real mess, with all kinds of unidentifiable junk lying in the weeds outside. It was dusk; coyotes started yapping away off somewhere. She wanted to turn back right then, but she had always accepted the consequences of her actions and decisions—Lisa was proof of that—and she'd see this adventure through.

Chris got out of the truck, went into an outbuilding, and turned on a generator. At least they had electricity. Then he took a big cooler from the back of the truck and showed her the steaks, the head of lettuce, and the sacks of tomatoes he'd kept on ice, and she thought that was very sweet and endearing. The camp was as clean and orderly inside as it was a mess on the outside. June was a good housekeeper—something she'd learned from her fastidious mother—and was impressed by how tidy Chris had kept the place with no appliances of any kind, just a broom and a mop, and no running water, only a hand pump over the sink, beside the butane stove. In a way the place was too orderly. The main room was stark: an Indian rug on the wooden floor, a plain table and chairs, and some shelves on which jars and canned goods were stacked—according to height, she noticed, with the tallest on the left, the shortest on the right. In the small bedroom, his bed was made so tightly that, he said, he could bounce a quarter on it. He took a coin from his pocket and demonstrated, and seemed very proud of himself. There was no closet. A pipe running the length of the shortest wall served as a rack for his clothes, which were hung exactly two inches apart, his shirts all facing the same direction. It looked like an army barracks.

Chris cooked the steaks and made a salad. Both were fairly good, though not as good as she could have made them. She would have rubbed the steaks in garlic and crushed black pepper, then splashed a little olive oil on them before taking them off the broiler. She was a good cook, if she did say so herself, and she loved to eat, which was plain for all to see. He had beer in the cooler, and asked if she wanted one with dinner. She took a glass of water instead, though she did accept the bourbon he offered after dinner. It was the only hard liquor he had—Early Times, she thought it was. He didn't have any mix, so she drank it straight, hoping it would relax her and help her get used to this odd situation: a dinner for two in the middle of nowhere, with coyotes howling outside—coyotes, for God's sake.

She had a second bourbon, then a third, and was soon more than relaxed. She began to feel wild and wanton, alone with him there in the cabin, looking at his lean-muscled body, his golden beard and hair. For a change, Chris was doing the talking, or trying to. The whiskey had loosened his tongue and inhibitions, and, she guessed, he felt free to talk on his home ground. He was attempting to describe some of his experiences overseas but was having trouble putting his words together—not, June realized, because he was drunk but because his experiences did not appear to make much sense to him and he was struggling to force some order on them.

The glimpses he gave her of the war reminded her of those she had seen on television in the sixties: disconnected images of a green land, its skies filled with plagues of helicopters, images of men running in the mud and bombs flashing in clumps of palm trees. She'd been in high school then, and had never been able to believe completely in the reality of what she saw on the screen. The running men seemed like actors, the news reports like war movies. In time, she lost interest in them, they were all so alike. Only one stuck in her memory. It was of a battle on a mountain, on whose slopes some sort of bombs were exploding in dense white clouds, as if gigantic bags of lime had burst open. Fireballs arced out of the smoke like meteors. There was an odd, fascinating beauty in the explosions. Having wondered for years what they were, she asked Chris about them, partly to satisfy her curiosity, partly as a way of getting him to talk.

"That was willy-peter—white phosphorous," he replied abstractly. "It's a chemical that burns at ninety-five degrees Fahrenheit. Get it? Three degrees below body temperature. The stuff gets on you, you can't put the fire out. You can roll in the dirt, you can jump into a lake, and it'll keep burning, right through you."

The thought made June squirm.

"Once, I saw a gook—a VC—hit by the stuff. It stuck to him. He rolled into a flooded rice paddy, but when he came out, he was still on fire . . . it . . . he . . . He was screaming, on fire, so we . . . then we. . . . Never mind."

That distant look came into his eyes. Her heart went out to him, but she wasn't sure if what she felt was love or pity, or a little of both. She stood and brushed his arm gently, giving him a chaste kiss on the forehead. She was almost frightened by the unexpected ardor of his response: He pulled her to him and, his hand cupping her breast, started kissing her as if he meant to swallow her whole.

Then he stopped himself and apologized. He hadn't touched a woman in so long, he explained, and she answered, Jesus, don't worry, it was wonderful, this isn't the 1950's anymore. He kissed her again, and she responded with as much passion. She was wet immediately, and when she took off her dress and panties, she could smell her own scent, salty and primordial, like a tidal pool. She went down to her knees, fondling him with her fingers, mouth, and tongue, taking an artist's pride in the change she brought about in him, his penis as big as the rest of him, outthrust at an aggressive angle. Chris took her the first time in the chair, she straddling him, and he exploded into her in seconds. God, it *had* been a long time for him. A lot of girls, like Sandy, would have been disappointed, those selfish bitches who wanted the man to hold back to satisfy them because that's what they had read in idiotic magazines. June reveled in the depth of Chris's need, and in the way she'd made him so hot that he went off quick and sharp, like a wild animal.

Maybe she would have been disappointed if that first time had been the only time, but Chris was young, and a terrific physical specimen, working and living in the woods, and that first taking was only the prelude to a night of lovemaking like none she'd ever known. He laid her on the floor, and then—Jesus, he was strong—picked her up and carried her into the bedroom and did it to her again, he lying on his back, she astride him.

And his desire, she realized, had less to do with his youth and strength than it did with the need to release emotions dammed up for too long a time. That had been the marvelous thing: how, joined to her, he escaped from the thing that imprisoned him, at least for the moment. After the third time—she guessed it was the third time; she wasn't a scorekeeper—he spoke of the beauty of her amber-olive skin, and her long black hair like an Indian's, and at last he told her he loved her. A lot of men said that, and after Ripley she'd learned to be wary; but she could tell Chris meant it because the words did not come easily. They were lying on their sides, his face on her breasts, when he spoke them, not gently or tenderly, but in a voice trembling from the pain and effort of it. He was almost crying; the old, old words came out of him like a confession.

His emotional abandonment made her more abandoned than she had ever been, shameless. She sat up, bracing her back against the wall behind the bed so she could watch herself make love to this strange quiet man who loved her. She stroked and caressed him until he was hard again, and when he pierced her once more, she kept her eyes open and, in the moonlight crashing through the small window, saw him plunging in and half out of her, loving the sight of his wheat-golden crotch against the blackness of hers.

Beast and angel. Mud and sky. She had always believed that every human soul was split in two at birth, and that the longing of men for women, women for men, was a longing for reunion with the missing half. And if you were one of the few lucky enough to find it, you joined with it in this act, at once holy and profane, and made yourself whole, and the other person whole, and together became one distinct being. That is what she saw, looking down past her breasts and belly to where their sexes met, two beings in one. He was her missing half, she his. She slid down onto her back, pulling him atop her, and coming in violent spasms. Her body quivering under his, she cried her love for him.

Chris rolled off her. She began to kiss him, over and over, because she did not want him to retreat back into himself. He returned her kisses, his lips touching every part of her, her mouth, her throat, her breasts and belly, her cunt and thighs and ankles. She turned onto her stomach and let him kiss the back of her neck, his hands parting her hair, and then he kissed her spine and hips until his face was buried between her legs, his tongue probing where his penis had been. She could not believe it, but she was aroused again, her hips rising to meet him so that her bottom and back formed a long, lush curve. Chris rose from his knees into a squat, his hands holding her by the small of her waist, and penetrated her from behind, like one of the wild things howling in the forest. All she could feel were the touch of Chris's hands, his crotch bristling against her buttocks, and his cock, pumping into her so deeply it touched her womb. She could not see him. He could have been any man, or any sort of male. Her imagination, as unrestrained in that moment as her desires, ran wild, and she felt she was living the unspeakable, unforgettable dream she had had long ago, about the bear-god in the Finnish fairy tales her mother had told her when she was young—the dream in which she was the human, mortal bride of the bear-god, locked in anguish and pleasure to the beast as he ravished her in a torch-lit cage. Pain and pleasure became one now, love and lust, man, animal, and angel as she joined his hard rhythm, holding her bottom tight against the god-beast, feeling his breath hot on the back of her neck, grinding her hips with sensual slowness, and when she felt his eruptions scalding her inside, she did not cry but screamed, savagely, joyfully.

Now, reliving that first night, all she could think about was making love to him as soon as she got home. Much as she wanted to, she would have to postpone it. The girls were home from school, she had to get dinner ready, and she was not sure Chris would be very responsive. Lately it was becoming harder for her to pull him out of himself in the only way she knew how. Even when he was with her, flesh joined to flesh, it was as if he was fulfilling an obligation.

His remoteness had begun to awaken her worst fear—of being left. Chris, she knew, would not desert her the way her father had, just walk out never to be seen or heard from again, or the way Ripley had, for another woman—several women actually. Ripley and his harem. True, Chris often behaved like a husband with a girlfriend on the side, furtive and secretive, but she would have known if he had a lover. Vieux Desert was so small that a man or woman couldn't keep a secret like that for longer than five minutes. She suspected that Chris had another sort of mistress: the war. The suspicion had been aroused by a few newspaper articles she'd recently read, and by Chris's bad dreams. More and more frequently he tossed and turned at night and mumbled phrases she recognized as military, though she didn't understand their meaning. Often he ground his teeth in his sleep, so loudly that the sound had awakened her. The war. That was where his soul went on its flights. The war called him and held his soul in an embrace he could not break. Or did not want to. She had asked him once about the small round scars on his back. He'd answered with one word—*mortar*—and refused to elaborate, giving her the impression that his wounding, like the war itself, had been an experience too intimate to be shared with her, or with anyone. The only comparable experience June could draw from her own life was childbirth. Perhaps war was to a man what labor was to a woman, a rapturous agony that belonged exclusively to the one who had endured it. If Chris had asked her what it had been like to bear Lisa and Christine, she could not have described it; nor would she have wished to. That helped her understand his reticence a little more; nevertheless she was jealous of the war. Given the choice, she would have much preferred a human rival. She could have taken care of an affair with another woman.

She was startled by the trumpet of a logging truck's diesel horn. She'd strayed over the center line, she'd gotten so lost in her thoughts. She jerked the wheel hard to the right, and the truck blew past her, buffeting the Jeep. That would have been a helluva way to go, she thought, her heart triphammering and her knees like water. HORNY WIFE, DAYDREAMING ABOUT SEX, KILLED IN HIGHWAY COLLISION. Several minutes later, she passed the sign that read VIEUX DESERT — POP. 942 — NATURE IN ABUNDANCE. That was for sure. In the winter, deer sometimes paraded down the main street, and in the spring, hungry bears prowled the outskirts, raiding garbage cans. Plenty of nature, folks, enough to make you sick. She drove through the dreary town and tried to restore her cheerful mood by thinking about how she would prepare the grouse and woodcock Chris had shot last week. She decided to grill the birds, and serve wild rice on the side with the last of the green beans from her garden. No more fresh vegetables from now on. The killing Canadian frosts were on their way.

Chris's truck was parked in the driveway. He usually got home before she did, a relief for her because she did not like the idea of the girls' being alone out here for too long after school. June got out of the Wagoneer, feeling out of place in this woodland setting in her heels and skirt, and went inside and announced, "Hey, everybody, Mama's home!" There was no answer. No one was around, although they had been: Lisa's schoolbooks were on the kitchen table and Chris's canvas jacket was hanging from its peg on the back porch. Maybe he'd taken the girls for a walk, which would have been unusual. Lately he paid even less attention to them than to her.

Upstairs, she took off her skirt and blouse, giving her near-naked figure a quick inspection in the full-length closet mirror. Not too bad for a big girl: large breasts still firm, and none of the ripples that made some women's skin look like bread dough. She wished, though, there was something she could do about her hips. Dieting helped only a little. She guessed it was her pelvic bone structure that gave her bottom its earth-mother breadth. Sandy, fanatical about maintaining her slim figure, had started aerobic classes in a gym someone had opened in Marquette, but June could not picture herself lifting weights or hopping around in tights to rock music. Anyway, she didn't like what that sort of exercise did to women's bodies. She'd seen these gorgeous girls in magazine ads, girls with perfect, athletic figures, too perfect and too tight somehow, all female roundness and sensuality sweated right out of them; she was willing to bet they made love as if they were doing push-ups.

She changed into her house clothes, a checkered shirt, Levis, and women's western boots—might as well dress the part of the country wife. As she started down the stairs for the kitchen she heard a gunshot and Lisa crying out Chris's name. Heart pounding, she ran outside and down the path that led to the junction of the Big and Little Firedogs, where the sounds had come from. When she'd heard the shot, the first thing to come into her mind was: Chris has killed himself.

She felt ridiculous for thinking such a thought, but was nevertheless relieved to discover that he had killed a fox. It was lying in the shadows of the firs alongside the river. Chris was standing over it with a revolver, while Butternut sniffed the carcass, and Lisa and Christine stared transfixed at the russet-furred animal, its head in a puddle of blood. Chris and the girls had been fishing; a spinning rod, braced in a forked stick, pointed out over the bank.

"Everyone all right?" June asked.

Chris looked up, a little surprised to see her, and she did not like the expression on his face. There were many, many things he had never told her, but she was smart enough to add two and two. Killing this animal had reminded him of something about which he needed no reminding.

"We're fine," he said.

"Well, is anybody going to tell me what the hell happened?"

Lisa, he explained, had heard the fox rustling in the underbrush after they'd started fishing. Apparently it had been hit by a car on the blacktop—both its hind legs had been broken—but had managed to crawl this far into the woods. It was so weak he'd been able to pick it up as if it were a kitten.

"So I got the pistol. Nothing else I could do."

"We could have brought it to the vet," Lisa said in the tone of the distraught adolescent looking for an excuse to argue with a parent.

"The vet is in Marquette," June reminded her. "He would have been closed by the time you got there. What then? Take the fox to the county hospital?"

"It isn't funny, Mom."

"Oh, Christ."

June turned her back on her daughter and strode off to the shed for a shovel, asking herself: Suppose one of the girls had been struck by a car, and it's such a long drive to the hospital over doubtful back roads? She came back, and without a word, rammed her foot down on the garden spade and flung a shovelful of dirt, then another, her long hair tossing with her movements.

"What are you doing, Mom?"

"I'm going to bury the poor thing—what does it look like?"

"We could have at least tried to save it before shooting it," Lisa whined, her eyes appealing for June's alliance.

"I didn't enjoy killing it."

"Then why did you make us watch?"

"I told you that you might as well see it. It's the way things are sometimes."

"The way *what* is?" asked Lisa.

June scattered another clod of earth as easily as if it were garden seed. Christine, who was as close-mouthed as her father, wanted no part of the argument developing between her parents and stepsister.

She sat down behind the spinning rod and pretended to be fishing, and the beauty of her pale blond hair against the green of the firs made June's throat catch.

"What your father means, Lisa . . . I mean, what Chris means is that there are things up here you have to get used to."

"Killing foxes? I'm supposed to get used to killing *foxes*?"

"You have to get used to not feeling sorry when feeling sorry doesn't do any good, or maybe makes things worse. That includes feeling sorry for yourself."

"There are some things I don't *want* to get used to." Lisa's balled fists went to her hips as she bent slightly forward at the waist, the gesture a tad artificial, as if she were imitating a stage movement she'd seen performed by some teenage actress on a TV show. "And I don't want to get used to them," she went on, "because I'm getting out of *up here* as soon as I'm old enough."

"I hope you do. That's what I wanted to do when I was your age. Then I was old enough . . ."

June caught herself, but Lisa, eager for a fight with someone, would not let it slide.

"Go ahead, Mom. Say it. In front of Chris and everybody. Say it."

"Go back to the house." June kept digging, though the grave was more than deep enough.

"Say it, Mom."

June drove the spade into the ground like a conqueror planting a flag, whirled, and went at her daughter, her hand poised to slap the girl's face.

"Get back to the house, dammit."

Lisa, only three inches shorter than her mother, physically an adult at fourteen but in all other respects a mass of sensitive nerves and hormonal confusion, burst into tears and ran off toward the house. June's first impulse was to run after her, put her arms around her and apologize for losing her temper, but that would only encourage Lisa to switch on the tear ducts when anyone spoke harshly to her or things did not go her way, and dammit, the way life was up here, tears were a luxury no one could afford, man or woman. June herself had not cried when Ripley told her he was leaving. She'd said, "There's the front door. Don't let it hit you in the ass on your way out." She cried later on, but not in front of him or anyone else.

She took hold of the spade to shovel the fox into the grave. Chris grabbed the handle.

"I'll finish up," he said.

"Christy," June said, "you'd better go too."

"I'm just fishing, Mom."

"Christy . . ."

The younger girl rose without further argument, a well-mannered child compared to her half-sister, and watched her father nudge the animal into the hole and cover it. June noticed that Chris was trying to avoid its eye, still-staring through the granules of loam, its teeth bared under the lips, curled in a last snarl.

9

"Will it grow back, Daddy?" Christy asked.

"What?"

She pointed to the mound of earth her father was tamping with the flat side of the shovel.

"How could the fox grow back?"

"When Mom buried her seeds in her garden, they grew back."

"It's not the same thing, sweetheart," June said, looking at her, not yet six years old, but already long-legged, and her heart seemed to swell to three times its normal size. She picked up the little girl and held her close before setting her down again.

"It's not the same thing, but it's a beautiful thought, Christy."

"The Indians believed something like that," Chris said.

"That dead animals grow back, Daddy?"

June knew her curiosity wasn't entirely genuine; she was trying to prolong their attention to avoid returning to the house, where Lisa would be sure to take everything out on her.

"They believed that everything alive has a master up in heaven. When something dies, its spirit goes to the master, who uses it to make a new creature to take its place."

Christine, half-comprehending, stared up at him with her blue eyes wide, their most common expression; it was as if she found every moment a surprise, which, June guessed, was the way a five-year-old ought to look at life.

"I'll bet that right now the fox-master is up there making a new fox, and that it'll be born pretty soon in the woods."

June sat behind the fishing rod, her hands clasped around her knees. She heard in Chris's voice an echo of gentleness with which he'd spoken to his infant daughter, years ago, rocking her to sleep. He'd been a good father then. Where had that man gone?

"Daddy, did the Indians believe people grow back?"

"No. Human beings don't have a life-master because human beings are different from other things. The Indians believed that, too, and I don't think any of it's superstition."

"I wonder what your father would think about that."

Chris smacked the grave again, harder than necessary—a reminder that his father was not to be spoken of.

"Christy," June said, "Please do as I asked and go back to the house."

The girl said, "All right, Mom," and turned and went on up the trail.

Chris put the spade down and sat beside June, the Big Firedog in front of them, wide and smooth except for the tips of sunken branches bumping in the current. The water was almost black on the far side, where a deep channel slid past the boards of a ruined wing dam under the shade of balsam firs.

"Any luck?"

"No."

Nope, yup. Gary Cooper. June reeled up to check the hook and, noticing it had been stripped, reached into the bait can and threaded on a fresh worm, then flipped the hook back into the water, the heavy split-shot sinkers taking it down faster than the current could pull it out. When it touched bottom she closed the bail and cranked up a few inches of line before setting the rod back in the crotch of the stick.

"Maybe that'll help," she said jokingly. "Nothing like a bare hook to turn the fish off. If we catch four or five brookies, I'll bread them in cornmeal and we can have them with eggs in the morning. How's that sound?"

"Fine, Jay-Jay."

Jay-Jay. She didn't like it when he used her old high-school nickname; it made her feel childish. June Josette. Jay-Jay.

"And I think I'll do those birds for tonight. With a little wild rice and green beans, a wild game dinner cooked by your big mama!"

"Okay," he said in a voice so flat you could have rolled a marble down it.

June, unable to sustain her play-act jauntiness in the face of his indifference, snatched the rod and yanked the bait out of the water, the line ripping across the surface.

"Miss a strike?"

"No," she said, tossing the bait out again.

"You'll spook the trout, jerking the line like that."

"I was trying to spook you. Lately it seems all you have to say is 'Okay.' I swear if I told you the house burned down, the girls have run away, and your dog got hit by a car, you'd say, 'Okay.' "

"Don't joke about things like that."

"That's exactly what you'd say."

"I never was one for talking. You know that."

"I know I know that. But the past few months you've been like an old radio. I have to give you a whack just to get a sound out of you." She gestured at the small mound of freshly turned earth. "Shooting that animal bothered you, didn't it?"

"Maybe Lisa was right."

"The vet would have put it to sleep, you know that. Lisa was just being a pain. I remember that age. She irks me when she puts on that injured act."

She moved closer to him, her hips shifting in the pine needles until her thigh touched his, a contact filled with longing. They could do it now, here in the woods on this fine warm afternoon, with her bottom on the soft loam of the forest floor. The top buttons of her blouse were open, and she could tell he'd caught the scent of her breasts, a warm, moist smell stronger than the cool perfume of the pines.

To try to cheer Chris up, she told him she'd had a great day and described what had happened in court. She was a good storyteller, funny a lot of times in the way she imitated the voices and expressions of other people. She tried to make Chris laugh by mimicking the gruff Finnlander accent of the defendant when he'd called her a bitch, but making Chris laugh was even harder than making him talk—impossible in fact. She might as well try to draw a chuckle out of one of the trees. Chris just sat there, staring out at the river while she talked, not listening to a word she said, and then, in the middle of her story, he pointed out over the water. Three otters were swimming downstream, only their small flat heads visible above the surface. Then they dove, the wet fur on their arching backs sleek as skin.

"They'll be a quarter of a mile downstream before they surface again," he said. "The Indians believed they were sacred."

"Otters?" she asked, thinking: all right, let's talk about otters, anything.

"Otters were kind of go-betweens between man and God."

"You're just full of lore today. Who told you that one?"

"What makes you think anyone told me?" he said defensively, his body tightening.

"That kind of thing isn't exactly common knowledge, so I figured someone told you."

"Nobody told me. I must have picked it up somewhere."

She put her arm around his waist, rubbing his back to relax the tension in him, but her touch seemed to make him more rigid. She could sense that he wanted to pull away, and she sat back a little so her blouse would open more and he could see her breasts, hoping that would arouse him in the old way, and he would want her here on the pine needles and escape himself, even if only for a few minutes. He would be totally hers for those few minutes; she would not have to share him. But he acted as if the sight and smell of her offended him, as if her scent were corrupt and disgusting, like a swamp's.

Resting on her elbows, her ankles crossed, she noticed the roll of midriff fat squeezed by the waist of her tight jeans, a woman's belly, distended by childbirth, tracked by stretch marks. Maybe he was beginning to find her physically repulsive. She considered an indirect approach to this subject, but she had always gone at things straight on.

"Do I disgust you?"

"What are you talking about?" he asked, glancing at her blankly.

"I touch you and you seem like you want to jump out of your skin."

"Maybe you ought to start those birds."

"You want to be by yourself, right?"

"Yes."

"You're always by yourself. You work in the woods by yourself. You're next to me in bed and you're by yourself. We hardly make love anymore, and the few times we have lately, you might as well have been by yourself."

He said nothing.

"I love you, Chris. I love you very much and I'm worried about you."

"Worried about what?"

"Do you know the first thing I thought of when I heard the gunshot? That you'd killed yourself. Don't ask me where that came from, but that's what I thought."

"If that's what you thought, maybe you ought to worry about yourself, Jay-Jay."

"Maybe I should and maybe I am, but something ugly has got into you. I don't know how long it's been there . . ."

"And I don't know what you're talking about."

"A few months ago you were grinding your teeth in your sleep. It was so loud, it woke me up, for God's sake. I thought it was some kind of animal scratching at the house. And you've done that I don't know how many nights since. You grind your teeth and toss and turn in a sweat, and when I shake you to wake you up, I can't, like you're so far away in your sleep that I couldn't wake you if . . ."

She paused, seeing him stiffen, as though he'd been hit with an electric shock.

"Tell me about the dreams, Chris," she said, her voice softening.

He picked up a flat pebble and winged it out over the river. It skipped once, skittered like some kind of aquatic insect, and sank.

"What happens in the dreams? Is it the dreams, baby?"

"I don't have dreams."

"I read someplace that dreams are a way of getting rid of our devils, like an exorcism or whatever."

"Sometimes they're a way of seeing the devil."

"What do you see in the dreams? Tell me."

"No fish in this river today."

He reeled in the bait, cleaned the hook, and stuck it in the cork grip of the rod. He stood, looking very outdoorsy with the rod in his hand and the revolver on his hip, and she saw his eyes turning inward and sensed him departing again, to that secret, impenetrable place where she could not go. She wanted to do something violent and dramatic to call him back, slap him, kick him, she was so fed up with these private silences of his. She got to her feet, sneering in her hurt and anger, and asked if his nightmares were why he'd been having such a tough time getting it up, or was there some other reason? It was as low and cheap a thing as she could have said, but she was glad she'd said it. There had to be some way to get through the wall around him.

Chris paused, looking at her with an expression that made her think he was going to spit on her.

"If that's what's got you worried, Jay-Jay," he said in a voice as dead as a slab of iron, "you can always go back to spreading your legs for whatever comes along."

He turned and walked up the path. June felt as if she'd been kicked in the stomach, although she knew she'd earned it—one cheap shot deserves another. Still, she was shocked because it was the first time he'd ever expressed any jealousy or revulsion about her past.

He'd never spoken a word about it, and his mentioning it now made her feel diminished, like a small-town slut, tawdry and stupid.

More stupid than tawdry. What was wrong with her as a woman that the only place she had ever been able to reach this man, the only place she had ever been able to make him hers completely, had been in the bedroom? She imagined that another sort of woman, one with greater mental and spiritual resources, would have found some other, better way. Another sort of woman would have been able to heal Chris's invisible wound, whereas she, June, had only been able to soothe it for five or ten minutes in bed, and now she couldn't even do that. She knew the signs of a deteriorating marriage—God, how she knew them—and she would have to be a fool not to see that hers and Chris's was in the first stage of decay at least. She wanted to fight to save it—she couldn't bear another divorce—but she didn't know what she was fighting against. Her adversary seemed, as she stood in the dimness of the pines, a menace without face, form, or name, as insubstantial as the shadows cast by the trees.

10

June did not grill the grouse for supper, because, Starkmann supposed, she was too upset to do anything complicated in the kitchen. Everyone ate her warmed-over macaroni and cheese in strained silence. Lisa was still sulking over his killing of the fox, and June over the remark he had made to her. Or maybe she was upset with herself for saying what she had to him. He couldn't tell. He didn't blame her for saying it or for feeling the way she did. He would have explained why he had become distant toward her if he could have explained it to himself.

After dinner he lay down on the couch in the living room while June and the girls cleaned up the kitchen. It was a warm night; there was no need to light the fireplace or the big oil heater that stood like some kind of metal altar in the middle of the living room. Starkmann picked up the *Detroit Free Press* and opened it across his chest to the sports page, but he could not keep his mind on the paper. The noise of the clinking glasses and clattering plates got on his nerves. Then, a restlessness overcoming him, he got up and went to the front door.

June asked where he was going.

"For a walk," he said.

She slapped a dish towel on the counter.

"Too many people here, I guess."

He said nothing and went outside. The night was clear and still; a tension in the air warned him that an autumn gale, the first of the season, was gathering up in Canada for its rush across Superior. The wind would be out of the north by tomorrow. The temperature would fall, and the firs that now stood motionless would be bending and quaking, the wind roaring like an avalanche through the pines. Starkmann walked down the gravel road, its khaki color darkened to pink by the light of a hunter's moon, a round red wound over the ridge bordering the Indian reservation. Butternut came panting up the road behind him. She needed the exercise and the company. He hadn't hunted her enough this season. Maybe she had hopes of scaring up a rabbit. She was pretty good at hunting rabbits, running them in circles, then cutting across their path to ambush them from the flank.

He stopped at the bridge over the Firedog and, leaning over the log railing, looked down into the water. Its riffles were a phosphorescent white in its blackness. He felt the old sadness of the sound of moving water, and continued on, trying to walk off his restlessness and sort out his thoughts. He regretted what was happening between him and June but could not think of any way to stop it. In the war, he remembered, you eventually learned to tell which men were most likely to die and which were not; it was as obvious as the dusty crosses Catholics wore on their foreheads on Ash Wednesday. He'd begun to worry that his marriage had been so marked, a possibility that terrified him, for the loss of June was the one loss he could not endure, if it struck him unprepared. Was it to steel himself against such a possibility that he had begun to distance himself from her? He did not want to be caught unaware. *Alert, alive.* Over there, you became most vulnerable when you felt most safe. That's when the earth usually blew up under your feet.

June complained that he didn't speak to her anymore. He didn't because he was listening to her and the way she said things, his ears tuned for those subtle changes in tone that signaled a change of feelings. So far, he had not heard or sensed anything that could be interpreted as a warning, although the way she spoke about Ripley sometimes made him nervous. She'd mentioned him the other day, something about how she helped other women get child support from wandering ex-husbands but had never been able to do the same for herself. She had sounded a little too bitter, as if she were trying to convince herself as well as him that she had lost all attachment to Ripley.

He felt she had, but would remain on his guard.

We do not need Christ to punish us for the pleasures we take in the things of this world. His father's words, hurled from the pulpit on a Sunday long ago, echoed in his memory. *We need Christ as our savior and guide, but the pleasures of this world, whether of the mind or body, charge their own price and inflict their own punishment.* If he never took anything for granted and never allowed himself to become too happy, perhaps he could hold on to her and all he had. He would keep his eyes on his flanks and glance over his shoulder to see what might be coming up from behind. Maybe that was to be the price and punishment of possession: constant vigilance.

Starkmann came to the blacktop. The moon had risen, its red fading toward white, and yet how dark the road was, how dark the woods, and comforting in their tranquil blackness. He'd intended to stop at this point and return to the house, but was drawn to hike up the highway toward the reservation. The stones on the shoulder of the road shone like precious minerals in the moonlight and crunched loudly under the tread of his boots. With Butternut tagging along, he walked as far as the road sign that read ENTERING VIEUX DESERT INDIAN RESERVATION, then paused, restraining an inexplicable impulse to go farther. Why on earth did he feel an urge to enter the reservation at this hour? He turned around and started back. The reservation was another country, and he did not belong in it any more than he belonged in town. He belonged right where he was: between the two.

He headed toward the house. The moon was so brilliant that the night was like twilight, and his and Butternut's tracks were clearly visible in the soft gravel. Now and then he looked down to check for strange footprints, just in case someone had tried to sneak up on the house while he'd been gone. There were none, and Butternut, sniffing the air, gave no signs of alarm. Then he was out of the forest and in the clearing where his house stood on a low rise, the lights burning brightly upstairs. He thought they looked very brave and cheerful, casting their glow into the surrounding darkness, and his spirits rose for a few moments. His house, his land, his perimeter of safety and solitude. As he walked up the path to the door, smelling the scent of wet grass, the lyrics to a Bruce Springsteen song lilted through his mind:

> My father's house shines hard and bright,
> It stands like a beacon calling me in the night.
> Calling and calling so cold and alone
> Shining 'cross this dark highway where our sins lie unatoned.

He opened the door and June called from upstairs, asking if it was he. He answered her, then went into the kitchen, took a bottle of Early Times from the cupboard, and poured a double shot. Though he had cruised five hundred acres of wild timber today and had just finished walking two and a half miles, he did not feel tired enough to sleep. He was afraid to sleep, afraid that the dream, after leaving him alone since its last call nearly two weeks ago, would visit him tonight.

The dream. Goddammit, why had she brought that up? The dream, the intruder he could not keep out. He wondered for a moment if it was his punishment, a scourging inflicted as payment for his acquisitions. Or was it a warning that he would lose all he had if he did not surrender a part of it, make a kind of offering. But offer what, and to whom? To clear his mind of these muddled thoughts, he stretched out on the couch with the whiskey and the sports page of the *Free Press*, and began reading a preview of the Lions' up-coming game with the Chicago Bears. He had begun to pay much closer attention to football since he'd discovered that King was trying to get him fired. He hoped King would think better of him and, perhaps, have second thoughts about canning him if he proved himself an avid football fan and joined in the almost daily office debates about teams and players. He would seem a regular fellow, just another one of the boys.

He took a sip of the whiskey and tried reading the story. It was some sort of analysis comparing the Lions' quarterback with the Bears'. It seemed like a pretty good story—he could use it tomorrow as a conversation starter. The trouble was, it did not hold his interest. He read and reread the first two paragraphs but could not get beyond them. He folded the paper on the coffee table and went into the kitchen to top off his drink. He took a healthy belt, then topped the glass again, and was going to give the article another try when he was seized by a recognition of how stupid this all was. It was stupid to feign an interest in a sport merely to please a boss, because, if losing his job was in the cards, then he would lose it. Just as he would lose June if that was in the cards. Nothing he did could make any difference. This waiting for something terrible to happen was driving him crazy. Each day that it failed to happen was making him more anxious rather than less. He was like a soldier, poised to go into an attack that is continually postponed, his nervousness heightening with each delay until the waiting becomes more awful than any attack could ever be, and he begins to wish for the event he once dreaded. And, as he stood in his kitchen, the whiskey scalding his throat as it clouded his brain, Starkmann wished that whatever was supposed to happen would happen, now. Let the axe fall. *Axe-time, sword-time.* Axe-time, sword-time? What the hell did that mean? Where had those words come from? He couldn't recall and could not have cared less where or when he'd heard them. Let the axe fall. Let June come down the stairs with the girls and her bags packed and announce she was leaving him. Let Harding telephone and tell him he'd been fired, and then let a bank manager send him a foreclosure notice. Let it all be lost! The nightmare had not troubled him in the days when he had nothing. Perhaps, if he returned to that purer way of life, it would cease to wrack his nights, and he would know a measure of peace.

Jesus Christ! He set his whiskey on the counter. He was thinking like a lunatic. He ought to avoid drinking straight alcohol like this. He emptied his glass into the sink, then climbed the stairs to bed.

The light was off but June was still awake, lying on her side, facing the door. He took off his clothes, put on his army boxer shorts, and slumped into bed beside her, expecting her to nag him when she smelled the liquor on his breath. Instead, she gently stroked his damp forehead, her hand cool, and asked him: "What's the matter, baby?"

"Nothing. Just needed a couple of belts to get to sleep."

"You feel like you've got a fever."

"I'm okay. I'd like to read for a little while."

She nodded.

Starkmann switched on the bedside lamp and removed his Bible from the drawer. He had long since lost all faith in organized religion, but out of habit continued to read Scripture now and then. He'd read it overseas. It had comforted him then, and comfort was what he sought now as he leafed through the Psalms, searching for a passage that might speak to him. He could not find anything appropriate and, his eyes whiskey-blurred, had trouble focusing on the small print. He turned to the book of Isaiah, half-remembering a message it had for him. He found it, chapter nine. *For wickedness burneth as the fire: it shall devour the briers and thorns, and shall kindle in the thickets of the forest, and they shall mount up like the lifting up of smoke.* He began the next verse but, unable to go on, slammed the Bible shut and turned off the light.

"Honey?" June asked in the darkness.

He stared at the ceiling in silence.

"Honey, I can help. I know I can."

"No, you can't."

He heard her expel a breath in exasperation, and turned his back to her. He kept his eyes open, fighting sleep. The room began to spin. He stared into the darkness for a long time, until the spinning stopped. When, against his will, his eyes closed, the bed lurched sharply to one side, like a boat broaching to, and the floor gave way beneath him and he felt himself falling, faster and faster into a blackness without end, nothing to grasp to stop his plunge. . . .

Starkmann's conscious mind had fallen asleep; his body was at rest, but some part of him, soul or subconscious, was traveling backward in time. It was the same journey it had made on many nights before, ending at the same date and place, as if it had been condemned to ride a train with only one destination: a dusty red hill near the Cambodian border on September 21, 1969.

The past becomes the present; then is now.

Starkmann is crouched in the foxhole with Captain Hartwell and Specialist Fourth-Class half-Pryce. It is light now, three hours after the attack began. The sun, to the backs of Starkmann's company, is splattering its blood into the sky. To the west, in front of them, a pale moon is still visible. The woods are brightening and the rusty strands of perimeter wire, severed in places, take on the color of the sun. Everyone in the company is unnerved by the organlike bellowing of the rockets, the bump and crash of the mortars the bushpeople are firing to keep the company pinned down and cover their retreat back into the jungle.

In the foxhole, Starkmann cannot move, paralyzed by the explosions and the sounds the shrapnel makes overhead, hissings and pluckings and crackings.

Once, as the shelling abates, he gets up the courage to lift his head and peek over the rim of sandbags. He sees the wire, and the red strip of no man's land between it and the woods, and the bodies of the bushpeople lying in the dirt or hanging from the wire. He remembers shooting at them, less than an hour ago, at first light, and the way they looked as they attacked through the woods, darting, dodging and ducking behind the trees, appearing and disappearing. Often it was difficult to tell which were real bushes and which camouflaged North Vietnamese, and so he fired his rifle at both. The woods became an evil thing, with the power of conscious deadly intent and he didn't care if his bullets were hitting vegetation or people—he wanted it all destroyed, leveled, flattened, blown to bits, the bits to dust, the dust to vapor. Some of the bushpeople made it out of the woods, and some died in the no man's land, and some right up against the wire, where, now, they resemble clumps of seaweed left by a receding tide.

The shelling intensifies again, and Captain Hartwell is trying to say something to Starkmann, but it is difficult to understand him because of the noise and because the captain's throat has been pierced by shrapnel. The shrapnel came from the same shell that killed Specialist Fourth-Class half-Pryce. Spec. 4 half-Pryce is the torso of Hartwell's radio operator. Not ten minutes ago, when the shells began to fall, he had been full-Pryce, and had been running with Starkmann and the captain toward the foxhole. They all three dived in, almost at the same time, full-Pryce a split-second behind, which was long enough. A mortar shell burst only a few feet away. As a result, only half of Pryce made it into the foxhole and a sliver of metal punctured the captain's throat. As he tries to speak to Starkmann, he rasps like a man with an artificial larynx.

By listening very hard, Starkmann is finally able to understand him: An air strike has to be called in on the rocket and mortar position. The captain points to a spot on his map, folded in a plastic case. That spot is the target. Hartwell then writes down the map coordinates in his notebook, which he hands to Starkmann, telling him that he will have to radio for the air strike. The captain almost passes out from the effort of giving these orders. A pink froth is popping from between his lips in a way that reminds Starkmann of a kid blowing bubble gum.

Holding the notebook in one hand, Starkmann reaches with the other over half-Pryce's shoulder and grabs the handset of the radio. The radio is still strapped to half-Pryce's back and, like his torso, has escaped serious damage. Half-Pryce looks just fine from the waist up, except for his set, staring eyes and the trickles of blood leaking from his nostrils.

Starkmann calls for the planes on the radio. He is nervous and unsure of himself because he is only a rifleman who has never before directed an air strike, and he is of course quite scared, lying in a foxhole under rocket and mortar fire with a wounded officer and the torso of a corpse. But he knows he must do this. He has to come through in this crisis, rise above himself and his fears. Once the mortar and rocket positions have been bombed, the company will be safe.

In a few minutes, a pilot's voice crackles over the radio: "Ironhorse Bravo Six, this is William Tell One, over."

The pilot sounds crisp, laconic, and competent.

"William Tell One, this is Ironhorse Bravo Six," Starkmann answers, hearing the suppressed panic in his voice. He does not sound competent; he sounds like a terrified nineteen-year-old boy.

The pilot asks for the location of the target. Starkmann glances at the notebook. The numbers aren't that easy to read; they're smudged with dirt and blurred by the tiny drops of blood that dripped from the captain's mouth onto the paper. He tries to check them against the map, but he's not an experienced map reader, and so squints at the numbers on the note paper and reads them off to the pilot.

Suddenly, from behind him, Hartwell reaches up and clutches at his arm. He is trying to shout something. A bubble of blood balloons in the captain's mouth. His words become a gurgling and gasping,

and Starkmann guesses he is pleading for a medic because he is
beginning to strangle in his own blood. At the same time, the pilot is
repeating the map coordinates, asking Starkmann if he has heard
them correctly.

"Roger, roger, roger," Starkmann replies, his panic almost out of
control now because of Hartwell's gagging and choking. He shouts for
a medic.

Then he hears the planes and, in a couple of seconds, sees them,
four of them, streaking in low over the jungle, lower and closer than
they should be. The target is a thousand yards away, but the planes
are coming in just in front of the perimeter, and in that instant,
Starkmann realizes what Hartwell was trying to shout to him. In his
dazed condition the captain had written down the wrong map coordinates. The howling drowns out the bursts of the shells. It deafens
Starkmann to the sound of his own voice, shouting into the radio,
"Pull up! Pull up!" That is all he can think to say. *Pull up, pull up!*
The planes screech over the woods, and the first two release their
bombs. Starkmann sees the bombs dropping, as if in slow motion,
from the racks beneath the camouflage wings, dropping and tumbling
like squat acrobats through the net of branches and leaves. He is so
hypnotized by this sight that he forgets to duck. Maybe he doesn't
want to duck. But he does remember to cover his ears. High explosive. A wall of smoke erupts; it's as if the earth itself is erupting, the
earth is heaving and quaking beneath him, trees crash as if felled by
the swipes of gigantic axes, and the shock wave, like a blast of wind,
plasters his shirt to his body, even pulls his skin taut around his
bones. Branches toss in the air, riding the crests of the explosions,
and invisible bits of steel keen through the air. Shrapnel sprays
across the perimeter like a sudden squall across a lake. Somehow,
Starkmann is not hit. Now there are screams in the woods, screams of
wounded North Vietnamese. As the first two planes climb and streak
away, the last two dart through the rising clouds of smoke, smoke that
has blackened the sky and engulfed the moon hanging low on the
horizon. The planes drop napalm. It bursts in oily red geysers, spreads
like a river of fire through the woods, its tributaries rushing across the
no man's land toward the wire. Starkmann watches it, mesmerized by
its eerie loveliness, gobs of flame arcing through the sky like comets,
watches the bodies of the bushpeople in front of the wood line
catching fire. He hears the screams, more terrible in their way than
the blasts of the bombs. Apparently not all of the North Vietnamese
had been dead. Now they are being burned alive. But other men, the
soldiers on a forward outpost, soldiers from Starkmann's company, are
also screaming: "God, help us. Stop it! Help us! Oh, Jesus God."

More napalm falls, and the cries stop. Starkmann feels the heat, so intense that, for an instant, he thinks he has caught fire. No, he has not. He is smothering, ravenous for air. The napalm is sucking the breath from his lungs. Only then does he duck, falling to the bottom of the foxhole and curling up like a fetus, trying to breathe through his seared nostrils.

BAWAJIGAYWIN

When the sun reached the middle of the sky, Wawiekumig would begin sweat-bath. Until then, he would read the story of the bear's breakthroughs, the beginning of the Midewewin, the Grand Medicine Society. Think about the beginning, he told himself, the Midewewin brought to the Anishinabe to give them a way to worship Kitchi-Manito, to show them how to cure diseases by balancing body, mind, and spirit, for all things are connected. If the mind is sick, body and soul suffer also; if the soul is out of harmony, body and mind will be as well. Ninoododadiwin, harmony. The Midewewin had been founded to show the people how to live in harmony with creation.

He held the scroll in his lap, rolled ends in his hands. The birchbark was dried, stiff. It was a copy he had made long ago from one of Red Sky's, pictures, not words, telling the bear's story, pictures etched into the bark with a bone stylus, the markings dyed in vermilion, the panels of each episode stitched together with basswood twine. As he read, Wawiekumig recalled the days of his early instruction in Red Sky's cabin, sitting on the cold dirt floor in the month called January in English, the big-manito month, the best time for teaching.

Red Sky, older then than Wawiekumig was now, a warrior before he'd become a holy man, one who had fought the Sioux in Minnesota. Red Sky—if ever there was a Man-Who-Knows-Everything, then it had been he, soft of voice and reserved of manner, but an exacting instructor, alert for the slightest mistake.

Wawiekumig remembered, his memories a meditation.

He remembered Red Sky pointing at five figures surrounding a circle in the first panel of the scroll and asking, "What's this?"

"The manito council," Wawiekumig answered. "They are meeting to figure out who is to take the Pack of Life across the sea to the people. They give it to the bear."

"Why?"

"The bear is strong. He can carry the Pack of Life."

"That's right. The bear can do anything, which is why he represents God. So the council gave it to him. Now you take the story from there."

Shivering in the drafts blowing through the chinked walls, bent like a hook over the scroll, Wawiekumig told of how the bear's fore and hind legs sunk deep into the earth. He could hardly walk, the Pack of Life was so heavy on his back. He carried it nevertheless, then came to a barrier, some kind of wall, and smashed through it with his paw—

"Wait," Red Sky interrupted. "You've made a mistake. Take another look."

Wawiekumig studied the picture more carefully. It showed a triangle piercing a line, symbolizing the bear's breakthrough. In a moment he saw the meaning.

"His head. He broke through with his head."

"Good. That's right. Keep going."

Wawiekumig continued the tale, describing how the bear, after overcoming the last obstacle, entered a lodge on the shore of the sea and planted a tree in its middle. An eagle landed in the top of the tree; then the Creator sent down a perfectly round rock and placed it at the foot of the tree and told the bear:

"This is the foundation of the Midewewin, the first Midewegun, the Sacred Lodge. This is where I will listen to the Anishinabe whenever they call upon me. This is where they will come to heal sickness or get rid of bad luck. This is where they will come to learn the secrets of how to live, and of those secrets, the bear will be guardian."

"No mistakes," Red Sky said with a smile of congratulation. "The next scroll tells about the white shell, the megis shell, which carried the secrets across the sea and brought them to the people, so the people would know what to do in the Midewegun. But we'll study that one tomorrow. You must be tired now."

Indeed Wawiekumig was. It had taken many hours to memorize just the one scroll, and he would have to memorize several more before he would be ready for initiation, at which he would be examined by a Grand Mide.

Red Sky, braids hanging like silver ropes from his head, took the end pieces of the birchbark and rolled it up, his deep-set eyes never leaving Wawiekumig's face.

"Understand the significance of the story you just told me," he said, his voice still gentle but full of import. "As there is night and day, winter and spring, so are there two sides to creation, the visible and the invisible, each as real as the other. As there can be no night without day, nor spring without winter, so can there be no visible world without its invisible opposite. Everything has its opposite twin. You have eyes in your head, but your spirit has eyes also, and it is with those a man can see into the invisible world. He can know things his reason and senses cannot tell him. Listen, now. The barriers the bear broke through were those between him and the world God created. The same obstacles exist within us, blinding us to insight. We are training your spirit eyes to be strong, so that, with each breakthrough, you will come closer to truth. Understand that this is the significance of the story of the bear's passage. Without the significance, it is just a fable, something we would tell children to amuse them."

The sun approached the sky's center. Wawiekumig, done with his meditations, furled the scroll and carried it into his wigwam, then walked down to the lake shore for a drink. The water was warm from the summerlike weather. The previous autumn had been a cold one; this autumn, hot. Everything changes; everything stays the same. Always there is autumn, part of the endless cycle, he thought as he gathered deadwood, as much as he could find. With an armload he returned to his camp and built up the fire in which he would heat the stones for sweat-bath. The flames growing, he followed a track a short distance into a swamp, where he stripped off several lengths of bark from a cedar tree, then walked back and sprinkled small amounts of it into the fire. Smell it, he said to himself, breathing in the sweet, purifying scent: geezheekindug, cedar, the healer.

The sun was now burning in the heart of the heavens. He would begin. His sweat lodge was shaped like a turtle shell, tarps and blankets drawn tautly over the bent-wood frame, only enough room in it for two—three men at most—sitting shoulder to shoulder.

Wawiekumig sat alone, naked in the steaming darkness. In former times his Mide brothers would have been with him to act as helpers, but they were dead now. He'd had to make all the preparations by himself: put down tobacco as an offering, lay cedar bark on the path from the fire to the lodge, carry the hot rocks inside and place them in the proper manner in the shallow pit that represented the womb of the earth, the three minor rocks on the bottom, the

Messenger on top. He'd had to do all these things by himself, as, now, he had to be all things: doorkeeper, man-who-leads, and firekeeper—duties that would have been assumed by his brethren had they been alive.

He smoked pipe for a while, reflecting on his purposes once again. To see into the future, to examine his past, and to end his grief—that above all. *It is this undying sorrow that puts you out of harmony, Wawiekumig.* He listened to his inner voice, the voice of ahmunisoowin. *It is unnatural to mourn for so long.* Holding this thought, he sprinkled water onto the Messenger stone and sang:

"Wee-wee-wee-way-way-yo-yo-yo."

Three times more he sprinkled water and sang, drumming the bottom stones with a stick in rhythm to his heartbeat. The fourth time, ascending steam filled the cramped space. He whispered:

"Now the Messenger is delivering my request to the Mide manitos, my prayer for aid in this undertaking."

He smoked pipe again, sweat erupting from every pore, fold, and crevasse in his decaying body, his memories carrying back to the sweat-lodge ceremonies that had preceded each of his four initiations, these recollections a form of reprofessing his beliefs, a going back to origins that would strengthen his faith.

Steam rising.

Understand the significance of this smoke that goes up from the heated rock, Red Sky had taught him. It represents passage from invisibility to visibility back to invisibility. The smoke is the outward form of our prayers; then it rises and vanishes into the spirit world. Understand the significance of the Madodigan, a place to purify body and spirit, making the soul more receptive to messages. The sweat-lodge is warm, moist, and dark, like a woman's womb. When you come out of it, it is like being born anew.

But Wawiekumig had felt anything but born anew when he'd emerged from his first initiation, weak from four days of fasting, almost suffocated from the heat, so dizzy as he walked the long path from the sweat-lodge to the Midewegun that he thought he would faint.

That had been at the big reservation in Wisconsin, Lac Court Oreilles; he and Red Sky had ridden there from Michigan on a train.

Wawiekumig, fifteen years old, walked the path with several other candidates, they and their families gathered for the fall Midewewin ceremonies.

Holy men, painted and feathered to represent serpents and other beasts, lunged from the woods howling and hissing to frighten the candidates. One man, cloaked in a lion's skin to symbolize Misshipeshu, the Great Puma, most evil of evil spirits, leaped from behind a tree, swiping at Wawiekumig's face with the claws strapped to his hands, a roar in his throat. Though he knew it was only a man, Wawiekumig almost jumped from the path in fear and fled into the woods. But he heard snatches of Red Sky's voice, singing from inside the Midewegun just ahead. All the initiates' mentors were in there, singing to the manitos to aid their pupils in traversing the path, to help them avoid being distracted or frightened by the holy men who stood in the place of the various evils that tempt a man to stray when he walks the path from youth to old age.

Other holy men stood by the eastern door to the Midewegun, near the pile of dogs sacrificed by the candidates. Wawiekumig could smell the dogs' blood, a salty, sickening odor, and hear the flies buzzing about the corpses.

The Midewegun was like a long tunnel but without a roof, its frame of hooped saplings open to the sky. At the bottom, a matwork of reeds and pine boughs reached up the walls to about half the height of a man. This matting served to hide from the crowd of onlookers the secret dance patterns of the holy men inside. Wawiekumig dared a quick glance at the audience, looking for Tcianung. He saw women in long dresses, men in dungarees and suits, as well as a few in traditional clothes. Buggies and wagons were drawn up at the edges of the gathering; wealthier families had come in automobiles, black Fords parked beside the wagons and buggies. Tcianung's face was not visible, but his son sensed his pride on this day, and allowed himself a smile.

"Hey, you, boy, what are you smiling about? Are you smiling at some girl? Is that who you've been looking for, a girl?"

The jeer came from one of the men grouped at the eastern door. He wore on his dancing bags the beadwork insignia of a second-degree Mide, and made an obscene gesture that drew laughter from the other men.

"Come on. Tell me. Can't you speak? Are you so full of lust for this girl that you can't speak?"

Again a peal of laughter. Wawiekumig, embarrassed that he'd been caught in a distraction, held his tongue and kept his eyes to the front. He was about to step over the pile of dead dogs into the Mide lodge when the man jumped in front of him, barring his way.

"Where do you think you're going? You can't go in there. The Midewegun is for men, not children. Do you think you can become a Mide brother at your age?" The mocker turned to his companions. "He is a child who knows nothing and seeks to know everything."

Another burst of laughter followed this taunt. Soon, the men were casting insults at all the initiates, who were expected to remain firm and quiet. The jeering went on for a long time, longer than Wawiekumig had expected, and the insults of these men were more serious than the play-act attacks of those who had imitated animal spirits; these men were trying very hard to provoke the candidates. Any show of anger or frustration would be proof of unworthiness.

At last the doorkeeper of the eastern door emerged and told the mocking men to leave. Only then, having shown their ability to resist both human and animal spirits, were the initiates allowed entrance.

Inside, Mide priests sat in their assigned places along the reed-and-bough sides of the lodge, their faces painted according to their degrees, wingbone necklaces around their necks, dancing bags slung over their shoulders, their pindgigossans—medicine-bundles made of otter and weasel skins, hides of beaver, muskrat, and bear—in their laps. The sacred pole occupied the center of the Midewegun, the center of all things, a smooth rock at its base. The Grand Mide, a man as large as the white lumberjacks for whom Wawiekumig had worked as cook's boy, stood before the pole, arms folded over his broad chest, a rattle in each powerful hand, a bearskin pindgigossan hanging from his belt, his face painted in the colors of the four quarters of the universe: north, white; south, blue; east, green; west, red. The fourth-degree cross-pole was sewn on the front of his deer-skin shirt. The Grand Mide was powerful of body and spirit, his face so strong in expression he looked as though he could shatter a mirror with one glance. Even his name was formidable; Manito-bijiki, Buffalo Spirit.

All was silent except for the hum of flies feeding on the dogs, the murmurs of conversation from onlookers outside. Wawiekumig, awestruck, was glad for Red Sky's presence in this place, in which all the mystery of the creation seemed gathered into a single force. Red Sky, hands on his pupil's shoulders, whispered instructions on how to behave in the sacred enclosure: He was not to smile, not to take his eyes from the pole, not to speak until asked for answers by the Grand Mide.

Someone blew a wingbone whistle. Its sharp cry silenced the crowd outside. The waterdrum sounded four times. The waterdrum—the voice of the Sacred Circle in which all nature moved, voice of the four-winds manitos. The priests rose and began to dance to the drumbeat, their feet tracing patterns meant to ward off and confuse any evil that attempted to enter the Midewegun. They danced and sang songs they had heard in dreams, each singing his own song, an interweaving of different voices, yet not unmelodious. Necklaces clattered as the holy ones danced around and around the lodge, rattles hissing and whistles shrilling. These sounds, the chants, the throb of the drum, the tread of feet, the movements of the dancers at the edges of Wawiekumig's vision had a strange effect. A looseness came to his knees, a lightness to his head. The strain of standing with eyes fixed on the pole, of resisting the impulse to look at the holy men, some of whom were breaking off and rushing at the initiates, pelting them with white shells from the pindgigossans, made Wawiekumig dizzy. The peculiar spinning in his head was like a childhood dream of tumbling from a high place.

Red Sky had warned him of this sensation, sign that he was approaching the edge between the spiritual and physical, between life and death itself. He was to retain balance between the two, and not to fall until struck by the megis shell shot from Manito-bijiki. Then he could fall. Then he *would* fall, dead.

"Understand," Red Sky had told him when they'd come down on the train, "your body will not die. Your heart will beat, your blood flow, but who you once were—that will die. And when you are struck a second time your new self will be born. Understand the significance behind this fall."

Four blasts from the bone whistle brought the drumming, singing, and dancing to a sudden halt. The Grand Mide swept his arm in a call for total silence. He approached one of the initiates and, pointing his rattle, asked a question. The young man answered satisfactorily. Manito-bijiki moved on to the next, his eyes stern. Wawiekumig, heart pounding, head swimming, belly crying out in hunger, was so nervous he was certain he could not give his own name if asked. Then the rattle was pointing at him. He had not heard the question, yet heard his voice giving the answer:

"The megis shell brought the secrets of the Midewewin to the people. It followed the bottom of the sea, and when it came to the other side, it climbed a hill and came to a little tent where a small boy lived with his mother and father. This boy's name was Minabozho." Wawiekumig stopped for a breath, his memory flashing pictures of Red Sky's scroll, his mind translating the pictures into words. "The megis-manito took Minabozho back across the sea, where he taught him everything about how to worship God and how to live through the Midewewin. It taught him until he reached manhood. Then he went back across the sea, to his home, and spent a long time searching for his father, who was very sad that he had lost his son. When they found each other, they were very happy. The father of Minabozho led him to the village, where the people were living in misery and sickness. Minabozho taught them everything he had learned from the megis-manito on the far side of the sea, and from then on the people enjoyed health and long life."

"Good," whispered Red Sky, standing behind him, hands on his shoulders. "Not a mistake."

Wawiekumig was amazed. How could he have answered a question he had not heard? Possibly he had heard, but with another sense. Anything seemed possible in the Sacred Lodge.

The whistle's piping brought him out of his self-absorption. The waterdrum throbbed again, and all the holy ones held out their arms to the east, the direction in which the salt-sea lay, and chanted prayers invoking the power of the megis-manito while the Grand Mide danced alone.

Bear, I am calling you.

The Grand Mide sang, shaking his rawhide rattles.

Bear, I am calling you
A song comes from my medicine-bag.

The mysterious song and Manito-bijiki's dancing entranced Wawiekumig. He felt as insubstantial as a leaf floating in a breeze. Only Red Sky, grip firm on his shoulders, prevented him from collapsing.

Here it is, the bearskin, intoned the Grand Mide, pulling his pindgigossan from his belt.

Through it I shoot the white shell
It never fails.
The shell strikes them
And they fall, and they fall.

Wawiekumig, as through a rain-misted window, saw the Grand Mide raise his pindgigossan, arm cocked like a man about to throw a stone.

It never fails
The shell strikes them
And they fall, and they fall.

Red Sky let go of his shoulders as the cowrie shell, flung from the medicine-bag, pelted him in the center of his chest. Wawiekumig went down into the dust as if clubbed, his eyes closed. Yet he remained conscious. He could hear Manito-bijiki singing *and they fall, and they fall* as each candidate was shot and killed. Lying flat, Wawiekumig thought: I could stand up now if I wished to. *Then go ahead*, an inner voice urged. *Stand up and prove there is no power in the shell. Prove this is all a magician's deception.* He closed his ears to the voice, recognizing it as a trickster spirit's; he shut his ears, knowing what the penalty would be if he gave in to its temptation: a short and miserable life. Then—for how long he didn't know—he did not hear anything. Fingers in his mouth stirred him from the sleep-like state. The fingers of the Grand Mide, plucking from under Wawiekumig's lips a small shell, singing as he did this:

> My Mide brother is searched,
> In his heart is found
> That which I seek,
> The white shell.

The shell, plucked from his lips. Wawiekumig was astonished. How did it get there? A magician's trick or a mystery?

> Here it is, the bearskin.

The Grand Mide, standing over him, singing again.

> Through it I shoot the white shell.
> It never fails
> The shell strikes them
> And they rise, and they rise.

There was a sharp blow to his temple. Without help, Wawiekumig leaped to his feet and knew the finding of the shell in his mouth had not been the work of some juggler, but a true mystery. His dizziness was gone; his blurred vision, gone; the weakness in his knees, gone. A new strength surged through him, like the energy that had flowed into him on Vision Quest, only more potent, a strength rising in him like water from a deep well, rising from his feet and through his legs to his chest, spreading from there into all parts of him. Spiritual vitality, power, the life-force of the Mide-manito.

Manito, spirit. Manito, body. Manito, all that is known and all that is unknown. Manito, all that is seen and unseen.

Manito, God.

All the spirits are one, and the one is Manito, he thought, watching the miraculous resurrection of his brother initiates, each standing in his turn when struck by the Grand Mide's shells. A thick dust yellowed the air in the Midewegun. Dust sparkled in the sunlight that fell through the wide spaces between the arched saplings. Wawiekumig smelled dog's blood, human sweat, and the fragrance of burning cedar from the sweat-lodge fires, the aromas intoxicating.

Manito-bijiki handed him the pindgigossan, inviting him to shoot to test his new powers. He took hold of the bearskin bag and flung a shell into the Grand Mide's chest. The huge man went down as if hit by a rifle bullet. He lay without moving. Wawiekumig struck him with a second shell, and when the Grand Mide jumped up, Wawiekumig felt his own soul jump out of his body. It sprang into the air above the hoops of the Midewegun and looked down. Through the hoops and the cloud of yellow dust, he could see himself from above. He could see everyone from above.

The power to take life and restore it had been given him, the power to heal: Mide power, to be applied with the strictest care, for good only, never to be abused.

I am Wawiekumig, he said silently, his soul slipping back into his physical self, but I am now one of the Mide brethren.

I am not as I was before.

I am still called Wawiekumig, but I am not *who* I was before.

Now, almost seventy years later, he meditated upon his first initiation and the three that had followed, each more difficult, each conferring new powers. With the second degree, power to see and hear great distances; third degree, power of prophecy; fourth degree, power to guide souls to the Ghost Lodge and to heal diseases of the mind and spirit. He acquired scrolls of his own, the migration scrolls that told the history of the Anishinabe, song scrolls that recorded the healing songs he'd heard in visions, medicine scrolls that gave the formulas for herbal cures—aster and calamus, dogwood powder, wild pea, seneca-snakeroot, root of dogbane.

He reviewed, in the sweat-lodge, all his learning, and this retrospection invigorated his faith.

Slowly at first, then more rapidly, the dizziness he'd felt in his first sweat-lodge ceremony came over him. He was once more balanced on the dangerous edge between the conscious and unconscious, between two states of existence. When he sensed himself about to lose equilibrium, he sprinkled more water on the sacred stones and spoke his requests to the ascending steam.

"I desire to look into the future and know if the world's end is near. I desire to look into my own past and know if I offended the Mide-manitos that all my family have died in terrible ways. I desire to restore harmony to myself by healing my sorrow. I desire to speak to my kinsman. It is I, Wawiekumig, who asks this, asks this."

His prayers sent, he opened the flap and crawled out. The autumn sunlight was dazzling after the darkness of the sweat-lodge. He put down a tobacco offering and rubbed his legs in powdered dogbane to keep them strong, tied on a leather groin-cloth, and began to dance. Today he would dance in honor of the north wind manitos, for north was the direction of wisdom. Tomorrow his dance would be to the spirits of the south, direction of trust; then to the east, direction of enlightenment; then to the west, gateway to the future and the Afterworld. After each day's dance, he would lie down beneath the branchless pine and fast, starvation of the body nourishing the spirit. By the end of the fourth day, he hoped, his spiritual senses would be heightened as never before, and he would be able to speak with his kinsman at the Ghost Supper.

Facing north, he danced, toe-to-heel, his feet moving to the rhythm of drumbeats summoned from memories of ceremonies long ago. He danced singing a hymn to Wayndanimuk-nodinjoon, the Four Sacred Directions, the circle in which all things moved. Four directions, four seasons to the year, four seasons to a man's life. South summer childhood, Wawiekumig sang. West autumn maturity. North winter old age and death. East spring rebirth.

His voice falling silent, his feet growing still, he paused to gaze at the top of the pine, then lay beneath the tree to begin his fast. For the next four days he would drink only a little maple water. He would eat nothing. He dreaded the ordeal even as he looked forward to the insights it would bring. And so he lay still, an old man, loose-skinned, bones age-stiffened, an old man, Wawiekumig, follower of an archaic creed, fasting alone and naked in the forest.

THREE

GIWAYDINNOONG

(NORTH)

11

June's spirits sank with the mercury. The temperature had dropped thirty degrees overnight, the cold riding a norther down from the Canadian tundras. Thirty degrees—that's what the man had said on her bedside radio; it would dip below freezing before tonight. She turned off the radio and got out of bed, shuddering as the air touched her bare skin; it had been so balmy last night she'd slept in only her underwear. She hopped across the bare pine floor as though it were an ice pond, put on her slippers, and belted her wool robe around her waist, the wool prickling her nipples. The middle of October and here it was already, for God's sake, winter. Outside, clouds the color of dirty dishwater were flying so low over the woods it seemed she could touch them, and the wind ripped the leaves from the trees in bunches. Wherever she looked outside, there were pinwheels of red and gold. The tumbling leaves deepened the sense of isolation she felt this morning.

Enough melancholy. It was gloom like this that gave the Upper Peninsula one of the highest suicide and alcoholism rates in the lower forty-eight. On with the day, she commanded herself, and went into the bathroom to wash. It was too cold for a shower. The house wasn't centrally heated; it had only the oil stoves in the living room and the two bedrooms, space-heaters in the bathrooms. She didn't have time for one of those little things to warm the room up. She douched without taking the robe off, giving herself a French bath, as her father called it. She didn't have to smell like Ivory soap today anyway. It was Friday, her day to go into the field and check up on her cases: that is, spy on them to make sure they were living at a level of poverty sufficiently low to warrant the generosity of the State of Michigan. In the cities, her professional counterparts specialized in office and courtroom work, leaving field visits to caseworkers. But the staff was short-handed up here, so she had to do both.

After she'd dressed and made the bed, with tight hospital corners, the way her mother had trained her to do, she woke the girls for school. Christy was no problem, Christy the morning lark, but waking Lisa was like performing a daily miracle of resurrection, and when you finally succeeded, you kind of wished she'd stayed dead, she was so sullen and grouchy. "Okay, Mom," she whined after June had nearly yanked her out of bed. "I'm *up*, okay?" On her way out of the bedroom, June glanced at her elder daughter—so tall for her age, as she herself had been—and tried to remember what she had been like at fourteen. She hadn't been any prize, either—not a complaining mope like Lisa, but wild and reckless, especially after Dad had left, reckless enough to get herself knocked up the last semester of her senior year. Fortunately, it had happened only two months before graduation, allowing her to hide her pregnancy and pretend that she was just putting on weight. If the school had known, they wouldn't have let her graduate. Still, Mom was brokenhearted when she found out, especially when she learned that the father was a twenty-seven-year-old pilot on an ore freighter. In Sault Ste. Marie, good girls did not get pregnant by sailors. Maybe now life was beginning to pay her back, what with these sulks of Lisa's. Payback is a bitch—that was one of Chris's expressions, something he'd picked up overseas.

She went downstairs and scrambled eggs. Recalling the mistakes she'd made as a young girl, she gave Lisa and Christine a breakfast pep talk, one she'd given several times before, about the necessity of paying attention in class and getting good grades and preparing themselves for college—meaning: Do everything you can to make sure you don't have to spend the rest of your lives in a no-place like these north woods. Giving the speech made her feel like a good, conscientious mother, and she really did want the best for both of them. Christy listened with wide-eyed incomprehension—she had just started first grade, and to her, college must have seemed like old age: so remote as to be impossible. Lisa chewed her eggs and read yesterday's *Free Press*, pretending not to be listening at all. June had to force herself not to roll up the newspaper and bop her over the head with it.

Breakfast done, the dishes put in the sink for Lisa to wash in the afternoon, June drove the girls to school, as she did every morning. They could have taken the school bus, but this little service seemed the least she could do to compensate them for being forced to live in the middle of nowhere, unable to have friends over after school or to go to their friends' houses, the way they had in Marquette. No, they had to get on the bus right away and ride it out here, to the end of the line, and then hike up a dirt road to the house and spend the afternoons alone until Chris got home. That was their fall and spring routine; in the winter they waited at school for Chris to pick them up because there was so much snow it was impossible to make the hike without snowshoes.

From the top of Hunter's Hill she looked down at Vieux Desert, and could almost see the wood and clapboard buildings hunching their shoulders against the wind. Even the bay had whitecaps, and out beyond it, Superior flung iron waves against the Coast Guard jetty and tossed spray as high as the top of the blinking lighthouse. It was a real nor'wester, all right. "The Witch of November," she'd heard that wind called, because November was the month of the big gales. Only it was October, and here one was, flying in early. June felt cold just looking at the lake, and turned up the heater as she drove down the hill. Neither of the girls talked much, except for Christy asking if the fox would grow back if she watered its grave, and Lisa telling her not to be so dumb. June kind of wished Chris was with them. She needed a hug, a big, warming hug, but Chris had been gone more than two hours, since before sunrise, stomping around by himself in the boon-docks. Probably he wouldn't have hugged her anyway. He would have just sat there, locked up in his private thoughts. He'd had one of those nightmares last night. He'd awakened her, grinding his teeth. She'd shaken him by the shoulder, but hadn't been able to rouse him. It was as though he'd been drugged. He'd kept right on, all curled up in a tight ball, gnashing his teeth, like it said in the Bible. It scared her; she thought he was going to grind his teeth into powder.

By midafternoon, June had put almost seventy-five miles on the Wagoneer, bouncing down back roads and through little towns. They were all the same: a cluster of ramshackle houses, a general store with a gas pump in front, and a saloon. There was always a saloon, no matter how small the town, shot-and-a-beer joints with tattered pool tables, mounted deer heads on the walls, maybe a stuffed bobcat snarling on a pedestal amidst the bottles of cheap whiskey and gin, and behind the bar, some big northwoods mama with the sex appeal of a logging truck. The great North was not a climate in which the erotic flourished; it was, June sometimes thought, among the reasons why she had always felt out of sync with life up here, as though she really belonged in some sensual place, although she didn't know where that might be. Somewhere in the South—New Orleans, maybe.

There was nothing but woods between the towns, woods and more woods, really grim-looking on bleak autumn days like this one. Once, when she was ten, June and her parents had taken a trip to visit her mother's relatives in northern Minnesota. They'd taken Route 2 out of Sault Ste. Marie, driving west for nearly two days, five hundred miles. The whole way June had seen only woods. She had the feeling then, that if her father had driven for the rest of their lives, they would never have gotten out of them, that there was no escape.

On her travels this morning, she'd called on the ex-wife of an iron miner who'd been laid off two years previously. The man had gone down to Oklahoma to work in the oil fields, and hadn't been seen or heard from since. The woman now lived on the dole with three kids in a shingle-sided shack at the edge of a railroad town where no trains had run for ten years. Next, she visited a young woman who claimed to be the common-law wife of a logger who'd gone west to top timber—for Georgia-Pacific, she thought it was— and then dropped out of sight. The young woman said she needed to know how she could have her child's "fraternity dejudicated," meaning *paternity adjudicated* so she could get after the son of a bitch and collect support. June's third call was to yet another woman, a ratty-haired blonde who knew where her ex-husband was but refused to file for support because he would come after her and "do what he done last time, hey"—that having been to fracture one of her cheekbones.

All this before lunch. June ate heartily, a thick beef stew served in one of those back-road diners where fast food, canned soups, or frozen vegetables had never been heard of. The stew warmed her and helped lift the depression caused by the weather and the misery of her cases. Eating, like making love, always cheered her up. Now and then it bothered her that her needs were so primitive. A good meal and a good night of love were all she needed to feel whole and harmonious; it seemed a sign that she lacked the complexity that made for a really interesting woman.

June sopped up the stew gravy with a biscuit and finished her third cup of coffee. Two middle-aged guys at the counter checked her out as she left, their glances making her aware of how big her rear end must look in her tight blue jeans. The old-timers up here liked big-sterned women, women who looked as if they could bear ten children and then go out and change a truck tire, but June reminded herself to watch her diet this winter. Whatever the local standards of feminine beauty, she didn't want to end up, at forty or forty-five, looking like one of those wide-load women who worked the bars.

Outside, the wind sliced through her. She jumped in the Wagoneer and cranked up the heater. Then she was on the road again, dropping in on more of the rural destitute. This was the part of the Upper Peninsula seldom seen by the summer tourists, the sportsmen, and the veggie-eating backpackers who came to admire nature's marvels. Not for nothing was the U.P. known as "the Appalachia of the North," for it bore many of the social and genetic ills associated with the hills of Kentucky and West Virginia. Here the dull, vaguely Mongoloid eyes that came from too many generations of first-cousin marriages, the superfluous fingers and toes, the dim-witted perversions and violence: incestuous rapes, the bloody horrors the sheriff's police described as "crimes of passion," the wife-beatings and child-batterings called "domestic disturbances." Here the suicide's pistol shot cracking in some snowbound house or cabin.

The first case she looked in on after lunch was a mob of half-breeds, known in local slang as "Finndians," part Finn and part Indian and all screwed up, the most marginal of marginals. There were eight or nine of them, related to each other in some way she could never quite figure out and didn't want to; their family tree would have looked like a bramble bush. The whole bunch, housed in a railroad car that had once been used as a logging-camp bunkhouse, lived on leftover chicken necks and whatever meat the older boys in the tribe could poach with their traps and their .30-.30's. June said hello, gave the place a quick look-over, and got out.

What we've got up here, she thought as she went down the road, are people who live about as hard as people did on the frontier, but without the promise that had made the frontier's hardships bearable, the sense of great possibilities waiting over the horizon; if things didn't work out in one place, there was always someplace else to go. No such illusions for people like that mob of Finndians. There were no possibilities, no place to go, and they knew it, the ones who had any brains at all, who were also the ones most likely to blow out their brains when the wind roared like God's judgment through the red pines and the drifts crept past the windowsills.

A few of June's co-workers, downstate girls, were almost moved to tears by the sufferings of these people, but June's reaction was unsentimental. She had come from a background almost as poor; she was northern white trash by birth, her father a common laborer in the Union Carbide plant in Sault Ste. Marie. She knew that only half of these people's misfortunes were caused by circumstance. The rest was their own damn fault. They were born losers, a lot of them. Granted, they had been dealt bad hands, but they'd done a bad job playing the hands they'd been dealt. Some of them were so in love with losing that they'd throw away an ace if they ever got lucky enough to draw one. And those deserted wives, with their bitter tales of mistreatment and their houses full of kids! Instead of patting them on the hands, June would lecture them about birth control. If the woman had had two or three men walk out on her, June would not shake her head in sympathy, but would wonder: "Well, what's wrong with you, sister, that you keep picking bums?" And she kept an eye out for the frauds, whose usual scam was to collect support, squirrel it away, and then go to Public Assistance and get themselves on the dole by pretending they weren't receiving a dime from the old man.

No, she couldn't bring herself to weep and bleed, the way some of the girls did, but she was very often scared by these abandoned women. They reminded her of what it had been like for her when Ripley left, and made her wonder what she would do if Chris ever did the same. She had her associate's degree and earned $10,500 a year, good money in this part of the country, very good for a woman, but not enough to take care of two kids properly. She sure wouldn't be able to keep the house. Not that she would ever want to keep it; her fear was that she wouldn't be able to sell it, just have to give it back to the bank. Why was she thinking like this? Chris wasn't the type who would take off. But then, you could never tell about any of them. Maybe all men were deserters at heart, and no woman today could count on the force of church, state, or society to hold on to her man. If she was good in the kitchen and fair in bed, she might be able to make him think twice when he started getting itchy. But once he got it into his head to walk, nothing could stop him.

She turned onto a wide gravel road called the Williams Trace, and headed for her last stop of the day, Edith Hermanson's. A U.S. Geological Survey map lay open on the front seat because it had been some time since she'd seen Mrs. Hermanson and she wasn't entirely sure of her direction. Chris had taught her to read the survey maps; ordinary road maps were useless once you left the county highways and plunged into the real back country, a maze of jeep and logging trails in which you could get seriously lost. You could, in fact, vanish without a trace, like that woman June had read about last year, the one whose car was finally found by some hunters, mired to the axles on a muddy two-track weeks after search-and-rescue teams had been sent out to look for her. Except for the car, no sign of her was found. It was as if she had drowned out in the middle of Lake Superior.

The thought of it gave June the creeps. The woods gave her the creeps. On the narrow, unpaved road, she sensed their power and vastness in a way she did not on the highways. Edith Hermanson lived about as far back into the wild as anyone could, in a deserted logging camp called Paulding's Crossing. It showed on the map as a few black dots clumped around a road junction, and all around it, stretching to the edges of the map, there was nothing but green, with here and there a squiggly blue line marking a wilderness river and blotches of crisscrosses that denoted swamps. The nearest paved road was twelve miles away; the nearest town, a tiny settlement called Elkhorn, another five.

The Williams Trace, full of sharp, unexpected turns and deep potholes, kept June's speed down to twenty miles an hour; and wouldn't you know it, the bumping and bouncing had given her kidneys such a knocking that she knew she couldn't wait until she reached Paulding's Crossing before going to the bathroom. She shouldn't have drunk so much coffee at lunch. She pulled over, got out of the Jeep, and walked a little distance into the woods, hiding herself behind a clump of balsam, just in case another car came by, although that wasn't very likely. The wind raised goose bumps on her bare thighs and bottom after she'd wriggled her jeans down and squatted to pee. Guys had it so much easier in situations like this. She was just about finished when she heard a branch crack somewhere behind her and got a panicked feeling that someone or something was watching her, eyes fixed on her buttocks. The wind was blowing from behind her, and, for a split-second, she thought she detected a rank odor souring the scent of pine and falling leaves.

Bear.

She was sure that's what it was. Too afraid to move a muscle, she stayed in a squat, the powerful wild-beast smell making her aware of her naked vulnerability. Nothing in the woods scared her as much as bears. Her father, who used to hunt them, had told some frightening stories about their incredible strength and persistence. He had also told her they had a keen sense of smell but poor eyesight, which reminded her that she was downwind and pretty well hidden in the balsam grove. Maybe it couldn't see her after all, if it was there. She stood very slowly, pulled up her underwear and jeans, then cautiously glanced over her shoulder. She saw nothing except trees and wind-whirled leaves, but she caught another whiff of animal rankness, not a disgusting smell exactly; like the stink of a marsh, it was sexual in some odd, primeval way. Careful to make as little noise as possible, her heart beating fast, she returned to the wagon, locked the doors, drove off, and did not breathe freely until she was a mile down the road.

In the safety of her vehicle, she began to feel pretty silly. Probably nothing had been there at all. It had just been her imagination. At the same time, her face burned with shame because she knew what caused her to be phobic about bears. Her mother was responsible for instilling this terror in her. Mom, June had grown to realize, had suffered from some form of sexual hysteria. All kinds of bizarre ideas snaked around inside the head of that outwardly proper, Evangelical Lutheran woman, ideas which had found an outlet in the Finnish folk tales and legends she had often told June when she was a child. Mom was a great storyteller (June had inherited her gift), dramatic and graphic. When she'd told those tales, she'd put her daughter right there, in those icy Finland forests, mist-bound and crawling with witches and hobgoblins. One of her strangest stories involved a fertility rite performed by pre-Christian Finns, blue-eyed pagans who believed that bears were not animals but the sons of the sky-god. A long time ago, one of these god-beasts captured a woman who had been gathering wood in the forests, mounted her as it would one of its own females, and made her its bride. She gave birth to a creature that was part deity, part animal, and part human, and it became the ancestor of a tribe called the Skolt-Lapps. (Where her mother, who'd never finished high school, had learned all this, June never knew.) In their fertility ceremony (torches blazing in the forest night, bear skulls stuck on poles, fur-clad people beating drums— Mom described it as if she had actually seen it), the Skolts would choose a tribal maiden to be the bride of a bear that hunters had captured. The animal would be kept in a stout wooden cage in the center of the village, the maiden would be brought out and stripped of her clothes, and . . . At this point, Mom would end the story, saying darkly, "And what happened afterwards cannot be spoken of by any decent Christian. It was to stop such disgusting things that the Lutherans converted the Finns to Christ." That was typical of Mom: She justified telling such lurid tales with some religious moral. Probably she was straitlaced and Bible-crazy because she knew she had some very weird impulses, and religion was the only way she could control them.

June, by the age of fifteen, was imaginative enough to picture the part of the story her mother refused to speak of. One night she'd had a dream in which she saw herself as the sacrificial maiden, naked and on all fours in the cage with the bear. The cage was surrounded by torches. In the flickering light she saw the skull-topped poles and a circle of brutal faces: the tribe watching her. The bear started licking her *there*, the way she'd seen dogs do it to each other, and the sickening thing was, she not only saw this in the dream but felt it, the rough tongue licking and licking. When the bear had finished that, she felt its warm breath on the back of her neck, its strong forepaws locking around her waist as it rose on its haunches and rammed itself inside her, its fur scratching her buttocks. It bumped and banged her painfully. She tried to scream, but, as in most nightmares, her voice was choked off. She couldn't move, the animal's embrace was so powerful, and the brutal people just watched, enjoying the hideous thing being done to her. Then the worst part happened. Her stifled screams became moans of pleasure; her bottom, responding to raw instinct, began to writhe and buck in rhythm to the bear's movements, and an orgasmic shudder quaked through her as the animal roared and shot its semen into her. That was when she'd awakened, paralyzed with fright at first, then overcome with shame when she touched herself and felt her wetness. She was so revolted with herself she wanted to die. She knew it had only been a dream, something she hadn't willed; she knew that even if such an abominable act were possible, she would never submit to it, let alone enjoy it. And yet, the mere fact that she was capable of dreaming such a dream seemed a symptom of a deep flaw in her nature, a hidden warp. A girl who had a fantasy like that locked up inside her head had to be sick, if not irredeemably sinful.

It had been so vivid, so, well, *real*. Even now, years and years after, she could recall the details of that dream as clearly as if she'd had it the night before, as clearly as she remembered that first time with Chris, when she'd acted out the fantasy, she'd been so abandoned. For some reason, that memory did not make her prickle with shame. She had never told Chris about the dream. It would have been too embarrassing, even dangerous. What would he think of her? Judging from the remark he'd made yesterday, he already had enough low opinions of her. On the other hand, maybe it would do her good to tell him, a sort of relief. And maybe her courage in revealing her secret nightmare would inspire him to reveal his. Maybe then she would find out what kind of monster violated him in his sleep.

12

She drove over a rise and saw Paulding's Crossing below: four log bunkhouses and a clapboard cottage in a broad meadow. Smoke coiled from the chimney of one of the log buildings, the one Henry Hermanson had converted into a house for his wife, daughter, and two sons. A pickup was parked in front. Laundry hung from the clotheslines, bed sheets billowing like sails in the wind. An American flag, which Edith ensured was raised each morning, cracked from its staff in front of the cottage. The cottage was to have been a grocery store for the hunters and fishermen who were to have rented the bunkhouses during the fish and game seasons. Henry Hermanson's dream, his grand plan for financial and personal independence, after he'd been laid off from his machinist's job at the Empire mine, had been to transform the derelict camp, which he'd bought free and clear for only two thousand dollars, into a remote lodge for sportsmen who wanted to get off the beaten path. He thought big, Henry did. Small craters pocked the back of the meadow, where he had dynamited the stumps of huge pine trees to clear the way for an airstrip for the sportsmen's private planes. The airstrip was never completed, and now there were only the craters and the fallen stumps.

Thinking of Henry's vision put June in a funk as she drove downhill toward "Hermanson's Lodge," the name Henry had decided on with less imagination than you would have . expected from a dreamer. Looking at the meadow and the woods encircling it, at the log buildings and the flag snapping under the low, smoky skies, June felt as if she were entering a settlement on some abandoned frontier.

The first time she had seen this place, she had been unable to understand how Edith could live in such desolation without going crazy. Then she'd met the woman and understood.

June parked behind the truck and went up the gravel walkway to the front door. Unlike most of the places she visited on her rounds, the Hermansons' yard was not overgrown and littered with rusty bedsprings, jerrycans, and castoff washing machines—all the cluttered junk of degraded people wallowing in their degradation. The Hermanson yard was as tidy as anything you'd see in the suburbs of Marquette. Whitewashed rocks bordered the walkway and there was even a small lawn, mown once a week by the two boys. Henry wanted it that way. Henry said it was important to make a good first impression on the rod- and gun-toting sportsmen who would be coming up from Chicago, Detroit, and Lansing. And because Edith was herself a typically fastidious Finn, as well as a good traditional wife devoted to her husband, she made sure the boys kept the lawn weeded and cut, just as she made sure they hoisted Old Glory each morning and that her daughter helped clean the bunkhouses and the "store," as well as iron Henry's shirts. "Hank, he's a stickler for ironed shirts, even out here in the woods, hey," Mrs. Hermanson had told June on their first meeting.

The daughter, Freya, answered the door. Freya was a sixteen-year-old knockout, tall and slender, with exquisite Scandinavian features and blue eyes and white-blond hair, like Chris's.

"Oh, Mrs. Starkmann, hello," Freya said, wiping her hands on a flour-dusted apron. June caught the aroma of blueberry pies baking in the kitchen.

"Hello, Freya. It's been a while. How's everything been?"

"The same," the girl answered, her eyes iced with the tired knowledge you'd expect to see in a disappointed woman of forty. "You might as well say hi to Mom first. Then we can talk."

"All right. I've got some information, but it probably won't be of much help."

"Has it ever been?"

June ignored the implied accusation—what could she do, she wasn't a one-woman detective agency, for God's sake—and walked with Freya into the kitchen. She glanced around for signs of a dramatic rise in the Hermansons' economic status: a new piece of furniture, a new rug, a new radio, a new this or that. The place was spotless—Henry liked a clean, orderly house—but there were the same old threadbare chairs, the same chipped table, the same frayed rugs in front of the fireplace, from which burning logs cast a little heat. Otherwise the house was chilly.

It was warmer in the kitchen, where the oven blazed. The smell of the pies made June's mouth water. Three of them had been set out to cool on the counter beneath the kitchen window. Edith, robust as ever, greeted her with a big grin and a motherly pat on the cheek, her chunky arms quivering like Jell-O. Freya must have inherited her slimness from her father. June didn't know. She'd never seen Mr. Hermanson.

"Sit down," Edith commanded, pointing at the kitchen table, its oilcloth smeared with blueberries. "Excuse the mess, but we've been baking, hey."

"Smells terrific."

"Well, you sit for a while and don't go runnin' off like usual. Those pies on the counter'll be cool enough to cut in a bit and you have a slice."

"Oh, no thanks, Edith."

"Ah, c'mon." Mrs. Hermanson set her sturdy bulk in the chair across from June's and brushed back a wisp of her hair. Once blond, it was now the color of the rocks lining the walkway, although Edith was still under fifty. The premature white, however, was the only sign of the difficulties she had been through. Otherwise, she was cheerful and energetic, full of the stamina that is sometimes granted the mad. "You sit a while," she continued. "Why, if it wasn't for you and the mailman and the people I see at church on Sundays, I wouldn't see nobody outside of Hank and the kids."

Freya slid three more pies into the oven without any show of emotion, but June could sense the girl's sadness and fatigue. She had become an emotional lightning rod, drawing into herself the sorrow and exhaustion that should have struck Edith.

Freya asked if she could go to her room to start her homework.

"Oh, yah. You do that. You know what your father says about doin' good in school."

Freya said nothing as she left. June wanted to follow her out of the madwoman's stifling kitchen, but contained herself. Like the children, she had to play along. How they were able to do it, day after day after day, was beyond her.

"She's a good girl," June commented. "I wish my oldest one was helpful around the house."

"Yah, that Freya, you couldn't ask for one better. And so pretty too. A lot of boys at school are chasin' after that one."

"So, you must have put up quite a few blueberries."

"Yah. Good season this season. We picked our last quarts last month. That Hank, how he loves his blueberry pie."

"Where is Mr. Hermanson, by the way?" June asked, searching

the woman's wide, coarse face for a vague twitch, a flicker in her green eyes, some indication that reason still dwelled in at least one small corner of her otherwise addled mind.

"Out in the woods, like always. He and the boys found a bear den, and they're out now baitin' a log."

Bear.

"We got some bow-hunters comin' for the weekend tomorrow, so Hank and the boys are gettin' that log baited up, buildin' the tree-stand, all that. Lotta work, hey, tryin' to make a go of a place like this."

"I'm sure, Edith."

"Let's see about that pie."

"Really, no thanks. I'm trying to watch my weight."

"Watch your weight?" Edith moved from the chair to the counter, where she speared one of the pies with a fork. Miniature geysers of steam rose from the holes. "You look okay to me. You don't have to watch your weight. Anyway, the pie's still a little too hot. Here. This'll cool 'em off quick." Edith's haunches loomed like the fantail of a fishing trawler as she bent over the counter and opened the window a crack. "Now it'll be ready to eat in a few minutes. I insist you have a piece, Mrs. Starkmann—you been such a good friend to me and Hank and the kids."

June, sensing an imminent collapse of her ability to play along with Edith's self-deception, said she'd be delighted to have some pie; but first she had to excuse herself to go to the bathroom.

As she passed through the living room, she noticed that Henry's hunting rifle still hung, Davy Crockett style, above the fireplace. There wasn't a speck of rust on it. Edith had seen even to that small detail, keeping Hank's rifle in good shape. Every last prop of her fantasy world was in place.

June climbed the log-and-board steps to the upstairs lofts which Henry had converted into bedrooms for his children, one for Freya, the other for his sons, Hank Junior and Tom. He'd also installed indoor plumbing and a septic tank because his wilderness lodge was to have had all the modern conveniences, but the expenses had eaten up every last nickel of his and Edith's savings before the lodge was half-completed. Besides the family's living quarters, only one of the bunkhouses had been renovated. The other two remained derelict, the would-be store a wreck inside.

As she looked around upstairs, June could not help but admire Henry's workmanship. It perplexed her because it suggested a careful, solid man, a responsible man, not a fly-by-night like Ripley who was incapable of such patient craftsmanship. So what had happened to solid Henry Hermanson? What secret devil had compelled him to strand his family out here? Had he planned it, like a murder, or had he done it on impulse, after he'd gone down south for that job on the offshore oil rigs in the Gulf of Mexico, the big-money job that was supposed to have provided the capital for finishing his lodge? Maybe, after all these months of breathing warm Gulf air and staring at beautiful blue waters, he couldn't bring himself to return to this forlorn place. Then why, if that had been the case, hadn't he brought his family down there? Men. You could never tell about them, never trust the bastards.

Freya's bedroom door was closed. June knocked, and the girl let her in. It was a small, bare room, shaped into a triangle by a steeply angled roof with cedar-log beams. June stood by the door.

"Well?" Freya asked. She had changed into a pair of faded jeans snug as a dancer's tights and an equally tight turtleneck shirt that flattered her small, well-formed breasts. With a figure and a face like hers, I would have been long gone out of here, June said to herself, recalling a high-school friend who'd taken off for Aspen, worked briefly as a waitress in a ski lodge, then married a rich condominium developer, a fairy tale come true.

June took the note out of her pocket and handed it to Freya, who lay down on the bed to read it, her back resting against the metal bedstead. Its tubular bars reminded June of a prison, which was kind of appropriate, considering the situation the girl and her brothers were in.

"What does this mean, Mrs. Starkmann?"

"It means he left Morgan City—that's in Louisiana—six months ago. The state's attorney down there did some checking. They're pretty sure he's in Oklahoma now, working for another oil company. They're trying to find out where, exactly."

"What then?"

"If they find him, the law in Oklahoma will haul him into court and issue a pay order. The amount will depend on how much he can afford. If he doesn't pay, he goes to jail."

Freya rose slightly from her lounging position to hand back the note. June noticed that the girl had changed more than her clothes; her manner was different. Up here, in her own private space, she wasn't quite the stoic, dutiful daughter she'd been downstairs. She seemed older, harder, and sexier, her movements almost slinky; and there was an odd flash in her blue eyes, a glare of daring and anger burning through the sadness and exhaustion.

"I wanted you to know that we're still trying. We'll find him eventually."

"You were right. This isn't much help. He's somewhere in Oklahoma. Great."

"It's the best we've been able to do so far."

This was the moment to leave, but June was held by the magnetism of Freya's eyes, challenging, naughty, and a little coy too. She looked like a girl who'd done something wrong and half-wanted someone else to know about it. June gave the room another once-over, her glance falling on a white booklet opened on the small table Freya used as a desk.

"You're not going to school, are you?"

"You're pretty smart, Mrs. Starkmann. Perspective, I mean."

"Perceptive."

"That's it."

"I know what a correspondence-course book looks like. I took a few. What's this in?"

"Math. I got a job waitressing at the café in Elkhorn," she confessed, a little too quickly. "Hank Junior is pumping gas at the station. It isn't much, but it pays the bills. Food stamps and the hundred-eighty you people send us just doesn't make it. Tommy's still in school. Sixth grade, even though he's supposed to be in eighth, but he flunked twice after, you know . . ."

"I know. How do you manage to pull this off? With Edith, I mean."

"It's a real small town. Three hundred people only. Everyone knows what's going on out here and they feel sorry for us. So they gave Hank and me jobs and they cover for us. Every morning, me, Hank, and Tommy drive into town in the pickup—I've got a license now and Hank Junior has a learner's permit—and we just drive in like we're going to school and then come back and nobody says nothing to Mom. It's no big deal. They're all part of the act, I guess you could say."

A whole town, June thought. A whole town has now become a supporting cast for Edith Hermanson's fantasy.

"Freya, you know that Hank Junior is only fifteen. Under the law, he's supposed to be in school. He's a truant . . ."

"So's my Dad."

"And, technically, you're no longer a dependent child. You're working full-time. If I mentioned that, the state would have to cut off the sixty a month your mother gets for you."

"But you won't mention it, will you, Mrs. Starkmann."

It was neither a plea nor a question, but an indirect statement of fact. June had decided she much preferred the Freya of the flour-dusted apron and quiet manner to this version, Freya the sly scammer.

"If I didn't, I'd be a party to welfare fraud. So I'll just pretend we didn't have this conversation. And you do the same."

"Thank you, Mrs. Starkmann."

"But you ought to stop pretending about your mother, you and your brothers. You can't keep this up much longer, this *act*. You've got to get out of this, Freya."

"You mean put Mom in the loony bin."

"She needs professional help."

The girl did not move, one long leg stretched out in front of her, the other bent at the knee.

"We're not going to do that. We just can't. I told you that last time. And with her gone, what am I supposed to do? Take care of all this by myself?"

June stifled an impulse to offer to take the children in, she felt so bad about their predicament.

"Some sort of arrangements could be made. And mental hospitals aren't like they used to be. They don't put people in cages, for God's sake, and they don't keep them there for years and years anymore. Sometimes just a few months. They use a lot of drug therapy now . . ."

"What're you saying? That some doctors will just give Mom a pill and one day she'll wake up and realize that Dad isn't here? That he's gone, almost two years now, and isn't coming back. All with a little pill, hey?"

"I'm saying she could be cured, in time."

"Do you want to know what would happen if Mom ever was cured? She would *really* go crazy. You don't need to be no doctor to figure it, and no social worker, neither. See, right now, she does everything she used to do. She cooks, she cleans, she washes, she goes to church, she takes care of us because she thinks *he's* still around. She sets a plate out for him at dinner! She even *talks* to him at night in her bedroom downstairs, and so she can do all the things she could do before. And that's why me and my brothers help her go on thinking he's still here. We figured out that that was the only thing to do, and we're just a bunch of dummies and dropouts. Why can't you figure it out, Mrs. Starkmann, if you're so per . . . per whatever it is?"

"Perceptive." June paused, sagging against the wall as the full weight of this entire day and of these children's impossible situation fell on her all at once. "All I'm saying, Freya, is that it can't go on forever. Eventually you'll have to do something, and when you do, don't think twice about calling on me for help. How's that?"

"Fine."

"Where are Tommy and Hank Junior now?"

"They're out baiting up a bear log, just like Mom said. We really do have a couple of bow-hunters coming in this weekend." Freya gave a little smirk. "Hermanson's Lodge's first customers, you might say. A hundred dollars, they're paying us."

"That's good to hear." June looked at her watch. "Well, I'd better go. I'll see you next visit, and I'll keep my mouth shut. I guess I'm part of the act too."

June had started to go out the door when Freya said to her back: "A couple of young guys who eat at the café a few days a week. They're not from town. Loggers, I think. They were talking bow-hunting, so I told them about our place."

It was the husky, languorous, imitation-Lauren-Bacall tone in which Freya had said *a couple of young guys . . . not from town* that made June turn to face the girl again.

"You don't have to answer this, but what's the hundred for?" she asked, as heartbroken as she would have been if Freya had been her own daughter.

"The cabin, the fixed-up one, for two days and nights, and my brothers' guide fees."

"I didn't know they were licensed guides."

"They're not. But out here, who cares?"

"Nobody, I guess. And you, Freya. You don't need a license, do you?"

The girl shifted onto her side, a provocative pose, with her elbow crooked and her hand cupping her lovely chin, her hips curving smoothly into the long fineness of her legs.

"I don't think I understand, Mrs. Starkmann." She was staring with a brilliant slutty rage.

"I think I do," June answered, restraining herself from throwing the girl over her knee and paddling her until she cried. "I'm very perceptive, remember? Just by the way you're looking at me now, I can tell that the money is going to be the least part of it. This is going to be your way of getting even, isn't it? You're just dying to let someone know, someone who just might tell Daddy when she finally finds Daddy . . ."

"Mrs. Starkmann," Edith interrupted, calling from downstairs. "You still in that bathroom? The pie's ready. I've cut you a slice."

"In a moment, Edith," June called back. "I've just been having a chat with Freya."

"Yah, sure, but you better come before it gets too cold. First too hot, then too cold."

"I'll be just a second," she said, and waited until she heard Edith return to the kitchen. "Well?"

"Honestly, Mrs. Starkmann . . ."

"You're lousy at being coy. You wanted me to know all along. Okay, listen, I said I can be of help, and I can be. Let me know now about what time of night you plan to sneak out of the house and go service your two merry bowmen. I'll be in the cabin with a Polaroid. I'll take shots of everything that goes on, maybe a good close-up of them handing over *your* fees. Then, as soon as we find out Daddy's address, I'll mail him the prints. Now *that* would be the way to get even. He can see in full color that he's turned his daughter into a teenage hooker and maybe come running back home, even if it's to beat your cute little ass for peddling it. What do you say to that, Freya?"

Freya sat up, the flashes in her eyes like the blue sparks given off by insects electrocuting themselves on an outdoor bug-killer.

"*Screw you*, is what I say." Freya did not raise her voice. "Screw you, Mrs. Social Worker. Screw your checks and your food stamps— they don't buy shit anyway. Screw you and screw *him*. Screw—that's what I have to say and that's what I'm going to do to those guys. For money. You said I needed to get out of this? I'm going to, hey. I'm going to screw my way out."

June, her Canuck temper overcoming her judgment, grabbed the girl by the shoulders and, with her superior strength, hoisted Freya to her feet. She was about to slap her face—an act that would have gotten her fired if she'd carried it through and it was reported—but she was saved from her rashness by an explosion of splintering glass and the loudest scream she'd ever heard.

13

She and Freya ran downstairs into the kitchen, where they saw something so incredible neither of them could move or make a sound: a thick coal-black foreleg groping through the shattered window, a huge paw clawing the countertop, and Edith, one of her arms slashed, either by the claws or by flying glass, swatting the paw with a broom and screeching, "Hank! Shoot it! Hank! Hank!" Two of the three pies had been knocked off the counter, splattering gobs of gelatinous blue across the kitchen floor, upon which hundreds of glass splinters sparkled. The bear whoofed, annoyed by Edith's swats, and smacked the wall outside with its other paw, the thud suggesting unimaginable strength. June absorbed all this in a split-second and, in the same fraction of time, asked herself if this was the bear whose presence she had sensed up the road. But that was ten miles away. Could bears move that far that fast? She didn't know what to do. She couldn't believe what she was seeing; as the bear in her dream had seemed real, this real bear seemed out of a dream, the ravaging beast of her nightmare sprung into life.

Then Edith, bravely taking another swing with her broom, slipped on a puddle of blueberries and fell heavily onto her rump, Freya crying, "Mom! Mom!" Without thinking, June snatched a big cast-iron skillet that hung from a nail in the wall and, raising it above her head in both hands—it felt as heavy as a maul—brought it down with all her strength, smashing the animal's paw against the counter. The bear bawled in rage and pain. June had never heard a more horrifying sound. She jumped back, thinking the animal was going to rip the walls down and come in after her. She was stunned to see that her blow had had no other effect than to make the bear angry; its foreleg was still stuck through the window. For God's sake, if she'd struck a man's hand like that, she would have crippled him for life, but there the paw was, rummaging for the last remaining pie. An instant later, the animal shoved its other leg through, and all June could see was a black as black itself, the blackness of both forelegs, the blackness of its chest, filling the window. Standing manlike on its hindquarters, the thing must have been seven feet tall.

June raised the skillet and threw it as hard as she could into the middle of all that bristling darkness. She might as well have thrown a wad of paper. The bear was undeterred. "Take it!" she screamed. "Take the pie, you bastard! Take it and get out!" This the animal did. The paws, guided by the acute sense of smell, at last succeeded in clutching the pie tin, and pulled it through the window as deftly as a man picking up an order at the carry-out window of a drive-in restaurant.

June stood in the middle of the kitchen, clutching for breath, her knees quaking. Edith, slumped in shock on the floor, skeins of blood roped around her flabby arm, was still calling for help from her vanished husband, not screaming anymore, but calling in a low, moaning voice. Freya, the would-be whore, the tough teenage cookie, was in tears and trying to bandage her mother's arm with a dish towel. June looked at the two women, then back out the window, and saw that the bear had not run off with its prize. It had ambled out to the middle of the side yard to gorge itself. Its black-and-tan snout was buried in the pie tin. On all fours, its tongue lapping up the blueberries, it did not appear a nightmarish menace, but looked like a big dog gobbling up its Gravy Train. This, too, was an unbelievable sight. It had clawed one woman and terrorized two more; it had been bashed in the paw with twelve pounds of cast iron; it had smelled human scent and heard human cries, and yet had not run away, just shambled off five or six yards and started eating. Its arrogance was intolerable. June hated it for its fearlessness, its strength, its possessive appropriation of the Hermansons' yard. It was a bear, lord of the woods, and could do as it pleased. Her knees stopped quaking as an unfamiliar rage surged through her. It was no hot, blind fury, but the sort of cold, clear-headed meanness that, she imagined, must be felt by a hired assassin.

She went into the living room and took Henry's rifle from the wall. Remembering the shooting lessons her father had given her long ago and a few things Chris had taught her about firearms after they'd moved to Vieux Desert, she fumbled the bolt backward, saw bullets racked in the magazine, and slid the bolt home, locking a round in the chamber. She returned to the kitchen without knowing what had overtaken her; it was as if she'd fallen under a hypnotic spell. "Bastard," she muttered under her breath as she bench-rested the weapon on the windowsill and leaned into the stock, the way Chris had shown her, to lessen the impact of the recoil. She centered the sights on the bear's massive shoulder. She was so calm! Her hand and aim were steady, and she knew the bear was dead even before the gun went off, with an explosion so piercing it was as though someone had poked pins into her eardrums. The recoil punched her shoulder, rocking her back on her heels. The bear went down, its squat legs flying out from under it, down on its belly, its jaw falling into the pie tin. The beast lay quivering for several seconds, then seemed to relax as a thick puddle of blood reddened the lawn. A little electric buzz traveled up and down June's spine. Except for a few grouse she had shot with Chris, she'd never killed anything in her life, and now she'd killed a bear! Just to make sure, she ejected the spent cartridge, jacked in a live one, and fired once more.

The shot sent Mrs. Hermanson back into hysterics, and Freya also let out a cry. June, in her triumph, looked at them contemptuously. She had done this for them—what were they whimpering about? She had struck a blow for them! As if to demonstrate her bravery further, she unlocked the kitchen door and went into the yard, the rifle in her hands. Any experienced bear hunter could have told her that this was a dangerous thing to do; a bear cannot be considered truly dead until its pelt is on the wall.

Nevertheless, hers was dead. Her first shot, she noticed, had struck to the right of her aim, piercing the animal's skull. Half of one side of its head had been blown away. Chips of bone and bits of brain tissue floated in the pool of blood. The animal looked harmless now, almost pathetic, even with its murderous fangs bared under the death-curl of its lips. "Stinking bastard." June raised the rifle and shot it a third time, point-blank between the eyes, gore spraying everywhere. She couldn't believe she was doing what she was doing; if anyone had told her she was capable of such butchery, she would have told him he was crazy. The rifle crashed again. She couldn't seem to get enough. It was so weird, but she felt somewhat the way she had when making love, those times when all her inhibitions and feminine restraints had flown and every part of her being was cast into a wonderful void; it was as if, between the transcendence of that beautiful act and the transcendence of this brutal one, there existed some bizarre connection.

"Bastard. You stinking bastard!" She fired a fifth round, so transported by her anger that she didn't notice the magazine was empty as she worked the bolt to load a sixth cartridge. She pulled the trigger again, heard the hammer fall with a click on an empty chamber, and then a winded male voice:

"It only holds five rounds, ma'am."

It was Hank Junior and Tommy, standing at the edge of the yard, their chests heaving. She stared without speaking. There were the two brothers in hunting garb, and behind them the browning meadow and then the pines, moving in the wind. The front was passing, the sky clearing, and a deeper cold descending.

"The rifle's empty, Mrs. Starkmann," said Hank Junior, "and that bear can't get no deader."

June stood without speaking, her hands gripping the rifle so tightly her fingers ached. Neither of the boys took a step toward her. Hank Junior, as tall as an average-sized man, was staring at her strangely, and the smaller Tommy looked frightened. Both were puffing. She could see their breath in the cold. It dawned on her that they had been on their way home when they'd heard the shots and had run the rest of the way, and had probably seen her pumping bullets into the dead animal like a madwoman. She glanced down momentarily, saw that the lower half of her jeans was splattered with blood, then raised her eyes back toward the boys. They were afraid, for God's sake! Afraid of her! She must have been quite a sight, shouting *bastard* and blasting away. Hank Junior held out his hand, as if he were begging her to hand over the rifle.

She snapped out of her trancelike state and started to shake again, more violently than before. The next thing she knew, tears flooded her eyes. Hank Junior took the rifle from her and tried to comfort her, as an adult would, patting her on the shoulder while she trembled and cried, irritated with herself but unable to stop the tears.

"You take it easy, Mrs. Starkmann," the boy said. He seemed a little embarrassed and awkward, unsure of how to go about soothing a woman who was falling apart. "What went on here?"

"Never mind that now," June snuffled. "Go inside and see to your mother. She's been hurt."

"Mom? Hurt?"

"Yes. I don't think it's too bad, but go inside. Please."

Hank Junior ran into the house. Tommy, the slowest-witted of the three kids, remained outside, apparently confused about what he was supposed to do. He looked at the bear and then at June, awe still in his eyes.

"You sure did mean to kill this bear, Mrs. Starkmann. Picked the right gun for it."

"Go inside and help your brother, Tommy. Your mom's hurt."
This did not seem to impress the boy greatly.

"That was my dad's bear gun. Seven-millimeter magnum. Two-hunnerd grains. Real bone-crusher."

"Your mother is hurt, Tommy! What're you talking about?"

She was a good woman! A decently married, respectable woman! She kept a clean house! She had a job and children of her own! What was she doing out in this godforsaken place with a dead bear and a half-witted kid?

"One good shot was all you needed. Didn't need five. Two hunnerd grains outa that rifle could blow a car off the road, hey."

"Get inside, Tommy!"

Inside the house, Hank Junior took command. He expertly dressed his mother's injuries, disinfecting them with hydrogen peroxide, taping gauze to them, then cinching a tourniquet around Edith's bicep to choke off the bleeding. Spots of her blood lay on the kitchen linoleum like red quarters, but her wounds were not as bad as they had looked at first; apparently the bear's claws had only grazed her when it punched through the window. Her son gave her a couple of shots of vodka to calm her nerves and walked her into the bedroom, where he instructed her to lie down and rest until he figured out what to do next. That done, he ordered Freya to clean up the kitchen and Tommy to fetch lumber from the toolshed and board up the window. The older boy was terrific, really in control of things, mature beyond his years: the man of the house. While Freya swept and mopped the floor, and Tommy, on a ladder outside, hammered the boards into place, June told Hank Junior what had happened.

"Mom shouldn't of opened the window with them pies there," he said when she had finished the story. A thoughtful frown knitted his blond eyebrows. He had his mother's thick build and coarse features. "I told her that before. Come this time of year, bears is real hungry and fattening theirselves for winter sleep, and they'll just come right in your front door if they smell somethin' good."

June, feeling like a fifth wheel but also anxious to start home—it would be dark in an hour—asked if there was anything she could do, perhaps drive Edith to a doctor.

"There's no doctor in town," the boy said, "but I figure she'll need one. Bear claws is filthy. She could get blood poisoning."

"I have to pass by Marquette on my way home. I could drive her to the emergency room at the county hospital."

Freya and Hank Junior stiffened at the word *hospital*.

"Marquette's fifty miles from here, Mrs. Starkmann," Freya said, as if she were speaking of a city in another country.

"I'm sure they'll keep her only overnight."

"All right," the boy said firmly. "Appreciate it. Freya oughtta go with her. Me and Tommy got to skin that bear out. Can't leave her in the yard, stinkin' up the place and drawin' every fox and coon and crow inside of a hunnerd miles."

"*Her?*"

"It's a she-bear, the one me and Tommy been watchin' all summer and was baitin' up for these bow-hunters we got comin' in." Hank Junior paused, looking at the window as Tommy nailed the last board, bringing twilight to the kitchen. "Sort of wished you hadn't of killed her, Mrs. Starkmann. She'd got what she was after and wouldn't of caused no more trouble."

It was a polite and mild reproach, but still a reproach, and June was damned if she was going to be reproached by a fifteen-year-old backwoods dropout.

"It *attacked* your mother, for God's sake! What'd you expect me to do?"

"Didn't attack her. That sow was just after the blueberries, and Mom kind of got in the way. And she ought not of left the window open, like I told her before."

"I don't believe this."

"Them bow-hunters would've paid up a . . . whatchewcallit . . . extra money if they'd of killed this bear. A tip, kind of."

"I'm sorry, Hank. I'm real sorry about you losing your tip. That animal hurt your mother, whether it meant to or not, and it wasn't going away. It was standing right there in the yard, like it owned this place."

"I know a lot about bears, Mrs. Starkmann. Black bears ain't like grizzlies. All you would've had to of done is fire a shot over her head and she'da been gone back into the woods. Bears is dumb, hey, but they ain't ignorant."

"I think it's time Freya and I got your mother ready."

As she helped Freya pack a small cardboard suitcase for Edith, June stewed over Hank Junior's criticism. It took all her willpower to refrain from telling the kid not to worry about his bear and his tip; his sister would be tipped generously for her services. Incredible. How could that boy criticize her? Hank made her feel as if she'd done something wrong, and the odd thing was, she had begun to think that she had. Her guilt made no sense to her, but then, the whole afternoon had been pretty senseless, the strangest afternoon of her life.

The packing done, she and Freya next had to rouse Edith, who was drowsy from the vodka and shock. They got her out of bed, wrapped her in a blanket, and led her out to the wagon. She sat in the back seat, muttering something about June not having to take her way up to Marquette—her husband could drive her as soon as he got home. June said that Henry wasn't available and that she had to get to the hospital right away, before infection set in. Edith was concerned: Hank would be worried when he came home and found her gone, and would June leave a note, explaining what had happened? June told her not to worry, the boys would explain things to Hank. "Oh, yah, the boys, that's right," Edith said. And, my God, that *thing* smashin' the window so all of a sudden, it was a wonder she hadn't died of heart attack right then.

"Please don't talk about it," her daughter said, sliding in beside Edith. "Just rest. Everything's going to be okay."

When June went out back to tell the boys she was leaving, she covered her mouth with a hand and wished to God she had just driven off. The boys had tied ropes to the bear's hind legs and had dragged it behind the toolshed, where they'd rolled it onto its back, spread-eagling its stubby limbs to gut and skin it. They had split its middle from the crotch almost to the chest, and where its innards had been there was now a steaming cavity, entrails, organs, and some slimy, half-formed tissue mounded off to one side. Blood gleamed in the meadow grass; the boys' hands and lower arms were blood-smeared as, now, Tommy peeled back the hide with his fingers, and Hank Junior, with his skinning knife, sliced through the white fat and cartilage that held the hide to the underskin.

Hank Junior, spotting her out of the corner of his eye, looked up from his butchering.

"Ready to go, Mrs. Starkmann?"

June nodded, her hand still cupped over her mouth. She could not take her eyes off the bear. Lying on its back, its fore and hind legs outspread, parts of its naked flesh exposed, the beast looked so human she felt as if she'd committed murder.

"Mom's going to be all right, isn't she?"

Unable to speak, she nodded again.

Hank Junior helped his brother free a stubborn patch of the pelt from the hindquarters, the two boys clutching it in their fingers, then ripping it back slowly. The sound of hide parting from flesh turned June to stone inside.

"C'mon, Tommy. Let's leave off this and say 'bye to Mom."

The boys stood and wiped their hands with a rag. Hank must

have noticed the pallor in her face because he said: "Guess you never seen this done before. It's a messy job, hey."

June did not say anything.

"Like to apologize for what I said in the house to you. Guess that was kinda dumb, considerin' what went on. You done real good for a girl. There's some men can't handle a magnum like that Remington. Your shoulder okay?"

"A little sore," she managed to say.

All three started to walk to the car.

"I figure we can use the hide and maybe some of the meat if we can dig out all the lead you put into it." Hank Junior grinned, to show that he intended no reproach this time. "No wonder that sow was so hungry to go bashin' into a house with people in it. She was eatin' for two."

Oh, Jesus Christ, June thought, an image of the slick, half-formed thing flashing in her mind.

The boys said their goodbyes. June drove off, never so happy to leave a place in her life. She had twelve miles to go before she reached the county highway. Pavement, asphalt, the twentieth century. The gravel road twined through the woods, dipping down into washed-out gullies. Each time the Jeep's wheels ground in a mushy pothole, she was stabbed by fear, thinking she was going to get stuck. But the four-wheel drive always pulled her out. Night, its darkness intensified by the forest, came down before she was halfway to the highway. June flicked on her brights and depressed the gas pedal as far as she dared. Black and white. Black of the woods, white of the headlights knifing into the crush of trees whenever she rounded a sharp curve, the beams sometimes illuminating pairs of green eyes that stared out from the forest with supernatural iridescence. Deer? Bobcat? Fox? *Bear?* What sorts of creatures did those eyes belong to? She half-expected to see the ghost of the bear she'd killed, she was so spooked. Or maybe its mate, towering on its hind legs in the middle of the road, a vengeful beast bent on clawing and crushing the life out of her. She could not understand her superstitious jitters. She had two years of college—she was educated, for God's sake—and she had not done anything wrong. She could not think of a single commandment or ordinance she had broken; and yet, she swore she saw a judgment in the spectral eyes that glowed in the headlights, as if she had violated a law after all, an unwritten one.

Overwrought, that's what she was. It had been quite a day. She needed a drink. A double shot of scotch straight up would straighten her out. She also needed, she realized, to call home and let Chris know why she was late. What would she tell him? Hi, honey, I'm running behind schedule because I shot a bear this afternoon? He would think she'd gone out of her mind. Maybe she had, at least when she was firing into the animal. Jesus, she could not believe she'd done anything so bloodthirsty. The experience now struck her as unreal, as if she'd dreamed the whole thing; but she couldn't deny the evidence of the dried blood on her blue jeans. She shouldn't have gone out back and seen what she had seen. Now she could not erase from her memory the picture of the half-skinned sow, so human in its nakedness. No wonder those pagan Finns had thought of the animal as more than a mere beast.

Two doubles, that's what June needed. That and a cigarette. She hadn't smoked since she'd become pregnant with Christine, but hungered to now.

"Freya, is there a bar in town, someplace I could make a phone call?"

"There's one next to the café. You can call from either place."

"If you're hungry, I can get you a hamburger to go."

"No thanks."

"How's Edith?"

"Out." The girl's voice was cool, a thousand miles away.

"Look, I'm sorry about losing my temper. I had no right to do that."

"That's okay."

At last the headlights revealed the highway, straight ahead. June stepped on the gas and shot for it, and covered the five miles into town in as many minutes.

A couple of bearded, shriveled, woods-rats were the only customers sitting at the L-shaped bar. Self-conscious about her spattered jeans, June stood behind the short leg of the L, ordered a double, and slugged it down like a lady lumberjack. She held herself to the one; then, with the change, she went into the phone booth and called home. Lisa answered.

"Mom, it's you!" It was the most enthusiasm June had heard in her voice in a year. "Where are you?"

"Some wide spot in the road called Elkhorn. Put Chris on, honey."

"He isn't here. He left."

"*Left?* Where?"

"He didn't say. What's the matter?"

"One of my cases was hurt in an accident and I have to get her to the hospital. I'll explain everything later. Be sure to tell Chris when he comes home that I'm taking her to the county hospital in Marquette. I'll be home as soon as I can. Don't worry. There's some leftover *pâté chinois* in the fridge. Warm it up for you and Christy for dinner."

"Chris made us peanut butter sandwiches before he left."

"That's not dinner. Have some *pâté chinois*. But when you're heating it up make sure the windows are closed."

"What?"

"Don't leave windows open when you're heating the shepherd's pie."

"That's really weird, Mom. The windows *are* closed. It's cold, remember?"

" 'Bye, honey. Mama'll be home as soon as she can."

June hung up, agitated that Chris had left their daughters alone, agitated and a little frightened. When Lisa had said "He left," June's stomach had turned a flip, as if she were on the edge of a cliff and had felt the ground giving way beneath her.

All right, calm down, she told herself, starting off for Marquette. He'll be back, steady Chris. He will be, won't he? she silently asked, without knowing to whom or what she'd put the question. If I have done something wrong, don't let that happen to me again. Not that, anything but that, please, please.

She drove northward and saw the glow of Marquette on the horizon much sooner than she had expected. In a moment she recognized the glimmering as the northern lights. They were arrayed in long wisps of greenish white, moving in a kind of rhythm. She had seen them dozens of times, and always thought they were beautiful. She remembered, from her school lessons, that they were caused by electromagnetic discharges in the upper atmosphere, but she did not see them tonight with the eyes of her mind; she saw them with the eyes of her heart, which is a much older organ than the brain; and to those eyes the aurora appeared as a sign of a disturbance that was not meteorological in nature. It resembled, in its dancing, the flicker of a pale and ghostly fire, and when it suddenly burst into brilliant colors that flashed off and on, June half-believed that something out there in the poleward heavens was sending messages, like the kinds that ships sent out on the lakes, signals whose code she could not decipher.

14

While June was driving to Marquette, Starkmann was making the rounds of the saloons that kept livers enlarged and minds from cabin fever in Vieux Desert. In his third stop, the East Bay Tavern, two unemployed loggers had asked him how the new mill project was coming along. "Just fine," he'd said, aware that he was slurring his words. "A-okay. They're going to build it even if they've got to clear-cut to make a go of it." His long arm swiped an invisible tree. "Cut every maple down between here and the Wisconsin line." The loggers said they were happy to hear that, and smiled at the way Starkmann tottered when he swung his arm. They would have been less amused if they'd known he was carrying a loaded .38 revolver in his coat pocket.

After talking with the two men, he had left the tavern for the Anchor Inn, across town on the West Bay Road. His eyesight slightly blurred, he drove slowly down Front Street past the big aluminum shed that was Jensen's Hardware store, and up over the hill where the bank, with its pillared facade and thick sandstone walls, stood as a reminder of better times. Below the hill, the street curved along the bay, its waters so black tonight it looked like a chasm, then ran by the county park, filled with the trailers of hunters up for a weekend of bow- and bird-hunting. Beyond the park the street merged into West Bay Road and went past the derelict sawmill, a row of clapboard cottages, the Anchor Inn, and the Coast Guard station before ending at the jetty, at whose tip the lighthouse's revolving beam gave glimpses of the lake heaving in the gale.

Starkmann parked on a side road near the station and the beach, where the surf crashed like a battery firing for effect. The Coast Guard's forty-foot patrol boat groaned and squealed as it strained at its mooring lines and slammed its bumpers against the dock. Warning flags cracked from their staffs. Starkmann walked to the bar, a distance of about a block, the stiff wind sobering him.

Inside, he shouldered his way through drunk and half-drunk Coast Guardsmen and lumberjacks, beer-swilling bow-hunters wearing camouflage suits, and the red-faced crew of a whitefish trawler that had put into safe harbor for the night. He found a seat at the far end of the U-shaped bar, where a dead lamprey eel coiled in its tank of preservative.

He ordered an Early Times, keeping his hand in the pocket that concealed the Smith & Wesson. He tossed back the whiskey. As he had eaten little since lunch, the liquor flowed straight into his brain, fuzzing his perceptions and stirring anew the jealousy, confusion, and fear that had driven him out of the house about two hours earlier. He looked across the bar and recognized the faces of Allen and Maggie Williams, owners of the fish market.

Williams waved to him and said, "Hello, Chris," mouthing the words in the manner of people speaking to the hard-of-hearing, because it was noisy inside. Voices buzzed, a video game bleeped and squawked, and country music whined out of the jukebox.

He returned Williams's greeting with a mechanical nod, and noticed that the little man was looking at him in the same way that the customers had in the other bars. Why in the hell did everyone stare at him as if he were a freak? Had King let the secret out? Did everyone now know he'd gone crazy in the war? Did they think he was one of those killers they'd read about in the newspapers, seen in trashy movies? If that was their image of him, he now had the power to live up to it: He had sudden death in his pocket. The nightmare had put him in a violent mood—that and Bill King, and then June, whom he half-suspected of cheating on him.

His morning had been an almost exact replica of the one after the dream's last visit. He'd made coffee at the office, sat down at the map table, and immediately suffered another dizzy spell. He'd come to hate and fear the unexpected attacks of vertigo as much as the nightmare. The wooziness had gone out of his head when Shirley Peterson waddled in, Harding and King a few minutes behind her. The two men discussed the Lions game coming up on Sunday, and Starkmann, hoping his ashen pallor did not show, had tried lamely to join in.

Later, Harding had held a private conference with King in his office to discuss the preliminary reports the cruiser from Eastern District had sent in. Starkmann had caught snatches of the conversation through the door. King spoke the loudest, not, Starkmann knew, because Harding was partially deaf but because King wanted Starkmann to hear that the revised estimates were more encouraging than his. According to the Eastern District cruiser, King had said, Starkmann had undergraded by a significant margin; there was plenty of high-grade hardwood out in them thar woods. Green gold.

The cruiser, Clyde Masson, was an old company-man who had been with Great Superior many years, and who, Starkmann had realized after overhearing King's comments, was doing what his type had done over in Nam: telling the boys upstairs what they wanted to hear.

He'd considered barging into the office and confronting the procurement manager. "You'd can me if you could," Starkmann wanted to say to him, "but you can't, so this is the way you're doing it, stabbing me in the back." But he restrained himself; a blowup like that would have played right into King's hands.

In the afternoon, cruising in the solitude of the forests, he'd stewed about what he'd heard, and could not shake the foreboding that he was going to be called in and fired any day now. *Messin' with my head*, Starkmann had thought as he paced through the woods. King is definitely messin' with my head. The phrase was not one Starkmann used in his daily speech. It was, he'd realized, one of D.J. Fishburn's idioms. "This jungle messin' with my head," Fishburn would whisper on patrol. Or, complaining about the army: "The big green machine is definitely messin' with D.J.'s head." Or, upset over some injury done him by First Sergeant Malnowski: "That Polack lifer messin' with my head—you hear me, Preacher, messin' with my *mind* definitely." Unsummoned, the scrawny ghetto kid from Philadelphia, dead these thirteen years, had entered Starkmann's thoughts and partly taken control of them.

In a few moments he'd begun to carry on an imaginary conversation with his dead buddy, as though his brain had divided in two, the one half speaking in the voice of Christian Starkmann, the other in the voice of Delbert Jones Fishburn. He'd told D.J. about the dream, about his troubles with King, his fears of some impending disaster. Fishburn, or the part of Starkmann that had assumed the role of D.J., had said nothing except to repeat that phrase: "Messin' with your head, Preacher—somethin's messin' with your head, definitely." The longer the fictitious dialogue had gone on, the more vividly Starkmann saw D.J. in his mind's eye: the thin body, spare and black as an

Ethiopian's, the bloodshot eyes, as if he suffered from a perpetual hangover, the way he would look off to one side and hold up his forefinger when he said "messin' with my mind." All the while, Starkmann continued to work with his usual exactness; somehow he'd been able to pace off the chains and talleys, measure densities with his angle-gauge, and drop the plots in the right places while speaking to . . . well, a ghost. But talking to that creature of his imagination had oddly made him feel less alone and apprehensive, so much so that a sadness had crept into him when, as he came to the end of the forty, D.J. had slipped out of his mind as swiftly and inexplicably as he'd entered it.

Starkmann had driven home around four and, following his normal routine, immediately checked up on the girls. Christine was in the living room, reading a picture book. Lisa was sitting on the floor in her room, a headset clamped over her ears as she listened to music on her Japanese blast-box. She looked like a World War II radio operator. Starkmann reminded her of her promise to finish her homework before dinner. The sullen girl pretended not to hear him. He repeated himself in a louder voice.

"I don't have any," she said. "We didn't get any assignments."

"Then what are those for?" he shouted, pointing at the textbooks on her desk.

"You're not my father." Her eyes, as dark as June's, had flashed defiance. "I don't *have* to do what you tell me."

His temper blowing, he tore the earphones from her head and flung them aside.

"Get off the floor and behind that desk!" he yelled, his voice taking on the sound of his drill sergeant's. "Got that? Get to god-damned work!"

"You can't talk to me like that," Lisa cried, rising to her feet. "You just *can't.*"

"I just did. And don't get any ideas that I can't tell you what to do."

It was an unequal contest. Lisa ran up a white flag, but her lips formed an adolescent pout that was, somehow, both self-pitying and sexy. As she bent over to pick up the headset, her blouse opened, offering a glimpse of her small breasts that sent a flash of desire through Starkmann.

He'd left the room, ashamed of himself, though the desire was natural: Not a drop of his blood flowed in Lisa's veins. But if there were no biological prohibitions against its fulfillment, the social and legal ones were considerable. He was, however, skeptical about the power of external restraints to modify human conduct. The war had taught him that the unthinkable not only could be thought and the unspeakable spoken, they could be *done*. Lisa was only fourteen, but what effect might she have on him in two or three years? What if, in a moment of weakness. . . ? He evicted the thought and entered his and June's room to get his Smith & Wesson. It was kept in the closet, along with the rest of his arsenal: two side-by-side shotguns, a .243 Winchester deer rifle, and, protected by a plain leather case, his old friend the semi-automatic carbine. The revolver in the pocket of his sheepskin coat, he went outside to exercise Butternut and walk off his agitation. Holding back the image of Lisa's breasts, he worked the dog through the meadow to the birch and aspen edges, where woodcock and grouse burst from their cover, brown wings beautiful against the yellow leaves. Each time a bird flushed, he fired into the air to give Butternut the impression it had been shot and thus maintain her interest in the game. Bred for waterfowl, she was poor at hunting upland game. Chipmunks and rabbits occasionally distracted her and she'd once committed the unpardonable offense of running a deer, for which she'd received a thrashing. She retrieved well, however, and had been inexpensive to buy. A finished pointer or Brittany spaniel would have cost half as much as a new automobile. Butternut had been the best he could get with what he had, and by training her he hoped to break her bad habits.

They worked toward the tamarack swamp. Just short of it, the dog put a pair of grouse into the air. Starkmann's heart jumped at the thunder of their wings. He fired twice, as if shooting the rise, then gave the retriever a rewarding pat on her crest. "Good girl," he said. "Good girl." They returned to the house.

Lisa and Christine were setting the table when Starkmann entered the kitchen. Engaged in this domestic chore with her young half-sister, Lisa herself appeared younger, a gangly adolescent. He poured an Early Times over ice and wondered why he had become upset merely because she'd stirred a fleeting excitement in him. He was in command of himself. He wasn't going to make advances to this awkward girl, now or in the future.

With his drink and the sports page of the *Free Press*, he stretched out on the sofa, half-listening for the sound of June's Wagoneer coming up the road. A happy thought entered his mind: After nine years of marriage, he still felt a little thrill when June returned from work. He finished the paper and, pleasantly tired from his walk, was about to doze off when Christine asked: "Where's Mom, Daddy?"

"On her way home."

"She's usually home by five," Lisa said. "She always calls if she's going to be late. It's almost five-thirty."

"She'll be here."

Starkmann poured another whiskey. Half an hour later, when June still had not returned or phoned, he became concerned enough to call her office. His only answer was a recorded message, informing him that the office was closed. Refilling his glass, he telephoned Vandy's, where June sometimes had a cocktail after work with Sandy Jackson. The bartender said he had not seen either of them. By six-thirty, Starkmann was distracted and a little drunk. He rang Sandy's house. She said she'd not seen June. Was anything wrong? No, he answered, adding another splash of whiskey to stiffen the drink. He'd now begun to wonder if she'd been in an accident.

"Where do you think she is, Chris?" asked Lisa. "We're hungry."

"I'll get you something."

His lips were numb; his brain was bobbing like a boat. He looked in the fridge but couldn't find what June had planned for dinner. All he could see was a vision of June's car, overturned in a ditch somewhere between here and Marquette. He made peanut butter-and-jelly sandwiches for the girls, and one for himself to soak up the Early Times. It tasted awful on top of the whiskey. When Lisa and Christy were finished, he sent them to their room, on the pretext that it needed straightening, while he called the sheriff's police. No, the dispatcher answered, they had no record of a traffic mishap involving a Mrs. June J. Starkmann. Starkmann hung up, not entirely reassured; if she'd run into a ditch on the lightly traveled road to Marquette, the police would not yet know about it.

Another whiskey failed to calm him; if anything, it heightened his anxiety. He had a tendency to think the worst, to expect catastrophe, as if life were a jungle trail with mines and ambushes around each bend. He paced the house, waiting for the phone to ring with terrible news. Unable to bear the tension any longer, he put on his coat, the revolver in its pocket a comforting weight—firearms made him feel better in a crisis—and went out, calling to the girls that he was going to check to see what had become of their mother.

He drove through town quickly and turned onto the Marquette road, sweeping the pickup's spotlight over the culverts in a search for wreckage, twisted metal, shattered glass, a bloodstained instrument panel—the shapes and colors of the disaster he was sure awaited him. He'd gone halfway to Marquette before giving up. He pulled off to the roadside, his stomach queasy. Shouldn't have drunk so much. He turned on the radio. If June had been in a wreck, perhaps it would be on the local news. Up here, where nothing much happened, collisions were major events. The news wasn't on, only country music, songs of heartbreak and faithless love moaning over the nighttime airwaves.

He started back toward Vieux Desert, uncertain about what he should do. The disc jockey announced that the program was going to play Willie Nelson's "The Red Headed Stranger." Willie Nelson was Starkmann's favorite country singer, as Bruce Springsteen was his favorite rock star; but he'd never heard "The Red Headed Stranger" before. Harsh and mournful, Nelson's voice filled the cab of the truck:

> It was the time of the preacher when the story began,
> 'Bout the choice of a lady and the love of a man.
> He loved her so dearly, he went out of his mind,
> When she left him for someone she'd left behind.

The lyrics riveted Starkmann, drilling into the core of his consciousness. "Preacher" had been his nickname in Nam; it was as if Willie Nelson were singing directly to him, sending him a message. *When she left him for someone she'd left behind.* Ripley. The name filled his thoughts. His head felt ready to explode. What if June was cheating on him, seeing Ripley again? No, that was a crazy idea. Ripley had disappeared. But only yesterday she'd insinuated that he, Starkmann, wasn't the man he used to be. Maybe she was getting itchy and had started seeing Ripley again. *When she left him for someone she'd left behind.*

He floored the pedal and raced back into town, where he parked in front of the old Lakeland Hotel, now a shabby boarding house, and called home from an outdoor booth. Lisa answered. Had her mother phoned? Yes, she had, only a few minutes after he'd left. One of her cases had been badly hurt. Mom had to drive her to the hospital in Marquette. She'd be home soon. How had this person been hurt? Lisa didn't know.

Starkmann hung up, head reeling while the lyrics to "The Red Headed Stranger" played back in his memory:

> He found them that evening in a tavern in town
> In a quiet little out-of-the-way place.
> They smiled at each other when he walked through the door,
> And they died with the smiles on their faces.

Taking one of her cases to the hospital—that was a creative lie, if it was a lie. He didn't know; but he did know he would kill her if he caught her with a lover. He'd kill them both. Kill her? His June? Could he do that? No. Yes. Anyone is capable of anything, he thought as he watched a drunken lumberjack, hard hat askew, staggering out of Swanson's across the street.

Back in the truck, he sat with his head resting against the side window. Crazy. Crazy to think he'd kill her. He'd drunk too much. Crazy to think she was being unfaithful. She was not a frivolous woman who would risk her marriage for a fling with an ex-husband, or with anyone. He remembered the gray suit she'd worn on the day of their wedding, its somber color reflecting her knowledge that marriage was a serious business full of pain, disappointments, and responsibilities.

He had worn highly polished cowboy boots, well-pressed jeans, a white shirt beneath a western-style leather jacket: a style of dress June had laughingly described as "high-hick." The ceremony had been simple to the point of drabness, performed in the offices of a county judge. Sandy and Rick Jackson had stood as witnesses. June's mother, a tall, rigid woman who reminded Starkmann of a stern high-school principal, had been the only guest. He had not invited his parents, certain that his father would have behaved as awfully as he had at Anne's wedding, and probably worse. If Lucius had been unable to approve of Ed Jenkins, he would have condemned June. Starkmann had not been raised to marry a woman like her, but a replica of his mother or of Anne, someone refined in speech and manner, without a questionable background. He wondered, as he sat in the truck, if he'd chosen her out of love alone or if his marriage had been another act of apostasy. It occurred to him then that he was his father's son, no matter what: a part of him disapproved of June. Though her marital conduct had been beyond reproach, he had always been a little scandalized by her past and afraid that the wildness of her youth would suddenly flare up, like some childhood disease of which she'd never been totally cured. He wanted to believe she'd been late tonight because she'd had to take someone to the hospital; in fact, the greater part of him did believe it. Whatever June's other failings, she wasn't devious or a liar. He dwelled on this thought for several minutes, holding on to it as if it were an invisible talisman against the evil of jealousy. But the charm did not work as effectively as he would have liked. He got out of the truck and crossed the street into Swanson's, which was to be the first stop on his tour of the town's bars.

Now, later, in the Anchor Inn, his doubts about June growing, he was building toward a good drunk and feeling meaner and more reckless by the minute. He looked across the bar through the cigarette smoke. Briefly, his eyes met Allan Williams's. Williams continued to stare at him in a way he didn't like. That Are-You-a-Crazed-Killer look. No, I'm not, but I can be, Starkmann thought, picturing himself drawing the revolver and shooting the lights out. The vision frightened him at the same time that it made him giddy.

Under his breath he sang the refrain to "The Red Headed Stranger":

So don't boss him, don't cross him,
He's wild in his sorrow . . .

How did the rest of it go? He couldn't remember. No matter. He liked the first line. *Don't boss him, don't cross him.* Don't boss me, don't cross me, he said to himself as a loud, familiar laugh came from the back of the room. He turned and saw Sam LaChance, hulking at a corner table behind the pool table with three of his crew in plaid shirts and suspenders, hard hats cocked at rakish angles. They broke into some lumberjack tune, probably to provide local color for the crowd of city-slicker hunters, who, in their camouflage outfits, resembled out-of-shape commandos. Jerks, all of them. Don't boss me, don't cross me. He ordered another drink from Billy Treadwell, the owner and night bartender.

Treadwell had been in Nam, the 101st Airborne. He wore a screaming-eagle tattoo on one of his muscle-streaked forearms, but the tense set of his shoulders and his watchful eyes, alert for trouble, were what told you he'd been *there*. Trouble occurred fairly often at the Anchor Inn. Treadwell never had a problem handling it. After the war, he had earned extra money as a sparring partner in Kronk's gym in Detroit, his hometown. Kronk's, Treadwell had once told Starkmann, made Nam look easy. The gym was in a neighborhood so tough, Treadwell boasted, that the welcome wagon was a Patton tank and the mail had to be delivered by the Michigan National Guard. He'd come to the Upper Peninsula after he'd gotten into serious gambling trouble with the fight mob, who'd suggested that ten years of clean wilderness air would be good for his health. Starkmann liked Treadwell because he was another fugitive, and a brother. Treadwell did not mess with his head.

Starkmann took a swallow from his fresh drink.

"Strange to see you in town, Chris," Treadwell said. "An unexpected pleasure. Still workin' in the woods?"

"Sure."

Treadwell, about six one, with a freckled face and wide, sloping shoulders, was standing in front of him, his big bruised hands on the bolster, his forearms looking as thick as an ordinary man's calves.

"Sometimes I think I shouldn't have quit that—cutting pulp. This business can be real bullshit, even if the money's a lot better. Liked workin' in the woods. Better'n gettin' banged in the face by fast niggers." He pointed to his broken nose, which, in the middle of all his freckles, looked like a peeled potato in a plate full of raisins. "And I liked it better'n this. No assholes to deal with, no books to keep, no liquor salesmen showin' up with their hands out."

A customer called for a drink. Treadwell paused, gesturing that he would serve him in a moment.

"Yeah, I finish up here at two A.M., four on weekends, and feel like hell," he went on to Starkmann. "But when I worked in the woods I always felt good at the end of the day. No matter what kind of trouble I had on my mind, it didn't make any difference after I'd been in the woods."

Starkmann heard a low buzz inside his head, like the sound of a distant chain saw.

"You told me that before, Billy." Starkmann's lips were numb, his speech slurred.

"Told you what?"

"That you always felt better after you'd been in the woods."

"Don't remember saying that."

"Well, you did, a long time ago."

Treadwell's brows pulled together, his eyes meeting Starkmann's, which shifted to the deer heads poking out from the wall above the mirrored back bar.

"You feeling all right, brother?"

"Sure. Do I look sick?"

"Hurt your hand?"

"What hand?"

"The one you're keeping in your pocket."

"My hand got cold. It's cold outside."

"It's warm in here."

"My hand is cold. I'm warming it up."

The neglected customer again called for his drink.

"Be easy, brother," Treadwell said before moving off to the other end of the bar. As he poured the customer's drink, he threw a sidelong look in Starkmann's direction. Billy, too? Was Billy, a brother, going to start messing with his head?

Things were starting to blur, and the noise in the place, the jukebox, the talking, and the cracks and booms of the video game were like sandpaper on his nerves. The singing of Sam and his crew rattled him most of all. They sounded as if they were in a German beer hall as they guzzled their Mooseheads and pounded the bottles on the table in time to their song:

My name is Jon Jonson, I come from Wisconsin,
I work as a lumberjack there.
And the people I meet, when I'm out on the street,
Ask me
WHAT . . . IS . . . YOUR . . . NAME?
I say,
My name is Jon Jonson, I come from Wisconsin,
I work as a lumberjack there . . .

It was the dumbest song Starkmann had ever heard, and when he couldn't listen to it for another second, he decided to drown it out with Willie Nelson. He weaved over to the jukebox and studied the rows of lighted title selections, looking for "The Red Headed Stranger." Once he found it, he would press the button, reach behind the machine, and crank up the volume control, blasting all that Jon Jonson crap out of the sky with good ole Willie. But he could not find "The Red Headed Stranger." He could not see the selections clearly. Things were blurred. Christ, he hadn't been this drunk in years.

"Hey, Mr. Starkmann!" LaChance boomed from his table, just ten feet away. "Didn't know you was here. C'mon over and have a drink with the boys."

Starkmann looked at him, so huge he almost filled the corner of the room, a smile arching like a crescent moon in his beard-shadowed face.

"Hey there, Mr. Starkmann, I know you're a man of few words, but at least you could say hello."

"Hello."

"Ha! See that, boys?" Black Sam banged the table with his palm, hard enough to make the bottles jump. "Told you he don't never say nothin'. Ask him to say hello, and that's exactly what he says. 'Hello.' Well, hello to you, Mr. Starkmann. C'mon over and have a drink on Sam."

Starkmann accepted the invitation because, all of a sudden, it seemed important not to have LaChance at his back. As no one was shooting pool, he leaned against the pool table, his glass in his free hand.

"Grab a chair, Mr. Starkmann."

"This is fine."

"Suit yourself. What're you drinkin'?"

Starkmann told him. Sam, roaring above the general noise, called to Treadwell for another round of beers and an Early Times.

"Do I look like a waitress?" Treadwell shot back from behind the bar. "You want service, you'll have to wait for it. And I'd best see a big tip."

"You will. We been hot-loggin' all week, makin' us some money for a change." Then, lowering his voice, he asked Starkmann: "You know my boys, don't you? Armand, O'Brien, my grandson David?"

With a nod, Starkmann acknowledged that he did. The 'jacks returned his nod, all of them a little red-eyed.

"Yeah, hot-loggin' all week, goddamn, and makin' a buck, Mr. Starkmann. The Dollar Bay mill got them a big contract from them bowlin' alley people, Brunswick. The mill can't get enough maple. Folks at Brunswick take the mill-run and ship it over to Japan where them little Nips work for nothin' finishin' the wood into bowlin' alleys and then ship 'em back to the States. Imagine that, them little Japs givin' us a hand up here in Vieux Desert."

Starkmann said nothing, on edge from the noise of the video game, some sort of space-war game with a battle-star under attack by alien fighters, laser cannons exploding and the fighters vanishing in flashes when they were hit. *Bang, crash, pop, boom:* An ambush is what it sounded like, light automatic weapons and grenades.

"Once that new mill goes up, we're gonna be hot-loggin' all the time. Town'll be rich again."

"You'll be, that's for sure."

"Don't believe I heard you, Mr. Starkmann."

"When was this town ever rich?"

"One time, it was richer'n it is now. So how you doin' with them rulers of yours? Gettin' everything measured just right?"

"Sure."

LaChance leaned forward, bracing his elbows on the table, his giant fists balled under his chin. He hadn't liked that crack about getting rich.

"Ain't what I been hearin'. I've been hearin' you got a few things measured wrong. I've been hearin' your outfit got another fella cruisin' these woods, an old-timer, not one of you college boys."

"His name's Masson."

Messing with his head, that's what Sam was doing. Sam always had, and now it sounded as if he'd been talking to King. Maybe King had told him; maybe the two of them were working together to get him fired.

"Yeah. Masson. Heard he's been measurin' things and sayin' we got more high-grade around here than you've been sayin'. Your outfit, I've been hearin', says the new mill could do seven million board feet a year, goddamn, and you tellin' me a while back it might not be built. You college boys." Sam polished off the last swallow of beer in his bottle.

"You know, Mr. Starkmann, I went to work in the woods when I was fifteen, back when contract cutters had to live out in the woods. Hired out to United Lumber, Big Bill Bonifas's outfit. I met Big Bill, goddamn. He was a man, strong as a horse, and no college grad-yew-eight like you. He couldn't hardly speak no English, but he was smart, hey. Come up to the U.P. with nothin' and retired to Miami Beach in 'thirty-six with twenty-five million bucks."

The buzzing returned to Starkmann's ear, and the video game was making weird noises: electronic bleeps, gulps, and pipings mixed in with the bangs and crashes. Out of his peripheral vision he saw a bow-hunter in mottled green-and-brown dropping quarters into the jukebox. Messing with his head—everyone was messing with his head. One of his bosses was trying to fire him. His wife wasn't home, maybe cheating on him. The last thing he needed was to take crap from this Canuck loudmouth. Don't boss me, don't cross me.

"I'm sick of your crap, you Frog son of a bitch," he said drunkenly, grinning and enjoying the startled hush that fell over LaChance's table.

"*What'd* you say?"

"I said you're a Frog son of a bitch and I'm sick of your crap."

"I believe you must be real drunk, young Mr. Starkmann."

"I'm sick of your crap about the good old days and your phony lumberjacks."

O'Brien started to make a move, but Sam laid a hand on the younger logger's forearm, restraining him. Sam was cool. Sam was in control. Sam had the calm that came from being six feet seven and two-seventy, and from knowing that he'd once killed a bear with nothing more than his hands and a knife.

"Phony lumberjacks? If we ain't lumberjacks, what the hell are you?"

"An inventory clerk," answered Starkmann, feeling pretty cool and in control himself; he had the confidence of a loaded .38 in his pocket. "I count trees. I add up what's in stock."

"I'd agree with that, but I don't agree that we ain't lumberjacks. Now let's see." LaChance ran the small finger of one hand along the track of his hook-shaped scar. "We don't fix cars, so we ain't mechanics. We don't build houses, so we ain't carpenters. We go inta the woods and cut down trees and haul 'em to the mills. My way of lookin' at things, that makes us lumberjacks."

Starkmann moved off the pool table and stood, facing Sam across the five-foot width of the round drinking table.

"It makes you gardeners, yardboys," he slurred, reeling a little on his feet. "The guys who cut 'em down with axes and drove 'em down the rivers were lumberjacks, but you guys, you're yardboys."

Sam pushed himself from the table and got to his feet, looming in the corner, three feet wide at the shoulders, an unmissable target.

"Maybe you and me oughtta talk this over somewhere else, young Mr. Starkmann. I might be sixty-two, but I ain't too old to handle a college boy, goddamn."

"Nowhere else, Sam. Right here."

Starkmann's heart beat rapidly, more from excitement than fear.

"I drink here a lot," said LaChance. "I don't want to cause no trouble here. But outside, this old Frenchman's gonna give you more trouble than you can handle."

Starkmann was aware of some nearby customers shifting in their chairs, either to watch the show or to be ready to move out of the way when it started. That was good; it lessened the chance of any innocent bystanders getting hurt. He hooked his thumb over the hammer of the hidden revolver, and smiled as he imagined the shocked expression that would come over Sam's face when he drew the Smith & Wesson and pointed it at the vast chest.

"Siddown, Sam. You, too, Chris. There isn't going to be any trouble. Here or outside."

It was Treadwell with a tray of beers and Starkmann's whiskey.

"This is between me and young Mr. Starkmann. Don't concern you, Billy."

"Anything that goes on here concerns me," Treadwell said, setting down the tray, his arms, loose and relaxed, falling at his side. LaChance, who had seen the bartender in action and respected the quickness and power in Billy's fists, remained on his feet long enough to let everyone know that he wasn't backing down, then dropped into his chair.

"Hey, for you, Billy, I won't start no trouble. But as far as you go," he sneered, turning to Starkmann, "the next time you come checkin' up on my crew, you remember it's gonna be just me and you out in the woods, goddamn."

"Cork it, Sam. Why don't you two shake hands and forget it. C'mon, Chris. Shake on it."

Starkmann could not move. His body felt as rigid as when he awakened from the dream.

Treadwell clasped his upper arm and whispered into his ear, "Take your hand out of your pocket and shake."

He could not make himself let go of the revolver; neither could he draw it. Every muscle in him was frozen. Only his eyes moved, side to side, up and down. At last they fixed on the group of bow-hunters, in uniforms like the kind the reconnaissance teams had worn. Splotches of green and brown—that was all Starkmann could see clearly.

"Be easy, brother. If you don't want to shake on it, maybe you and me should go outside for a little air." Treadwell tightened his grip on Starkmann's arm and tried to turn him to walk him out the door, but it was like trying to turn a statue cemented to the ground.

"Think you got one real drunk college boy on your hands, Billy."

LaChance's voice sounded far off, so distant it was nearly inaudible over the racket of the video game, which grew louder by the moment, duplicating the thud of grenades, the tapping of machine guns. Soon, that was the only thing Starkmann could hear, a noise that made his skin crawl. Then his ears caught another sound, one that, more than any other, brought everything back, ramming his conscious mind into his memory so that the distinction between remembered experience and immediate event grew blurred. The sound was coming from the jukebox, playing that Billy Joel song "Goodnight Saigon." A snare drum was imitating the rhythmic whisper of helicopter rotors in the distance, the whisper swelling in volume until it became a noise as of someone loudly and rapidly tapping his fingertips on a thick pad of paper. For an instant the bar transformed itself into the inside of a helicopter, the faces of LaChance and the others into those of D.J., Ramos, Hutchinson, and someone else—another man whose features were hidden in the darkness at the rear of the aircraft. The jukebox was in the helicopter; the helicopter was plunging into a hot landing zone. He heard his voice and the voices of his buddies singing along to the refrain of "Goodnight Saigon." The swift descent of the chopper wrung the song from their throats, in the way that the downhill run of a roller coaster forces its riders to scream. It was a hymn of terror, defiance, and brotherhood:

And we would all go down together!
We said we'd all go down together!
Yes, we would all go down together!

*   *   *

The helicopter tipped to one side, then the other, and suddenly became the inside of the bar again. The room tipped to one side, then to the other. Nausea choked him. Jesus, not now, not one of those vertigo attacks now! He looked for something to hold on to, and fell backward, his skull bouncing against the floor. He saw a white flash.

The line demarcating the remembered from the immediate vanishes altogether.

Starkmann is lying in the burned woods, covered in ashes. It is four days after the attack. He is lying alone in the woods, because an inner voice had commanded him to. It commanded him to desert his post, take off his helmet and flak jacket, remove his cartridge belt with its magazine pouches and bayonet, lay down his rifle, and walk off into the woods where the stripped trees looked like blackened spears. He walked until he came to a shallow ravine and obeying the voice only he could hear, knelt, scooped up the ashes of the earth, and poured them over his head. He rubbed them into his face and into his arms and hands until he looked almost as black as D.J. Then he lay on his back, his arms outspread and legs forked.

He lies in that position until D.J., Hutch, and Ramos come up to him. They have come after him because they saw him leaving the perimeter unprotected and unarmed.

"Preacher, what you doin'?" D.J. asks, his small dark face pinched into an incredulous expression. "What *is this?*"

He attempts to answer, but his mouth won't open; he tries to gesture, but cannot move a muscle. *They have mouths, but they speak not*, Starkmann thinks as he lies in the ashes. Psalm 115. *They have hands, but they handle not: feet have they, but they walk not: neither speak they through their throat.*

"Preach, you hearin' me?" says D.J., kneeling beside him. "What you doin'?"

"Yeah, what da fock is dis?" he hears Ramos interject. "You stoned, man? You been smokin' some bad shit or what?"

"He ain't stoned. The Preacher don't smoke—you know that, you dumb greaser. Hey, Hutch," D.J. says to the medic, "you the doctor, you the medical *expert* in this outfit. What's wrong with him?"

"Hell if I know," Hutchinson replies; then, squatting next to D.J., he asks Starkmann: "Can you talk, Chris? What's going on? You're outside the wire, brother, without your piece or flak jacket. Chris?"

He battles to respond, but the tyrannical voice within his mind decrees that he lie without moving or speaking.

"We're going to have to carry him back to the perimeter," Hutch declares. "Whatever's going on, it ain't no job for a medic. C'mon."

They lift him up, Hutchinson and D.J. holding him by the arms, the powerfully built Ramos by the legs, but this proves an unworkable arrangement; Starkmann sways in the middle so that his buttocks scrape the ground.

"The dude's too *long*," D.J. complains, puffing.

"I'll get his arms, hold him around the waist," Hutch orders. "C'mon, let's get the hell out of here."

In that way they carry him through the woods, Starkmann's body now rigid as a pipe. Above, the tips of the scorched trees point toward the sky, a sky as cool and blue as water. Water. Starkmann feels parched. Water. Words form in his head, then on his lips: "Water . . . Saved me . . . Fire, killed with fire."

"Hey, he said somethin'!" exclaims D.J. "Preach is talkin'! What'd you say, Preacher?"

"He didn't say shit," Ramos declares. "Can't you dig it, man? Preacher's crazy. *Loco*, y'know."

A helicopter is soon hovering overhead, its rotor wash raising clouds of dust as it lands. D.J., Hutch, and Ramos shift Starkmann onto a stretcher. *Water . . . Saved me . . . Fire, killed with fire.* "The fire," he mumbles as his three comrades lift the stretcher and slide it into the chopper. Hutch, who is a medic, is shouting into a radio: "Roger, roger, Raven One. He's aboard, dust him off, get him out of here!" The helicopter rises. Starkmann feels weightless and, in the wind buffeting through the open hatches, sees the ashes on his flesh peeling away, blowing out of the hatch, falling earthward in dark flurries, flakes of cindered snow.

There was no transition between unconsciousness and consciousness, past and present. Starkmann came to, aware that he was lying on the floor of the Anchor Inn. He heard Billy Treadwell ask, "What did he say?"

"I didn't quite get it," a strange voice answered. "Something about a fire. Putting water on a fire—something about a dust-off."

Starkmann, the taste of vomit souring his mouth, remained on the floor, staring at the ceiling fan as it whirled against the smoke.

"You all right, Chris?" Treadwell asked. "Man, you went down like a guy hit with a sneak left hook."

Starkmann nodded to signal that he was okay, then propped himself on his elbows. The back of his head ached.

"Told you he was one drunk college boy," LaChance said. Starkmann could not see LaChance, only Treadwell standing next to a man he did not recognize.

"Back in the land of the living, Chris? Brother, you must have been ripped to the tits when you walked in here to go down like that."

With the other man's help, Treadwell hoisted him to his feet. His legs were shaky. Treadwell draped one of Starkmann's arms across his shoulders. The other man, who was too short to do this, held him around the waist. The stranger was one of the bow-hunters, dressed in camouflage. He had moderately long hair, the ends of which curled out from under the back of his hunting cap. He and Treadwell walked Starkmann out of the bar like trainers helping an injured ballplayer off the field.

Outside, the air helped to revive him. Air. Air and wind. The front had passed, the clouds had blown away, and with the clearing of the sky, the true cold had set in, arctic and penetrating. Starkmann took several deep breaths and spat to purge the salty taste from his mouth. Northward, above the black seam between the sky and the lake, the aurora glittered a boreal green.

"You sure do a good job of pretending you're not drunk," Treadwell said, shivering in his shirtsleeves. "Thought you were sober when you came in. Or did a couple of whiskeys do that to you?"

"I don't think it was just the whiskey," the short man said, blowing into his hands.

"Who're you?"

"Eckhardt," the man said cordially. "Dr. Jim Eckhardt. Not the medical type. A Ph.D."

"You an expert on drunks?"

"No, not on drunks."

"I am."

Treadwell turned from Eckhardt to Starkmann.

"I'll ask you straight, Chris, you answer me straight. What's in your pocket?"

Starkmann hesitated a beat, worried that he'd be arrested for carrying a concealed weapon. He did not understand what had happened to him. He'd blacked out, and then had gone on another journey backward in time, but to a different destination from the usual one. He'd gone back to the day he'd cracked up. Now, to his fear of arrest was added the fear that he'd said something while unconscious, let out the secret of his breakdown. He began to shake all over. The next thing he knew, he was doubled over at the curbside, vomiting.

"You're in some great shape," Treadwell said, laying an arm across his back. "Hey, *Doctor* Eckhardt, if it isn't whiskey making him puke like this, what is it? The flu?"

"Was this guy in Nam?"

"He doesn't like anybody to know about it."

"It's not something you advertise. I was over there."

"So was I."

"Yeah. I can see the tattoo. Hundred-and-First Airborne. I was with the Third Marines."

"So what is this? A meeting of the Veterans of Foreign Wars?"

"I was just wondering if he'd been over there," the man called Eckhardt said, his voice that of a salesman speaking to a difficult customer. "I heard him say something about a dust-off when he was out."

Dust-off was military slang for a medical evacuation by helicopter.

"I don't care what he said. I'm freezing my ass off." Treadwell, while Starkmann was still doubled over, dry-heaving, deftly slipped his hand into the pocket of the sheepskin and pulled out the revolver. "I'm freezing my ass off and I've got a stone drunk on my hands with a loaded gun on him."

"Christ," said Eckhardt.

Starkmann straightened up, too weak to do or say anything in his defense, and watched Treadwell flip open the chamber, empty the shells into his hand, and put them in his shirt pocket.

"Guns and drunks don't mix," Treadwell said, placing the weapon back in Starkmann's coat. "I'm not going to ask you what you had in mind, Chris, and I'm not telling anyone about this, but I am telling you that I've got to eighty-six you from the Anchor Inn. Sorry, brother, but I'm not running a Wild West saloon. No hard feelings, okay?"

"Okay." Starkmann wiped his lips, relieved. Jesus, would he have drawn the gun on LaChance? What had gotten into him? Would he have pulled the trigger?

"Good enough," Treadwell said. "Dr. Eckhardt, thanks for your help. Next round is on the house. I've got a bar to tend and I have to figure out some way to get my friend home."

"My truck's by the station. I can make it all right."

"The hell, Chris. You're a living example of why I carry dram-shop insurance. I don't want you killing yourself or somebody else on the road. What's your number? I'll call June and ask her to pick you up."

He watched the plumes of Treadwell's breath exploding into the air. June! He couldn't let June know about this. His June. He didn't care where she'd gone tonight, what she'd done. All he wanted now was to go home and fall into her arms. He felt as fragile as a shattered mirror still in its frame; but June would make him whole again.

"Hey, Chris, answer me. You've got a phone out there, don't you?"

"Don't call June. . . ."

"I understand. I'd drive you back, brother, but I haven't got anyone to watch the place for me."

"I can take him," Eckhardt offered. "My car's just around the corner."

"He lives a ways out of town. Eight, ten miles."

"No sweat. I could have guessed that," Eckhardt said. "It fits the profile."

15

When she pulled into the garage and saw that Chris's truck was missing, June climbed out of her Wagoneer, flung the door shut, and covered the ten yards to the house in about five strides. As soon as she was inside, she took the stairs two at a time to make sure the girls were all right. They were overjoyed to see her. Even Lisa exclaimed, "Mom!"—which made June almost happy that Chris had taken off, it was so unusual to feel wanted and needed by the girl. But Christine, frightened by the bangs and moans of the wind, had hidden in the closet when she'd heard the front door slam shut, not knowing it was her mother.

"She's such a wimp," Lisa said haughtily, sitting on her bed with her schoolbooks.

"You don't look so brave yourself," June chided, then hugged them both and told them not to worry anymore, Mama was home.

Lisa, folding her legs, asked in anticipation of a good story what had happened to the woman June had brought to the hospital.

"Later. You won't believe it."

"Mom, what's that *stuff* on your jeans?"

"Mud, Lisa. It's mud," June answered, striding out of the room and back downstairs, where she tore off her quilted jacket and tossed it on the couch. *Goddamn him*, she thought. Leaving two young girls out here by themselves.

She picked up the phone and called Swanson's, asking if Chris was there. No, he wasn't. He'd been there a while ago—had a few drinks and left. No, he hadn't said where to. June didn't know the numbers to the other bars; she went into the kitchen, where the phone book was kept, and saw that Lisa hadn't cleaned up after dinner; she'd left the dirty plates on the table, the ceramic dish in which she'd reheated the *pâté chinois* on the counter. The mess, though minor, almost drove her over the edge.

"Lisa! Get down here and clean this kitchen!"

Lisa responded that she was finishing her homework. June shouted back that she didn't care, she was to clean up immediately. Lisa, restored to her normal sullenness by her mother's tone, slumped downstairs into the kitchen, muttering something to the effect that one parent yelled at her for not doing her homework; now the other was yelling because she was. She started the dishes, pokey as a discontented maid, while June called the East Bay Tavern. The line was busy. Then she phoned Pedersen's Resort, from whom she got the same story she'd gotten from Swanson's. She resisted the impulse to ask if Chris had been with anybody; that would have really put the small-town gossip mill into high gear. Her calling like this had, no doubt, started tongues wagging already. *June and Chris are having troubles—she was calling all over town for him the other night.*

Lisa, in the meantime, had managed to wash only one dish. June flared at her again and sent her back to her room.

She finished the dishes herself and then, to keep occupied, swept the kitchen floor. When that was done she paced from the kitchen, through the combined living and dining room and back again, rubbing her arms against the cold. The oil stove was turned to low. She turned it up, then went out into the windy night, took an armload of split logs from the woodpile, returned to the house, and stacked them in the fireplace. Soon she had a fire going. She squatted in front of it, warming her hands and waiting for the sound of Chris's truck or the flash of headlights coming up the road. Once, she stood by the front door, gazing into the darkness, as if this act would hasten his return. When that failed, she resumed her pacing, digging her boot heels into the pine floors. The monotonous throb of the generator outside irritated her. Everything in the house began to irritate her, especially the furniture, most of it the secondhand junk she'd bought for her bachelorette apartment in Marquette. She'd wanted to get rid of it for a long time. The trouble was, she and Chris didn't have the money to buy anything to replace it, despite their dual income. There were the payments on the house, on the Wagoneer, and on the forty acres. The forty acres—that's what did it. If they didn't have that burden, they could afford new furniture, but no, Chris had to have his own forest. Chris the land baron did not want any neighbors crowding him. What did he think would have happened if he hadn't bought the acreage? Was some developer going to build condos or a subdivision on it? The land had been derelict for decades, centuries probably, going back to the Indians.

She returned to the kitchen, opened the cabinet where the liquor was kept, and poured a scotch. With her glass in her hand she climbed the stairs to the bathroom and began to fill the tub. A hot bath was what she needed. The well-water smelled of iron and sulphur, as if it were being piped up straight from hell. She yanked off her boots and shimmied out of her jeans. About to drop them in the clothes hamper, she rolled them into a tight ball instead and tossed them in a corner. She'd decided to throw them out; the taint in them was not the kind that could be removed with laundry powder. She could not overcome the shame she felt about killing the bear, although when she thought sensibly about what she'd done, it seemed pretty brave, nothing to be ashamed of. Maybe she could even consider herself a heroine, though she had no desire to be known as one. At the hospital, one of the doctors had said that the Department of Natural Resources would have to be notified of the bear attack so that game wardens could be sent to track down the animal and kill it. June quickly told them that it had been killed by Mrs. Hermanson's sons, and she later asked Freya to support her in this lie. Bear attacks always made the newspapers, and the last thing she wanted to see was the real story printed in the Marquette *Mining Journal* or—who could say?—in the *Free Press*. She'd never hear the end of it from the men in her office and in the state's attorney's office. It would only enhance her Amazonian image. June the bear-slayer.

The tub filled, she eased herself in. Within minutes the hot water had begun to soothe her nerves, to massage her tense muscles and loosen the tautness in her spine. She luxuriated in the bath, sipping her scotch, but each time the wind made a sound, her heart would jump happily because she thought it was Chris. The girls, as accustomed as she to his punctual habits, were also anxious. Christy called to her from across the hall, asking when Daddy would be home.

"Pretty soon," June answered, trying to keep the sharpness out of her voice.

"Where is he?" asked Lisa. "It's past eleven."

"He's probably out having a few drinks. Every man should be entitled to get drunk once in a while. Every woman, too, as far as I'm concerned."

"You never go out and get drunk, Mom."

"I might just start."

"Something's the matter with Chris, or between you and Chris, isn't there? He looked a little drunk when he left tonight."

"The only thing the matter is that I'm trying to take a bath in peace and quiet and you keep pestering me. That's what's the matter."

"Cheeze," Lisa said in her most persecuted tone. "Sorry for asking."

June told herself that she was not responding to any of this at all well. Her private monsters, old fears and insecurities, had begun to creep out of their hiding places. Loneliness was her greatest fear, loneliness and the blues; not the bittersweet loneliness that came at the end of an affair you wanted to end anyway, but the bone-deep aloneness that followed desertion or divorce, the solitude that could start you shivering at high noon in August; not the blues sung by piano-bar crooners, who always sounded as if they were enjoying their melancholy, but the howling heartbreak blues, which could strike anyone but which only blacks could sing authentically, wailing about empty beds, empty houses, and the sense of internal collapse that hit you when the sun went down; the shrieking-in-your-guts blues, out of whose depths some women clutched for any man who came along, some for a glass, a needle, or a line, and others for a bottle of pills. Those were the kind of blues that had rolled over her like a late-night express about three days after the front door had closed behind Ripley. That was what she feared most of all.

She feared it, not because she didn't think she could survive it again but because she knew she would. She also knew *how* she would: the same way she'd survived it after Ripley. She was the clutch-for-any-man type, any and all: Just stay with me till I'm asleep, baby; then you can go if you want to or have to. That was the kind of woman she would become if Chris ever left her, and that life eventually created its own kind of emptiness. Maybe it was a better cure than drugs, booze, or pills, but it wasn't the best way. Hell, it was doing what Freya planned to do without charging for it.

Freya. Maybe she ought to think about Freya to take her mind off herself. Freya—what a lovely northern name. The hospital had agreed to allow her to stay with her mother overnight. June had left the hospital, hoping Edith's injuries would frustrate the girl's first venture into a life of lay-for-pay. Probably they would, but only for the time-being. Freya, though pretty and smart, was another loser, determined to throw away her best cards. She shouldn't have taken such a personal interest in the girl, especially to the point of almost striking her. She could stay on the trail of Freya's father and make sure the checks arrived on time, but she could not save the girl from herself. Only Freya could, and June didn't see much chance of that happening. The way she felt now, she didn't see a whole lot of salvation for anyone.

16

Eckhardt was as talkative as he was affable. He'd begun talking almost from the moment he and Starkmann got into his car, the words tumbling from his lips in the genial salesman's tone that appeared to be his habitual mode of speech. He wasn't, however, a salesman; he was a clinical psychologist, practicing in Ironwood as a volunteer counselor with something called the Outreach Program, which was affiliated with the Veterans Administration.

"Affiliated, understand me. Not strictly a part of, but affiliated, Chris. Is it okay if I call you Chris?"

"Sure."

"You can call me Jim."

That also was okay with Starkmann. Now they were Chris and Jim.

"What I mean, Chris, is that we're not part of the V.A. bureaucracy." Eckhardt took one hand off the wheel and held it up, palm forward, as if he were giving testimony under oath. "We know how a lot of you guys feel about the V.A., and we don't blame you. A lot of us feel the same way."

The remark mystified Starkmann. What guys? And how was he supposed to feel about the Veterans Administration? He didn't feel one way or the other about it. It was like the Bureau of Labor Statistics or the Department of Health, Education and Welfare. He opened the window, spit out the putrid residue in his mouth, and said: "Turn left here."

Eckhardt turned and drove slowly up Hunter's Hill. His car was a new Subaru, four-wheel drive, so Starkmann assumed that the sluggish pace had nothing to do with the condition of the automobile; apparently Eckhardt wanted to prolong the ride to give himself more time to talk. He seemed eager to establish his credentials as a combat veteran and, despite the "Dr." prefixing his name, as an ordinary guy. He said he'd been raised in a blue-collar neighborhood in Pontiac, where his father worked on the line for Chrysler. He himself had been a delinquent and high-school dropout before he'd joined the marines, who sent him to Vietnam back in 'sixty-five. The war and the marines had given him "religion." After his discharge he returned to school and, by age twenty-eight, had his doctorate in psychology. Now he was applying his skills and education to helping war veterans with emotional problems.

Starkmann sat tightly against the door, tightly enough to feel the revolver jabbing him in the side. He was also vaguely nervous about Eckhardt's profession, wary of the short man's friendly garrulousness; it was as if, with all those words and all that sincerity, he was trying to lull his passenger into a false sense of security. Starkmann wasn't sure if he'd said anything compromising after he'd lost consciousness, but knew the psychologist had to be curious about why he'd been carrying a weapon. Perhaps, now, Eckhardt was trying to trick him into confessing that he'd come close to shooting a man tonight. Starkmann remembered that there was a big V.A. hospital in Ironwood. Did the small blond man have the authority to bring him in for an examination? He would leap out of the car and live like an animal in the woods before he again submitted to the humiliations he'd suffered in the hospital in Nam. Injections, pills, babbling maniacs for bunkmates, creeps asking him how he felt about his mother and how many times he'd masturbated at night when he was a kid. Goddammit, why hadn't Treadwell kept his mouth shut?

"Who were you with over there, Chris?"

"Bravo Company. First of the Seventy-seventh," he replied, surprised at how easily he volunteered this information. Eckhardt somehow or other had put him at ease, made him feel dangerously comfortable. That's why Billy had opened his mouth. This little runt could make you talk even when you didn't want to.

"Light infantry, huh? You guys got moved around a lot."

"That's why we were light infantry."

"Where were you mostly?"

"Seven Mountains area. Near Cambodia."

"When was that?"

" 'Sixty-nine, 'seventy."

"What'd you do?"

"Whatever I was told. What do you want next? Rank and serial number?"

"Hey, take it easy. Just rapping—you know, one ex-grunt to another."

They had descended the hill by this time and were on the straightaway, but Eckhardt was not driving much faster than he had going up the hill, thirty miles an hour at most. Sensing that he had touched a nerve in Starkmann, he fell silent for a few seconds, then changed the subject to bow-hunting. He loved bow-hunting; it required more strength, skill, and, if it was bear you were after, more nerve than hunting with a rifle. He also loved to fish. Bass, pike, trout—it didn't make any difference. Hunting and fishing were among the reasons he'd taken the counseling job in Ironwood. You couldn't beat the Upper Peninsula when it came to hunting and fishing; it wasn't like the woods in Wisconsin or the Lower Peninsula, but wild country, real bush.

"You must know what I mean, Chris. You live here. Look at these woods tonight. Spooky, huh? You get a feeling of their power. I'll bet it doesn't look much different than when those Indians were here, the Chippewas. A night like tonight, you can almost see 'em, like they're still here."

"They are still here. I live next to a reservation. Ojibwa."

"How's that again?"

"Ah-jib-away," he enunciated. "Chippewa is a corruption. Ojibwa means 'puckered moccasin.' It comes from a type of moccasin they used to wear."

"Where'd you pick that up?"

"Somewhere. How come you're driving so slow?"

"I'll speed up if you want."

"That's okay."

Starkmann, still sitting snug against the door, one hand resting lightly on the handle, had decided the snail's pace would work to his advantage in case he had to jump out and make an escape. It would also give him time, before he saw June, to piece together what had happened to him tonight, to make sense of it and master it. His flesh prickled when he thought about what he'd almost done. The blackout also frightened and perplexed him. He could swear he actually had experienced that moment when he was evacuated, just as he actually experienced the attack in his nightmare. As if some part of him had been in another dimension where terms such as *past* and *present* had no meaning. As crazy as it sounded, there seemed no other way to account for the clarity with which he had seen and heard things, the *bop-bop-bop* of the helicopter, the voices of his friends, the sharpness of the smells, the precise reproduction of the sequence of events.

He'd become so absorbed in his reflections that he didn't realize they'd passed the crossroads until he saw the sign marking the border of the reservation and heard Eckhardt ask: "This the reservation you were talking about?"

"Where're you going?"

"I'm driving you home."

In Starkmann's eyes, the dim glow of the panel lights gave a somewhat diabolical cast to Eckhardt's face.

"Why didn't you turn off? The turnoff's back there."

"You didn't tell me to turn off."

"Turn around."

Eckhardt made a U-turn and headed back in the direction from which they'd come. Starkmann opened the door as soon as he saw the crossroads.

"Wait till I stop, for Chrissake," Eckhardt said, braking at the shoulder of the highway. "If you're in such a hurry, I can drive you to your house."

"I'll walk. It isn't far."

"Good enough. Nice talking to you, Chris."

With a smile, he extended his hand, but Starkmann was already out of the car and about to start up the gravel road.

"You're welcome for the ride," Eckhardt called from behind him. Starkmann turned and saw that the psychologist's lips were still bent by a smile, a knowing, deceptively friendly smile, reminiscent of the deceitful grin of the man in the maroon Plymouth.

"What?"

"You're welcome."

"Oh, yeah. Sorry. Thanks for the ride."

Through the open door, Starkmann gave him a quick hand-shake. Eckhardt's hand felt small and soft in his.

"Here," the psychologist said, holding out a business card. "Give me a call sometime—you know, if you feel the need to rap with a brother."

Starkmann hesitated.

"Hey! It's only a business card."

He took the card and folded it into his coat pocket without looking at it. Then, as Eckhardt drove off, he hiked up the road, stretching his legs in long strides to put distance between himself and the highway. He did not slow his pace until the sound of the car faded into silence.

He had to hand it to Eckhardt. The little man was a sharp one, with his glib, easy manner. Without any effort at all he'd gotten

Starkmann to disclose the name of his unit, when he'd served, and where. Given time, he might have compelled him to admit that, yes, he'd almost shot a man tonight, and yes, he'd been hospitalized once—acute depressive reaction, they'd called it. It hadn't lasted long, thanks to heavy doses of Amitriptyline, but his heart froze at the thought of divulging such information to a man with Eckhardt's credentials. It seemed an odd coincidence that the short blond man just happened to be in the same bar tonight. He'd been too eager to drive Starkmann home, had asked too many questions. Maybe Eckhardt had been hired by King to check up on him. That made sense. King could then go to the regional office and not only tell Furman what he knew, but also present supporting evidence from an expert, a clinical psychologist for the Veterans Administration. "This guy is not only falling down on the job for us," King would say, "but take a look at this: He cracked up in the war. He's a nut case, probably from smokin' that dope they had over there. We'd better get rid of him."

Starkmann tripped on a rock lying in the middle of the road and kicked it as hard as he could. Startled by the noise, a coon or fox thrashed off into the woods. He picked up the rock and winged it in the direction of the animal. King. He had to stop thinking about him, and about Eckhardt as well.

To imagine a conspiracy between the two men was crazy, as crazy as imagining that his dreams were a form of time-travel. He cautioned himself against allowing his mind to run in overdrive. He would see June in a few minutes, and he had to appear calm. His big, beautiful June. She must never know or suspect the thing he'd come within a hair's breadth of doing tonight.

He continued up the road, the north wind cracking his face. Soon he heard the river, its bump and tumble mixing with the roar of the wind through the trees. He would tell her that he had gone into town to tie one on, like any other woodsman on a Friday night. She would forgive him. Then they would make love. He would show her he was still the man he used to be, and she would restore him. He would be all one piece again.

When he reached the bridge, he sidestepped down the ravine, squatted, dipped his hands into the river, and splashed the freezing water onto his face, once, twice, three times. It was so cold it made his cheekbones ache, and the sound of the river took him back to a day in his thirteenth year, when his father was teaching him to double-haul with a flyrod. They were fishing the Ontonagon below Agate Falls.

"What you do, son," Lucius said, "is tug on the line with your left hand when you make the back-cast, then follow it back. Then, when you snap for the forward cast, give it another pull and let it go. That's what shoots the line. Like this."

He demonstrated, his movements as effortless as a trained athlete's. Leader and fly, looped tightly back over the line, hissed through the air, straightened, and dropped delicately into the water seventy-five or eighty feet downstream.

"It's all a matter of timing, Christian. Now you give it a try. Remember to strip off enough line. It's the weight of the line that moves the fly."

He handed the rod to Christian, who made a mess of his first attempt. Mistiming his forward cast, he whipped the fly into the back of his father's neck. Lucius yanked the tiny hook out of his flesh.

"You're supposed to hook the fish, not me," he laughed. "Okay. Try again. I know it's hard. It's a little like trying to pat yourself on the head and rub your tummy at the same time. But I know you'll get it."

Christian made another attempt and another mess.

"You'll get it. Keep trying. Wait till the back-cast is all the way back before you come forward."

Lucius had been so patient then, Starkmann recalled. He could be patient, even affectionate and attentive when he was out fishing the wild streams. Perhaps the release from his pastoral duties, family obligations, and political obsessions allowed a kinder, warmer side of his nature to manifest itself.

Starkmann stopped thinking about his father as other, less pleasant memories about the man began to filter into his consciousness. He could not allow himself to dwell on those, any more than he could on King and Eckhardt.

He rinsed out his mouth to sweeten his breath, and scrubbed the stains from the front of his sheepskin. The waters of the Big Firedog made him feel much better, more clearheaded. He was only a woodsman, coming home after a drunken Friday night. He might have gone a little crazy, but he wasn't anymore, and he would not permit himself to go crazy again. The prevention of madness was a matter of will, of watching yourself, being careful. Look at Harding, with his condition. Every day he lived with the knowledge that instant death lurked inside his chest, but he watched himself, didn't push himself past his limits, and stayed alive. Starkmann would do likewise to stay sane, because the brain was an organ, like the heart. If it was faulty, all you had to do was take care of yourself. Everything is going to be all right, Starkmann told himself.

An owl in a wind-shaken tree offered a derisive hoot.

"Hoo, yourself," Starkmann said, feeling lighter hearted. Everything would turn out all right after all. He drew the revolver from his pocket, aimed it at the tree in which the owl perched, and pulled the trigger.

"Hoo-hoo," he called as the hammer fell with click.

Junc had just finished drying herself when she heard Butternut's bark, then the front door open, and Chris announce that he was home. His voice sounded odd, warmer than normal, but with a forced, false warmth—the voice of a husband doing a bad job of trying to sound not guilty. Naked, she stood in the warmth of the space-heater, rapidly debating how she should greet him: Should she be accusatory or indifferent? But even as her mind was sorting through these options, her heart impelled her to dash into the bedroom, slip on the pair of midnight-blue panties he thought were sexy, and arrange her hair so it fell in two jet-black lengths over her breasts— which, she suddenly feared, had begun to sag, to look bovine. Down the hallway she heard him and the girls speaking briefly together. Dammit, the kids were still awake. Then he came into the room, and it gave her a rush to see him and to know he was back. Bye-bye, blues. He looked a little wild, his hair tousled by the wind, his face wind-reddened, his eyes wild-looking, too—glittering, kind of, but with what or from what, she couldn't tell. He reminded her of the day she'd first seen him, the Viking god, and this impression had the same effect on her as it had then; but a new element entered her attraction. His rupture of his habitual routine, which had had her so upset minutes ago, revealed a streak of unpredictability in his nature that now excited her. She couldn't understand it; she thought she hated unpredictability in men. Neither could she understand why his tangled hair and untamed eyes pierced her with a thin blade of fear, nor why this keen sensation heightened her desire for him. She neverthe- less kept herself under control and asked him where he had been. There was no bitchy bite to the question, nor even expectation of an answer. She'd asked it more or less by rote, out of a sense of obligation to her womanly self-respect.

"Looking for you," he answered, pulling off his sheepskin coat and shutting the door, his eyes never leaving her—which was another strange thing, because his eyes hardly ever stayed in one place longer than a few seconds. "Where did you think I was?"

"I didn't know."

He draped his coat on the chair by the dresser and switched off the light. The bathroom light was still on, casting a half-glow into the bedroom that coppered June's olive skin. "I didn't know where you were, either," he said.

"One of my cases was hurt. I had to drive her to the hospital. I called, but you'd already left."

"Lisa told me. It doesn't make any difference." He peeled off his shirt and threw it on the chair, atop his coat. "Everything is going to be all right now."

She was trying to figure out what he meant by that, but the sight of his lean torso, his muscles twisting like vines under his skin, bemused her. Still, she was determined not to let him off until she'd heard an explanation; nor was she going to surrender easily, not to him or to her own lust.

"Were you with anyone tonight? Should I check for lipstick on your collar, or whatever a wife does when her old man comes in at midnight?"

"I just tied one on, that's all. Like any other woodsman on a Friday night."

Like any other woodsman on a Friday night? What kind of talk was that? He must have drunk a lot; even from a few feet away she caught the whiskey-stench of his breath.

"I don't think it was right, Chris . . ." she began, but he had stripped below the waist. God, he was a beautiful man, standing naked before her. ". . . leaving the girls here alone. It wasn't right."

He embraced her—seized her, really—pressing her to him so tightly that her bruised shoulder ached. He kissed her no less violently, a devouring kiss, his tongue in her mouth, lunging for her throat. She pulled her lips away and pushed his shoulders back in token resistance. She wanted him to know that she wasn't some bimbo who could be left sitting home alone while he wandered the bars, and who would then compliantly fall on her back and spread her legs when he decided to come home.

"Ah, June. June. I love you, June. June Josette."

He kissed her again. His hands dug under the waistband of her panties, clutched her buttocks, and parted her legs; and when his finger penetrated her, she stood on tiptoe, pressing her crotch against his. But his kisses scared her, almost smothering her with their animal urgency. She had never seen him this abandoned; more than abandoned—desperate. Something was the matter. She wanted to free herself from his arm and ask what it was, but her will was gone, obliterated by her own urgent longings. He ripped her panties off, reached down to hold her by the backs of her thighs, and lifted her up off the floor, she clamping her legs around his waist, the two of them falling on the bed. They had not made love for such a long time, his entering of her went through her like an electric shock. She didn't care any longer if he was drunk; his intoxication intoxicated her. She drank in the smell of her arousal, as Chris raised himself on his arms, dipping his head to suck her breasts, then, shuddering, erupted into her. She arched under him, moaning, and threw her head back, her hair falling over the edge of the bed.

Afterward, they lay on their sides, her leg over his narrow hips. She had started to talk, curious about what had lit this fire in him, but he stilled her with more kisses—kisses on her lips, her shoulders, her belly, whispering her name and assuring her over and over that everything was going to be all right. She stroked his cock, slick with her dampness, and he entered her again, making love to her side-by-side, as furiously as he had the first time. By the fourth or fifth time, she was bent over the bed, her knees on the hard pine floor, Chris's hand around her ribs as he thrust into her from behind, like the bear-god. *June, June, June.* Hearing her name so constantly on his lips brought small cries of happiness from hers. It was like an incantation, a prayer in this rite that was theirs together. His thrusts grew more rapid, harder. The rhythm of their movements, the hoarse chanting of her name, the scent of their love on the sheets, acted on her like a drug. She felt limp, dreamy, floating free of her body. It was as if her body, like his, had only been an instrument in this ritual, through which their souls were released to dance in the true marriage of the spirit.

He burst again in hot spasms, but June, in a delirium, hardly made a sound.

She did not come to her senses until some time later, after Chris had fallen asleep. She lay awake, looking at him and tenderly smoothing the tangles in his hair. She ought to have been exhausted, and yet she could not sleep. She should have been satisfied, reassured that he loved her and would not leave her. She was all those things, but now that it was over, the lovemaking that had so inflamed her made her a little uneasy. Had she been loved, or merely used? The way he had embraced her the first time, those consuming kisses, and the violence with which he'd entered her suggested a hunger for something more than her alone, a desperation that made her doubt that everything was "all right." What had he meant by that? What had changed?

She pulled the blankets over her and turned onto her side, looking at the window rattling in the wind. After dozing fitfully, she woke up sometime before dawn out of a dream that fled her mind the moment she opened her eyes. The wind was still blowing. Clouds had moved in again, and she saw, tumbling past the window, the flakes of the year's first snow.

17

The long white settled in. In late October and early November, the snow lay over the woods like a pale dust continuously blown clear by the autumn gales. The maple, birch, and aspen surrendered their leaves to the high winds and cold, giving Chris several fine days of bird shooting. Their natural cover gone, the grouse and woodcock were easier to bring down, although the tiny woodcock, with those abrupt dips they made in midflight, challenged even the most experienced wing-shots. June, who went along on a couple of trips just to be alone with Chris, missed them every time; but she'd downed three or four grouse with the twelve-gauge. Whenever she made a good shot Chris would congratulate her, and Butternut would seem to nod in approval after retrieving the birds; but she took little pleasure in killing them. She had never been an enthusiastic huntress, and was even less so this season. Each time she fired the shotgun she heard in her memory the crack of the magnum, saw the bear crumpling, and felt her heart tighten with apprehension.

She'd told Chris and the girls the story of the bear's raid on Mrs. Hermanson's kitchen, but had deleted the part about her killing the animal. It still struck her as a shameful thing to have done.

Chris had undergone a change for the better since the night he'd gotten drunk in town, though it was a transformation of degree rather than kind. He'd become less closemouthed, less imprisoned in himself. He took more of an interest in the girls, talking to them amiably at dinner and occasionally helping Lisa with her homework. His nightmares appeared to have ceased; at least she wasn't awakened by that awful grinding of his teeth. He'd become an eager lover again, though there continued to be a disturbing urgency in his kisses and embraces, a want she could not satisfy. She always felt a little used afterward; once, when his lovemaking bordered on cruelty, Chris kneeling between her thighs and pinning her wrists to the bed with his hands, she'd felt as if she'd been raped. Though she would have preferred more tenderness, June didn't complain; better that he love her in this way than not at all.

Of course, a lot of things about him had not changed: his eyes still had the habit of flicking back and forth, like some cautious animal's, and he never laughed. In all the years she'd known him she'd never heard him laugh, not that she could recall. He smiled now and then, but there was no laughter in him. She wondered sometimes where it had gone.

The first of the big snows fell in the middle of November, the blizzard attended by an awesome gale. The sky appeared to drop to within a hundred feet of the earth. The wind shrieked off the lake, driving the falling snow horizontally as it whirled the drifts into cyclones until no one could distinguish the whiteness in the air from the whiteness on the ground. Schools closed; roads closed; the whole town closed, battening down like a ship weathering a storm. Telephone lines went down. Power lines snapped, and windows glowed at night with the antique flicker of kerosene lamps. Superior hurled itself against the heights of Radisson's Point, swallowed ten acres of earth and timber, then spat the debris across the mouth of the Little Firedog, creating a dam that forced the river to cut a new channel and turned its old outlet into a stagnant pond. Everyone agreed it was the worst winter gale since the one that had sunk the *Edmund Fitzgerald* seven years earlier.

It ended three days after it began. The skies took on a clarity that made the eyes ache. County road crews were called out, their snowplows building artificial drifts on both sides of the roads so that the roads looked like wide trenches after they'd been cleared. People began to dig themselves out of their houses, their faces red and cheerful in the biting air, and talked excitedly about the storm. A river's course had been changed practically overnight; and Radisson's Point, which had jutted into the lake like a freighter's bow for as long as anyone could recall, had been sheared off entirely. The Point was no longer a point, but a blunt slide of mud and loam strewn with fallen pine trees. Why, the big lake had washed away so much land that the shoreline had advanced a hundred yards closer to the old veneer mill. The people of Vieux Desert had experienced an *event*, a thrilling break in the monotony of their lives, a diversion from worries about layoffs, mine shutdowns, declining demands for timber, and foreclosure sales.

June, who'd gone grocery-shopping the day after the storm, found nothing to get excited about. As she pushed her cart down the aisles of the IGA, she grew irritated by the meteorological conversations she overheard from other shoppers stocking up for the winter. Couldn't they find some other topic? And what was so interesting about going three days and nights without power or phones? The people up here loved disastrous weather and weather disasters. Every would-be artist on the Upper Peninsula had done at least one watercolor of the *Fitzgerald*'s sinking, and the ballad Gordon Lightfoot had written about the catastrophe was still played on every jukebox in every dive in the north woods.

She lugged her packages into the station wagon and drove home through a world white as the moon and, it seemed to her, as cold. The earth had died, interred under three feet of snow. She mourned its loss, the earth she would not see, smell, or touch for another six months. Already, on this day of winter's baptism, she yearned for the spring thaws and the day when she could once again turn the soil in her garden, dig the seed-trenches with a stick and her hands, the dirt and the smells of peat and manure clinging to her fingers. And after the seeds had been planted and her prayers for rain and no frost answered, there would be the magical dawn when the first green shoots sprang from the rich warm earth. Six months, she thought, six months. Full of longing and envy, she watched a skein of Canada geese, each bird a black arrow in the sky, shooting southward.

Starkmann loved the winter, the purity of the air, the whiteness of the drifts, and the beauty of dead branches sheathed in ice, pristine as bone. He loved the isolation most of all. Even in the height of summer, only a handful of tourists visited the Upper Peninsula, but in winter no one came at all except a few adventurous cross-country skiers. Snowmobilers committed the only disturbing intrusion, their buzzing machines a metaphor for everything he hated about the pig's world called civilization.

Almost every day he cruised the woods, in his boots when the snow wasn't too deep, on snowshoes when it was. He measured and graded the timber, and read on the pages of the forest floor the history of the previous night's events: the prints of a hare outrunning a fox, the hard-packed depressions where deer had yarded up to browse on cedar bark, the tracks of the wolf pack that had hung on their flanks, studying the herd for the half-starved does, the buck too feeble to run far or to fight.

When he wasn't in the woods he was in the office, making maps, filing tally sheets, and feeding the computer. The football debates between King and Harding ended in early December, when it became a mathematical impossibility for the Lions to make the divisional playoffs. King handed over the twenty-five dollars wagered in September. It gave Starkmann some satisfaction to see him lose the bet; for King's efforts to put him on the unemployment line had not ceased. Clyde Masson's reports had been sent to the regional office, but Starkmann had not been called to Marquette to explain why his estimates had been fifteen percent lower than Masson's; nor had his pink slip come in the interoffice mail. Having failed with one tactic, King tried another, and it was typical of the man's guile and craft.

One leaden morning before the holidays, while Shirley was decorating the office Christmas tree, King mentioned that the regional and district managers had been asked by the home office to submit names of qualified applicants for an executive training program. If accepted, a college-educated field man would be sent at company expense to graduate school at the University of Michigan for a master's in business administration. Once he had his M.B.A., he would be guaranteed a management position at G.S.I.& T.'s Detroit headquarters.

"You're the only guy in the region with a degree," King said with his fraudulent smile. "It's a great opportunity, hey. You don't want to spend the rest of your life walking in the woods."

Starkmann did not say anything. His eyes moved toward Shirley, draping tinsel on the tree, then slipped past King's rodential face to glance at the survey maps papering the walls. He was trying to figure out what snare was concealed in this apparently generous offer. The fact was, he had every intention of spending the rest of his life in the woods. The image of himself wearing a suit as he sat behind a desk in some steel-and-glass building would have been laughable if it had not been so frightening.

"What do you think?" King asked.

"I'm not sure."

"I can understand that." King sidestepped into his office, where he took a thick manila envelope from his In-basket. "It's kind of sudden. There's a memo in here explaining the program, along with an application. Look 'em over and talk it over with your better half and let Ralph or me know as soon as you can. The deadline's March first."

Starkmann took the envelope, deciding there could be no harm in that.

"You won't regret it, Chris." He winked and gave Starkmann a locker-room poke in the ribs. "But if you become a big-time exec, you'll have to clean up your act. No picking fights in bars and passing out flat on your ass."

"I just tied one on," Starkmann said defensively.

The story of his drunken confrontation with LaChance had been known by everyone in town the morning after it happened; but, true to his promise, Billy Treadwell had not told a soul about the gun.

"I was only ribbing you, hey," King said. "When I was your age, I must have done that twice a week."

Later in the day, after Starkmann had thought things through and studied the long, detailed application—it asked too many dangerous questions, like "Have you ever undergone treatment for an emotional or mental disorder?"—he formulated a plausible theory about King's intentions. King knew he had undergone such treatment. If Starkmann answered no to the question, King would tell the main office he had lied, and he would be fired on that score alone. If he answered truthfully, the company would do a background investigation and uncover the record of his hospitalization. That, too, would end his job. It was as bad as a prison record. If he filled out the application, King would have him, coming or going.

Shirley plugged in the lights of the Christmas tree, stepping backward a few feet to admire the twinkling colors that cheered the bleak office.

"That makes the place look a lot better, doesn't it, Chris? It looks like Christmas."

"Uh-huh," Starkmann answered absently. Sitting at the map table, he replaced the papers in the envelope, pleased with his perceptiveness in seeing through King's latest ploy. The stocky man was smart, but Starkmann was smarter. He would be able to stay one step ahead of King, though he cautioned himself against overconfidence; he would have to remain alert. *Alert, alive.* But there was no doubt that his mind was the quicker of the two. His life had been going more smoothly since the night in the Anchor Inn; it was as if the confrontation with LaChance had expelled some mental virus. He had not dreamed, the vertigo spells had ceased, and on those nights when his serenity began to crack, June was always there to love and restore him; in the hot, wet detonations of orgasm, he would feel whole again. The Bill Kings would persist in trying to strip him of what he had, but he was confident now of his power to outwit them. His troubles had begun to leave him. He wondered how long he would have to wait before they ended entirely, and he could grasp happiness, certain he would never lose it.

Christmas and New Year's passed, to June's relief. The holiday season heightened her feeling of isolation; not just the geographical isolation, but the separation from families that brought on a sense of disconnection, absences. June's mother had come to Christmas dinner two or three years, and was distant, always looking at June with reproachful eyes. Lisa got the same looks, Lisa the love child, the living evidence of June's teenage trespass. Mom created so much tension with her silent judgments that June was just as glad not to have her around.

Holidays were also the time of year when ghosts of vanished fathers haunted June and her elder daughter. Lisa had no memory of Ripley—she'd been a toddler when he'd taken his walk—and did not miss him so much as she missed the *idea* of having her own Dad around for Christmas. Relations between her and Chris always grew strained during this season; Lisa put him at arm's length, treating him as if he were an intruder.

As for Chris's family, well, June had never met them and knew next to nothing about them. His father was a minister, his mother a leisured lady who did church charity work; he had three sisters, one older, two younger. That was the extent of her knowledge. Chris had not even bothered to tell them he had gotten married; June had had to make the announcement, and only after she'd pried their address out of Chris, as if it were a state secret. The card that had come in response simply said, "Wishing you happiness forever," and was signed, in a woman's hand, "Mother, Dad, Anne, Stephanie, and Jennifer." The same signature appeared on the cards that arrived on Chris's birthday and each Christmas. Never any gifts, messages, or letters—just the cards and the names. June's mind attached great mystery to these terse and infrequent communications. Only an orphan could have had less contact with his family. What had happened to cause such a breach? Her imagination had written a number of scenes; finally, one evening shortly after their marriage, her curiosity had gotten the better of her. She'd been wiping off the dining room table after dinner when she'd asked Chris why he and his family had so little to do with each other. She would never forget his reaction: He struck her with a cold stare and told her, in as glacial a voice, that she was never to ask him that question again, nor mention his family, especially his father's name. His relations with his father and his family were his private business. June, who had an independent character hardened by years of being on her own, lost her temper. Who the hell did he think she was to go ordering her around? One of those obedient geishas or whatever they were called, those little Oriental slaves he'd screwed overseas? She was married to him, and his family was as much her business as it was his. That was when Chris, exploding in a fury she'd never suspected existed in him, had picked up the dining room table and flung it into the wall, breaking off two of its legs and knocking holes in the plasterboard. The next thing she knew, he was crying, and begging her to promise not to speak of his father or his family again. June, stunned by his rage and strength—he'd thrown the heavy wooden table as easily as he might have a card table—didn't know what to make of him. But, afraid of doing anything that might strain her new marriage, she eventually gave him her word: She'd never mention them again.

Except for a few slips now and then, she'd kept her promise, becoming an accomplice in his exile from his family, and in her own exile as well. There were only the four of them, cut off in a house in the wilderness.

To prevent herself from wallowing in self-pity, she busied herself with holiday cooking and baking: the traditional turkey and pumpkin pie, and also some of her favorite French-Canadian recipes, *tortiere*, *pâté chinois*, maple-sugar pie, roast venison from the buck Chris had shot in November. It was far too much for her small family, so she distributed some of it among her cases. It seemed the right thing to do: to feed the hungry, one of the corporal works of mercy that June, who had been raised a Catholic at her father's insistence, had learned as a child. She gave a potful of home-baked Cornish pasties to the mob of degraded Finndians, a *tortiere* to the girl attempting to "dejudicate fraternity" for her bastard child, a maple-sugar pie to the ratty blonde with the fractured cheekbone.

She drove to Hermanson's "lodge." In its winter meadow, the log house looked as desolate as an Antarctic weather station. She had not brought any food—that would have insulted Edith's pride in her cooking. She brought a much better present: Henry Hermanson had been found, in Corpus Christi, Texas, where he was earning twenty-five thousand a year working as a skilled laborer on an offshore oil rig. He'd been hauled into court and a payment order for child-support issued. As Edith remained a prisoner of her indestructible delusion, June gave the information to Freya (whom she refrained from asking about her part-time profession), Hank Junior, and Tommy. The children received the news stoically. So now they would be receiving checks from the old man instead of from the State of Michigan—big deal. June wished them a merry Christmas anyway, and left.

On New Year's Eve day, she attended a couple of office parties. She made the most of them—Chris refused to go out on New Year's. By the time she got to the state's attorney's party, one too many scotches had awakened some of her old recklessness; she flirted with Erickson, more seriously than she should have, and gave him her patented look, more or less to see if nine years of marriage had diminished its powers. Apparently they hadn't, because Erickson spent a good fifteen minutes talking to her, instead of flitting around the way people usually did at cocktail parties. And when she started to leave for Sandy Jackson's, her last stop before going home, he kissed her on the cheek, about a second longer than a friendly peck ought to have lasted, his hand holding the small of her back in a way that appeared, but did not feel, innocent.

Outside, the copper dome atop the courthouse blazed in the clear winter light, and the ice on the lake reached out so far that Superior looked like a polar cap. June walked briskly to her station wagon, feeling an excitement she shouldn't feel. It hadn't been the scotch, Erickson's lingering kiss, the flattery of his obvious attraction to her, or his good looks which had stirred the forbidden emotion. It had been something he'd told her during their conversation: He was leaving Marquette in the summer to set up private practice in Ann Arbor, where he would also teach part-time at Michigan State Law School. He'd no sooner mentioned this than June's mind, acting on a wild inspiration, formed a picture of her married to him. She saw herself living in a university town in a lovely house, next to well-off, intelligent neighbors, doctors, professors, bankers, other lawyers. People. Civilization. An interesting life. She saw Erickson, in a lawyerish three-piece suit, pulling out of the driveway to go to work while she dressed for her classes at State, where she would get her bachelor's degree and then maybe build a career of her own—a real career, not a life of wage-slaving for a government bureaucracy, dealing with backwoods halfwits. The whole image flashed before her with a suddenness that shocked her. If the picture was a bit corny—the successful hubby pulling out of the suburban driveway—it expressed yearnings that had been stifled in her for a long time, too long.

She felt guilty enough about her not-so-mild flirtation that she confessed it to Sandy almost immediately.

"Oh, you poor Catholics," Sandy said with a shake of her head, a small oval framed by long waves of chestnut hair.

They sat on the living room sofa, in front of a glassed-in wall that looked out on the lake.

"What do you mean by that?"

"Catholic guilt. You Catholics feel guilty about waking up in the morning. What's your New Year's drink, Jay-Jay?"

"Scotch. And make it light."

While Sandy mixed the drinks in the kitchen, June sat on the sofa, staring through the glass at the lake, ridges of ice piled up along the shore like frozen waves. The Jacksons' beach-front house, modest but modern, was in one of the choicer sections of Marquette. With its contemporary furnishings, its decorative objects picked up on the couple's travels, its splashy paintings, it seemed ten thousand instead of thirty miles from the rusticity of June's house.

Sandy and Rick were both trust-fund babies, descendants of British mine owners who'd emigrated to the U.P. from Cornwall and made killings in copper and iron. The interest from the inherited fortunes was supplemented by Rick's high salary as an ore-freighter pilot, a job he'd taken because, like any bored rich kid, he needed adventure. For the same reason, he engaged in drug smuggling now and then. To keep herself occupied, Sandy worked part-time selling stereos and computers at Radio Shack, mostly to the college crowd from A.& M. After New Year's, when most of the Great Lakes were closed to shipping, the couple escaped to warm climates for three or four months: Florida, Mexico, the Southwest, places where Rick made connections for his illegal enterprises, and Sandy, an expert horsewoman, did a lot of riding as well as a lot of mushrooms, "grooving on the sun," as she put it.

June did not approve of their drug-taking and rich-brat outlawry, but they had an aura of adventure about them that provided a fascinating contrast to the usual run of drab, small-town folks. If she could not run off to Florida or Mexico, the next best thing was to be friends with people who did. Merely to know them and hear about their travels reminded her that there was indeed a world outside these woods.

Sandy returned with the drinks, a sexy woman in a scrawny sort of way. June was jealous of her fashion-model figure, her finely cut upturned nose, and graceful movements. Beside her, she felt coarse-looking and clumsy, a big country-girl.

"So tell me more about your little encounter with Marquette's most eligible bachelor." Sandy lounged with her drink in a corner of the couch, a wicked curiosity in her brown eyes.

"There's nothing more to tell. Out of nowhere I got this flash in my head that I'd marry the guy and get the hell out of here. I've looked at a few guys since I married Chris, but I've never even thought about going to bed with them, let alone marrying them, for God's sake."

"It's only natural," Sandy said reassuringly. "It must get pretty frustrating, living in the boondocks with Gary Cooper."

June bristled at the criticism of Chris, despite, or perhaps because of, its truth. She frowned inwardly when Sandy set her drink on the glass coffee table, plucked a plastic bag of coke from a lacquer box, then laid out a line and snorted it up through a short straw. What right did this doper have to comment on her marriage?

"Look," Sandy said, daubing the white powder that ringed her nostril, "don't make yourself crazy over an office-party flirtation. Maybe you should get it out of your system. Have an affair with the guy."

"What?"

"An affair. Ever hear of them? They were invented about the same time as marriage. Hell, every single girl in town, and a few who aren't, would like to get that hunk in bed."

"How about you?"

"Not my type. I'm sick of these blond, blue-eyed Scandinavians. That's all I see up here. Half the time I think I'm in Oslo. The ones who turn me on are those Cubans down in Florida, the Chicanos in New Mexico. Black hair, skin like nutmeg, dark chest hair, gold crucifixes on their necks. I *love* lying underneath them and looking up and seeing that old cross of Jesus, all bright gold, swinging back and forth in front of my eyes."

"I'll bet Rick loves that too."

"We've got an understanding."

"Chris isn't the understanding type."

"I'm not suggesting you put your business on the street. A discreet affair."

"I don't believe you sometimes. Just like that?" June snapped her fingers. "I cheat on Chris because I got hot pants for a few minutes at an office party?"

"Catholics," Sandy said, bowing her head to greedily inhale another line. "Jay-Jay, after living all these years with a guy who says maybe two words a week, you deserve a little fun."

"If I weren't buzzed right now, I wouldn't say this, but it bothers the hell out of me when I hear you talk about Chris that way. Why do you dislike him so much?"

"He scares me."

"What did he ever do to scare you?"

"Nothing. It's those eyes of his, the way they keep moving. And that weird quietness. He reminds me of those old westerns when two cowboys ride into a canyon, and the one cowboy says, 'Sure is quiet, Tex,' and the second cowboy says, 'Sure is, Jake.' Two seconds later, all hell breaks loose. That's how he scares me. I get this feeling that he's going to do something any second."

"What?" asked June, seeing in her memory the dining room table flying through the air.

"I don't know. He seems dangerous, I guess. Dangerous in the wrong way. Freshen up your drink?"

"No, thanks. I could use a cup of coffee before making that drive."

"This'll perk you up a lot quicker. It's hardly been stepped on." Sandy gestured at the plastic bag, the contents of which, June thought, cost as much as the child-support the Hermanson kids received each month. "One line won't kill you."

"You know I don't do that stuff."

"It isn't only the high, Jay-Jay. It's the adventure. To snort this coke is to suck a little high adventure into your brain. Here we are on the border of Canada and this white lady came all the way from Colombia. Think of it. Dashing Latin smugglers in the jungles, swashbuckling Yankee pilots flying it across the Caribbean, Cuban dealers moving it north to Chicago, then my sweet Rick sailing it up on a Great Lakes freighter. You could make a movie about it."

"I don't make movies."

"Oh, you Catholics. Instant coffee okay?"

"Instant would be fine."

18

In January and February, winter's grip tightened into a stranglehold. Under iron skies, people did not see the sun for two weeks at a time, and some, like June, had begun to wonder if it had burned out and died. When it did shine, its light was weak and exhausted, without the power to melt even the surface of drifts that were six feet deep in places. Herds of starving deer wobbled out of the woods and down Vieux Desert's street to browse on the dune grass by the lake shore, where the winds had thinned the snow. The mercury sought the bottom of the thermometer: twenty below, twenty-five, thirty. On one still, cloudless night, it reached minus forty-two, cold enough to thicken the antifreeze in cars and send ice creeping up the inside walls of the houses. Trees froze straight through to their hearts and exploded, trunks and limbs bursting under skies so clear and white with stars it was as if the earth had become as airless as the moon.

The extreme cold was good only for the bar business; the taverns were packed almost every night, always with the same people, who eventually grew sick of looking at each other and of listening to the same tired stories, the same complaints, the same gossip. On edge from their imprisonment, their emotional temperatures rising from cabin fever, wives and husbands squabbled over petty irritations, and old friends became temporary enemies, turning the Anchor Inn into an arena for a couple of brawls as rough as anything Billy Treadwell had seen in Kronk's gym.

Out in the woods the bears slept, deer died of hunger, scavengers

fed on the winterkills, and coyotes and wolves sang their mournful arias.

June took up cross-country skiing to keep her weight down and herself from going crazy. Because she had a poor sense of direction, she stayed on the highways and back roads unless Chris went with her. Skilled in the sport, with what seemed like a built-in compass in his head, he broke his own trail, avoiding the trails maintained by the county; he did not want to encounter other skiers.

June took surprisingly few spills for a novice. The sport was in her Finnish blood, she guessed; cross-country had started in Finland thousands of years ago. She grew to love the stretch and flex of her muscles when her legs pumped to build up speed, the cleansing sear of cold air in her lungs, the rush of straight-running or of a downhill glide, the skis hissing. Sometimes, on a fast run through the stands of red pine near the Indian reservation, her knees bending and shoulder dipping to round a sharp turn, she felt so swift and graceful that she pretended she was Undurridus, the Norse ski-goddess, racing through the forests of heaven. Inevitably, that's when she would take a tumble, as if the real goddess had tripped her to punish her presumption and remind her of her mortality.

After she'd been at it for five weeks, she stepped on the bathroom scale and was thrilled to see she had lost several pounds. Her new trimness so pleased her vanity that she stripped to her underwear, studied her figure in the mirror, and pronounced her body voluptuous. If she got her teeth straightened and her hawk's-bill nose fixed, like those Jewish girls did, she could be a real knockout.

She bought skis for the girls, deciding the sport would be good for them as well. Christine was eager to learn, and she looked so lovely with her face wind-reddened and her golden hair flowing out from under her cap. Lisa rebelled, naturally; she thought it was dumb. She wanted to hang out with the kids at Swanson's, pumping quarters into the video games. June forced her to learn regardless and organized family ski outings on weekends.

Those were the best times, the four of them together, Chris out in front breaking trail. In the winter woods he seemed almost happy, relieved of his secret suffering. He gave nature lectures to the girls, pointing out the different species of trees and explaining why they grew in certain types of soil. He interpreted the animal tracks: the webbed hind feet of beaver, the human-looking prints of coon, the twin teardrops of white-tailed deer.

She only wished he could be as extraverted in the outside world, maybe take the family out to a decent place for dinner after skiing. But dining out with Chris always meant Burger King or Wendy's

where they would eat in the car, suffocated by the warm blasts of the heater. A couple of times, forcing down a tasteless lump of Whopper, June caught herself thinking about Erickson. He would not have taken them to some crummy drive-in but to a real restaurant, drinks before dinner, wine with, a brandy afterward. She criticized herself for daydreaming about him and for finding fault with Chris over so small a matter. Her fantasy of gracious living as the lawyer's wife had long since lost its fascination and had taken on the garish Technicolor of a cartoon, comic nonsense. Nevertheless, uninvited, Erickson entered her thoughts now and then.

He did not merely enter them but broke into them on the Saturday morning after she'd run into Bill King at the bank. She'd been standing at the back of the line, silently giving thanks that she was there to cash a paycheck, not a welfare or unemployment check like half the others in front of her, when King stepped in behind her, said hello, and asked if she was excited about the possibility of becoming a big-shot's wife. Her first reaction was panic; Sandy, the bitch, had been gossiping. Then she remembered that Sandy and King did not know each other; furthermore, Sandy had been in Florida for the past month.

"I'm afraid I don't know what you're talking about," June said with righteous formality, just in case an account of her little flirtation and fantasy had somehow reached King's ears.

"C'mon, June. It's not top secret. It's a great opportunity for the both of you, if he gets that application in on time. Only a week left, hey."

June bent one leg, shortening herself so she could look directly into King's eyes.

"Maybe you'd better remind him to fill it out this weekend," he said. "I'll make sure it goes out to the regional office on Monday."

After she'd wheedled the story out of him—King, when he'd learned that Chris hadn't spoken a word to her, had been reluctant to tell her; sometimes a man had reasons for not consulting his wife, he'd said—June drove home in a high temper that opened the door to thoughts of Erickson. She saw his handsome face, remembered their New Year's conversation and the way he'd held that kiss just long enough for it to be more than friendly. Erickson would have consulted her. If he'd been in Chris's position, he would not have waited this long to send in the application. He would have seized the chance right away, whereas Chris's procrastination was typical. He tended to

drift, to let things happen rather than to make them happen. If she hadn't come into his life and prodded him to return to school and make something of himself, he would still be living in that shabby deer camp, hand-to-mouth.

He was splitting firewood by the shed as she came up the road. From a distance he appeared woodsy and Lincolnesque in his wool mackinaw, his long arms rhythmically swinging the maul; but when she got closer, and he looked up to wave hello, she noticed the unusual narrowness of his head. It resembled a rectangle standing on end. This unattractive feature had somehow escaped her attention all these years, and the discovery of it now added to her disappointment in him.

She climbed out of the station wagon, stomped through the snow toward the shed, and confronted him. Why in the hell hadn't he mentioned this to her, why did she have to hear it from King, and why was he waiting till the last minute to do something about it? He had only a week left, for God's sake.

Chris stood a sawn log on the stump he used as a chopping block, tapped in the wedge, swung down on it with the maul, steel ringing on steel, and split the log with one stroke.

"How about an answer, Chris? How about a few words from Gary Cooper?"

He gave her one of his furtive glances, his pupils scurrying from one corner of his eyes to the other like caged rats.

"That goddamned King," he muttered under his breath as he added the log halves to the pile he'd started.

"Tell me you wanted to surprise me. Tell me you didn't want to raise my hopes in case you got turned down. Tell me you're a macho woodsman who doesn't have to check with the little woman before he makes a big decision. Tell me to get into the kitchen where I belong, but tell me something."

"Hard to explain," Chris said, pulling another log from the stacked cords and splitting it with another sure, powerful stroke. June thought he was trying to intimidate her, and she resented his strength, as she'd resented it the night he'd thrown the table into the wall.

"Try explaining. Graduate school at company expense. Then a job in the main office. We could live like the rest of the human race. We could get the hell out of here."

She focused on his face, trying to arrest the constant dart and dodge of his eyes. His head really was too narrow to call him truly handsome, she thought, and wondered why he had once made her weak in the knees.

"I don't want to get the hell out of here," he answered tightly. His eyes held fast for a moment and cast a peculiar light.

"What about the girls? Maybe they need to get out of here."

With one arm only, he twirled the ten-pound maul as easily as a majorette her baton, driving its sharpened end into the stump.

"The girls seem okay."

"Do they? They're lonely and bored stiff, if you want to know, stuck out here. That's one thing. Another thing is that they could go to a really good school downstate, not to this bumpkin-yard full of kids who've got IQs about as big as my shoe size."

"They're doing all right." He sat on the stump, gazing downward and squeezing his gloved hands.

"Well, I'm not. I've lived on the godforsaken peninsula all my life and I want *out*. O-U-T. I'd like to go grocery-shopping where the heads of lettuce aren't a month old. I'd like neighbors to talk to. I'd like to go into the city and see a movie that isn't ten years old. I'd like not to have to go to the bathroom in an outhouse because the pump is down because the generator is down. I'd like to live in a place where bears don't break into people's kitchens. I'd like a little grace and comfort. All this back-to-nature stuff is great for those spaced-out hippies who've never had to live in it, but when you've had to, it starts to suck."

"I never did like your trashy mouth, June."

"Is that right? Well, I'm sick of your quiet mouth. Say something, goddammit."

He kept squeezing his hands as if he were kneading an invisible lump of dough. There was such tension in this movement that her heart jumped when he abruptly turned his gaze on her and reached behind him to grip the maul handle.

"I belong here, June, and you belong here with me," he said finally. "Right here on these forty acres. Nowhere else."

"What? On the whole planet?"

"I suppose I could find a better position, but this is a pretty good one."

Position? She didn't get that at all. The cold creeping through her boots and into her bones, she hopped from one foot to the other. For the first time, she understood Sandy's fear of him. The way he looked now, his hand clutching the maul, the strange light in his eyes disturbingly like the expression he'd had the night he'd come home drunk—he did seem capable of doing something awful and unpredictable at any moment. A few seconds ago she'd thought he was going to explode and split her head as he did the logs: with a single stroke. Now she saw the nature of the hidden turbulence she'd always sensed in him, the violent current roiling under the ice; and this inner flaw was far uglier and more disturbing than the outward one she'd discovered.

"We're off the track," she said in a more moderate tone, afraid of provoking him and, at the same time, affronted by her fear. "I want to know why you didn't even talk to me about the offer and why you're waiting till the last minute."

"Because it didn't make any difference. It didn't and it doesn't."

"It's a chance you—we—might never get again. At least you could fill out the application this weekend so King can get it in on Monday. Then we could talk all this out and see what happens."

"I burned it, June. The day he gave it to me, I put it in the fireplace and burned it."

It took her several seconds to absorb this; then she didn't know if she wanted to cry or seize the maul and split his skull, that ugly, narrow skull.

"Oh, Chris, why? Why, for God's sake?"

He pondered a long time before answering. A chipmunk hiding in the stacked cords poked out its head as if to see what all the conversation had been about, then ducked back in.

"I can trust you, can't I?" Chris asked finally.

"I hope so, after all these years."

"Can I trust you not to think I'm crazy?"

"What kind of a question is that?"

"Because what I have to tell you will sound crazy, but it's true. Can I trust you?"

"Yes," she said with exasperation. "Yes, yes."

"All right. The application was bull. It was another one of King's tricks. I know things about him you don't, and one of the things I know is that he's been trying to get me fired for months. That's what this 'offer' was all about. Another one of his tricks to get me fired."

June had no reaction to his explanation; he might as well have been speaking Swahili.

"Don't mention that to anyone," he went on. "It's a confidence. And I don't want you to worry. Everything's going to be all right. He'll never get me canned. I'll always be one step ahead of him."

"Chris? I don't . . . A man gives you a chance to go to grad school and get ahead, and you're saying he's trying to get you *fired*?"

He stood, freed the maul, and readied another log for splitting, as if he considered the matter settled.

"That's the truth of it. I can't tell you why it is. There are a lot of things I can't tell you, but you'll have to believe me if you trust me."

"I do, but . . . these things you can't tell me . . . I don't understand."

"All you have to understand is that the man is out for my ass," he said sharply. "He cornered you in the bank today because he's getting nervous. *He's* got only a week left—not me. Without the application filled out, he hasn't got a case against me. Another one of his tricks down the chute. So he figured he'd get you to pressure me. But, like I said, I'm one step ahead of him. Always. I burned the application." With the maul's blunt end, he drilled the wedge into the wood. "Don't worry. We'll be all right."

These were perhaps as many words as Chris had ever spoken to her at one time, and after she'd heard them and saw him raise the maul overhead, she stepped back a pace or two, her heart beating fast. The log parted with a sharp, dry crack.

"I told you it would sound crazy, but you don't think I'm crazy, do you, June?"

"No," she answered, softly and tentatively. "Maybe I'd understand better if you told me these things you say you can't tell me."

He did not seem to hear. The maul rose and fell again, cleaving another log, and another, the steel's chimes striking across the yard and the white meadow beyond.

After that conversation, June returned to the house, where, to calm herself, she started to prepare dinner. She soon gave it up. She then tried to vacuum the rugs, but was so distracted that she caught herself standing in the middle of the room staring off into space while the Hoover hummed at her feet. Realizing she had to get out, she gathered a bundle of clothes, piled them in the Wagoneer, and was about to head for the dry cleaner's in Marquette when she remembered her daughters. She did not want to leave them with Chris; but because the excursion to the dry cleaner's was a pretext for her to be alone and order her scattered thoughts, she didn't want to take them with her. They would only add to her distraction. The solution was to drop them off at one of Lisa's friends in Vieux Desert. This she did, both girls delighted by the temporary escape from their confinement.

During the drive to Marquette, June disputed her suspicion that Chris was either out of his mind or close to it. That she and her two young daughters were living in an isolated house with a disturbed man—one who was, moreover, six feet five and over two hundred pounds, strong enough to hurl a dining table across a room and to swing a wood-splitter's maul as if it were a croquet mallet—was a possibility too appalling to contemplate. She reminded herself of his predictable habits, his punctuality and conscientiousness. He'd never been late for work, nor missed a day of work. Lunatics couldn't hold down any sort of job, let alone a job that demanded as much care and precision as his. And if he were mad, why would his company have offered to send him to graduate school, promised him a position in the home office? She began to doubt her own sanity. By the time she reached the cleaners, she'd half-convinced herself that Chris was possibly right about King; every company had its office politicians and back-stabbers. Her department was full of them.

But her rationalizations unraveled when she emptied the pockets of the clothes before she gave them to the woman behind the counter. In Chris's sheepskin, she found a folded, soiled business card.

J.T. ECKHARDT PHD.
CLINICAL PSYCHOLOGIST
VETERANS OUTREACH CENTER
IRON MOUNTAIN, MICH.

His home and office numbers were printed in the lower right-hand corner. June put the card in her purse. God! Had Chris been undergoing treatment without her knowing about it?

On the drive back she worked hard to persuade herself that that was not the case. Mental illness—what could be more frightening or mysterious? You could see, or at least imagine, a broken bone, a clogged artery, a cancerous cell, an enlarged liver. But what did a diseased mind look like? What intangible, immeasurable, invisible bacteria infected the mind? Mental illness. Madness. Insanity. Mania. Psychosis. Dementia. Derangement. The very words were charged with terror. The card, she hoped, immediately transmuting the hope into fact, had no significance; it had probably been handed to him by some guy he'd bumped into, some guy who just happened to be a clinical psychologist. Her efforts at self-deception bore fruit. By the time she saw the sign VIEUX DESERT, POP. 942. NATURE IN ABUNDANCE, she'd concluded that Chris, at the worst, was suffering some minor, passing crisis, a kind of psychological head-cold. Her fears of leaving the girls alone with him had been foolish; he'd never laid a hand on either of them. He was all right; everything was going to be all right, she told herself. Nevertheless she asked Chris who Eckhardt was when she returned home. He said he couldn't recall the name—why was she asking? She told him about the card.

"What's the matter, Jay-Jay? Do you think I'm some nut case? One of those screwball vets you read about in the papers?"

"No . . . No. I was just wondering who he was."

"Some guy who drove me home the night I got drunk. You've got the card. Call him and ask him."

She didn't, because that was the answer she wanted to hear. But she made sure to keep the card hidden in her purse.

During the following weeks their life outwardly went on as before, its established domestic rhythms undisturbed. The weekend ski trips continued well into March, for the blizzards kept falling on the northern earth, ignoring the passage of the first day of spring. But inwardly, June began to detach herself from her husband. She found herself studying his facial expressions at the dinner table and looking for a demented glimmer in his eyes; she monitored his voice for a peculiar phrase, an off-key note. Her observations extended even into the bedroom, where, withholding her heart from him, she watched his reactions as if she were some sort of sex therapist. Or a whore. Quite often she felt like a whore, offering only her body, and out of fear that he might notice the change in her, turning in a credible masquerade of sexual climaxes.

She hated feeling such distance from him. Even more she hated living in doubt—so much that it would have come almost as a relief to her if he'd done something overtly crazy; but he remained in some margin between madness and sanity, which bound her to a twilight of uncertainty. Once—again it was at a chance meeting in the bank—she cornered Bill King, after he'd mentioned that he was sorry Chris had not taken advantage of the "great opportunity." June almost broke into tears but held her composure and covered for Chris by saying they'd talked it over and decided they enjoyed small-town life. It was good for the kids, what with all the drugs in city and suburban schools. King nodded and, with a shrug, said, "Well, to each his own, I guess." She asked how Chris was doing at work—were they satisfied with his performance? King replied that he was one of the best they had. Oh, he was a little slow in submitting his estimates because he was so careful, and he tended to come in on the conservative side, but that was to be expected from a Lands Department man—they were all Johnny Appleseeds these days, forgetting that a timber company was in the business of cutting down trees, not keeping them up. Other than that, he was a real asset to Great Superior. She should be proud of him.

June said thank you and left, unsure what to think. The next weekend, the last one in March, something happened that began to move her out of the twilight—in the direction she did not want to go. She and Chris had driven into town to run errands. They were on their way home, stopped at the light at Front Street and East Bay

Road, when she remembered that she needed to buy stamps. She asked him to pass by the post office, three blocks down on East Bay. He started to turn when the light flashed green, then froze at the wheel and broke out in a nervous sweat. He said he'd forgotten to pick up something at Jensen's Hardware. He would go there on foot; she could drive to the post office. A car behind them honked its horn. June said the post office would take only a minute; then he could go to Jensen's.

"I don't drive the East Bay Road," he answered, his breathing rapid and shallow as he opened the door. The other car weaved around them, its driver cussing. "I never take it."

"You take it every day to work."

"No, I don't," he insisted.

She was about to ask him the reason for this when he jumped out and went loping across the street toward Jensen's.

June got behind the wheel and turned onto the road, searching for some reason that would cause a man to become phobic about driving a small-town street. On one side there was a general store, a row of frame houses, Saint Joseph's Catholic Church, the VFW Hall, then the post office. A narrow park separated the opposite side of the road from East Bay Beach, but she saw nothing out of the ordinary there: an historical marker informing visitors that the French fur trader and explorer Pierre Radisson had discovered Vieux Desert Bay in 1657; a war memorial across from the VFW Hall; and opposite the church, a huge forked anchor, salvaged from a sunken schooner, with a marker beside it describing the history of Lake Superior shipwrecks.

That was it. Nothing to cause a grown man to panic. After June had bought her stamps she went to the post office pay phone and took Eckhardt's card from her purse, alarmed enough to consider calling him. She decided against it. What would she say to him? There's a street in our town my husband refuses to drive on for no reason I can think of. Can you help him? Christ, he'd probably send the white wagon after her.

The last three days of March brought a brief false spring. Southerlies raised the temperature to a balmy forty-five, the ice broke up on the rivers, and the floes sailed lakeward down currents gorged on melting snow. June, cheered by the thaw, took a ride to the shore to watch the jagged chunks twirl into the bay and collide with the blocks of cracking lake ice. The sights and sounds of winter's end, the ice groaning like the timbers of a grounded ship, made her happy and hopeful. Her fears about Chris would be proven groundless.

When, on April Fool's Day, she saw her first herring gull soaring high as a hawk on its gray wings, she drove to the garden shop in Marquette, bought seed packets and bags of peat and fertilizer, and lugged them home to await the day when the white vanished from the earth. She should have known better; a frost descended the next morning, a Sunday. The wind ripped out of the north, propelling clouds that skimmed low overhead like gray bombers dropping payloads of new snow. By late afternoon the crystalline surface of the old crust was covered by more than a foot of it, wet and thick, a white mud.

Chris went into the garage, hitched the plow to the mini-tractor, and started to make a path down the gravel road so they could get to the highway in the morning. He was so long of leg that he looked a little comical atop the small vehicle, like an adult riding a tricycle.

June retreated to the sanctuary of her kitchen to rummage through her cookbooks for a recipe exciting enough to overcome the depression brought on by winter's renewed assault. Everything that interested her was too complicated, requiring ingredients she didn't have. She didn't have them because the damned IGA in this damned hick town didn't carry them. Too far from the downstate markets. This was pure meat-and-potatoes country, the reason the incidence of stomach cancer up here was as high as the alcoholism rate. All right, she would do a meat loaf, spicing it up with Worcestershire and garlic. Thank God for garlic.

She was mixing the ground beef and eggs by hand when the phone rang. She told Lisa to get it.

"It's for Chris, Mom," Lisa sighed, as if answering the phone had expended most of her emotional reserves.

"He's out plowing the road. Take a message."

Lisa passed this on, then said, "Whoever it is won't leave a message. He wants to talk to Chris. Now."

June wiped her hands and picked up the phone. The voice at the other end asked to whom he was speaking. Not "Who'm I speaking to" but *to whom*. June identified herself, which caused the grammatically correct gentleman some confusion.

Oh, his wife . . . of course . . . We've never met. I'm Ed Jenkins—Chris's, your husband's brother-in-law. I'd like to speak to him, please. It's urgent."

When she recovered from her amazement at this, the first direct communication she'd ever heard from someone in his family, June explained why Chris could not immediately come to the phone. Ed

Jenkins said he understood, they were having a little snow in Chicago, too, imagine, snow in April. June heard a woman's voice in the background, and another woman crying.

"What's happened, Mr. Jenkins?"

"Ed. Ed will do," he offered. "I'm afraid something has. Please ask your husband to call me right away. I'm at his father's house. The number's the same, *if* he remembers it."

It was impossible to miss the rebuke in the last phrase.

"Could you give it to me in case he doesn't?"

He gave her the number, which she scrawled on the back of the phone book.

"Would you mind telling me what's wrong, Ed? I am his wife, after all."

"It's his father, June. It's all right if I call you June, isn't it? It's his father, I'm afraid."

"Yes?"

"We think it's high time your husband—Chris—ended this . . . well, I don't know what to call it . . . this estrangement from us. Do you know I had to go through two special operators to reach your number?"

"The number's unpublished. Chris wants it that way."

"We think it's time he ended that kind of thing. We'd like him to come home—down here, I mean. Rosemary—that's his mother— Rosemary's taking it very hard. She needs to see him, especially now. It's been ten years."

"What about his father?"

"It happened a few hours ago. A cerebral hemorrhage. A severe one. He's in a coma now, in the intensive care unit. The doctors are giving him two days, three at most."

Starkmann, snowshoeing across the meadow, glanced over his shoulder, past the outbuildings, and saw June watching him from the front porch, her arms folded over her quilted jacket. He motioned to her to go inside, but she didn't move; either she had not seen the gesture through the curtain of snow, or had chosen to ignore it. He turned and plodded toward the tamarack swamp. June had been upset with him for weeks. She thought he was nuts—he sensed that. Now, he supposed, she thought him heartless or worse. Half an hour ago, after she'd run down the path he'd plowed and had broken the news, she'd said she would take the sick days she had coming and find someone to watch the girls so she could accompany him to Chicago.

He was silent at first, trying to absorb the shock; then he told her he wasn't sure if he should go. He needed time alone to think it over. June, with a swing of her arm that almost knocked him off the tractor seat, flayed him in her most strident voice.

"Not sure? You're not sure? It's your *father*, for God's sake! What's wrong with you?"

He'd been unable to answer, his vocabulary too limited to explain that he did not feel whatever you are supposed to feel when you learn that your father is near death. He felt an upsurge of hatred, a hatred that had risen because the first thing to enter his mind had been the memory of Lucius's behavior at Anne's wedding reception. Starkmann could not fathom why that, and no other remembrance had come to him; nevertheless it had, and the picture was so vivid it was as if the reception had been held yesterday instead of sixteen years ago.

Lucius was standing alone near the exit of the country club's banquet room, his hands clasped behind the tails of his dove-gray tuxedo. His posture and unsmiling lips suggested a man restraining a powerful grief, as if he were at a funeral instead of a wedding. The standard rituals had been performed—the cutting of the tiered cake, the tossing of the bridal bouquet—and now the band was playing, forties foxtrots for the older guests, rock tunes for the younger. Everyone was attempting to have a good time, but it was difficult to ignore the tall man whose very presence seemed to cast a spell on the crowd and to lower the emotional temperature in the room to below freezing. Under his censorious stare, young as well as old danced stiffly and awkwardly, as if hesitant to let go and enjoy themselves. Christian, dancing with his date, wished Lucius had stayed home. He had disappointed Anne enough by refusing to perform the ceremony. If further objection to the wedding had been necessary, he could have registered it by his absence. But no, he had to make a public display of his disapproval, as if the marriage were on the same level as the racial inequalities and unjust wars he'd protested most of his life. He had to stand apart, drawing attention to himself and the sacrifice he was making. It's difficult for me to be here, he said with his rigid stance and pained expression, but it's my obligation and I'll fulfill it.

Anne, though, was handling her father's rudeness with grace. Tall and slim, she looked regal in her bridal gown as she waltzed with Ed, the Black & Decker tool salesman. When the musicians struck up the traditional songs that signaled the end of the celebration, she danced a few bars with Christian, whispering to him that she wanted Dad to take the floor with her, just for a short while. Since he was Dad's favorite, would he please, please ask him to do that for her?

Christian did not think it was such a good idea, nor had he ever considered himself his father's favorite; but, flattered, he agreed to act as her intermediary. He straightened his tie and cummerbund and strode purposefully toward Lucius. It was the first time he had worn formal dress, and it made him feel grown up, a sense of maturity augmented by the four inches he'd grown in the past year. He was now the same height as his father, a physical accident that gave him the illusion that they were equals.

"I'm afraid I'm not much on a dance floor," Lucius said after he'd passed on Anne's request.

"It isn't a dance contest, Dad," Christian responded, affecting a bantering, man-to-man tone. "Annie just wants a few minutes with you."

"I'm afraid I can't do that."

Lucius looked past the now-empty dais and out the wall of windows that offered a view of the swimming pool and the sunlit fairways beyond, where pennants fluttered in the breeze and golf carts scuttled like toy automobiles. "You know, sometimes I think I should have taken up golf instead of fishing."

"What's golf got to do with this?"

"It's a more sociable sport, wouldn't you say? It would keep me in contact with people in the community. But then, I'm not the sociable sort, am I?"

"I don't understand why you're acting like this. What's wrong with Ed? He seems okay to me."

"You've asked me that before. I told you then, and I'm telling you now, it's between me and Anne. And your mother. Understood?"

His resolve faltering, Christian turned his glance to the dance floor, seeking in his new brother-in-law's appearance an outward sign of a character flaw that would solve the mystery of Lucius's antipathy to the man. Ed, who was waltzing with a bridesmaid, looked as bland and unremarkable as a junior sales executive was supposed to look— trim physique, conservative haircut, handsome but undistinguished face.

"I don't get it," Christian said, facing his father again. "Excuse me, but I think . . . what you're doing, I mean . . . I mean the way you're acting—it's wrong, Dad."

Lucius's chin jerked as if he'd been struck.

"I am *not* going to stand here and be lectured to by a sixteen-year-old. It's bad enough that I've had to—"

It was Anne who cut him short. Apparently she'd noticed that her brother's efforts were failing and had decided to make a personal appeal. Striking in her height, her long hair the color of wheat against the creamy white of her gown, she glided across the floor holding up her hem as her train whispered behind her. She stood in front of Lucius, her heels elevating her eyes to within two inches of his, and held out her hand.

"Come on, Dad. It won't kill you," she said with false lightness.

Her father looked down, pretending to examine the shine in his shoes.

"Anne, don't . . ."

"Please. Just for me. Only for half a minute."

She gave a radiant smile so artificial that Christian was embarrassed for her.

"Anne, don't spoil it with this, this . . ."

"This what?"

"Sentimentality."

"Sentimentality? Is that what you call it?" she asked, her voice dipping into the icy regions inhabited by her father's. Her smile had begun to crumble. Her attempts to hold up under the weight of her sadness and hurt reminded Christian of someone straining to support a collapsing beam. "I want my father to dance with me on my wedding day, and that's sentimentality?"

"Anne, please. This is embarrassing. You know how I feel."

"I certainly do. Everyone here can tell how you feel." At that moment Christian wished he had the power to become invisible. He was sure his sister was going to fall into hysterics; but she was a Starkmann, ever in control. "And since everybody can see how painful this is for you," she went on, her eyes glistening but her voice steady, "you're making it painful for them. And for me. So why don't you do all of us the courtesy of leaving?"

She whirled around in a rustle of antique satin, and without another word or glance, returned to the dance floor and her husband's arms. Her audacity—it was the first time Christian had seen anyone in the family stand up to Lucius—had left his father stupefied. He stood for a moment in injured, silent amazement at Anne's defiance, then turned on his heel to walk through the foyer toward the front door. Looking at his back, his hair like polished pewter in the sunlight, Christian felt an inexplicable pity, though his sister's courage had won his admiration.

"Dad," he called, following Lucius outside. "She didn't mean to—I mean, she was upset."

"Go inside and tell your mother we're leaving."

The command caused Christian to undergo an emotional somersault, anger overcoming pity.

"You could have done that, you know. That one little thing, but no, not you, you . . ."

"You *what?*" asked Lucius, without breaking stride as he marched toward the parking lot. "*What* were you about to say, Christian?"

That voice. Christian shriveled under it, down to the size he'd been at nine years old.

"Nothing. I wasn't going to say anything."

"That's what I thought. Because nothing is precisely what a sixteen-year-old has to say about anything. Go inside and tell your mother we're leaving. Now."

"All right." Christian looked out toward the golf course, where a man in a pastel shirt and checkered pants was hunching over to make a putt. "Whatever you say, *Father.*"

Now, as he trudged through the tamaracks, the same resentment boiled inside Starkmann as hotly as it had then, a dormant fever reinflamed.

"You bastard," he muttered, climbing a small knoll that overlooked the Big Firedog and the ridge beyond. He removed his snowshoes, rammed one heel down into a drift, and used the other to shovel out a dry space between the forked roots of a hemlock.

"Bastard!" He flung the snowshoe aside. "You bastard!"

He punched the tree, bruising his knuckles, and punched it again, and a third time, until his knuckles bled.

"Bastard! Bastard!"

He embraced the trunk, laid his cheek against the bark, and prayed silently. *Don't die, you bastard. Don't let him die.* He wept, prayed, and cursed. The strength passing out of his legs, he flopped down in the dry space between the roots. A trickle of blood fell from his knuckles, speckling the snow with red. *You stiff-necked bastard, don't die. Please don't let him die.* June was right. He had to go to his father's side, but it would be unfitting to go with this much hatred in his heart. He had to overcome it somehow. *Please don't let him die*, he repeated, looking up through the laden branches toward a sky low, heavy, and opaque. He packed snow on his hands to staunch the bleeding. *Don't let him die. Not yet. Not till . . .* Till what? Till we've made peace with each other, Starkmann thought. Peace, peace, peace with one another. He smashed his fist into one of the roots, opening new cuts in a self-mortification for the blasphemy he had uttered years ago, for his failure to express his contrition that night when Lucius had entered his room as he was packing, for his blindness in not foreseeing the remorse he would feel if his father were struck down before they'd reconciled, and for the rage that frothed in him now.

Not until this hour had he known how deeply he needed his father. Whether as a source of safety and comfort in his childhood, in his boyhood the standard against which he had measured himself, or as the authority against which he'd rebelled in his early manhood, Lucius had always been a reference point in his life. He dreaded losing him, but dreaded even more the thought of his dying estranged from his son. Was it too late for them to mend the breach? Could they reach down through the crust of misunderstandings, old hurts and disappointments, the words that should not have been spoken, the words that should have been but never were, silences turned to stone, and find at the bottom of all that petrification some remnant of a love still living? Starkmann hoped so, more than he had ever hoped for anything; but such a labor required love at its start, which demanded that he cut the anger out of himself. He wondered how to perform that emotional surgery, and how long it would take. There was so little time. Two to three days at most, June had said.

A gust of north wind shook the trees. Shivering, he drew his knees to his chest and clasped his arms around his legs, huddling for warmth. But the cold was nothing compared to the ache in his chest brought on by the feelings contesting for possession of his heart, his hopes for reconciliation wrestling with his fear that the time for it had already passed, his resentment of his father grappling with his need for him. So violent was the struggle, he felt as if two hands had reached inside him and were tearing him in half.

He wanted to return to the house and the solace of June's arms. He needed to talk to someone about these confusing thoughts and emotions. Who else would listen to him but she? He half-rose to go to her, but something held him back: his dread of intimacy and of sharing his deepest feelings with another, the invisible barrier June had once been able to break through but could no longer, for it had grown thicker in the past year, becoming impenetrable even to her.

He sat down again, the wind and cold making him drowsy. His eyes closed as he bowed his head to rest it on his bent knees, a position in which he sat for several minutes. He began to drift off and, in a state midway between consciousness and sleep, heard himself speaking to someone. *He's had a massive stroke. They've got him in intensive care. I should go and see him, I know I should, but I can't bring myself to do it. What can I do? What should I do?*

Starkmann's eyes opened and his head snapped back, like a puppet's yanked by a cord. A warning mechanism in his head had startled him awake. He'd been speaking to a ghost in his half-sleep, and the last time he'd conversed with the dead, he recalled all too clearly, had been on the day of the night he'd gone into town, drunk, with a loaded gun in his pocket. He held the tree roots tightly, as if clinging to them would help him retain his grip on himself. Yet, even as he clutched them, a corner of his mind beyond his control again asked the question—What should I do?—and awaited an answer. Another gust of wind hissed through the trees. A miniature avalanche fell from their branches into the river.

"What should I do?" He was startled by the sound of his voice. The words had come out of his mouth independently of his will.

He was aware of a presence in the woods, unseen yet perceivable, like a magnetic field. A shadowy movement caught the corner of his eye. He turned to see who or what it was. Nothing was there. The movement came again, a movement as of someone ducking behind a tree; but when he looked, he saw that it had only been a branch, quivering in the wind.

"*Preacher.*"

The voice seemed to be calling from across the river, from somewhere up on the ridge. Goose bumps crawling up his neck, Starkmann peered through the dense flurries. No one was there.

"*Preacher.*"

Impossible, he told himself. Who could be calling him by his old nickname out here?

Then he saw three vague but definitely human figures walk down the ridge, jump over the river—a leap beyond any ordinary man's abilities—and climb up the knoll to stand in front of him. In a moment their features grew distinct, like faces brought into focus by a camera lens. Their forms assumed a three-dimensional reality, or the illusion of it. Starkmann would have screamed but he was too horrified to make a sound, horrified not by the figments themselves as much as by the insanity they represented. He could see the snow, the pines, the river—the real world—and yet he also saw *them*, not six feet from him, so clearly it was as if they had been reincarnated. Tim Hutchinson, with his sandy hair and beardless chin; D.J. Fishburn, stringy and hollow-cheeked; Alessandro Ramos, wearing a flak jacket over his bare, muscular chest. Impossible! They had vanished from this life years ago, in a departure so thorough that hardly a fragment of their bones had been left to bury. By what sorcery had they been made whole again?

He blinked to make the apparitions disappear, and when that had no effect, he began to pray again, now petitioning the heavens to return his sanity. *Please not this. Please, please, please.* He shut his eyes, envisioning his brain as a kind of ship floating in a sea of cranial fluids. One of its compartments, damaged and flooding with madness, had created the hallucinations. He had to seal it off, dog its hatches, to save the rest of his mind. His efforts to do so were so strenuous they set his teeth on edge, his muscles growing as rigid as the roots to which he clung. Vertigo overcame him; he was near to passing out when the hatches burst with a roar, and he saw the waters of madness, as foul as any swamp's, surging through his mental passageways, a deluge he was powerless to stop. Utterly spent, he abandoned himself to it, sinking into a darkness in which he could not see, hear, or feel a thing.

When his eyes reopened, the cold had become the heat of a tropical afternoon, the snow a monsoon drizzle. The snowdrifts had darkened into mud, the hemlock had changed into a wild tamarind, and the river flowed between galleries of pale bamboo.

"Preacher."

He looked up into D.J.'s gaunt face.

"You know what you gotta do. Don't need us to tell you."

D.J. squatted beside him, bloodshot eyes peering out from under the cowl of his poncho. Hutch and Ramos remained standing, Ramos hunching his shoulders against the rain, the medic cupping a cigarette.

"You're not real!" Starkmann shouted. "None of this is real."

"We are and we ain't," D.J. said with a spectral grin.

"What he means, Chris, is that you're just imagining all this." Hutch inhaled on the cigarette and blew a cloud of smoke into the warm, moist air. "You're imagining us, but that doesn't mean we aren't real. We're real to you."

"That's crazy. It's craziness."

"Crazy? I don't know. I'm just a field medic. What difference does it make anyhow?"

Hutch's voice, gentle with the accents of coastal Virginia, quieted Starkmann's fears. He relaxed, and his mind, working with supernatural speed, grasped the truth in the apparent contradiction that the three men were real and illusory at the same time. He had entered a realm in which distinctions between the imaginary and its opposite did not exist. The instantaneousness with which he came to this understanding astonished him. The spirits of D.J., Hutch, and Ramos lived in his imagination, and what was more, he could speak to them, they to him. He was not alone. He could share his thoughts and feelings with them, his comrades in the only brotherhood he had ever known.

"So let's hear what's on your mind," Hutch drawled.

Starkmann told them and asked what he ought to do.

"Like I said a minute ago, you don't need us to tell you. You know."

He looked quizzically at D.J.

"It's in your Bible," Hutch said.

"Yeah. You the Preach, y'know, all a time readin' the Bible. Where's your Bible?"

Starkmann reached into his pocket. His Bible wasn't there. It was back in the house. The tranquillity he'd felt a moment earlier left him, panic taking its place. How could he return to the house from wherever he now was?

"Be easy. You don't really need it," Hutch reassured him. "You know the passage by heart. The prodigal son."

"Luke. The book of Luke. Chapter Fifteen."

"I guess that's it. How's it go, Chris?"

" 'And when he came to himself, he said . . .' " Starkmann paused. He knew it verbatim, but his memory had failed him. He tried again. " 'And when he came to himself, he said, How many hired servants of my father's have enough—' No. 'Have bread enough and to spare, and I perish with hunger! ' "

"Sound like you got it," Ramos said. "Le's hear the rest."

" 'I will . . . I will . . .' "

"C'mon, Chris."

"I can't remember."

"Preacher, you got to remember."

" 'Arise.' That's it. 'I will arise and . . .' "

"C'mon, Chris."

"Le's hear it, Preach."

"You gonna arise and do what, Preacher?"

He tried to recall the verse, but the harder he struggled for the words, the more they eluded him. His panic mounted. It seemed everything hinged on his memory. He grew short of breath and began to quake.

He was lying under the hemlock when he awoke, still trembling and gasping for air. He lay for several moments, bewildered by what had happened to him, then sat up to shake off the feeling of disorientation. He looked about. Nothing had changed except the sky, its gray shading toward black as the early northern dusk descended. He wondered how long he had been asleep. *Had* he been sleeping? He could not recall any passage into unconsciousness, and yet he must have fallen asleep, probably after he'd lowered his head to his knees. He'd fallen asleep and dreamed. He'd only dreamed that he had gone mad, as he had dreamed the conversation with his brothers. A dream within a dream. He was sane after all, a discovery that so overjoyed him that he temporarily forgot about the predicament that had brought him out to this spot. He stood, brushed the snow from his clothes, and basked in the sight of the pines, the sky, and the white earth. It had been nothing more than a dream. A part of him clung to it, to that moment when the presence of the three ghosts had dispelled his loneliness. He missed that feeling of comradeship, but in the end was more than glad to trade its illusory comfort for the painful reality of this solitude, in which he at least had full ownership of his mind.

Happy that he had not lost it, happier than his conscience thought the son of a dying man should be, he remembered the verse that had evaded him in the dream. *I will arise and go to my father, and will say unto him, Father, I have sinned against heaven, and before thee, And am no more worthy to be called thy son. . . .* It was remarkable, as plain to him as if he were reading it from the printed page. *But the father said to his servants, Bring forth the best robe, and put it on him; and put a ring on his hand, and shoes on his feet: And bring hither the fatted calf, and kill it, and let us eat, and be merry: For this my son was dead, and is alive again; he was lost, and is found.*

That was it, word for word. Starkmann's heart beat from the excitement of discovering the message in the dream. It had been like a message from God, telling him that if he went to his father and confessed his wrongs, Lucius would recover and forgive him. Then they would be reconciled at last. This was, he saw, more than a mere hope: it was a prophecy.

He strapped on his snowshoes and shuffled through the tamaracks as quickly as the clumsy footgear would allow. Ahead, the generator hummed as the lights went on in the house, the windows casting elongated rectangles on the drifts. He could not wait to begin packing for the drive to Chicago, where a miracle awaited him.

19

All color had been leached from Lucius Starkmann's face. It looked like paper. The once vigorous white of his hair now had the unhealthy paleness of an albino's. *And I looked, and behold a pale horse*, Christian thought as he entered the room and gazed at the figure on the bed. *And his name that sat on him was Death.* But he did not believe it was the nearness of death that gave his father his ghostly pallor; it was the hospital room. Its walls were white, as were the contour Fiberglas chairs beside a bed covered in white sheets. A white gown cloaked his father's body. The nurse escorting him wore a uniform bleached to the whiteness he'd seen on TV commercials for laundry detergents. The life-support and monitoring machines hooked to the Reverend Starkmann were either white or off-white, the respirator tubes in his nostrils and the IV tube in his arm clear plastic filled with clear fluids. A sickly city sun shone through the window, heightening the colorlessness of the room and his father's face.

Looking at the face, Starkmann noticed that the jaw was as firm and defiant as ever, confirming his belief that his father would not die. As he had challenged the cattle prods of the mounted troopers in Mississippi and the bayonets of the National Guardsmen here in Chicago a long time ago, so was he now defying death itself.

The nurse left. Starkmann stood alone in the room. He had bathed before coming to the hospital, in the hottest water he could stand, scrubbing his skin until it almost bled. He wanted to appear clean and presentable when his father awoke and saw him. He was wearing his western-cut leather jacket, jeans, a blue-and-white striped shirt, and cowboy boots—the "high-hick" outfit in which he'd been married. Perhaps he did look a little too countrified for Chicago, but his boots had been buffed to a high luster—he'd spit-shined them himself—and the Holiday Inn had starched and pressed his jeans and shirt, the creases in both as sharp as the edges of an envelope. He and June were staying at the Holiday Inn, at his insistence. He did not want to stay at his father's house in Oak Park, at least not yet.

Lucius had been moved from the ICU to the terminal ward. It was on the seventeenth floor, near the top of the building, as if the doctors wanted dying patients to be a little closer to heaven in their final hours. The hospital had liberal visitation rules on the terminal ward. Relatives were allowed to stay as long as they desired, to keep vigil, a kind of deathwatch. Anne and Ed had done that this morning and were now at the house with June, taking care of his mother, who was under sedation. After Anne and Ed, Jennifer and Stephanie had taken over. He'd seen his two younger sisters in the lobby as he was coming in to take his turn. He'd hardly recognized Jennifer, who'd been fourteen when he'd last seen her. Or maybe she'd been fifteen. He couldn't quite recall. Anne had welcomed him kindly, but his younger sisters had greeted him with cool animosity; when he'd said that he was going upstairs to be alone with his father, Stephanie, with tears in her eyes, asked, "It's a little late for that, isn't it, Chris?"

He forgave the condemnation implied in her question, because she did not understand the reasons for his exile and because he knew it was not too late.

Starkmann sat in one of the contoured chairs, looking at the white figure on the white bed, and at the array of white machinery. Northside Hospital was one of the best and most expensive in Chicago. It had all the latest equipment, but Starkmann did not like the high-tech gadgetry, the wires, tubes, and electrodes attached to his father. It made him look like an experiment in a science-fiction story. One machine monitored his heartbeat, which registered on a gray videoscope as a series of peaks and valleys, like a constantly moving mountain range. His pulse made green blips on another scope. A third machine recorded the bioelectric impulses of his brain, displayed as gentle waves on yet another scope. The respirator bellowsed his lungs, his mechanical inhalations and exhalations making a sound like a scuba diver underwater. The life-support systems were gruesome-looking, all right, but they would be necessary until the miracle took place; God would not allow a man who had preached His word to die without knowing that his son had returned.

Starkmann closed his eyes and sat quietly for a quarter of an hour, clearing his mind; then he concentrated on transmitting his thoughts into the wires patched to his father's head. The doctor had told the family that Lucius was not yet brain-dead; a part of his mind continued to live under the layers of unconsciousness, like an ember beneath a mound of ashes. Christian attempted to fan this faint coal into a flame with his own thoughts.

Dad? Hey, Dad. It's me, Chris, your boy. I've come back, after all these years. I'm right beside you. If you can understand me, say "Yes" in your mind. Think it real hard, Dad. "Yes."

Christian opened his eyes, fixing them on what he believed to be his father's brain waves flowing across the videoscope. He did not notice any change in their pattern. Maybe he had not concentrated enough. He tried once more, focusing his thoughts, imagining them to be like sun rays burning through a magnifying glass; but when he reopened his eyes, he saw that the brain waves were continuing their gentle oscillations across the screen. Maybe he was using the wrong method of communication. Maybe his thoughts could not travel through the wires like radio signals. Or maybe the machine could not register his father's thoughts. It was also possible that the waves were not brain waves at all, but some other bodily function.

After reflecting a while, Starkmann recalled that he had read or heard somewhere that the last sense to go in coma victims was hearing. *The Reader's Digest*—a story about a woman who'd been in a coma for days, but who came out of it when she heard her husband's voice. He pulled the chair to the bed and took his father's hand, the one without the IV tube, in both of his. The hand was limp and speckled with liver spots. His father had grown old! Sixty-five, Starkmann remembered. Well, that wasn't terribly old nowadays.

"Dad? If you can hear me, it's Chris, your son. I'm back. Yeah, I'm back, finally. I know it's awful that it took something like this to bring me back, but here I am, right next to you. I'm holding your hand."

Pausing to gather his thoughts, he gazed out the window at the crush of buildings and, beyond them, at the shimmer of Lake Michigan. Snow from the spring blizzard that had followed him down from the Upper Peninsula lay melting in the streets, a brownish-white mush like undercooked oatmeal.

"I wish we could forget the past ten years and the thing that drove us apart. Do you remember when I was a kid and you were teaching me how to double-haul with a flyrod? You said it was like trying to rub your belly with one hand and pat your head with the other at the same time, but if I kept at it, I'd get it. You were so patient with me then, so I hope you'll be patient with me now.

"I love you, and I'm sorry for hurting you. I did what I thought was the right thing, but I guess it was the wrong thing after all, especially if it hurt you. I'm sorry for that and for the hard thing I said the last night I saw you. I don't know what had got into me, but I am sorry for it. I still remember my scripture, Dad. Luke: fifteen, twenty-one. *And the son said unto him, Father, I have sinned against heaven, and in thy sight, and am no more worthy to be called thy son.* That's pretty much how I feel right now, but everything's going to be all right.

"God is going to pull you out of this because He's not going to let you die without knowing I came back to you. I dreamed that the other day, and I know it'll come true. He won't let you down. And He's not going to let me down, either. He's not going to let you die before you put your arms around me and say 'Welcome home, son.' We'll throw our arms around each other, no kidding—you're going to wake up and that's going to happen. I saw a father and son do that when I came home from the war. This kid came off the plane and he and his father ran into each other's arms. They were Spanish, I think. I don't know, I couldn't read the kid's name tag, but he and his dad looked Spanish. The Latins are like that—emotional, I mean—and I know we're German and English and not like that, but we're going to embrace each other anyway as soon as you wake up and you don't need these machines anymore."

He caught his breath after this, perhaps the longest speech of his life. Apparently, Lucius still had not heard him: The mountains of his heartbeat peaked and dipped with the same rhythm as before; his brain waves maintained their smooth undulations. God, what could he say to get through to him?

"Maybe I'd better tell you something else. There are some people who think I'm a little crazy. June, for example. She doesn't know that I know that she thinks I'm a little crazy, but I can tell by the way she looks at me sometimes that she thinks I am. I want you to know that I was crazy once, but I'm not anymore. I'm . . . I'm . . ." He paused again, searching for the right phrase to express the insight that had come to him during the long drive from Vieux Desert. The self-discovery had so excited him that he remembered precisely where he'd made it: two miles outside the town of New London, Wisconsin. Now he tried to articulate it in a way that would make sense to Lucius. On the slushy streets far below, traffic was piling up; it was rush hour. "I'm kind of not in one piece—split in two, I guess," Starkmann said. "See, all of me never came home, Dad. I mean, I'm here and I've been here in the States, what is it now? Thirteen years. But a part of me is still *there*. I don't know why, but it is. That part of me hasn't come home. Not too long ago, I—the most of me that's here—used to go back there, in my dreams. They weren't dreams, exactly, but like trips back in time. I know. That sounds like a crazy man talking, but it's true. What happened, I think, is that the most of me that's here would get lonely for the part of me that's still there and would take these trips to join it. I haven't made one of those trips in a while, but that part of me is still, well, sort of MIA— Missing in Action—and what I want is for it to leave there and join the most of me that's here. That's going to happen when you wake up and say 'Welcome home, son.' Kind of like the prodigal son, Dad. Luke Fifteen again. *And he arose, and came to his father. But when he was yet a great way off, his father saw him, and had compassion, and ran, and fell on his neck, and kissed him. . . . For this my son was dead, and is alive again; he was lost, and is found."*

That'll do it for sure, Starkmann thought. He must have heard that. But he saw no reaction from the long, pale figure on the bed; nor did the videoscopes register any change in his pulse, his mind, or his heart.

How badly he wanted his father to speak! How strange it was not to hear his clear voice, the voice that froze and burned, that scourged and cleansed like an arctic wind. He knew he would have to be patient and wait for the miracle to happen in its good time. He let go his father's hand. He braced his chair against the wall, arranging the other so he could stretch out and prop his feet on it. He needed to sleep; he'd driven all night, but he couldn't get comfortable in the hard chairs. Also, he was so tall that when he extended his legs their full length, he sagged in the middle like one of the suspension cables on the Mackinac Bridge. He pulled his feet from the second chair, stretched his legs out in front of him, his heels on the floor, and finally managed to fall asleep.

Someone shook him gently by the shoulder. He opened his eyes, blinking against the bright overhead light. Outside, it was dark.

"Mr. Starkmann?"

It was the nurse, not the same one as in the afternoon, but an older woman, gray-headed. There were two other people in the room: a doctor and another nurse, a black woman who was removing the respirator and the plastic drainage tubes. Starkmann jumped out of the chair when he saw the blue of his father's open eyes.

It had happened! The life-support systems were no longer needed. A miracle on the terminal ward!

"I'm sorry, Mr. Starkmann," said the older woman.

He looked down at her uncomprehendingly.

"*Sorry.* He's come out of it!"

"No, Mr. Starkmann. Your father's gone."

His eyes ranged the room, taking in the doctor, who extended a hand in sympathy; the black nurse, who was now removing the intravenous tube; his father's motionless chest; and the videoscopes, all displaying straight lines, straight lifeless lines, the peaks and valleys leveled, the waves flattened to the flatness of a pond on a day of no wind.

"We picked it up a few moments ago at the monitoring station," the doctor explained. "There's a phone there, if you'd like to notify your family. Or I can, if you prefer. We promised to let them know as soon as it happened."

The black nurse, her uniform startlingly bright against her skin, had begun to detach the life-support machines.

"Stop that! Stop it, goddamn you!"

"What's the matter with you?" she shouted as Starkmann tried to reattach the complex array of wires and hoses, plugs and tubes. He couldn't figure out what went where, flung them aside, and started to cry in frustration.

"Mr. Starkmann, please! He's gone," said the gray-haired woman.

The doctor took hold of his elbow as if to lead him away, but he jabbed the elbow into the doctor's ribs, hard, the way he used to, fighting for a rebound under the boards. As the doctor fell back, clutching his side, Starkmann reached under his father's back, scooped him up into a sitting position, and held him tightly against his chest.

"Dad? Dad? Dad!"

The corpse's head fell to one side, the jaw dropping open as if he were about to speak.

"Say it, Dad, say it!"

Both nurses and the doctor were trying to pull him away; they were trying to tear him and his father apart. He shook them off, then reached with one hand to wrap one of his father's arms around his waist.

"Hold me and say it." He shook the corpse, its white head flopping like a broken doll's. "Welcome home, son. Say it, damn you!"

The older nurse ran outside to call Security.

BAWAJIGAYWIN

Nights are cold, high in the Hurons in the month of the shining leaf, but there was no shivering in Wawiekumig's flesh as he walked naked out of his wigwam to hear the birds singing up the sun. After three days of sweat and starve, his spiritual side had gained ascendancy. His belly had ceased its calls for food; his throat no longer commanded him to drink from the jar of maple water. Only one physical demand this morning: Wawiekumig went off a short distance to relieve himself against a tree, his piss almost red, as if blood itself were draining out of him. Maybe I'll die before today's done with, he thought. Maybe that's the way to achieve breakthrough.

He went to the fire and blew the embers into flame, piling on ironwood logs. He did not want to die, though he had no fear of it. Death was natural, and he had lived more than a man's allotted years. His fear was of what might happen afterward; with no one to perform the Ghost Rites for him, his soul could stray from the Path of the Dead and become lost, wandering the swamps for eternity.

He banished the morbid thought as he heated the rocks for sweat-bath and watched the sun spread its light over the lake. Such thinking was a distraction on this day, the day when he would hold the Ghost Supper.

While the rocks warmed, he walked down to the shore to check the trotlines he had set out last night to catch fish for the Supper. Exhausted by the trial he'd put himself through, a trial not yet ended, his legs wobbled as he squatted to pull in the lines. He felt the weight of fish on both, the first one yielding a good pike, four, maybe five pounds; the second a much smaller fish; the two together more than enough. After filleting the pike, leaving the green white-speckled skins on, he scooped coals and smoking chunks of ironwood into a big pot, building up a thick layer that would burn for hours. He laid the fillets on a pie tin, which was fitted over the pot, then covered the tin with another and set the pot next to the fire. In a few hours, the fish would be smoked.

The savory smell made his belly grumble, but a short time in the sweat-lodge stilled temptation, spirituality reasserting itself. When he came out, Wawiekumig sprinkled bits of sage leaves into the fire, the powerful sweetish smell overcoming the aroma of the fish, the sage smoke purifying the camp.

Then, facing the branchless pine, his back to the sun, he spread his arms like wings, singing to the spirit of the eagle, singing to the manitos of the west. He began to dance again, his movements awkward, with only a suggestion of the suppleness his limbs had once possessed. He kept on, unmindful of how well or badly he danced. There was no one here to admire or criticize him. Dancing ever in a circle, eyes on the earth, the spirit of the past, dancing and reflecting upon his life, seeking to recall if he had succumbed to one of the seven temptations that come to a Mide on the path from youth to old age.

And he thought about his dead.

His wife had died of tuberculosis two years after giving birth to their son. Wawiekumig had sung her his healing song, given her remedies for the coughing-up-blood disease, all to no effect. He buried her in the proper way, her feet to the west, and sang to her: "Your feet are now on the road of souls, my wife." His first mourning, his face blackened for a year. His second had come a year later, with the death of his father.

Wawiekumig never remarried, and so had no more children after Ka'wa, who had brought him another kind of sadness by turning his back on the Mide path, adopting Christianity, and insisting everyone, red and white, address him by his English name, Clement. Clement had returned home from the big war against the Japanese full of greed, his only purpose in life self-enrichment. He slaughtered trees, not for fire or shelter but for money, an evil against which Wawiekumig had warned him. Everything has a right to be on the earth, he'd told his son; everything possesses its own spirit, its own mystery. To kill without necessity was a violation. Wawiekumig had seen the consequences of such destructive greed in his youth, when the whites had butchered the white pine in the north woods, a massacre so vast in the visible world that it had an effect in the invisible world: The life-master of the white pine died. The life-master, to which the spirits of dead trees would have flown to be regenerated and sent back to earth as new trees, had been destroyed—this the reason so few white pine now grew in the woods. To this, Clement had made a mocking answer, scoffing at his father's beliefs, saying that making money was a necessity. Did not Wawiekumig earn a living by trapping, by guiding hunters and fishermen who came to the woods to kill and catch only for the sport of it?

"Yes, I do," he'd replied quietly in English, as Clement refused to speak his native language. "But only to eat."

"Well, old man," Clement had said, "I want to do more than just eat."

Then came the day, the inevitable day, when one of the trees, raging like a bear from the wounds Clement had inflicted on it, turned on him and killed him. His crushed body lay in the woods a week before it was found, half-eaten by crows and coyotes. Wawiekumig blackened his face for the third time in his life and, worried that his son's soul might not be admitted to the Christian heaven, held the Ghost Rites, guiding Clement's spirit down the Path of the Dead.

Madeline died within a few months of Clement, but for her, there had been no blackening of the face, no Ghost Rites performed. Madeline had never been a faithful wife to his son. Her conduct had been scandalous. She was never a good mother to Boniface. A drunk with a wildness in her, her drunkenness had led to her death in an accident. No, there had been no mourning for her by Wawiekumig. Madeline, also a Christian, had called him a superstitious fool when he'd counseled her to amend her behavior. She had laughed at him, her breath stinking of whiskey, an insult that had almost provoked Wawiekumig to curse her through the rites and incantations of mudjimushkeeki. It had taken all his strength to resist the temptation, but when Madeline's father, also a Christian, had come to him, pleading that he hold the funeral ceremonies for his daughter, Wawiekumig could not resist laughing. He refused the man's request. Neither you nor she needed my medicine before, he'd said, his heart like granite. You don't need it now. Go away. Go to your church. Go to your priest. Maybe he can help you.

That had been an unfitting thing to say, an unfitting thing to do, Wawiekumig thought, dancing. A Mide was supposed to be above anger and petty revenge. Also unbecoming had been his hidden wish, after Madeline's insult, that misfortune befall her. True, he had never practiced mudjimushkeeki to bring it about, but the truth was he'd wished it, and had been glad when she died in the accident. A selfishness had mothered both the desire and the gladness and had come with its fulfillment. Long before Madeline's and Clement's deaths, he had wanted Boniface to live with him; he was disturbed by the way his parents were raising him. They had baptized him and had sent him to the white schools. One more Ojibwa was going to be lost to the Mide path; and Wawiekumig, already past the middle of his life, foreseeing its end, had begun to long for someone to whom he could entrust his scrolls and medicine-bundle, whom he could teach the old language and customs, someone who would hold the Ghost Rites for him.

Eyes on the earth, mind on the past. Suddenly Wawiekumig stopped dancing. He stood, his heart beating with the quickness that always preceded the reception of a message. Looking at the bare tree, his spiritual senses made alert by the punishment of his flesh, he waited no more than a few moments before it came. *You never practiced mudjimushkeeki to bring death to your daughter-in-law, but your desire for her death, your desire to become father to your grandson— those were so powerful they were equal to an actual going-through of the rites by which one causes harm to another. That was your offense, Wawiekumig, and the out-of-season death of the grandson you coveted its consequence.*

The voice, the voice of insight, had never deceived him. It spoke the truth now, but he did not reproach himself. Its message had not been an accusation but insight, and an insight was more cause for rejoicing than reproach. Yet he did not rejoice either. He had reached only the first level of awareness on this quest of his. Instead, Wawiekumig rested briefly, refreshing himself with a little maple water, and pondered that which he had just learned about himself, his musings taking him back to the day when Boniface had come to him, asking his advice.

His grandson's dilemma had confused him. The little that Wawiekumig, isolated and illiterate, knew about the war to which Boniface had been called he had learned by overhearing snatches of conversation at tribal council meetings and mutterings of discontent from the young men who idled about the reservation store. His sense of dignity prohibited his admitting his ignorance to Boniface, whom he told to wait a few days while he meditated on the matter.

Wawiekumig had studied the migration scrolls, in which were recorded the many battles the Original Men had fought against the Iroquois and Sioux. Red Sky had taken part in one of these fights as a very young man, and in his old age looked back with happiness on the glory of his war party's victorious return, Sioux scalps flying from their rifle barrels as they came upriver to their home village. The women launched canoes, which they paddled in zigzag patterns in front of the returning warriors', the women singing a song of welcome, *Ojibwa our brother brings back*. The Seven Grandfathers, Red Sky had said, had taught that war was natural to man. So was peace. There was a time for each, just as there was a time when the Big Lake should be calm, a time when it should be wild with storms. But the Grandfathers had also taught that war was natural only when fought against natural enemies; engagement in the conflict of others was an offense. Red Sky had witnessed the consequences of such a trespass during the Civil War, when many young Ojibwa joined the American Army. Almost none came back, and those who did returned without arms, legs, eyes, and some were crazy. There was mourning throughout the villages and, what was worse, no way to avenge the deaths and restore balance. The white man declared the war was over; the Ojibwa had no recourse but to grieve, their grief the penalty for their trespass. It was that experience that had turned Red Sky to the Midewewin.

Wawiekumig had thought about this, and about Clement coming home from the war against the Japanese tainted by alien influences, a changed man, full of greed. The same army that had called him was calling Boniface to fight another distant people with whom the Anishinabe had no natural quarrel. He was considering flight to Canada to avoid this war. That seemed the proper thing to do, and yet he came from a warrior race of men who had never fled from danger. Wawiekumig's confusion grew. Sioux and Iroquois, natural enemies, but the world had taken many turns since those distant battles. Who were his grandson's natural enemies? The question prompted another: What was his grandson, Ojibwa or American? Or both?

With these conflicting thoughts in his head, Wawiekumig had gone off to fast and pray for a clarifying vision. In time, one came: He saw great fires burning in a forest and a fierce hawk flying into the flames, then flying out, its wings on fire, yet flying. Intuition having shown him a vision, his reasoning mind had to interpret it; and his reason told him that the fires were the war, the hawk Boniface, and his plunging unafraid into the blaze a sign that he should go, not run. That is the counsel he gave to his grandson, taking care to leave him room to make his own decision.

"Think about going to Canada," he had said. "And if you can't imagine it, don't do it. A man shouldn't try to do anything he can't *see* himself doing."

In itself, that had not been false advice, but Wawiekumig's interpretation of the vision—that had been false. He saw that now. The evil he had wished upon Madeline had come full circle, had opened him to misleading voices, which had tricked him into thinking the vision was ninbawadjige, a medicine vision, when it had been ina'puwe, a dream-warning of Boniface's death. Those deceivers had so blinded him that he had not seen the truth even when he'd spoken with the soldier who'd come to the train station with Boniface's body, the corpse in a metal box draped in an American flag. Ten, twelve of Madeline's relatives were there also, uncles, aunts, cousins. The soldier explained to them how Boniface had died: in a fire—"friendly fire" was what the soldier had called it in English, a peculiar and baffling phrase. Airplanes had dropped firebombs in the wrong place, killing Boniface. Madeline's family had been more angry than sorrowful at this news. One of the men almost attacked the soldier, as if he were at fault. Bombs dropped in the wrong place—"What kind of story was that?" shouted a woman, a younger sister of Madeline. What was the reason for such a mistake? It made no sense for Boniface to die in such a way, only nineteen years old. Someone was to blame. Someone should be punished.

Numb with sadness, Wawiekumig at first had listened to their rantings in silence. All he could do was stare at the metal box and the flag and choke back his tears. Outward displays of grief were unbecoming a Mide brother. But Madeline's relatives began to get out of hand, frightening the soldier and compelling Wawiekumig to attempt to restore calm and reason. The soldier, he'd told them, was only a messenger. Why shout at him? Why shout at all? This death called for dignified mourning, not loud voices. The death was not an accident without reason, for nothing happens without a reason; when a reason for something could not be found, then it was called mystery, beyond human understanding but still a part of the Creator's plan. The Seven Grandfathers had taught that, as they had taught that a death out of season was a sign of trouble in the world. If Madeline's people wanted a reason, then they should look into their own hearts. If they wanted someone to blame, then they should blame themselves. They, all of them, had strayed from the Mide path, and the untimely death of their kinsman was a sign that the Mide-manitos had been offended by their deviation.

His listeners had looked at him as if he were crazy. He knew his wisdom had not reached them, maybe because he'd had to speak in English, which did not supply him with the words to express his true thoughts, true feelings.

And because, Wawiekumig thought as he sat near his fire, in any language I had not spoken the truth that day. There had been a trespass, but it was mine, not theirs—I know that now.

He took another sip of maple water, offering a silent prayer of thanks for the revelation of his offense. At least I know more now than I did this morning, he said to himself. Maybe by this evening I will know more than I do now.

He stood up, ignoring the shooting pains in his legs, and walked to his fasting-place, where he lay down, the sun directly above. When it set, he would call Boniface to the Ghost Supper.

Concentrate all your thoughts on him, instructed his inner voice. Think only of him. Imagine him as he was when he lived on the earth. If you imagine well enough, then you will see him, hear him, when he comes.

Wawiekumig chased down memories of his grandson. Boniface sitting at his feet and learning how to read the etchings on the scrolls . . . Boniface smiling the day he'd caught his first fish, a big brook trout . . . Boniface tramping behind him through winter woods to check what the traps had caught . . . Boniface crying after he had heard the tale of Minabozho's search for his father, crying and asking Wawiekumig: "Mishomis, if I go across the ocean when I grow up, will I find my father?" . . . Boniface, a man, shaking hands goodbye when he'd left for the war.

Boniface's funeral. Wawiekumig remembered that. Madeline's family, taking advantage of an old man's sorrow, had given the boy a Christian burial in the cemetery of the reservation Catholic church, an outrage, a theft of body and soul.

Some nights later, Wawiekumig, accompanied by Eshkwaykeezhik and Endusogijig, both alive then, and by three younger men, had sneaked into the graveyard, this bold act almost like a war party's raid in the days of Red Sky's youth. The young men dug up the metal box, tidying up carefully so the grave would not appear to have been disturbed, then loaded Boniface's corpse onto a truck and drove to an ancient Ojibwa burial ground far in the woods. Wawiekumig and the other old men, his Mide brethren, followed in another truck. At the burial ground, where small huts and stakes bearing clan do-dems marked the graves, the box was opened. Wawiekumig, masking nose and mouth against the smell, took a paint jar from his medicine bag and smeared a vermilion stripe across his grandson's forehead—this according to the old customs. He worked by the light of kerosene lamps held by the young men, the lamplight disclosing his grandson's face, almost unrecognizable, so badly had it been burned. He wanted to weep, but showed strength, and with another paint jar drew two brown circles on each of the charred cheeks, then cut off a lock of singed hair, enough for the spirit-bundle he would carry during his year of mourning. The body was then lifted out of the box, wrapped in birchbark, and with the feet pointing westward, was lowered into a grave dug beforehand. A grave house built by one of the young men was placed atop on the mounded earth, a marker with the whooping-crane symbol of the Bird clan staked in front of the house.

"Now your feet are on the Path of the Souls," Wawiekumig had said when all was done. Then, for the fourth time in his life, he blackened his face with charcoal.

The young men were paid—they'd had to be bribed to do what, in the past, would have been an honor—and sent off, leaving the three old men to conduct the Ghost Rites in secrecy. Endusogijig beat the waterdrum while Eshkwaykeezhik took the place of Boniface's spirit, acting out its journey to the Village of the Dead, while Wawiekumig sang warnings to the soul.

"You will come upon four fruits on your journey, Grandson: heartberry, plum, Junecherry and blueberry. Resist temptation to eat them. If you do, you will become lost in the swamps."

Eshkwaykeezhik mimicked the soul encountering the fruits, reaching out to taste them, then withdrawing his hand and walking on.

"Now you are approaching the Village of the Dead. There is a river, a bridge across it," Wawiekumig chanted. "Beware this bridge, which appears to be a log but is not. It is the tail of Kogagoupogun, the water serpent. It will roll under you as you cross it. Keep your balance. If you fall, you will be lost forever."

Endusogijig beating the drum, Eshkwaykeezhik danced an imitation of the spirit tottering as the serpent's tail rolled and thrashed, the spirit recovering its balance and entering the Village of the Dead, passing from there into the Ghost Lodge.

Drum and songs ended.

The three old men remained in the woods for four more days, the time it would take Boniface's soul to complete its journey, all three fasting and praying for its safe passage.

At the end of the fourth day, Wawiekumig presided over the Ghost Supper, providing food caught in his traps, setting out a place for Boniface. When all were done eating, he passed around a jar of maple water and then spoke, showing strength, restraining his tears.

"Grandson, for as long as I remember you, I will remember you in this way, the way we, the Original Men, once commemorated our dead. I am happy you could eat with us today, but now the feast is done and it is time for you to return to the Ghost Lodge. I ask you to leave us. I ask you to go home."

That had been fourteen autumns ago. Fourteen years I have grieved, Wawiekumig thought, lying in his fasting place.

He lay until the sky blushed red. He rose and went to his

fire to prepare for the Ghost Supper. He could not feel the ground beneath his feet, nor smell the smoked fish he took from the pot and placed in two pie tins, setting both on a log. He had almost no physical sensations now, as if he were turning into pure spirit, a good sign that he would achieve a breakthrough. After he tossed some of the fish into the fire as an offering and put down tobacco, he took powdered dogwood and sage from his medicine-bundle, rubbing dogwood into his eyes, sage into his ears. You will close your eyes to all outside movements, shut your ears to all outside sounds, his inner voice said. You will allow no distractions. You will see and hear only that which you desire to see and hear.

He returned to the fasting place and stood facing west, eyes shut.

"Grandson," he called in a voice so soft it would not have startled a deer ten feet away, a voice quiet in this world but making itself heard in the world of the manitos. "Grandson, the feast is prepared. I invite you to it, as I have every year. I invite you to leave the Village of the Dead and join me in this feast. Come. I wait."

He stood for a time, motionless, hardly breathing.

Come. I wait.

A woodpecker tapped into a tree—woodpecker, herald of the woods, its hammering an announcement: Someone approaches.

Come. I wait.

Soon Wawiekumig sensed a heaviness in the air. The air was a weight bearing down on him, pressing against him on all sides.

You are here.

Wawiekumig, eyes clamped shut, standing fixed as a pole, speaking spirit-to-spirit.

Grandson, now would be the time I would invite you to eat beside me, I content with knowing you are here. This time I wish to speak to you, to see you. I wait.

Think about him, Wawiekumig. Think only of him. Imagine him as he was when he lived on this earth.

Grandson, there are things I wish to know. Who will carry my medicine-bundle when I am dead? Who will care for my scrolls? Who will guide my spirit as I guided yours? These are among the things I wish to know. But my greatest wish: the joy of hearing your voice once more, the happiness of seeing your face once more.

Nothing, only the heaviness in the air.

I am lonely and uncertain. I wish to speak to you. All the old men are dead. My wife is dead. My son is dead. You are dead.

"Grandson, I am old. I am alone!"

His spirit-voice had become his body's voice, cracking, trembling as the tears he had held back for fourteen years burst from his eyes—tears, the blood of a wound unhealed. His sorrow poured out of him in a flood, and he saw through his tears a form, indistinct at first, then assuming recognizable shape. Not Boniface, but migizi, the eagle, swooping down from the crack between night and day, talons extended. Wawiekumig felt himself rising swiftly. Migizi had snatched him in its claws and was carrying him upward, higher and higher, toward the crack between night and day. He looked down, seeing his body, fallen on the ground, not stirring. A wolf howled. Wawiekumig understood. Myeengun—wolf—was guardian spirit of the Afterworld. *I am dying.* He did not feel dread, but exhilaration. His corpse lay far, far below. *I am pure spirit now. I am dead. This is how the manitos are answering my prayers. They are sending me to him. This is not mere mystery, but a marvel, a rapture.*

Then, abruptly, the eagle opened its talons. Wawiekumig fell as rapidly as he had climbed, down and down, soul plummeting back into his flesh. Then darkness.

When he opened his eyes, the sky was still light, the sun dyeing the clouds a deep red. His flight could not have lasted more than an instant. He sat up, tried to stand, collapsing as his legs folded like reeds. A wolf sent up its cry, not myeengun, the Great Wolf, but a wolf of this world, the old, familiar world of the visible, of loss and suffering. Wawiekumig made another attempt to stand. Unsteady, he took a step, then another, and one more, like an infant learning to walk. He hobbled toward the fire, again aware of physical sensations: the chill of the evening, the earth beneath his feet, the raging hollow in his stomach. He had failed to achieve a complete breakthrough. He would not hear the voice for which he'd longed; he would not learn to whom he could leave his sacred objects, but he was not disappointed. *I am not as I was before,* he thought as he sat on the log, warming himself by the fire. He had obtained a medicine vision, in which he had shed his sorrow. His inner voice told him that the body he had seen fallen to the ground had not been he, but his grief. That was what had died, its death cause for thanks, a thanks he gave, singing softly. Migizi, my guardian and guide, I am not as I was before. My mourning is at an end. It is I, Wawiekumig, who says this, says this, I who flew around the world with you.

Then he dressed and ate as one no stranger to hunger.

FOUR
ZHAWANOONG´
(SOUTH)

20

Earth. The smell of it, as June broke ground for her garden, cleansed her lungs after a week of breathing stale office and courtroom air, and the mild exercise of hoeing was a tonic to muscles used Monday through Friday for nothing more than shuffling her case reports, the paperwork of poverty. She'd turned the ground first thing after breakfast with a rented Rototiller; then, with the hoe, she began breaking up the clods of dirt. It was a cloudless morning in mid-May. The warm sunshine drew sweat from her forehead as she chopped at the chunks of loam and clay. The garden formed a thirty- by twenty-foot rectangle behind the garage, and merely standing in it brought out a proprietary feeling in her. Although the house and the timber acreage was in both her and Chris's names, she considered her part-ownership in them a legal one only. In all other ways, they belonged to him; but this small patch of cultivation was hers alone, her equity measured not in dollars but in the sweat, worry, and care she put into it. There had been no spring this year, none to speak of. The weather had stayed chilly throughout April and early May, when it had abruptly turned hot. It was as if the months had leaped from December to July, with no seasonal transition.

This year she was going to risk planting corn and tomatoes to supplement her cold-weather crops of potatoes, radishes, and spinach. Corn required at least three months to mature, tomatoes about half that; the growing season at this latitude—almost forty-seven degrees north—lasted only two months, with the first frosts striking in August. Her Old Farmer's Almanac, however, had predicted a warm summer, which persuaded her to take a chance. Fresh tomatoes—she could almost taste their sweetness now. What a change from the bland tomatoes she bought at the IGA, picked green and then dosed with chemicals to give them an artificially red color. Full of hope, she swung her hoe and breathed the musk of the earth.

Her cross-country skiing had toned her muscles; when she took a break, it wasn't to rest so much as to savor the balmy sun and the sight of the awakening maple and birch, with their branches draped in the lace of reborn leaves. She also wanted to prolong her pleasant labor, wishing she were a farmer with a hundred and sixty acres to plow and plant instead of a mere six hundred square feet. As she stood, her gloved hands curled around the handle, she caught a flicker of beige in the pine woods that picketed the far side of the meadow. A doe cautiously stepped out of the trees to browse on the grass, until some sound or scent frightened it into a series of swift, graceful bounds across the meadow; then it turned sharply and vanished back into the pines. The odor of the earth, the budding trees, a wild deer running— life in the woods was not without its simple pleasures, June supposed, and she was determined to enjoy them to the fullest; there had been few other pleasures in her life since the funeral.

After she finished hoeing, she poured peat and manure into a lawn spreader, which she pushed along the length of the garden, humming tunelessly to herself. The fertilizer made a whispery sound as it sifted through the spreader, its smell calling to mind the odor of fecund bogs, protean life. Nature had never intended this sandy northern earth for domestic crops; it was a sterile womb, and June enjoyed the idea of enriching it, preparing it to receive the seeds she would plant this afternoon. There was, she believed, a morality in vegetable gardening; in the architecture of furrow and troughs she saw order wrested from chaos, a valiant little patch of civilization in a wasteland where everything grew wild.

The fertilizing done, she picked up a spade and turned the crumbled dirt over once again, mixing it with peat and manure. Then she gave the garden a light sprinkling with a hose, to prevent the enriched topsoil from blowing away in case a wind came up.

She set her tools in the wheelbarrow and called for Christine, whom she had to drive to a catechism lesson, her last one before she made her First Communion. Christy was keeping her father company in the back part of the forty, where he'd begun to string another section of the barbed-wire fence that would eventually surround their property and make it look like what, in June's opinion, it had always been: a minimum-security prison. The project had started two weeks ago, after he'd caught two fishermen trespassing and had driven them off at gunpoint. *Gunpoint*, for God's sake! As if they'd been burglars instead of a couple of bumbling anglers who'd strayed onto private land. June had witnessed the last part of the episode, when Chris was marching the fishermen down the road toward their car, a rifle crooked in his elbow so that he looked like a guard escorting criminals to a paddy wagon. Later, he'd declared his intention to ring the property in steel—a perimeter, he'd called it—and showed up the next day with his truck-bed full of stakes, No-Trespassing signs, and rolls of barbed wire.

She called Christine again. When the girl failed to answer, June started across the meadow toward the back of the forty, a dim tamarack swamp below the pine-prickled ridge of the Indian reservation. She'd reached the edge of the swamp when she saw Christine, with Butternut, coming up the log walkway Chris had built across the boggy ground. June loved the way her daughter looked hopping over the logs, her hair flouncing, hair as gold as the spatterdocks that bloomed amidst fan-shaped leaves in the places where the sedge mat thinned, opening to form lily-tangled ponds. The girl bent down, picked a sprig of bog laurel, and handed it to her.

"A bouquet for Mom."

"Why, thank you, Christy," June stuck the laurel in her buttonhole and could not resist lifting Christy up, holding her close to her breast, and lavishing her cheek with kisses.

"You're so pretty, I could swallow you whole."

"Me and Lonnie gave Dad a bouquet too. Laurel and leatherleaf. The leatherleafs looked real nice. Like tiny white bells."

"You're going to have to change those muddy shoes and those jeans before you go to catechism," June said as they returned to the house. "And put on a dress."

"Does Lonnie have to change too?"

"No. Lonnie can come the way he is."

Lonnie had entered their lives after June and Chris had returned from Chicago. June had been a little troubled, thinking Christine too old for imaginary playmates. She'd consulted Sandy, who, though she had no children of her own, kept up on all the modern trends in child psychology. Sandy had reassured her that a make-believe friend was perfectly normal for a seven-year-old. June still wasn't convinced; it was normal only in the sense that it was a natural reaction to an abnormal situation. Christine was lonely out here; lacking real friends, she'd had to invent one.

"Lonnie's pretty messy. He had to give Dad a lot of help building the fence because Dad's friends are kind of lazy."

"Dad's friends?"

"D.J., Hutch, and Ramos."

"Where did you come up with names like that, Christy?" June asked with a laugh.

"Those are their names," Christine said as she slipped into the dress. She looked so lovely in it that June stopped worrying about the condition of her fantasy life.

Christine stood in front of the mirror, admiring herself, or perhaps trying to get used to the picture of herself in a dress, she wore one so seldom.

"Do I look all right, Mom?"

"Pretty as can be."

"Lonnie thinks so too. And I'll bet D.J., Hutch, and Ramos would, too, if they could see me."

"I'm sure they would, but just remember, they're only pretend." June laughed again. "I just can't imagine how you came up with names like those."

"Those are the names Daddy gave them."

"Oh. You mean Daddy named them for you."

"No, Mom. They're Daddy's friends. He talks to them sometimes. That's how I found out their names."

An unpleasant tingling shot up June's arm, as if she'd been shocked by one of those electric buzzers practical jokers concealed in their palms.

"What does he say to them?" she asked, trying to keep a note of alarm out of the question.

"I can't tell you because he uses bad words when he talks to them." Christy's face turned crimson. "He uses the name of the Lord in vain, like they teach us not to do at catechism, and . . . the F-word. He uses that too."

"Honey, it's kind of important if you tell me what he says. You can leave the bad words out."

"Okay. Sometimes, when he's working on the fence, he says, 'G-D, Hutch, this is tough work.' Or he'll say the F-word and ask D.J. and Ramos why they can't be here to help him because it's hard, building the fence all by himself."

"Can you remember anything else he says, Christy?"

The girl paused, knitting her brows, then shook her head.

"When he talks to them, is it like they're really there, or is it like he's talking to himself?"

June rubbed her thumbnail with her forefinger while Christy pondered the question.

"I don't understand, Mom."

"Does he talk to them the way you talk to Lonnie, or like he's just talking to himself?"

"I don't know. Daddy hasn't committed a mortal sin, has he, using the name of the Lord in vain and the F-word? He won't go to hell, will he?"

"No, he won't go to hell, honey."

She drove into town, those three odd names filling her mind, and dropped Christine off at Saint Joseph's. The catechism classes were held there one Saturday each month, a three-hour session taught by a nun from the parochial school in Marquette.

As she pulled away from the small building with its stubby bell tower and its shabby shingles painted a nondescript yellow, she recalled the great stone church, Grace Lutheran, where Chris's father had been a minister and where his funeral had been held. Inside, every pew had been filled with clergymen and dignitaries, with liberal politicians and civil rights leaders whom June had known only as names in the newspapers. She'd had no idea the Reverend Starkmann had been so famous. Three or four people delivered eulogies, praising his works, and from the loft an organ and choir rattled the stained-glass windows with Protestant hymns like *A Mighty Fortress Is Our God* and *Amazing Grace* as the pall-bearers, Chris among them, carried the bier down the aisle toward the hearse waiting outside. Her most painful memory was of the way Chris had looked, bearing his father's coffin: His eyes had ceased their restless movements and stared straight ahead, still as blue stones. He did not seem aware of where he was, or of the mourners in the pews on either side of him; it was as if he were still drugged on the tranquilizers shot into him after his outburst in the hospital.

She'd learned very little about what had caused the breach between her husband and the man buried that April afternoon. Chris's mother, in a state of nervous collapse, couldn't speak about anything; his sisters were as tight-lipped as he—especially Anne, who, with her bright blond hair and narrow face, also bore the closest physical resemblance to him. The only thing Anne had said was "My brother left for the war in 1969, but somebody else came back, and we've never found out who that is." Her husband, the grammatically precise Ed Jenkins, had been slightly more informative, describing the Reverend Starkmann's passionate opposition to the war, his hopes that his son would follow him in the ministry, and his "profound disappointment" when Chris had quit divinity school to enlist in the army. June had told him that she found a disagreement about the war an inadequate explanation for a father and son not speaking to each other for so many years. Something else must have happened. Ed had agreed: Probably there was something more to it but he'd never been able to figure out what it was; he wasn't sure if anyone in the family had, and even if they'd solved the riddle, they were such an intensely private bunch they would not have told even him. "Lucius and I never did get along," Jenkins said, adding that, among the Starkmanns, he often felt more like an interloper than a member of the family. When June had thought about it, that had been the way they'd made her feel. She'd loved Chicago and the decorous old suburb where the Starkmanns lived in their Tudor-style house, the sort of house she pictured in her fantasies of middle-class grace; but the family were so standoffish, their animosity toward Chris so obvious, that she'd been relieved to say goodbye.

Relief had turned to apprehension during the drive back to Vieux Desert. To have called Chris withdrawn would have been the greatest of understatements; he'd disappeared in all ways but physically, his personality vanishing so completely it was as if the car were on remote control and the man behind the wheel one of those lifelike dummies that auto makers used to test the effects of collisions on the human body.

In the weeks since then, he'd shown no signs of reemerging, and June had come to know a strange kind of loneliness, an alien species of the blues: the ache of living with a man who'd deserted her in his heart and soul but whose outward form remained with her. It was, she thought, somewhat like sharing a house with a ghost.

Now, returning home, the county road parting the dense hordes of trees, she could recall only one occasion in the past month or so when he'd said anything. Three weeks ago, after the local weekly had announced Great Superior's decision to build the new sawmill, June had mentioned at dinner that half the town was already out in the bars, celebrating as if it were the Fourth of July. Wasn't it wonderful that the men would have work again? Chris shot her one of his glares, said that he saw no reason to celebrate, and muttered something about a plan he'd worked on being thrown out the window, and how loggers were going to clear-cut, "massacring" trees to make bowling alleys and roller rinks. He got up from the table, pulled an old book from their meager library in the living room, and, returning to the kitchen, commanded the girls and June to listen. He was going to read from a poem written by a north woods preacher back in the days of the logging boom, when the white pine had been "butchered" and fires consumed the acres of stumps and slashings.

"*Green leaves evaded storms but not the race of zero greed*," he began and then went on in a tremulous voice:

*   *   *

"Heart-sick, I hold my place
And take my bitter scourge upon your face.
Timber! You groaned and trembled over the yell
Of gloating lumberjacks when martyrs fell
And years of grandeur fed the fires of hell."

With that, he placed the book back on its shelf and stalked out of the house, leaving his stew congealing on his plate and June and the girls dumbfounded.

He'd done a few other peculiar things. The eviction of the trespassing anglers and the decision to ring the property in barbed wire were only two of them. One day he'd rearranged the kitchen, lining up jars and spice bottles according to height, as he'd done in his old camp, and labeling the shelves in the refrigerator: the top one for catsup, mustard, and mayonnaise, the second for pickles and peppers, and so on down to the bottom, reserved for dairy products. He'd hung a garment bag in the closet to divide her side from his, and spaced his shirts and trousers two inches apart, the shirts all facing the same direction, like soldiers on parade.

Whiskey had replaced June as his solace. He had not made love to her, or touched her, since his father's death. Three nights out of four, he sat up in the living room to all hours, sipping Early Times and listening to a Bruce Springsteen tape on the portable cassette player—the same song over and over again. The sound invaded the bedroom where she lay alone, trying to sleep. After a while, each phrase and note had engraved itself so deeply in her mind that she found herself humming the mournful tune at odd hours of the day—on her way to work, cooking dinner. Sometimes she felt that she would go crazy herself if she had to listen to it one more time.

And maybe, she thought as she turned up the gravel road, going crazy would not be a bad idea; maybe then she could communicate with Chris. If you can't beat 'em, join 'em. The thought was of course facetious. Too much depended on her holding herself together, and if Chris didn't climb out of whatever ditch he'd fallen into, everything could end up depending on her. Twice in the past month he'd gotten so drunk that he'd been an hour late for work, and had gone in red-eyed and hung-over. Two other times he hadn't bothered to go in at all, staying in bed till past noon. June had covered for him by calling him in sick, but Ralph Harding and Bill King, apparently, had not believed her: They'd been overheard discussing Chris at Swanson's one night, something to the effect that they thought he was taking his father's death pretty hard and that they were willing to tolerate his tardiness and absences for that reason, but there were limits to their patience. June had relayed this intelligence, or gossip, to Chris. His reaction was to look at her with silent indifference and then to spend another night of solitary boozing while Springsteen's dirge groaned through the house:

> Last night I dreamed that I was a child
> out where the pines grow wild and tall.
> I was trying to make it home through the forest
> before the darkness falls.
> I heard the wind rustling through the trees
> and ghostly voices rose from the fields
> I ran with my heart pounding down that broken path
> with the devil snappin' at my heels.
> I broke through the trees and there in the night
> My father's house stood shining hard and bright.
> The branches and brambles tore my clothes
> and scratched my arms,
> But I ran till I fell shaking in his arms.

And now there was this business of his conversing with the three invisible personalities: D.J., Hutch, and Ramos.

She parked in the drive and hopped out of the Wagoneer, with half a mind to sneak up on Chris to find out if these were what she suspected—some sort of hallucination. She thought better of it, mostly because she feared confirming her fears. Without another pause she resumed her gardening. She felt more in control as soon as she entered the box of broken earth, her sanctuary. Here, her actions had a visible effect; here she could make things happen; here she could nurture and protect. She turned over the soil once more, this time with a rake, its tines like extensions of her fingers as they stroked the earth. The sun had reached its height, and she was soon sweating through her denim shirt.

A clanging pealed from out of the tamaracks beyond the meadow: Chris driving in another fence stake. Cold steel on cold steel. *Clang, clang, clang.* The shrill ring grated on her nerves. It made her feel like crying because it struck her ears as the sound of her loneliness; yes, if the emptiness she'd felt these past weeks could be transformed into a sound, it would be that harsh and hollow *clang, clang, clang.*

She fought back the impulse to cry and continued raking, working up a dense sweat. The hammering had stopped for a moment. She paused to enjoy the silence and the sight of her tools stacked in the wheelbarrow, the bags of peat moss beside it, the seed packets and sprigs of tomato plants. Sweat stung her eyes. She pulled a kerchief from her pocket, tying it above her eyebrows like an Indian headband, then took off her shirt and cast it aside. Although there was no one to see her, she felt daring in doing this. An excitement began to overcome her sadness. She started raking again, reveling in the movements of her muscles, in the warmth of the sun that embraced her shoulders, massaged her back, and caressed her breasts as she turned her beloved earth.

The raking done, she got a stick and garden spade from the wheelbarrow, knelt on both knees, and began the furrows in which she would plant the seeds. The sun pierced her winter-paled skin, entered her like a lover, and made her burn. The sun and the smell of dirt, peat, and manure, so powerful it was as if the air were becoming earth, brought on a druglike euphoria. Chris's hammer struck another stake, but its sterile tolling did not, this time, make her ache. She would not allow it to spoil her joy in this, her own rite of spring.

After she had made two neat rows, she stood to stretch and, wanting to feel the silt beneath her feet, kicked off her sneakers. As she wriggled her toes in the dirt, an urge to strip seized her. She undid her jeans and tossed them beside her blouse; then, naked, knelt again to begin the third row. The earth kissed her knees. Its scent drugging her further, she spread her ankles so her buttocks touched it. Was she really doing this? She'd only an hour ago dressed her little daughter and brought her to catechism; in another hour or so she would pick her up. What would Christine think if she saw her like this, kneeling naked in the dirt? But it felt so good, God, yes, so good. She held a lump of earth to her nose, inhaling its perfume, and thrust her bottom against the furrow. She rocked back and forth, her hands going between her thighs to masturbate; and that felt good, too. God, it had been so long since anything living had touched her and now the living earth was caressing her buttocks, the sun her breasts—it all felt so good, weeks of tensions and heartache releasing themselves. Her climax was like a flood, and rising into a squat, she allowed the streams from within her to trickle upon the earth, God, yes, the earth.

21

On Tuesday morning Starkmann drove out to the forties he'd surveyed the day before. He'd run the property lines with some college trainee, some kid named Ellmore or Elwood, who'd objected to Starkmann's frequent nips from a hip flask of Early Times. The hell with Ellmore, or Elwood; drunk, he could run lines better than some undergraduate could sober. Today Starkmann had to make sure the logging crews had started cutting in the right places. He was tired because he had worked on the perimeter most of yesterday afternoon after work, then into the night after dinner. He'd finished the strongpoint on the knoll overlooking the Firedog, high ground. Stringing wire and digging foxholes had been rough but enjoyable work; but now his muscles ached and his eyes were bleary, making it difficult for him to negotiate the rutted, rocky road. It passed through spruce and tamarack bogs, where returning mallards and black ducks rested in dark ponds, then climbed gradually toward the distant ridges whose hardwood slopes, dotted with stands of upland pine, looked like emerald canvases daubed with splotches of dark green and blue. Bruce Springsteen sang on the portable cassette player Starkmann had wedged between the seat and the parking brake so it wouldn't fall when he hit a bump.

After crossing the Yellow Dog River over a bridge built of discarded railroad ties, he hooked around a cedar swamp, then passed through the Yellow Dog Plains, a flat stretch of jack-pine barrens where he almost skidded off the road to avoid hitting a doe and two fawns that seemed to materialize out of thin air. Shaken by the near

miss, he pulled off to the shoulder, took his thermos and pint from the glove compartment, and poured a pick-me-up, half coffee and half Early Times. He should have seen the deer sooner. He had to start getting more rest, which meant he had to complete the perimeter soon. Building the fence was like holding down a second job. He finished his eye-opener in two swallows, and started off again, crossing the winding Yellow Dog a second time before going up the first steep ridge into the tall maple, beech, and mountain ash.

When he reached the top he saw the Hurons rising away from him, their green changing tone as broken clouds passed across the sun. A granite bluff thrust through the trees in the middle distance, a cavern where wolves denned showing as a giant skull's eye in the bluff's gray face. Farther off, a chain of lakes linked their blue beneath glacier-scarred ridges. The Hurons, the high lonesome— wildcats in the draws, wolf and coyote country, uninhabited, never touched by the plow, Indian country.

A memory like a near-forgotten rhyme from childhood brushed the edges of his mind, and the sadness commonly aroused in him by the sound of rushing water rose from the deepest part of his being, gorging his throat until he thought he would choke. He again pulled off to the roadside, where he swilled another coffee-and-whiskey cocktail to force back the sadness. When that medicine failed, he guzzled the whiskey straight, and when that had no effect, he rammed the truck into gear on impulse, floored the gas pedal, and rocketed down the back side of the ridge, trying to scare the sorrow out of himself.

Down, down, leaning far back in the seat, arms extended their full length like a race-car driver's, the speedometer sweeping toward forty, then past forty toward fifty—fifty miles an hour on a dirt grade dangerous at half that speed, down, the bottom of the ridge lunging up at him, the descent like a helicopter assault into a hot LZ. *We'll all go down together, we said we'd all go down together.* Starkmann screamed, his heart slamming against his chest, when he saw the water-filled pothole, big as a flooded shell-crater, in the fold between this ridge and the next. He wasn't going to make it, was going to flip over in the pothole or slam into the trees. D.J.! Hutch! Ramos! he bellowed in his mind, downshifting at the same time, the engine almost blowing at the higher RPMs and the truck skidding while the cassette player bounced to the floor silencing Springsteen's voice. D.J.! HUTCH! RAMOS!

"*Downshift!*" He heard Hutch's voice, but he couldn't tell if it was coming from within his own imagination or from outside him-

self. He did know that's what Hutch, if he were alive, would have told him to do.

Starkmann slammed the clutch and shoved the gear into first, the motor screeching so loudly he was sure he'd thrown a rod. The truck spun from the sudden decrease in speed, turning a complete three-sixty just before the front wheels splashed into the soup of the pothole, then leaped across, the shocks almost breaking. He cut a hard right, fishtailing around a curve, and then came to a stop.

If he'd intended to scare himself, he'd succeeded: His hands were shaking, his legs so weak it was as if an invisible knife had cut his hamstrings. To settle his nerves he took a swig of whiskey. Hutch, the medic, would have prescribed a hit off a Thai-stick, but the Early Times would do.

Drinking slowly, swishing the whiskey like mouthwash, he pictured Hutch, whose hairless, freckled complexion made him look like a prep-schooler, and D. J., with his sardonic grin, and Ramos, his physique like a Renaissance statue carved out of mahogany. Starkmann no longer feared that communing with his three dead friends was a sign of madness; if anything, his make-believe talks had helped to keep him from going over the edge.

They'd begun about two weeks ago, when the weather had turned warm. One night he'd gone wandering through the wooded forty acres, thinking about his father's death and trying to understand why God had forsaken him by failing to work the miracle. No answers had come to him, and he'd never felt so alone and abandoned. His more or less aimless stroll had brought him to the log pathway he'd built across the tamarack swamp. There, in the darkness, with the raucous chorusing of frogs in his ears, the numbness he'd felt since burying Lucius peeled off like blistered skin, and the reality of the death struck him full force, as hard as a punch to his solar plexus. He'd doubled over, fallen onto his knees, and cried.

He cried for a long time, and found his thoughts turning to his brothers. The mere remembrance of them eased his sense of isolation as it soothed his sorrow for his father—and for himself. Closing his eyes, he conjured an image of them: Hutch with his medical kit snapped to his belt. D.J. and Ramos with M-16's slung over their shoulders, dressed in green uniforms faded by the sun, cracked, mud-crusted boots, web gear, and camouflage helmets. Softly he began to speak to them, expressing the pain he could not to any living person. His need for them was so urgent it seemed as if he could actually summon them from whatever heaven they'd gone to, and he had wondered if his grip on reality were slipping.

His doubts were dispelled one afternoon several days later, when

he'd observed Christy talking to her make-believe friend, Lonnie. Christine's Lonnie existed only for her, but she wasn't crazy; neither was he. His mind, he'd realized, wasn't failing; rather, his imagination had reverted to a purer, childlike state unhindered by adult prejudices as to what was real or unreal, mad or sane.

And who, he thought, taking a last sip of whiskey, could argue with what his figments had just done for him? They had probably saved his life. If he'd not thought of Hutch at the critical moment, he might have struck the pothole at full speed and flipped over.

He capped the bottle, and drove over the next ridge, bumped across the Yellow Dog once again, and turned onto a skid-trail, its junction marked by the amputated corpses of maple trees. We stacked the bodies like wood over there, he thought, and over here we stack the wood like bodies. Question: What is the kill ratio between men and trees? Must be pretty high in favor of men; trees can't shoot back, although they can fall on you.

When he heard the chain saws and the screech of a forwarder slashing the felled maple into log lengths, he tucked the Ford into an earthen ramp gouged out of the embankment by a bulldozer, and went the rest of the way on foot, stumbling over the broken ground. Up ahead, a maple shuddered, gave its death shriek, and went down in a long, stately fall. Starkmann, woozy-headed, almost fell himself when the skidder came crashing out of the woods and he had to leap out of its way.

The driver went on a few yards, then stopped and looked at him from atop the yellow monster.

"You the cruiser?" he shouted.

"Sure."

"Boss has been waitin' on you. He's got some problems."

Starkmann, watching the skidder growl toward the road, hewn logs bouncing behind it, tried to steady the rocking motion in his head through force of will. He went around a bend in the trail and saw Sam LaChance and the foreman arguing over a map spread out on the hood of Sam's truck. What the hell was Sam doing here? His outfit hadn't contracted for this job.

"Well, well, 'bout time." LaChance transferred his eyes from the map to Starkmann. "Keepin' banker's hours now, are you?"

"What's your problem?"

"It ain't mine, hey. It's yours."

"He says we're cuttin' his timber," the foreman explained, pointing a pencil at the map. "But I dunno. I cut where I'm told to cut."

"This is company land. I ran the lines yesterday," Starkmann slurred.

Sam studied his face and smirked.

"You been drinkin' again, college boy? Sounds to me like you been drinkin'. Smells like it too. Maybe you was drunk when you ran these lines."

"I ran this forty yesterday."

"Yeah, that's what this fella been tellin' me, but you run 'em wrong, Mr. Starkmann. You didn't measure things right this time."

LaChance's speech was reverting to its Canuck origins, *things* coming out as "tings," *that* as "dat."

"This here is a *short forty*. Part of it belong to your company, part of it to me, and right now these fellas cuttin' on my part."

Starkmann's eyes flicked to the map. He couldn't recall anything about a short forty from the survey notes. He'd set that corner only yesterday and, goddammit, he didn't make mistakes.

"What you done was to run your line the full thirteen hunnert twenty feet, right onto my land." LaChance dug his toe into the dirt and crossed his arms over his chest. "Know what that means, don't you?"

"Sure. And I know what I'm doing. I know how to run a property line."

He tried to keep an interval between his words, but somehow they bumped into one another in a series of rear-end collisions.

"He wants us off," the foreman said.

"That's right. I want this crew off. I already got you on unwillful trespass and cuttin' private timber. That's triple damages your outfit owes me already for every tree cut this mornin'. You're the cruiser, Mr. Starkmann. You tell this crew to clear off, and you be right behind 'em."

"You have a survey proving this is your land?"

"No, I don't got no survey, but I can have a surveyor out here by tomorrow, goddamn. Then I'll have you on willful trespass. That's a crim'nal offense."

Starkmann said nothing at first, his glance angling away from LaChance's face toward a lumberjack who was topping a felled maple. The saw bit into the tree's skin, into its meat, through its brown, sap-swollen heart, chips splattering everywhere. In a rush, the whiskey in Starkmann's gut raced up through his throat into his brain. The hell with this big loudmouthed Frog, he thought. The hell with this business. The hell with all of it.

"Keep cutting," Starkmann told the foreman, then pivoted and started back toward his truck.

"Willful trespass, I said—a crim'nal offense, hey. Now get your ass and this crew's ass off this land, goddamn."

From behind, Sam gave him a shove that almost knocked him over. Starkmann spun, winged a haymaker, and clipped the lump of scar tissue where LaChance's ear had been. Sam stepped back a foot or two, more from surprise than the force of the glancing blow. The foreman, a merely average-size man, bravely inserted himself between the two to hold them apart.

"Out of the way," Starkmann said, giddy with booze and excitement; something was going to happen. "I'm going to get the shit kicked out of me."

"You got that right, college boy."

Without effort, Sam pushed the foreman aside and charged, his fists flailing. One punch caught Starkmann in the shoulder, numbing his arm down to the wrist; another shot to his ribs knocked half the wind out of him. He hooked an elbow around LaChance's neck, thick as a stump, and tried to trap him in a headlock, but the giant broke his grip, slipped behind him, and, squeezing him in a bear hug, lifted him into the air and flung him face down into the dirt. He rolled from the big man's kick. Sam's boot, missing his kidneys, thudded into his hip with exquisite pain.

"Get up. Get up and get some more from this old Frenchman. You ain't nuthin'."

Starkmann thrust himself onto all fours, raising his eyes toward LaChance, who stood rolling his fists over each other like a nineteenth-century boxer.

"Get up! You an' me been comin' to this a long time."

Starkmann forced himself to his feet, his hip throbbing. Head down, he rushed Sam in an attempt to tackle him, but the two hundred and seventy pounds were immovable. LaChance banged him with an uppercut that closed his left eye, then smashed him across the back twice with clasped hands, hammering him to the ground once again. And once again he struggled to his feet, his head reeling, his good eye fixed on Sam. The foreman and two lumberjacks lingered a respectful distance away, watching the uneven brawl.

"Had enough?"

Sam was gasping for breath. The old man was powerful, but he didn't have the wind anymore.

"C'mon, Sam," Starkmann wheezed. "Beat the shit out of me."

LaChance, his face hidden by the balls of his raised fists, circled with a motion at once comical and menacing, like the movements of a bear. Starkmann circled in the opposite direction. A jab connected with Sam's grappling-hook nose, drawing a seepage of blood; then he threw a wild overhand right, aiming a kick at the giant's knee at the same time. The punch missed; the kick, low of its mark, cracked into

LaChance's shin. With a yell of pain and fury, Sam dug the fingers of one hand into Starkmann's face. Clubbing his temple with the other, he dropped him for the third time and raised his foot to Starkmann's face. Starkmann rolled away in time to evade the boot that drove into the ground, inches from his head. Back on his feet, the leg with the bruised hip nearly buckling under him, he managed a defiant grin as he put up his fists.

"Do it, Sam. Beat the shit out of me."

"I just did, goddamn." LaChance, circling him, sucked desperately for air. "You want more?"

"More. Kill me. You're going to have to kill me, you Frog son of a bitch."

Starkmann lunged, grazing the top of Sam's head with a left hook as LaChance grabbed him by the shirt and rammed him into the side of the truck. Clutching him by the throat to pin his head against the side window, Sam cocked a fist to throw a punch that would have shattered Starkmann's face if the foreman, shouting "That's enough! He's had enough!" hadn't leaped on him at that moment and, with the help of the two lumberjacks, wrestled him off.

Starkmann, rubbing his throat and leaning against the truck to hold himself upright, focused his right eye on LaChance and jerked his lips into another provoking grin.

"Didn't do it, Sam. Didn't kill me."

Sam made a move toward him, but the foreman and the 'jacks hung on to the big man.

"Next time, you crazy bastard—next time I kill you." He wiped his bleeding nose with the back of his hand, then turned to the foreman. "I don't give a damn what this crazy bastard tells you—you quit cuttin', goddamn, and get your crew off my timber."

"We're off, hey," said the foreman. "We're as good as off."

Still grinning, Starkmann lurched down the skid-trail toward his pickup.

"Keep cutting, boys," he laughed. "Bowling alleys. Racquetball courts. Roller rinks. Cut 'em all down."

"Next time," LaChance hollered to his back. "Next time you're gonna be one dead college boy, goddamn."

His side and hip ached as he got into the Ford, but he felt pretty good overall, cleansed inside, at least for the moment. Something had finally happened. He turned on the Springsteen tape and drove down the skid-trail toward the road. Each bump sent a jolt of pain through his sore ribs, through the tender lump bulging from his temple, ugly as a tumor; but the pain was a delight somehow, his bruises and battered eye badges of a just and honorable suffering, like his old shrapnel wounds or the injuries he'd received in his football days. Black Sam, bull of the woods, bear killer, hadn't been able to kill him. He smiled through his pain as he turned onto the road. The way Sam had looked, rolling his fists like he was John L. Sullivan—that was pretty funny.

In the distance, the Hurons rubbed the sky. It was a fine spring day.

22

Wednesday, a day in court. June sat in the front row softly tapping the bench with her fingers while she thought about her garden to keep her mind off Chris and the dreary hearing about to begin. Two weeks had passed since she'd planted, and the garden was thriving; the radishes and spinach had pushed their first shoots through the earth sometime during the night. She'd seen them when she left the house this morning; and as she gazed at their pale shoots and the two rows of darker tomato plants, she'd felt an emotion like the rush of love. This year she would weed, water, and thin with more attentiveness. She would not overwater the tomatoes; she would bind the plants to stakes in midsummer. She would pray harder against flood, frost, and drought, leaving the rest to God or nature. She would nurture the plants as if they were children; they were almost literally her offspring, for the waters of her womb had mingled with the earth in which they grew. What, she wondered, would Judge Lundquist, so proper-looking in his black robes as he assumed his seat behind the bench—what would he think if he knew that she, proper-looking now in her gray suit, had squatted naked over her garden's furrows, masturbating until she'd climaxed? And Erickson, with his fair hair glowing copper-yellow in front of her— what would he think? Probably that she was horny, a desperate woman in need of a good lay; and he would, of course, present himself as the best man to fulfill that need.

Judge Lundquist opened the hearing. The initial formalities had become so familiar to June that she paid little attention to what was being said, allowing her eyes and mind to wander.

"Mrs. Larsen is currently receiving public assistance," Erickson droned from the witness table, where the plaintiff, Elaine Larsen, sat beside him in a polyester outfit, her hair done up in a women's bowling-league bouffant. The opposite table was occupied by a public defender and Mr. Larsen, who slumped in his seat and occasionally flung hostile glances toward his ex-wife and June. Lundquist, his bench bracketed by the state and national flags, rested his head on his hand and tried not to look too bored.

". . . and we're here, Your Honor, to obtain a court order for child support from Mr. Louis Larsen. We're asking the court to issue an order to Mrs. Larsen to pay . . ." Erickson paused to glance at his notes ". . . Twenty-five dollars per month for each of his three children . . ."

The back of June's neck prickled when she heard that. The woman turned to face her with an expression at once startled and angry.

"Is that what you want?" June, bending forward, asked in a whisper.

Elaine Larsen shook her beehive head.

"Did Erickson talk to you? Did he ask you what you needed?"

The woman's lips formed a silent "no."

Same old story, June thought, leaning back in resignation. Twenty-five per kid per month; at today's prices, that might keep the family in corn flakes.

June was then called to testify. She was wearing her low heels, and she slouched in an impossible attempt to make herself appear small and nonthreatening as she approached the stand. Sworn in by the bailiff, she took her seat, demurely crossing her legs. Erickson recited his litany of questions: Are the allegations true and correct to the best of your knowledge? How much is Mrs. Larsen receiving in public assistance? What is Mr. Larsen's delinquency, and how much in back support is owed? June answered each in her professional tone of voice, like a receptionist answering telephones, but made sure to fire a few bullets into Erickson with her eyes. Twenty-five a month, for God's sake. At the same time, she could not help but be impressed by the lawyer's blown-dry good looks, the assurance of his gestures, the way his mere presence dominated the room.

When she'd finished her testimony, Mr. Larsen hobbled to the stand with a feigned limp, claimed he was employed by the Empire mine but was on temporary disability and didn't have a dime to spare.

Lundquist listened sympathetically, instructed Larsen to bring in verification of his disability, and continued the case for a month.

"Well, damn it all," Elaine Larsen muttered, watching her former husband file out of the courtroom with the public defender.

"Same old story," commented June, feeling the same old helpless anger as she picked up her case file and strode into the polished granite hall, where Larsen gave her a triumphant smirk.

"What are you grinning at?" she snapped.

"A big cunt."

"Look down at your fly and you can smile at a little prick," she said over her shoulder, the clatter of her heels echoing down the hall.

She tried to calm herself by returning her thoughts to her garden, but the only thing that could tranquilize her now would be a scotch, straight up. A big cunt. She should have cracked that fraud across his foul, grinning mouth.

Erickson caught up with her outside, under the pillared portico, where foreclosure notices papered the bulletin board beside the doors.

"I heard that exchange in the hall," Erickson admonished. "You're not going to help the case with that kind of talk, June."

"You've been a terrific help. Christ, Don, you could have asked her how much she needed. Twenty-five a month. What gave you that inspiration?"

"I figured it was all he could afford."

"You mean you talked to him. You talked to him, but not to her."

Erickson dug a finger under his collar, as if it were too tight. "Yeah. The guy's on disability. . . ."

"A month from now he'll come in without the limp and with some new excuse and the judge'll continue the case again. Meantime, the Larsen kids live on generic peanut butter."

She started down the steps.

Two jet planes roared low over Lake Superior. The interceptors were from Sawyer, a Strategic Air Command base not far away, its planes and the blue-suited flyboys who came into town on passes, reminders that small, remote Marquette had probably earned a place on Russian war maps.

"You take these things too personally," Erickson said as the sound of the jets faded. "You know how the system works."

"I sure do. All you boys side with the men. Way down deep you're thinking, 'Hey, that could be me someday, with some bitch trying to get her hands in my wallet.' "

Erickson paused and lightly touched her elbow. "Why don't we talk about this over lunch?"

The invitation, a first, caught her unprepared. She felt flattered but did not answer immediately, pulling her eyes to the side to look at his profile. Automatically she compared it to Chris's, and then criticized herself for making the comparison because it came out in the lawyer's favor.

"What do we have to talk about?"

"We're supposed to be on the same side in these things, not arguing with each other. Maybe we need to set a few things straight."

They reached the bottom of the steps and turned down the sidewalk, heading in the direction away from her car.

"This had better not be a pass. Let's get that straight from the start."

An enigmatic smile bowed Erickson's straight, thin lips.

"It's not a pass, June. It's lunch."

He took her to the Northwoods Supper Club, one of the few decent restaurants in Marquette, an old-fashioned place that called to mind the woodsy elegance of a twenties-era hunting resort. On the edge of the city, it was discreetly hidden in a grove of pines well off the highway. As Erickson went up the long, winding driveway and into the parking lot, June was happy to see Cadillacs and Lincolns instead of the usual Jeeps and pickups with gun racks fastened across the rear windows.

She made sure to carry her file folder inside; Erickson his briefcase. Marquette was a lot larger town than Vieux Desert, but it was still small; their working lunch not only had to be one, it had to look like one.

They were seated at a linen-covered table by a waiter in a spotless uniform who asked, "Would you care for a drink before ordering?" instead of "Whatchagonnahave, hey?" June called for a Johnnie Walker Black, Erickson for a vodka martini. The waiter returned with the drinks, menus, and a wine list. She could not recall the last time she'd been to a place with a wine list, or if she'd ever been to one. About all she remembered from her recent dining-out experiences with Chris were McDonald's and Burger King bags, spotted with grease. The scotch, the quiet atmosphere, and the cedar-log walls, oiled and varnished to the richness of a yacht's woodwork, rounded the edges of her anger toward Erickson. She found herself admiring the way he handled himself in a restaurant as much as she did his conduct in a courtroom: There was the same self-assurance, a confidence that wasn't quite arrogance as he studied the menu and the lists, the same aura of command when he summoned the waiter with a subtle gesture of his hand.

June ordered whitefish fillets sautéed in lemon butter; Erickson, broiled lake trout. He asked if she preferred a Chardonnay or a Pouilly-Fuissé with her meal.

"Whatever you decide, Don." She deferred because she didn't know the difference between the two, an ignorance that embarrassed her and—a further embarrassment—made her realize how presumptuous she'd been to have implied that the luncheon invitation had been a pass. Why would a man like him, soon to become a successful private attorney and law professor in Ann Arbor, bother making a pass at a not-very-attractive married woman too dumb to know one wine from the other? She counted up her personal and social flaws, and the number of them so overwhelmed her that she apologized for the accusation.

Erickson, slowly chewing his lake trout, absolved her with a casual flick of his fingers (strong, masculine fingers, she observed, but not ones she could picture curled around a wood-splitter's maul).

"I wrote it off to the tension you've been under lately," he said.

"Tension?"

His blue eyes, darker than Chris's—water rather than ice— regarded her analytically.

"The last few times I've seen you, you've seemed as wound up as a rubber band on a kid's model airplane."

"Thanks. Should I appreciate your frankness?"

"June, every case that comes up, you argue with me or with the judge, or both. You're arguing with the court clerks because you don't think they're getting the cases on the docket fast enough. Pardon the candor, but you're getting a reputation around the courthouse as . . . well . . ."

"A bitch. A pain in the ass."

"That's a little strong." He winced ever so slightly, to let her know that he did not like hearing vulgar language out of a woman's mouth.

Just like Chris, she thought. Men could cuss a blue streak and no one thought anything about it. If a woman did, she was branded as a tramp.

"If it takes bitchiness to get these women a fair shake, then you and the judges and the clerks haven't seen anything yet."

"That's my point," said Erickson, his voice—the voice of a man used to being in control—assuming its oracular courtroom tone. "It's okay to push hard, but you do reach a point at which you can push so hard you'll only end up doing less good for them. Counterproductivity, it's called."

"Is this business or a lecture?"

"Call it professional advice. I think you take these cases too personally. There's a lot of them and only one of you. You ought to remember: 'Too much spreading his passion, he shallows it.' "

"Is that an original?"

"Hardly." He laughed gently. "Herman Melville. *The Confidence Man*. What he meant by shallowing . . ."

"I understand what he meant," she interrupted. "I'm not that well-read, but I'm not stupid."

"I didn't mean to sound patronizing, so you can sheathe the sword."

She drank half the wine in her glass to cool her temper.

"Sorry. Maybe you're right. I guess I have been tense, uptight."

An awkward silence followed, during which she cast anxious glances around the room, then drank the rest of the wine in one swallow. She ought not to have made that remark; it put a key in a door best left locked.

"Is anything wrong, if you don't mind my getting a little personal?" Erickson asked, softly turning the key and easing the door open a crack. "Maybe I could help."

"It isn't a legal problem."

"I like to think I'm more than just a lawyer. I think I'm your friend." His voice had thickened, becoming more intimate. "At least I think I can be."

"I have a friend."

"A woman?"

"Of course. I don't think men and women can be friends, pals, buddies. Maybe for a few weeks or months. Then it ends up in a motel room."

"A *motel* room?" With the grace of a skilled seducer, he drew the Chardonnay from the ice bucket and refilled June's glass. "Motel rooms aren't my style."

"Now what am I supposed to say to that? Ask what your style is? Your apartment? A suite with a Jacuzzi? It sounds to me, Don, like you're sneaking up on a pass."

"Why do you keep insisting I'm making a pass?"

June poked at the crumbled remains of her whitefish, but her stomach was fluttering so much she'd lost her appetite. Out of nowhere, the notion of marrying him had again popped into her mind. Where did they come from, these silly middle-class aspirations for the big suburban house, the car in the drive, the successful hubby?

"I suppose you think a woman like me, married and not too good-looking, is flattering herself if she thinks that Marquette's most eligible bachelor wants to make a pass at her?"

"Your marriage is one thing, June, but I ask the court to note for the record that I don't think you're unattractive."

"And I don't think that Marquette's most eligible bachelor is much of a title as a sex symbol," she jibed to cover up her delight in his compliment. "It's like being a star quarterback on a team nobody ever heard of."

"Your sword is out again," he answered, unperturbed by the wisecrack. He'd spent too much time parrying quick, clever thrusts in the courtroom to be ruffled by the clumsy swat of a confused woman.

Confused she was, and not only by her conflicting emotions toward the man seated across from her. Despite her avowal of the impossibility of noncarnal friendships between men and women, she in fact felt in need of a male confidant, one whose intelligence she respected, whose opinions she could trust. A man, she thought, would have more insight than a woman into what was happening to Chris; a man could better explain why he'd become indifferent toward her; a man could give her some idea of what Chris had gone through in the war. His sister had said he'd come back a stranger. What could have happened to have done that to him? Was the war the beast that violated his sleep? Did the war explain his behavior yesterday, when she'd come home to find him with an eye swollen to the size of a golf ball and a bruise on his forehead? He'd refused to tell her what had happened. She hadn't been able to get a word out of him until this morning, after he'd crawled out of bed grimacing in pain, and she'd noticed more bruises on his ribs and hips. She nagged him until he finally admitted that he'd been in a fight with Sam LaChance. The weird thing was, he seemed happy about it. "I got the shit kicked out of me," he'd said with a smile, "but he couldn't kill me." Was that some sort of machismo, or just plain craziness? Only a man, she thought, could answer these questions, but she wasn't sure Erickson was the right one to turn to. You don't trust lawyers; you hire them, she thought.

"I really don't understand this defensiveness of yours," he was saying as, with a turn of his head, he called the waiter over for the check. "I'm offering to be a friend."

"Because I don't believe that. Why do I get this feeling you'd like to get me in bed?"

She regretted the words as soon as she spoke them.

"I don't know why. Maybe you *are* flattering yourself. Married women aren't my style, either," Erickson bristled with insult.

She couldn't tell if his offended manner was genuine or a bit of lawyerly theater. It didn't make any difference: She'd made a fool of herself. To hide her chagrin, she went to the ladies' room, where she immediately began to cry. What a dumb thing to have said to him, and now she was in tears, for God's sake, and her mascara was streaked.

She wiped her eyes, composed herself, and returned to the table. Erickson was filling out a credit-card receipt while the waiter hovered a discreet distance away.

"Don, I'm sorry for what I just said," she apologized, after the waiter took the receipt and walked off with a nod of thanks for the generous tip. "That was really dumb."

"That's okay," he said as they went out to the car. Although she was slightly taller than he in her heels, she felt small, diminished. "All I was trying to tell you is that if you need to talk something over, I'm willing to listen."

"I know. Sorry for running off at the mouth."

Again, he granted her dispensation with a flick of his wrist, a gesture so casual it was demeaning, as if anything she said could not possibly make much difference to him. She got into the car, disliking his capacity to make her feel insignificant. As he slid into the driver's seat, she looked for flaws in his appearance, and settled on his blown-dry hair. That convinced her that he wasn't the man she could confide in. She couldn't trust a man who used a hair dryer.

He dropped her off at the county building, where the State Department of Public Aid rented its office space, and repeated his offer of friendship. June, thanking him perfunctorily, went inside, in too lousy a frame of mind to do anything but groan inwardly when she saw Henry Hermanson, Jr., sitting in the waiting room in his greasy station-attendant's uniform. What now? she thought, but put on a smile and asked him what he was doing in Marquette.

He gazed at her, as surprised to see her as she was him.

"Mrs. Starkmann?"

"Yes? Did you come to see me?"

"Oh . . . I never seen you . . . I mean, it didn't look like you, hey. Dressed up . . ."

"What is it, Hank?"

Fidgeting with his baseball cap, he haltingly explained that he needed her advice, that's why he'd taken off work early and driven all this way, and could they talk somewhere private, hey?

She took him to the snack bar down the hall, where they sat at a plastic table beside a bank of vending machines. June bought a Coke for Hank Junior, a cup of murky coffee for herself.

The boy, after a few stumbling false starts, finally came to the point: A week ago, after coming home from work, he'd checked the mailbox—like usual, hey—and found a letter from his father. Although it was addressed to his mother, he'd decided it would be a good idea if he saw it first. So he'd opened it, and because he didn't read so good, he asked Freya to make sense out of it, and Freya told him that Dad was filing for a divorce, that he'd said as long as he was being forced to pay out all this support money, he might as well be a free man so he could get married again if he wanted to, which, Freya had said, meant that he'd already got him another woman down there in Texas, and Dad had also claimed that the lodge and the property belonged to him, so he'd got in touch with a lawyer because he wasn't going to get screwed out of no more money.

"I just don't know what to do, Mrs. Starkmann," Hank concluded.

"There isn't much you can do, Hank. Did you show the letter to your mother?"

He shook his head.

"Did anybody explain to her what was in it? What about Freya? She would be the best one to tell Edith what's going on."

"Freya's gone," he said matter-of-factly.

"*Gone?* Where?"

Hank Junior, twirling his cap between his legs, looked down and shrugged.

"You have no idea where she is?"

Still staring at his cap, the boy said that two days after the letter arrived, his sister had taken off early from her waitress job and had last been seen, with a suitcase, climbing into a car.

"Some guy was driving the car, but I couldn't find out who it was. I figure she must've packed the suitcase the night before and hid it in the back of our truck when we drove into town that mornin'. Anyway, she ain't been back, hey."

June felt a sense of personal loss as luridly dramatic scenes flashed in her mind: Freya raped and murdered by the mysterious "guy," her body dumped in a field. Freya in tight shorts and spike heels hustling tricks on a street corner in Detroit or Chicago; Freya, in the thrall of some big-city pimp, shooting heroin in a seedy hotel room. Screw my way out of here, that's what I'm going to do. She must have saved up getaway money from waitressing and her illicit sideline, and now she was gone.

"We've got to find out where she is, Hank. I'll get in touch with the sheriff."

"It ain't Freya I'm worried about. I don't blame her for runnin' off. Sometimes I want to, but I can't leave Mom too. She's been real upset since Freya took off, cryin' all the time."

"At least she realizes she's gone," June said, laying her hand over the back of Hank Junior's. "It's more important than ever that Edith starts seeing things the way they are."

"I just don't know what to do now, Mrs. Starkmann. I thought maybe you would."

She sat back, staring at a bright-blue candy-bar dispenser and thinking: Not even sixteen years old. This kid isn't even sixteen yet. A murderousness rose in her. It was criminal what Henry Senior had done to that family. Criminal. If she had the power, she'd try and then hang him. The hell with a trial. Just hang him.

Calming herself, she advised the boy that his mother would need a lawyer.

"Half that property is rightfully hers. I know you can't afford a private attorney, but I can call Legal Aid for you. I can do that and contact the sheriff about Freya. She's a runaway."

"I don't mean that kind of thing, hey. I don't know how I'm goin' to keep Mom from knowin' about this divorce thing and this woman Dad's maybe got in Texas. She'll really go crazy then, and you know we just can't put her in no hospital. That just ain't goin' to happen."

"Look at me, Hank. Stop staring at that cap and look at me."

He raised his slanted blue eyes. When June saw the dampness in them, she recalled Erickson's admonition about taking her cases too personally, and contained her impulse toward a useless pity.

"If your mother has to go to a hospital, then that's the way it'll have to be. There isn't any way you can keep her from knowing about this divorce. She's going to have to sign the papers, for God's sake."

"Mrs. Starkmann—"

June stood abruptly to cut him off.

"I have a lot of work to do. I have a lot of cases, just as bad as yours, and some a lot worse. I can call Legal Aid and the sheriff, but I can't help you keep this from Edith. I can't and won't."

Hank Junior, his eyes falling again to his cap, nodded.

"I'm sorry. I really am."

"Is it all right if I have another Coke?"

"Of course." She dug into her purse and gave him the change. "You can have that."

23

It was three days since the brawl. His face still showing its effects, Starkmann sat in Ralph Harding's paneled cubbyhole gazing out the window, which framed a picture of a demolition crane that gawked above the trees at Radisson's Point as it swung a wrecking ball into the smokestack of the old veneer mill. Harding, who'd called him in first thing for a talk, was hunched over his desk, flipping through some papers with one hand. He took a sip of coffee, flipped through the papers again, then, frowning, rubbed the back of his neck like an actor in a TV commercial advertising remedies for tension headaches.

"You know, fistfights used to be a kind of sport in the logging business," he said, looking up, not smiling. "That was a long time ago, and even then the boys did most of their fighting off the job."

Silent, Starkmann dropped his glance to his hand. It was scarred by the teeth of the barbed wire despite the heavy gloves he wore while working on the fence.

"Do you get my drift?"

"What?"

"Fighting on the job. The company doesn't like it."

"That what you wanted to talk about?"

"Part of it." Harding tapped a finger on the papers. "This is the surveyor's report. LaChance dragged him out there right after you two had your go-around. That end of the forty *is* his. The company's looking at triple damages. Then there's the PR aspect—one of our cruisers duking it out with the guy we're leasing the mill property from. And you, Chris, may be looking at charges of criminal trespass if Sam pushes it."

"I ran that line right."

"It's pretty hard to argue with this survey." Harding shook his head, his voice growing sharper. "It's a short forty. A snot-nose kid wouldn't have fouled up like this. You got any explanation, hey?"

Starkmann did not say anything. Harding stood and, leaning a shoulder against a wall, looked out the window toward the distant wrecking crane, which swayed above the trees like the neck of a steel brontosaurus.

"Maybe I've got one. You haven't been yourself lately, Chris. I know you took your dad's death pretty hard and all, but you've also been doing some drinking. Isn't that true, Chris? Maybe you were a little drunk, or hung-over, when you ran those property lines? Is that it, Chris?"

Starkmann's eyes careened around the cramped room, resting again on his hands. The strong-point's finished, he thought. Now I've got only one side of the forty to fence in, and I'll hang tin cans with pebbles in them so they rattle and warn us in case anybody tries to cut the wire.

"How about an answer?"

"Who said I was drunk?"

"That kid who was working with you. Ellwood. He said he saw you nipping at a bottle," Harding said.

"I had a few, sure, but I wasn't drunk."

"Dammit!" Harding bumped the wall with the side of his fist. "What about the next day? LaChance told me he smelled booze on you, and the foreman said you didn't look too steady to him."

"I wasn't drunk. Just had a few, that's all."

"First thing in the morning? Christ almighty."

He sat down, and now massaged both his temples, as if his TV headache had moved to the front of his skull.

"Chris, we're going . . . dammit . . . I don't have any choice. . . ." He stopped rubbing his temples to fiddle with the brass-and-oak antique compass. "You know I've thought a lot about you and your work, but the past couple months, you've come in late three sheets to the wind, you've been absent, now fighting on the job, drinking on the job, and this foul-up. It's like you're throwing this job away. Just throwing it away."

"I didn't make any mistakes."

"That's all you have to say?"

"I ran the line right."

The tension headache had moved once more; Harding was

rubbing the back of his neck again. Starkmann felt sorry for him. He seemed in a lot of pain.

"We're going to have to let you go," Harding said, lowering his voice. "I've already talked it over with Furman and King, but I wanted to hear your side of the story first. I'm sorry as hell, but I haven't got any choice."

Starkmann, without saying anything, stared past him and through the window, watching the top of the smokestack collapse, bricks tumbling; now the jagged stack looked like a big red tree that had been struck by lightning.

"I'm afraid the severance is immediate. I'll have Shirley figure out what we owe you in back pay and get the check out right away. You'll have to turn the truck in. Give the keys to her on your way out—I mean when you leave. I guess that's about all. I'm sorry, Chris. No kidding."

Starkmann did not move or say a thing.

"Listen, if you need a letter of recommendation, give me a call. I'll be happy to give you one. I'll . . . Well, I hope there's no hard feelings between you and me. I had no choice, Chris."

He extended a hand across the desk. Starkmann was confused. Why did Harding want to shake his hand? What was going on? He'd had a few drinks this morning, his usual waker-upper of coffee and Early Times, and it had made him a little foggy.

"Okay, okay," Harding said. "Maybe later. Remember to turn in the keys to the truck, Chris. I'll give you a lift home."

Harding rose from his seat, jiggling his car keys, and started to walk out, pausing in the doorway when he saw that Starkmann hadn't moved.

"Chris, the severance is effective immediately. You'll have to turn in the truck keys. I can give you a ride home."

Starkmann got up, really baffled. Why did Ralph want to drive him home at this hour of the morning? He had three hundred acres of timber to cruise today. Maybe Ralph meant that he had to drive himself home because of his tension headache. That was it. Starkmann followed him, past the frosted-glass cubicle where Shirley's typewriter tick-tacked, and out the door into the parking lot. As Harding got into his car, Starkmann climbed into the truck and called to the older man to take care of his headache.

"What?"

"Take care of that headache," Starkmann repeated, raising his voice. He started the engine.

"Where the hell do you think you're going?" Harding shouted as he jumped out of his car and strode toward the truck.

"I've got a lot of timber to cruise, Ralph. All those forties west of here."

"What in the hell . . ." An astonished look on his face, Harding grabbed for the door handle as Starkmann put the pickup in gear and sped out of the lot, gravel exploding under the tires. When he pulled out onto the paved road, he glanced in the rearview mirror and saw his boss, standing in a cloud of dust, waving at him. He stuck his hand out the window, returning the wave, and shot on down the blacktop, past the town dump, where ravens wheeled above the mounds of trash.

Two hours later he was in a red-pine forest, where the trees grew straight as telephone poles. He paced off his chains and talleys. Eight, nine, ten, eleven, chain. I ran the line right, Starkmann thought. That surveyor didn't know his ass from a teacup. Nine, ten, eleven, chain. Every two chains, he dropped a plot.

After he hammered the stakes into the ground, he measured the forest's density with his angle-gauge. He had trouble squinting through the trapezoidal aperture because of his bad eye, which was swollen nearly closed. He could get along with one eye. He knew what he was doing, unlike the idiot surveyor who'd said it had been a short forty. Nine, ten, eleven, chain. He was still a little confused about what had gone on in the office, but he assumed he'd understand it once the whiskey mist lifted. Nine, ten, eleven, chain. Nine, ten, eleven, chain. Talley.

He broke for lunch in the early afternoon, sitting on a bed of pine needles with his back against a giant pine that must have been as old as God. Starkmann munched on his sandwich, washing it down with coffee and Early Times, and raised his eyes toward the first branches, spreading nearly seventy-five feet overhead. When some puny lumberjack executed this tree, it would not become a bowling alley; it would go down to the Meade paper mill in Escanaba and be mashed into pulp for newsprint, magazine stock, toilet paper, books. What would become of it? he wondered. Would it wind up wiping someone's ass or become a book of, say, poetry?

Finished eating, he capped his pint and thermos, stuffed both in the back flap of his jacket, and continued pacing. Nine, ten, eleven, chain. He felt happy; he was by himself in the woods, where he belonged. The woods were silent, except for the wind's rustling and the screeches of some ravens up ahead. Now and then the wind bore a strong ammoniac stench. Something had died not far off; it lay rotting under the trees. He went on, climbing over brush piles, windfalls and deadfalls, the odor present, then gone, then present again, depending on the eddies of the wind.

Fifteen minutes' walking brought him to the end of the section, on the lip of a sandy bluff that angled steeply twenty or thirty feet into a grove of spruce, then down another ten feet into a cedar swamp. As he pushed through a patch of second growth, a dozen ravens cried and rose out of the spruce below, where he saw the deer at the same time that he smelled it on a gust of wind lofting out of the swamp. Only its upper half remained; its hindquarters had been taken by the poacher who'd shot it, its entrails eaten by scavengers.

Starkmann sidestepped down the bluff, his feet loosing miniature landslides, and the mysterious sadness caught his throat when he saw that the doe's eyes had been pecked out by the blackbirds. He had a strange feeling that he'd seen this before, but could not remember where and when. The inexplicable sorrow crept into him once again, the sadness without object. Perhaps the dead deer was its cause. A fine-looking doe she must have been, shot out of season. He noticed tracks in the hard, dry ground, but could not identify them. A gray squirrel scampered about the base of a spruce while the ravens, black as priests at a funeral Mass, watched silently from their high pulpits in the branches of a pine. Swilling whiskey to hold the sadness at bay, Starkmann followed the tracks to where they entered the swamp, in whose mud they had made a clearer impression. No poacher had made them. As soon as he recognized them, the sorrow flushed out of him, fear rising to fill the vacuum. There were legends about these animals; though they were supposed to be extinct on the Upper Peninsula, now and then people claimed to have sighted them in remote places and to have heard their hiss and scream in the night. Out of the corner of his eye he saw the squirrel suddenly blur up a tree. One of the ravens screeched and flew off, the others following. His attention diverted by their noisy flight, he looked around, puzzled by their alarm until some ancient instinct brought a tingling to his scalp, tensed his muscles, and wadded his guts into an adrenal knot. He hadn't heard or seen a thing, yet knew somehow that *it* was close by. He looked into the swamp. Berry bushes choked its near edge. Beyond, its mossy earth lay flat under the shadows of the cedar trees. Rotten stumps and logs floated on the mud like wreckage on a mold-green sea. None of the trees grew straight; they slanted at precarious angles or crooked into sleigh-runner bends, the bark scaled by fungus. Starkmann's eyes moved back and forth, sweeping the gloom in widening arcs until his gaze met a wall of tag-alders. Through their tangle, nothing could be seen. If it had not been for the wind rasping through the pines, the stillness would have been absolute.

He turned and started to climb the bluff, forcing himself not to panic and run. *It* had its eyes on his back—he was sure of it. When he reached the top of the bluff he glanced over his shoulder, but saw only the swamp and the spruce and the half-devoured carcass of the deer. He paused to listen, as intently as he'd once listened on night ambush. Hearing nothing unusual, he started walking along the edge of the bluff, looking for a trail back to his truck, parked four miles away on a logging road. The swamp paralleled the bluff, conforming to its contours, a kind of muddy lake to its wooded shore. The sensation of being watched clung to Starkmann like a damp, invisible shirt. More than just watched, he was being followed. *It* was padding soundlessly through the cedars below, hanging on his flank. He pictured it, its eyes yellow, its muscles flowing with deadly grace under a tawny-red hide, in the design of its body the terrible efficiency of the solitary killer. Cougar. Puma. Mountain lion. *Panther.* The image of the cat was so clear it seemed to have been projected into his mind by the animal itself, some form of extrasensory communication.

Its intentions perplexed him. Was it watching him to make sure he left its territory, or was it hunting him? If it was stalking him, why hadn't it attacked? It could charge out of the swamp and lunge up the bluff in seconds if it wanted. Maybe it was waiting for a signal from him, for the moment when he realized beyond all doubt that he was a hunted thing with no chance of escape, and, through a nervous movement, or an odor given off by some atavistic gland, he signaled to the panther his readiness to die, inviting it to kill him. Then, its ears laid back, claws extended, fangs like white bayonets, it would come at him. For a moment an urge to go down fighting pumped renewed strength into his legs. He saw himself charging the cat, a warrior's yell in his throat. But the thought of confronting the beast in those somber thickets so appalled him that lumps of his half-digested lunch, soured by the whiskey in his belly, rose into his windpipe.

He walked faster, and when he couldn't find a trail, turned into the woods and started to run. He was lost. He ran and ran, the weakness in his knees making him stumble. *Lost.* The sun. Where was the sun? He stopped, breathing hard, and spun in circles, searching for the sun through the bristling green far overhead. There it was, past the zenith. That direction was west. The wind was out of the south. He'd entered the woods with the wind to his face. North, he had to run north.

As he lunged ahead, his heart punched against the inside of his chest and sweat dripped into his eyes. These woods did not seem anything like the woods he'd entered just a short time ago; they were darkened somehow, but in a way that had nothing to do with the lowered angle of the sun. He could do nothing but keep running north. Roots thrust out of the ground, tripping him. Branches tugged at the sleeves of his jacket, clutching as if to hold him, and then, as if angered by his headlong rush to escape, slapping him in the face. Up ahead, a huge, wind-shaken hemlock leaned over his path. Starkmann slowed, half-certain the tree would fall and crush him the moment he passed under it. He circled around it, its exposed roots like a nest of coiled snakes. He clawed through dense saplings that whipped his swollen eye, drawing tears, and then he saw a trail, winding northward.

He sprinted down it for a quarter of an hour without a sign of a road. The possibility that it was the wrong trail almost made him scream. He lost the sun momentarily. As he searched for it, a part of him expected to see the panther, leisurely tracking him, waiting for the moment of recognition, of submission, of invitation: *kill me*. But he saw only the old sun, burning over his left shoulder: he was headed in the right direction. In another five minutes he noticed a light through the trees, then stumbled through a clump of smoke weed and a stand of sapling birch onto the logging road.

He double-timed through the reddish dust, his nerve ends popping through his skin. The forest, crowding the road on both sides, wore a threatening mask. He had never carried a gun for his own protection in the woods; now, for the first time, he felt in need of one: his old carbine, with its taped double magazines. He held a mental picture of himself, bent at the knees, the flat of the carbine's stock against his hip as he fired into the woods on rock-and-roll—full automatic—sweeping the muzzle back and forth, the carbine a thing of magic power in his hands. He annihilated the phantom panther hiding in the trees; he shot the trees themselves, the bullets chipping the bark, scissoring branches and severing trunks until the trees looked like splintered spears.

As he jogged around a bend, he saw his truck, perhaps a quarter of a mile away. It was a wonderful, welcome sight, that familiar old Ford, leaning to one side with its right wheels up on an embankment at the edge of the woods. Two young grouse burst from their cover in an aspen stand ten feet from him. The whir of their wings, sudden and loud, snapped the stays of what little self-control he had left. He bolted for the truck, jumped in, and locked the doors. For half a minute he sat with gulping lungs, both hands firmly on the wheel.

When he regained his breath, he looked out the windshield and saw the flicker of one of the birds as it winged from a branch. Scared witless by a grouse. He switched on the ignition, turned the pickup around, and headed toward the highway, his shoulders hunched, his nose almost touching the glass, as if he were driving through a heavy rainstorm. A couple of times he thought he saw flashes of beige as the big cat streaked through the forest alongside, keeping pace with the truck. Low branches scraped the fenders; another reached out to swipe the windshield. The wilderness had somehow acquired the power of intention; it was only a wilderness—earth, water, rocks, and woods— and yet it seemed aware that his presence in its midst had always heralded death: men with chain saws had followed the paths he'd blazed with his ribboned stakes, had entered the forest to murder the trees. Now the wild had roused itself against this violation, and was expelling him.

The woods, in whose fastness he had always experienced a sense of belonging and of sanctuary from the world would from now on deny him their refuge.

A patch of asphalt showed through the trees ahead. He punched the gas and, the instant his tires touched pavement, jerked the wheel to the right, spinning onto the highway. As if trying to outrun whatever had spooked him in the forest, he floored the pedal until the broken lane-dividers blurred into a single white line beneath him. Where was he going? Where could he go now? Where?

Nowhere.

He took a turn at fifty-five miles an hour, pushing the Ford up to seventy on the straightaway. A distance ahead, a logging truck blew diesel fumes from its stack as it came on fast from the opposite direction. Starkmann drifted over the center line, into the truck's path, but some last shred of self-preservation pulled him back into his lane as the truck roared past with a bray of its horn.

He pulled to the shoulder of the road and sat there for a while; then, in a delayed recognition, it came to him that he'd been fired this morning. His stomach dropped. Fired. Canned. Sacked. Out of work and luck. He pounded the steering wheel with the edges of his hands. *King*. King had finally won. He felt a powerful desire to race back to the office and break the man in two; but he did not act on the desire because he knew his battle with King had been a hopeless one from the start. This loss had been coming for a long time. First his father, now his job. What was next, and what could he do now? Where could he go? If his brothers were alive, what would they advise? He banished all distracting thoughts, allowing his memories of them to sweep over him. He experienced one of those mystical moments when, out of the depth of his longing for their comradeship, it seemed within his power to raise them from the grave itself. But they did not appear. He saw his house instead: his house, with its weathered boards and shingles, and the bridge over the Big Firedog, and the forty acres he claimed as his own. Chill-bumps rose on his arms and the backs of his hands as a sense of great urgency came over him. His house and land—that was where he had to go immediately. He had to finish the fence without delay before he lost the last sanctuary left to him.

24

On a Sunday afternoon late in the month after which she'd been named, she knelt in her garden, weeding by hand while Chris's skill-saw shrieked in the tool shed. The sound ripped her eardrums like an alarm. It would not allow her to rest or think and seemed to be telling her that the time for thinking was over; if she did not have her talk with Chris today, she never would. She'd planned and prepared for it for a week, rehearsing her lines like an actress. She'd arranged for Sandy and Rick to take the girls sailing on Lake Superior for the day, and she'd gone to Mass this morning to pray for strength. Church had made her feel virtuous, but her emotions now, as she shuffled down the rows on her knees, were those of an adultress about to confess to her husband that she'd been seeing another man.

Her meeting with Dr. Eckhardt, ten days before, had had the aura of a lover's rendezvous. The secrets she'd told him about Chris and the way she'd poured out her own feelings had been an adultery of sorts: a sharing of confidences with an outsider, a betrayal of trust.

She yanked a weed. Little rain had fallen in the past two weeks, yet the weeds flourished; they always did. The vegetables, thanks to her diligent irrigation, were, however, holding their own: The corn-stalks stood about two feet high, hung with the spike-shaped pistils that would mature into ears. The radishes, potatoes, and spinach were thriving; only the tomato plants showed signs of needing a sunnier, warmer climate.

She plucked another weed, and another, as the skill-saw screamed through a four-by-four, or two-by-four, or six-by-one, or whatever he was cutting in there. If this scene were being filmed, she thought, it would look perfectly commonplace: a husband and wife pursuing their weekend hobbies. But the gardening had ceased to be a hobby for her: with Chris out of work, it was no longer a labor of love; it was just plain labor, pleasant enough, she supposed, but it was a labor attended by the knowledge that any mistakes she made, or the capriciousness of the weather, could mean the difference between eating and hunger. Well, that was an exaggeration, a little melodrama on her part. The difference between living with dignity and suffering the humiliation of applying for food stamps was closer to the truth of the matter.

She had gone grocery-shopping yesterday, and when, after returning home, she balanced the checking account and then found in the mail their first notice of an overdue mortgage payment, she'd become sick and dizzy. Sickness had turned into resentment an hour later, with the arrival from Jensen's Hardware of a load of concrete mix and lumber for the gate Chris had decided to build across the entrance to the gravel road. It wasn't cheap, ordinary lumber, either, but redwood. Nothing weathers like redwood, he had said; the gate will last forever. She saw the bill, which amounted to almost half his weekly unemployment check, and yelled at him: "What the hell do we need a gate for? What the hell do we need that fence for?"

"Security," he'd answered calmly, as if the reason were self-evident.

That reply had helped bolster her courage for what she had to do today. His dull tone of voice had reminded her of the afternoon, almost a month earlier, when he'd come home and flatly told her: "I got canned today. What do you think we should do now?" What did he mean, what did *she* think they should do? she asked. *What* were they going to do? How would they pay the mortgage, the bills, the insurance premiums? His only answer to these questions had been to say: "Well, King won, that goddamned King." She'd wanted to strangle him, seeing in her mind's eye the notices that advertised family financial disasters on the courthouse steps. She'd pictured collection agents repossessing the Wagoneer, goons confiscating their furniture.

She considered herself a pragmatic woman by nature, and Chris's obliviousness to the catastrophes facing them had diminished rather than heightened her initial panic. *Sisu*, June, you've got *sisu*, and you're going to need it: That's what her mother would have said. *Sisu*—a Finnish word for guts, grit, determination, the capacity to endure any hardship—was the virtue that had given Mom the strength to raise a difficult daughter on her own, as it had given Mom's parents the courage to survive the Great Depression after the lumber barons had deserted the U.P. for fatter pickings out west, leaving the unemployed loggers to get along any way they could. Mom had said that Grandpa used to poach deer and dynamite lakes for fish so his family could eat, but he never gave up. That was *sisu*.

After Chris's announcement, June had gone to banks, exploring refinancing schemes; through Erickson, she'd contacted a lawyer to represent Chris and her in the event of a foreclosure (though she half-wished the loan company would kick them out; maybe it would take that to awaken Chris to reality). She'd talked to real estate agents about putting the place on the market, brought home the contracts one afternoon, and begged Chris to sell off the forty acres, at least. He wouldn't hear of it. The land was his. It was the only safe place left to him in the world, he'd said; he wouldn't sell, and if anyone came to repossess it they'd best come with a police escort, because he meant to fight for it, and not in court. As if to prove his resolve to her, he'd spent a couple of hours that day cleaning his guns and stacking boxes of ammunition. She'd watched him, disturbed by the look on his face as he rammed cleaning rods down the barrels, oiled the metal parts, and lovingly rubbed the stocks with linseed oil; a look not of determination but anticipation, as if he were eager for some John Wayne shootout. She'd argued with him that he would have to land another job if he wanted to hold on to his property, not battle it out with a SWAT team or whatever, for God's sake.

But he'd made no effort to find work. He never left the confines of his forty acres except to drive to the unemployment office in Marquette to pick up his weekly check. Other than that, he did nothing but work on his fence by day and, by night, lie on the couch, drinking Early Times while listening to his Springsteen tapes.

June more than once had considered leaving him, just packing her own and her daughters' clothes and getting out. She'd begun to question if she loved Chris any longer. The doubt alone seemed proof that she did not; maybe she was sticking with him out of *sisu*, a gritty perseverance, which was not to be discounted as a marital virtue, but it wasn't love.

She wondered now if she had ever loved him. Possibly she had been drawn by the mystery of his silences and by the impression he gave of a man with a secret hurt, an air of noble suffering that intrigued her. Now she suspected that his silences did not arise from a deep, reflective character, but had a more prosaic source: he had nothing to say; and if he had suffered an emotional injury, in the war or somewhere else, it had probably been self-inflicted. At best, he was a troubled man, nothing more nor less; at worst, another crazy one, and June despised his illness because it had caused him to abandon her.

She stood, brushed off her knees, and stretched, watching Butternut playing her usual cat-and-mouse games with the woodpile chipmunks. It was an unusually warm day, windless; there wasn't a flutter in the leaves of the birch in the meadow, and the pines beyond stood so still they looked like a photograph. Almost lunchtime. She should take the sandwiches and potato salad out of the fridge, call him inside, and get it over with. The saw whined again as she entered the kitchen. The noise forced upon her the recognition that she despised more than Chris's illness; she despised him for the stupid, almost deliberate way he'd lost his job. The gossip mill had filled her in on the details. He'd all but begged to be fired. Mostly she despised him because she was afraid of him.

Now, as she set out the plates on the table, it chilled her to recall the fevered expression in his eyes when he'd cleaned his guns, the perverse tenderness with which he'd stroked the barrels and polished the stocks.

Her most disturbing memory was of the evening when she'd resolved to call the psychologist. Chris had failed to answer her calls to come to dinner, so she'd gone out to look for him. She'd walked down the corduroy path through the swamp, a place that always gave her the creeps. She'd seen barbed wire glinting through the undergrowth on a knoll that humped out of the mats of moss and sedge grass. She'd called him again and, receiving no answer, climbed the knoll and noticed that the underbrush had been cleared from its top. The barbed wire had been staked in a rough circle around the clearing. Four deep holes had been dug, one at each point in the compass, with cut saplings piled up to form parapets around them. In the low evening light, she hadn't been able to tell what it was at first. On initial glance, it resembled a kid's fort. Then she realized that it *was* a fort, an adult's. It reproduced the hilltop perimeters she'd seen in news photographs of Vietnam. He'd been building a fort—all that time and effort to build a fort; and as she looked at it she pictured him in one of the holes, with his guns blazing away at people who'd come to evict him from his land. She supposed this was her imagination running wild, fueled by newspaper accounts of berserk veterans. But she knew the time had come for her to stop pretending that Chris was merely passing through some temporary crisis.

So she'd arranged the appointment with Eckhardt. They'd met in Ironwood, where they'd talked over lunch and drinks in a phony-rustic chalet favored by skiers. Her first impression of the psychologist had not been favorable. "June Starkmann?" he had asked when she'd walked in. "Boy, you weren't kidding when you said you were tall. Why do you suppose you got all that height and I got shortchanged?" June nearly groaned, thinking: This little twerp ought to be selling encyclopedias instead of dealing in troubled minds. But her respect for him increased after they'd sat down and he interviewed her, putting her so at ease that she confided things about Chris she had never confided to anyone. She left nothing out, except for the business of his talking to imaginary people. She had only Christine's word on that, and a seven-year-old wasn't a very reliable source.

As she talked, Eckhardt slouched in his chair, one of his stubby arms hooked over its back, and occasionally made notes or interjected a question about Chris's background. Was there a history of mental illness in his family that she knew of? What was his religious upbringing, if any? That sort of thing.

When she was through she pressed him for an opinion, but he refused, saying that it would be unprofessional to make a diagnosis without speaking to Chris first. He then described his counseling program and gave her a short course on war-related neuroses. There were, he'd said, thousands of veterans suffering from something he called Post-traumatic Stress Disorder, which he described as a delayed reaction to terrible experiences that had happened five, ten, even fifteen years in the past. Post-traumatic Stress Disorder—it was quite a mouthful, and though June did not care for clinical psychobabble, preferring to call a spade a spade, her heart quickened at the possibility that Chris's affliction had a name. To be able to identify it lessened its power to frighten her. But she could not understand how the effects of a bad experience could take as long as ten or fifteen years to show themselves.

"Soldiers—warriors—aren't supposed to express their emotions," Eckhardt explained. "But they feel them all the same. They bottle them up inside, and eventually they start to manifest themselves, sometimes in odd ways."

"This delayed stress—that's what Chris has got?"

"I couldn't say one way or the other. I'd have to interview him. Anyway, delayed stress isn't something you get, like the flu."

"Don't patronize me, Jim."

"I'm not, and I'm sorry if I sounded as if I was. Look, most of the guys I treat saw things over there that defied their understanding. They did things that didn't fit in with their own images of themselves, things they couldn't justify. They were only boys, remember, and their way of coping with these experiences is to forget them, or try to. In some of the more severe cases, they've buried these memories so deep that even they don't know they have them. It's a form of self-induced amnesia. We had one guy in the group who'd gone berserk over there. Burned down a hut with civilians in it. They all died, a woman and three kids. He was court-martialed for it, but whenever I brought it up, he not only couldn't recall burning down the hut, he denied being court-martialed. He wasn't lying. He genuinely couldn't remember. He couldn't allow himself to remember, because he couldn't accept that he'd done something like that. So he put it out of his mind. Like erasing a tape. What we do, basically, is to get the guys to unearth those memories, face them, and come to terms with them."

Burning a woman and her children alive. The picture made June shiver.

"Chris. He couldn't have done anything like that, could he?"

"How can I answer a question like that?" Eckhardt said with detachment. "I don't know what's bothering him, if anything is."

"Then what was your card doing in his pocket?"

"It's like I told you when you called. I just happened to run into him. He'd had one too many. I drove him home. I gave him my card."

June had a feeling that Eckhardt knew or suspected more than he was letting on, but she decided not to pursue it.

"I wonder if you even know why I'm here, talking to you," she said.

"I've got a pretty good idea. *You* need somebody to talk to."

"You're damn right I do. I'm scared. Sometimes I think I'm going off the wall myself. Living with him is like living with someone who's got a fever that won't get any better or any worse. It just keeps going on and on, and I'm getting sick of it." Her eyes dampened. She dried them with a cocktail napkin, embarrassed when she noticed a nearby customer staring at them. We probably look like we're having a lover's quarrel, she thought. "Sorry for the tears. It's just that I was happy with him once and I want it to be that way again. And I want to know if you think you can help him. That's all."

"Not if he doesn't come in. The program's voluntary. It wouldn't work otherwise."

"He won't do it. He won't do it because he doesn't think anything's wrong."

Eckhardt folded his hands and looked at her earnestly. "I probably shouldn't say this, but my guess is that he does, deep down. All of these things you tell me he's doing might be his way of asking for help. He doesn't know which way to turn. He's probably begging for someone to show him."

"Me."

"You seem like a pretty resourceful woman," Eckhardt said.

But she did not feel very resourceful now, as she cut the ham-and-swiss sandwiches in halves and arranged them attractively on the plate. She didn't have any idea what she was going to say.

She placed a bowl of potato salad in the center of the table. Potato salad was one of Chris's favorites. That done, she folded the paper napkins, laid a fork on each one, and quickly washed and stacked in the drying rack the dirty breakfast dishes she'd left soaking in the sink. An atmosphere of cleanliness and order was necessary—for her if not for him.

She went to the garage. The place was a mess, full of sawdust and bits of cut lumber. Off in a corner, Chris's reloading machine stood on a bench, its lever giving it the appearance of a strangely shaped slot machine. The bags of powder stacked beneath it concerned her; what if they spontaneously combusted? But that was the least of her worries now. She had to wait for the saw to scream through a board before she could announce that lunch was ready. Chris, with a pencil behind his ear and a carpenter's apron hung from his neck, looked the picture of a *Family Circle* handyman as, guiding the saw, he bent over the triangular horses supporting the plank. If he can do this, she thought in a pique, why can't he find a job? A chunk of wood toppled into a mound of sweet-smelling sawdust on the floor. The saw went silent.

"I've got lunch ready."

His pale hair, paled further by the dust, his face lightly powdered, he looked up, startled, as if she'd just told him the house was on fire.

"June. Didn't hear you come in. Don't sneak up on me like that."

"I didn't sneak up on you. I've got lunch if you're hungry."

Without saying anything, he braced a four-by-four across the horse, measured it with his tape, marked it, and started cutting again. The sound of the saw was deafening in the enclosed space. June resisted an impulse to jerk the cord from the socket; that would have gotten things off to a bad start. *Sisu. Sisu* also meant patience.

When he'd finished, she repeated her announcement.

"In a second. I've got to wash up."

She left, giving the earth a few light kicks with her sneakers on her way back to the house. Waiting in the kitchen, her fingers quietly drumming the table, she rehearsed her lines again. Stage fright. She had no appetite; the very sight of the sandwiches and the smell of the potato salad almost nauseated her.

At last the moment arrived. Chris, his hands and face scrubbed but the woody talcum still powdering his hair, sat down across from her and began eating. Was it her imagination, or had his table manners deteriorated? He seemed to be wolfing everything down, smacking his lips, and she couldn't help contrasting this with Erickson's decorous behavior at lunch the month before.

"How's it going?" she asked, nibbling at the edges of her sandwich.
"What?"
"The gate."
"Fine."
"Is that all? Fine?"
"I've got the posts and the cross-braces cut."
Wonderful, she thought, struck again by the unattractiveness of his rectangular head.

"I still don't get it. The gate, I mean. We've gotten along without one all this time."
"Things are a lot different now."
"Right. You're out of a job, and instead of looking for another one, you're building a gate we don't need."
He said nothing, shoveling a second helping of potato salad onto his plate. June warned herself not to scold; scolding wasn't the way to lead into it.

"All right, Chris, what's so different that you've got to turn this place into a jail with gates and a barbed-wire fence?"
In answer to her question, he mumbled, "You know," with his mouth full, a half-grin baring lumps of unchewed ham and cheese.
"I forgot to get you something to drink. How about a beer?"
"Sure."

She rose, opened the fridge, and wanted to jump into it, slamming the door behind her. How do you do it? she asked herself. How do you tell a man you've lived with ten years, the father of your child, that you think he's deranged and that you'll leave him if he refuses to see a doctor? You tell him, that's how. Flat out.

She popped a can of Budweiser, set it on the table in front of him, sat down, and blurted, "Chris, there's somebody I want you to see, a doctor."
But the words came out so quickly they crashed into one an-

other, merging into a single word: *ChristheressomebodyIwantyoutoseeadoctor.*

He lifted the can to his lips, looking over the rim with the neutral expression he assumed whenever he heard something he didn't want to hear.

"Did you understand me, babe?" she asked more slowly. "I'd like you to start seeing a doctor."

"Which doctor?"

"Dr. Eckhardt. He's not a doctor doctor, he's . . . You remember him. He drove you home from the Anchor Inn last fall."

"I don't remember any doctor driving me anywhere."

"He's a little guy. Blond hair. You told me so yourself months ago. He drove you home. You'd gotten a little drunk . . ."

"I wasn't too drunk to drive. I'd just tied one on. Friday night. I wasn't that drunk, Jay-Jay. I came home and *screwed you* silly. Drunks can't screw a woman silly."

She flushed at the remembrance of that night; at the same time, the hostility with which he'd said "*screwed you* silly" brought a compression to her chest.

"Eckhardt still drove you home. You must remember him."

He raised the beer can again, half-emptying it in one swallow.

"Stop the games, Chris. You were drunk and he drove you home and gave you his card. How do you think I found his number?"

"A little guy who talks like a salesman. A clinical psychologist. Works with the V.A., right?"

"Yes," she answered, nervous but relieved at having gotten him over the hurdle of his selective amnesia. "That's him."

"Why should I see him?"

"I think you need to talk to somebody, a professional."

"Did you talk to him, Jay-Jay?"

"Yes."

"What'd he have to say?"

She glanced over his shoulder at the counter upon which he'd lined up the spice and seasoning jars like toy soldiers.

"Quite a lot. Delayed stress. Maybe that's what you've got. He wants to talk to you, and *I* want you to talk to him."

"What's delayed stress?"

"It's a kind of, well, a sickness."

"Sounds like bull to me. Know what I think, Jay-Jay? He wants to lock me up in that V.A. hospital down there."

"Chris, that's—"

"Are you two in cahoots? Do *you* want me locked up? Maybe

you've got something going on the side and want me out of the way. Is that it, Jay-Jay? Do you and that little turd have something going?"

"For God's sake, if I had someone on the side, it wouldn't be a man who comes up to my chin."

"Everybody's the same height lying down."

"I'm not sleeping with him or anybody else, and nobody wants to lock you up in the hospital, all right?" She reached across the table and took his hand; it was cold and unresponsive, like his eyes. "I love you, Chris, and I think you need to see him. I need you to see him. I can't stand living this way."

"This one doesn't have any mustard," he interrupted, turning over the top slice of his second sandwich.

"I made one with mustard, one without."

"Where's the mustard?"

"In the fridge. Where else?"

He stood up, opened the refrigerator, and gazed blankly at the top shelf.

"It's not here."

"It's there. Look, for Christ's sake."

Recognizing the faint tremor that passed through his body as the prelude to a violent outburst, she was not too shocked when, finding the mustard, he yelled, "It was supposed to be on the top shelf! Why the hell do you think I labeled them, goddammit!" He flung the jar across the kitchen, the glass exploding, gobs of yellow slithering down the wall.

"Stop it! Chris, for God's sake—"

"Nothing's where it's supposed to be. Look at this mess!"

He snatched the catsup she'd bought yesterday and winged it with all his strength over her head. The bottle crashed into the wall where the mustard jar had burst, the catsup streaming like lava as Chris, with a single swipe of his arm, knocked everything off one shelf, pickles, mayonnaise, peppers, horseradish, and grape jelly crashing to the floor in a multicolored explosion.

"Not a thing where it should be!"

He tossed a bottle of salad dressing like a hand grenade.

"Not one goddamned thing in order. You've got all the time to go talking to shrinks, back-stabbing me, but you haven't got the time to put things where they belong, do you, Jay-Jay?"

A jar of blueberries, which she'd picked and preserved the previous September, sailed through the archway into the living room. That did it for her. Her Finnish side surrendered to the Canuck, forbearance to fury. Leaping on him from behind, screaming, "Stop it! Stop it!" she tried to pull him away from the refrigerator, but he shoved her backward into the counter. Its metal-stripped edge jabbed her spine.

"Go ahead," she cried. "Smash all of it. It's only food. It's only money and we've got money to burn. You crazy bastard!"

She grabbed a bottle of barbecue sauce by the neck, cocked her arm, and hurled it at him. It missed, struck the door, and bounced onto the linoleum, shattering in a splash of brownish-red. She lunged for a jam jar for another try at hitting him, and was stopped cold when he whirled and slapped her across the side of the face with a blow powerful enough to buckle her knees and make her ears ring.

It was the first time he'd ever struck her.

"You son of a bitch!" She cupped her ear in her hand. He raised his arm to strike her again, then lowered it.

"June . . ."

Hitting her appeared to have spent his fury. He stood dumbly, as stunned as she by what he'd done.

"You son of a bitch, the next time you do that, you'd best cold-cock me or I'll take a knife and cut your guts out."

"Jesus, Jay-Jay . . ."

He lowered his eyes to the mess on the floor, staring as if he could not figure out who had made it.

"Except there won't be a next time. I'm leaving." She backed toward the entrance to the living room. "Did you hear that, you crazy bastard? I'm packing up and leaving. Now."

"Don't say that, June."

"I'm not going to say it. I'm going to do it."

His arms out to the sides, palms forward, the pose of a suppliant, he took a step toward her but slipped in a puddle of mayonnaise and pickle juice, falling against the counter and dropping to his knees.

"Don't, June. Don't you leave me, June Josette," he muttered, pulling himself up. He slipped and fell again, like an ice-skater who couldn't regain his balance.

He was both pathetic and comical at that moment. Her instinct was to help him to his feet, but, her ear still ringing from the force of his slap, she turned and ran upstairs to their bedroom. After locking the door, she started pulling her clothes from the closet and drawers, tossing them on the bed. She could not believe he'd hit her, though she was, in some perverse depths of herself, gratified that he had. After all the months of mute indifference, any reaction out of him, even a violent one, was better than none at all. She took her two suitcases from the closet shelf and began to shove her dresses, jeans, and underwear into them without order. As she did this, the old phrase *beside oneself* assumed a new meaning for her; she felt that one part of her had literally separated from the other, that she was watching herself stuffing clothes into suitcases. The picture was a little ridiculous, a soap opera.

Then Chris knocked at the door. When she refused to answer, he pounded on it. She cast her eyes toward the closet, where his shotguns and rifles were stored in tooled-leather cases, and wondered if she could use one to defend herself. Every story of domestic violence she'd seen on the TV news, read in the newspapers, or heard about from her cases reeled through her mind—crimes of passion, love haywired into bloodshed, paramedics carrying shrouded corpses of Mom and Pop out of conventional little houses into ambulances with pulsating lights. She had to get a grip on herself. She wasn't a killer, and neither was he.

"Jay-Jay. *Jay-Jay.*"

"What? What do you want?"

"Don't leave. You can't leave, June. You belong here with me."

"I'm over it, Chris. I'm packing."

"Don't leave."

His voice did not sound human, his plea a cry of animal pain, like the bawling of the bear after she'd smashed its paw with the iron skillet; only this cry filled her with remorse and pity instead of fear. She sat on the edge of the bed. One of her suitcases was the same one she'd packed years ago, when she'd left Sault Ste. Marie on the Greyhound. The sight of its worn locks and its musty smell reminded her of Ripley, of desertions, loneliness, transience, the impermanence of love. She could not quite believe, after ten years of marriage, that she would leave without a struggle. Pack up and quit. She couldn't do it—walk out on him as Ripley had walked out on her. *Sisu.* Endurance. Perseverance. Grandpa dynamited lakes for fish to feed his family, but he never quit or ran out on anybody.

"Promise me you'll start seeing Eckhardt," she offered. "Promise me that and I'll stay."

He said nothing. To underline her resolve, she snapped shut the locks to her suitcase.

"June . . ."

"You heard me. Promise me you'll start seeing him and I won't go anywhere."

After a pause he asked, "Will you give me time to think about it, Jay-Jay? I need to think. Let me think about it."

"What's that mean? A week, a month, a year?"

"A little while. Give me a little while to think about it."

"No!" she shouted, then opened the door. Without looking into

Chris's face, afraid that the sight of it would weaken her, she shoved past him and went into the girls' room to gather their things. "There's nothing to think about."

"June, what're you doing?"

"Lisa and Christy are going with me," she said, yanking their dresses from the closet. "You like being alone so much, you can have this place all to yourself."

"You can't do that. You can't take Christy."

"I can and I will. If she means so much to you, if I mean anything to you, you'll promise."

He hesitated, mulling it over while she continued packing, her back to him. She didn't dare turn around.

"All right," he said tiredly. "I'll see him."

She hadn't expected so swift a surrender. Maybe he felt guilty about striking her, or maybe Eckhardt had been right about him—he secretly wanted someone to push him in this direction.

"Call him now," she said, worried he would change his mind if he waited. "Call him and make an appointment."

He said nothing. She could only guess at the expression on his face, for her back was still to him. He went downstairs, and when she heard his voice asking to speak to Eckhardt, she wanted to cry from relief, an impulse she restrained. This was no time for displays of emotion. Chris called up to her that the appointment was set for a week from today—was that quick enough for her? Before she could respond, the back door slammed shut as he went outside. He was angry, and maybe had a right to be. She'd blackmailed him into it, not the most subtle tactic, but the situation did not call for diplomacy. She rehung her daughters' clothes, then walked down to the kitchen and took a mop and bucket from the broom closet. She had one hell of a mess to clean up. *Sisu.*

25

The following week, dreading the interview but seeing no alternative but to go through with it, Starkmann made the drive to Iron Mountain. The psychologist's office was in the Outreach Center, a converted storefront not far from the V.A. hospital, a menacing, mustard-brick building surrounded by well-kept lawns and a landscaped parking lot. The Center had two rooms in addition to Eckhardt's office: a small kitchen with a hot plate for making coffee, and a meeting room containing a cafeteria table and some folding chairs. Posters decorated the walls. One showed a photograph of a GI carrying a wounded buddy over his shoulders and bore the caption HE AIN'T HEAVY, HE'S MY BROTHER. Another displayed an artist's rendering of the Vietnam War Memorial in Washington, two huge slabs of polished black granite upon which the names of nearly sixty thousand dead were inscribed—as if, Starkmann thought, they'd been nothing more than the victims of some enormous industrial accident, like a refinery fire or a gas-plant explosion. Well, maybe that was all they had been. Modern war was an industry, soldiers mere workers on its bloody assembly line.

Eckhardt greeted him cheerfully and offered him coffee in a Styrofoam cup like the cups in Burger King. Starkmann sat in a vinyl lounger, the psychologist in a large desk chair that made him look like a boy trying on his father's office for size.

"Tastes just like mess-hall coffee," he said with his disarming smile. "Makes you feel right at home, doesn't it?"

"Yeah."

Eckhardt tried to ease into the interview with small talk about the poor fishing season this year. Such unusual heat, so little rain, the trout sluggish.

"Let's get this over with," Starkmann said, cutting off the chitchat.

"You sound like a man who's going to have his appendix out."

"I'm here because I have to be."

"I assumed you called me because you *want* to be here."

"My wife said she'd leave me if I didn't come in. I guess you gave her that idea."

"I talked to her, Chris." Eckhardt folded his hands over a file on his desk. "But I sure as hell didn't suggest that she threaten to leave you. We don't operate that way. Do you know what we do here, what this is all about?"

"No."

"We think of ourselves as human reclamation experts. A lot of guys got messed up over there, in their heads. And messed up by the way they were treated when they got back to the States. They were made to feel like outcasts, and a lot of them think of themselves as outcasts, pariahs. We try to bring them back into the fold, so to speak, but not with the standard Freudian crap. We use rap groups, private counseling, drug-clinic referrals, the whole nine yards. Most of our people are veterans themselves, brothers helping brothers, reestablishing the bond of combat in a civilian setting. The idea is to make these guys feel good about their service, to show them that they're valuable human beings."

"That's some sales pitch, Eckhardt," Starkmann said, a little baffled by the jargon.

"This job requires some salesmanship."

"Are you saying I'm messed up?"

"Maybe we ought to start by finding out if you want to be here, regardless of what June wants."

Starkmann did not say anything, disliking Eckhardt's reference to June by her first name. His eyes ranged around the room for something to divert his attention. The office was sparsely furnished, its walls as bare as prison walls except for one small window flanked by a pair of potted ferns, a few more posters, and Eckhardt's degrees, framed in black.

"Look, if you don't feel you need to be here, you're free to walk out." Eckhardt gestured with a cock of his head. "There's the door. If you're having problems, you can stay where you are. Up to you."

"What problems am I supposed to be having?"

"I don't know. June thinks you are. Do you agree with her or is it just her imagination?"

"I wouldn't know about her imagination. Why don't you ask her? You two sound like you've gotten on pretty friendly."

"Let's forget I talked to her. Let's start from scratch. You haven't walked out of here, so maybe there's something you need to get off your chest."

"Like what, for instance?"

Eckhardt gave it some thought. "Maybe we could start with the night we ran into each other in the bar."

Starkmann crossed his legs and pulled a loose thread from the cuff of his jeans.

"I remember you passing out and mumbling something about a dust-off. I couldn't quite make it out. Do you remember why you were calling for a dust-off?"

"No. I was out."

"You were wounded over there, weren't you?"

"Yeah."

"How about elaborating?"

"Mortar fragments. It wasn't very serious. I was in the hospital only a couple of days."

"Three, to be exact." The small man opened a file and read from it: "Admitted to Fourth Field Hospital July 24, 1969; returned to full duty July 27."

"What is that?"

"It's a summary of your two-oh-one file," he answered, using the army term for a soldier's service record.

Starkmann felt as if tiny flames had begun to lick up his arms. How much did the psychologist know about his record? Did the file contain a report of his crackup? He hadn't counted on this, and regretted not having left when he'd had the chance. He wanted to leave now, but if he bolted, Eckhardt would know he had something to hide. Control, he warned himself. Stay in control.

"Where did you get it, the two-oh-one?"

"Washington. I called for it after you phoned me."

"Why? What for?"

"Standard procedure. Unfortunately, we get our share of frauds in here—guys looking for a free lunch. You know, supply clerks who never left Saigon and cooks who dished out pizzas at the staff officers' club coming in and claiming they're emotionally shattered from all the hell they'd seen in the jungle and then hoping we'll certify them for a psychiatric disability."

"Listen, I was there."

"I know." He read from the file again. "Arrived in-country June

2, 1969. Assigned B Company, First of the Seventy-Seventh. Wounded in action July 24, then the three days at Fourth Field."

"What else does it say in there?"

"That you were in the hospital a second time, from September 25 to October 10, then reassigned to brigade headquarters. Were you wounded twice, Chris? It doesn't say so here."

"The second time in the hospital you mean."

"Yeah."

"Malaria," he lied, pleased with his quick thinking. "I had malaria. I wasn't in good shape after I got over it, so they assigned me to brigade."

"What did they have you doing there?"

"Perimeter security detail. Night watchman stuff."

Eckhardt, clasping his hands behind his head, leaned back and looked up at the ceiling. "Going back to that night you passed out. Were you dreaming about the time you were wounded? Is that why you were calling for a dust-off?"

"I don't know. I was pretty drunk."

"I'll say. You were ready to take on that big son of a bitch. What was his name?"

"Sam LaChance."

"Biggest son of a bitch I've ever seen."

"He's big, all right."

"Of course, you had that revolver in your pocket. Evened things up a bit. What were you doing with it, by the way?"

The fire again crawled up his arms and now spread to his face. "I'd left it in my pocket. I'd been exercising my bird dog, and I'd left the gun in my pocket when I went into town. I wasn't going to use it on Sam if that's what you mean."

"Hell, no. You're not here on a weapons charge, and I'm not interrogating you. I was just curious."

"Okay."

"Once more going back to what you were saying when you passed out: Do you know what a flashback is?"

"Remembering something all of a sudden."

"It's a special kind of memory. *Reexperiencing* is the professional term for it. Experiencing a past event as if it's actually happening."

The dream. Did that explain the unusual clarity of the dream? Was it a reexperience and not a journey into the past? He wanted to explore this idea, but held his tongue; if he so much as suggested that he'd thought his dream was a form of time travel, Eckhardt would lock him up for sure.

"I heard you use somebody's name," the psychologist was saying. "T.J. or P.J. Something like that."

"D.J.," Starkmann corrected, thinking: There can't be any harm in telling him that. "D.J. Fishburn."

"Do you remember calling his name?"

"I'll take your word for it."

"All right. Do that. Was he a buddy of yours?"

"Sure."

"Have any others?"

Starkmann nodded.

"I don't know what kind of soldier you were, Chris," Eckhardt said, exasperation roughening his voice. "But you would have made a fine P.O.W. The bad guys would never have gotten anything out of you."

"Is that supposed to be a compliment?"

"It's a request for a little cooperation. If I'm going to do you any good, you'll have to meet me halfway. Maybe you could tell me who these buddies were and if you were tight with them. Something, for Christ's sake."

"There was D.J. and two other guys. Ramos and a medic, Hutchinson. And yeah, I guess we were tight."

"Do you still stay in touch?"

A part of him longed to cry out, Yes! I talk to them. I speak to the dead, Dr. Eckhardt! I commune with ghosts!

"They were killed. All three of them together. A booby-trapped two hundred and fifty-pound bomb. Blew them into gas."

"When was that?"

"When I was in the hospital. The second time."

"With malaria."

"Right."

Eckhardt found this information interesting enough to note it down. "How do you feel about that—their getting killed while you were in the hospital?"

Starkmann glanced around the room like a student stumped by a quiz. A bar of sunlight leaned through the window, brightening the leaves of the ferns. "How am I supposed to feel?"

"However you do feel."

"I don't think about it. I guess I don't feel anything." He paused, plucking another thread from his cuff. That answer did not sound appropriate. Eckhardt might think him unnaturally callous. "I felt bad about it when it happened is what I mean. But it was a long time ago."

The small man rose and pulled a book from the small case

beside his desk. "Homer. *The Odyssey*," he said, turning the pages. "Here it is." He held the book out in front of him and read aloud: " 'Would God I, too, had died there—met my end that time the Trojans made so many casts at me, when I stood by Achilles after death. I should have had a soldier's burial and praise from the Achaians, not this choking waiting for me at sea, unmarked and lonely.'

"That's Ulysses speaking," the psychologist said, resuming his seat. "Wishing he'd died with his comrades instead of being cast adrift by Poseidon. 'I should have had a soldier's burial and praise from the Achaians.' We didn't get either, did we, Chris? We survived the war, and instead of being praised, we got cursed. We were treated like shit, weren't we?"

Starkmann heard a low roaring, as when you hold a seashell against your ear. *I should have had a soldier's burial*—the words moved him deeply.

"When I got back . . ." His voice broke.

"When you got back what, Chris?"

"I was hitchhiking from Travis . . . Never mind."

"It won't kill you to talk about it."

"Just never mind. All right?"

"All right. But you know what I mean. We had rocks thrown at us. We were spit at and called killers by undergraduate punks, but the funny thing is, some guys felt they *deserved* that kind of treatment. A man goes to war, his friends die, he lives, and he feels guilty about it."

"That's screwy."

"No, it isn't. But that kind of guilt can drive a man crazy if it goes on long enough."

"I'm not crazy, Eckhardt."

"I'm not suggesting you are. I was suggesting that possibly—"

"And I don't feel guilty that those guys got killed and I didn't."

"I wasn't trying to put thoughts into your head. You might say I was trying to prime the pump."

"I guess it came up dry."

"Maybe so. Maybe you don't need to be here, but in case you think you do, we're holding our next rap session day after tomorrow. You're welcome to come."

Starkmann went, and continued to go off and on for the next several weeks. He was puzzled by what drew him to the weekly assemblies of invisibly maimed men. It was something beyond the fear of losing June, a compulsion he could not understand, all the more so because he found the sessions an ordeal. He didn't even like the term *rap session*.

It was linguistic camouflage, a use of casual contemporary slang to give the sessions the atmosphere of friendly get-togethers, just a bunch of the boys telling war stories. In fact, the sessions were a type of group therapy. The men would talk and smoke over coffee, with Eckhardt skillfully guiding the conversation. Sometimes he would choose the topic and manipulate everyone to stay on it; at other times he would allow the men to ramble on and on, then cut in with some sage advice or psychological wisdom. At other times he would select one man and ask him to describe his experiences, or how his life had gone since coming home, and then everyone was supposed to comment on the man's revelations about himself.

Starkmann, with his reticent nature, was ashamed for the men who exposed themselves and their lives to virtual strangers. How eager they were to talk about their experiences, their relations with their families, wives, or girlfriends. He wondered what the point of all this public confessing was supposed to be. Eckhardt was always reassuring them that none of them was crazy; they had simply suffered normal reactions to abnormal experiences and he was there to help them "work through" and lead normal lives—whatever that was supposed to mean. If they weren't crazy, then what were they doing there? What good did it do anyone? None that Starkmann could see. The same men came in, night after night, and talked and talked, but their lives did not appear to change. The ones who were out of work stayed out of work; the drunks stayed drunk; the dopers kept getting stoned.

As for himself, Starkmann said very little. Quite often he spent an entire session without speaking more than a few words. The idea of spilling his guts to people whom he hardly knew disgusted him. Nor did he care much for his comrades, or whatever they were supposed to be. Except for one, an ex-Special Forces medic named Mike Flynn, they were long-haired and scruffy, and their speech, like their sloppy mode of dress, seemed frozen in the sixties. Starkmann liked Flynn because he, too, was reserved, not given to these shameful revelations. Then, one night, Flynn was maneuvered into talking. His story came out in fragments, disconnected phrases interspersed with gasps, as if he'd run ten miles at top speed.

He said he'd been on a patrol in 1969, and had cracked up after a soldier in his unit had been shot in a night ambush during a monsoon storm. It had been so dark and the rain so heavy that Flynn couldn't see where the casualty had been wounded.

He'd had to feel along the body with his hands, and discovered, when his fingers dipped into a gob of brains that the top of the soldier's head had been blown off. He couldn't pull his fingers out, he'd said. Something held them there, clutching the brains that felt like lukewarm oatmeal, and he started screaming in the middle of the jungle night, the enemy all around, firing at him as he screamed and screamed, unable to move, a man's brains in his hand.

After telling his story, the ex-medic fell into tremors, then started choking and crying as he collapsed on the floor. No one could do anything for him. He lay on the floor wheezing. Eckhardt called for an ambulance, which arrived in a short time and took Flynn to the hospital. That was the last the group saw of him. Although Eckhardt later assured them that he'd suffered a "temporary anxiety reaction," from which he'd completely recovered, Starkmann had his doubts: Mike Flynn was probably in the psychiatric ward, locked up for the rest of his life.

After that incident, he stopped attending the sessions, suspecting that their purpose might be to trick the men into saying or doing something crazy so they could be put away. America wanted to get rid of them, human refuse from an unpopular war, men indelibly stained by the muck and filth of where they'd been.

June forced him to go back with more threats and nagging, making his life more miserable than it had been before. He returned after an absence of two weeks, but kept a cautious eye on Eckhardt, watching him as he'd watched the paddy farmers in Vietnam; you never knew which of them was only a farmer, which a disguised guerrilla who would set off an electrically detonated mine the moment you turned your back.

A couple of times, in his usual cordial way, the psychologist tried to pry information out of him. "Chris," he once said with an affable smile, "we haven't heard much from you. Is there anything you'd like to tell us?" Starkmann replied that there wasn't. "There must be a reason why you decided to come back," Eckhardt said. Starkmann answered as he had in their first interview: his wife had threatened to leave him if he didn't. This drew laughter from a couple of the guys, which surprised Starkmann. He'd made a joke! Except he didn't think it was very funny. "Why do you suppose she did that?" Eckhardt asked. Starkmann wanted to vanish. He wished he could reduce himself to the size of a microbe. He responded to the question with a shrug. When Eckhardt pressed him, he snapped that what went on between him and June was no one's business but his own.

"Sure, Chris, sure, we'll change the subject," Eckhardt said agreeably, but Starkmann had noticed him write something in his notebook.

The only thing he liked about attending the sessions was going to Burger King after they were over. A Burger King stood on the highway, less than a block from the hospital. He could see the hospital through the window and sometimes wondered how Mike Flynn was doing, if that's where they'd put him. He would sit, munching a Whopper and fries, and feel, in the neutral atmosphere, almost as safe as he did within his perimeter. Often, he renewed his fantasy of becoming an Interstate nomad, surviving on hamburgers and tacos. Interstate 95, Interstate 10, Interstate 65—there were dozens of them, a concrete trailwork forty thousand miles long, a country unto itself, a domain of strangers.

As much as he disliked the rap sessions, they became habitual, part of his routine, like his weekly visits to the unemployment office. At home, he put the finishing touches on his perimeter, clearing fields of fire where he could, attaching empty beer and soda cans to the wire. The gate was finished, and he was proud of his workmanship. Anchored on four-by-four posts cemented into the ground, it straddled the gravel road, solid as the gate to a frontier fort. It had a six-by-one across the back as a bar, a feature that got on June's nerves because she had to remove it when she left for work in the morning. To keep her happy, Starkmann walked down to the gate every evening about the time she returned, and did her the courtesy of opening it so she wouldn't have to honk the horn. That, too, became part of his routine.

Barring the gate after June left, opening it when she came home, going to the center and the unemployment office—these chores and activities helped him get through the depression that dropped on him like a collapsing tent-top when the perimeter was at last finished and there was nothing more to do.

To keep himself occupied and to make sure everyone was safe, he started to run regular security patrols in the early-morning hours when June and the girls were asleep. He would crawl out of bed in the predawn darkness, get his carbine and a flashlight, and then stalk along a quarter-mile section, looking and listening, alert as a cat. *Alert, alive.* The patrols did not take long; he would be back in bed within an hour.

Despite his faithful attendance of the sessions, June remained unhappy with him. If he wasn't going to look for a job, she complained, why didn't he do some of the housework, or help her get dinner ready instead of loafing around all day? And why, for God's sake, did the gate have to be barred? She felt like an inmate, and the girls, out of school for the summer, were going nuts, bored and alone out here, and if he found at least part-time work he could buy a secondhand car so he could take them to their friends' houses in town while she was at her office.

Starkmann had begun to feel toward her as he had felt toward the civilians back home when he was in Nam: aggrieved and unappreciated. He had built the fence for her protection, but she didn't realize that, nor did she seem aware of the sacrifice he was making, for her sake, by attending Eckhardt's morbid gatherings. He wondered if she thought him less than a real man because he wasn't working, bringing home the bacon. Once, to prove he could still take care of her and the girls, he went fishing in the Firedog, where he caught a mess of brook trout and a three-pound rainbow that took nearly ten minutes to land. He gutted the fish on the riverbank, stuffed them in his creel, and returned to the house, triumphant. He emptied his catch in the kitchen sink, calling June, Lisa, and Christy to come take a look. "Enough for a week," he exulted. "I can still bring home the bacon." June picked up one of the rose-speckled brookies, slapped it back into the sink, and said, "What good is this going to do? Fish. We're three months overdue on the mortgage, and you bring home fish." Then she broke into tears. Starkmann was disappointed and baffled. He couldn't understand what the matter was. Maybe she was going crazy. Or maybe his early suspicions had been on the mark: she had something going on the side, and now that he'd satisfied one of her demands, she was looking for some other excuse to leave him.

On a muggy night at the end of July, after falling asleep to the strumming of mosquitoes, Starkmann went on another journey in time, the first he'd taken in months. He relived that terrible dawn, from the moment he leaped into the foxhole with Captain Hartwell and the torso of Spec. 4 Pryce, to the instant when he saw the napalm's fire, the trees uprooted, and the smoke swallow the sun and moon.

It was still dark when he awoke, his rigid body bathed in sweat. The mosquitoes continued to hum outside the window screens. After his muscles had relaxed, he crawled out of bed and stood by the west window, through which he saw wisps of fog slithering through the meadow. Beyond was the ridge, darker than the sky, a black hole in space, a gravitational whirlpool drowning all the light in the world. The smells of where he'd been clung to him once again, smells of mud and blood, of scorched flesh and flaming gasoline. Why had the dream returned, after all this time? For every question, there was an answer, and the answer to this one came in a few minutes when Butternut let out a bark. The dream had come as a warning: trespassers, concealed by the fog, had sneaked under the wire.

Starkmann quickly dressed, got his carbine and a flashlight, and went outside, quietly locking the back door behind him. With Butternut out in front as a tracking dog, he patrolled the entire perimeter, creeping through the mists in search of footprints and breaks in the wire, but found nothing. First light had begun to gray the sky by the time he was done. Worn out, Starkmann returned to the house, cutting across the meadow, whose dew-wet ferns brushed him like clammy hands.

Inside, he found June already awake, sitting in the living room in her bathrobe. Her eyes widened when she saw him in muddy boots and wet trousers, a gun in his hand. He asked what she was doing, awake before sunrise.

"I heard you go out," she answered, her gaze fastened on the carbine. "Chris, what were you doing with *that* in the middle of the night?"

"Thought I heard something. Butternut was barking. I was checking it out. It's all right, though. You can go back to sleep."

He thought she was going to start nagging him again. Instead, as he detached the magazine from the carbine, she got up from the sofa and embraced him tightly. The smell of her body, of her nearness, repelled him.

"What's happening to you? Tell me, what's happening to you?"

He didn't answer. The question made no sense to him.

June, slipping a hand between them, undid the belt to her robe, letting it fall open so that her uncovered breasts pressed against him.

"If you can't tell me, then make love to me. Now. Right here. On the couch, on the floor. I don't care. Make love to me, Chris. Do it, Chris, now, please."

He stroked her black hair, wondering what she could be thinking. He'd just come in off a patrol, muddy, wet, and tired. How could she ask him to make love? He pulled her arms from around his waist.

"You can be one cold son of a bitch," she said, then ran upstairs. He heard her slam the bedroom door.

June was stopped at the light at Front Street and East Bay Road, her hands opening and closing on the steering wheel while Tammy

Wynette wailed on the radio. June switched it off. She enjoyed listening to the blues, when she could pick up the good, gritty black stations in Detroit or Chicago, but hated the country music that monopolized the airwaves up here. Piss-and-moan music, she called it—anthems of self-pity, manufactured sorrow, and sentimental hogwash churned out by the electronic studios of Nashville. She had a special dislike of Tammy Wynette, who had made "Stand By Your Man" a hit. "Stand By Your Man," that hymn to blind feminine steadfastness. Go ahead and stand by him, Tammy, but you'd better take a look to make sure he's still there, June thought, still burning from Chris's rejection of her this morning. She had never felt so unwanted and unneeded. And what had he been up to, creeping around before dawn with that army rifle?

The light seemed unusually long. She waited, tapping her unpolished nails on the dashboard and dreading the hours ahead of her. Today was her day in the field, her day to visit the backwoods dispossessed, with whom she might soon have more in common than she'd ever feared: The last letter from the loan company had threatened foreclosure if the default on the mortgage wasn't cured in thirty days. The lawyer referred by Erickson had assured her that she had more time than that; at least six months would pass before the bank repossessed the property. The default could be paid at any time during that period, he'd said. Terrific. Before that could be done, Chris would have to get off his butt, on his feet, and find a job, which now appeared about as likely as her winning a million in a lottery. Anyone who wanted to buy his prison farm was welcome to it, as far as she was concerned; but she did not want the place sold for petty cash on the courthouse steps and have to start over from scratch.

The light was still red. It must be stuck, she decided. Ridiculous. A stoplight in a one-horse town through which a couple of dozen cars might pass in an entire day. She punched the gas and shot through the intersection, the squeal of her tires loud enough to startle two early-bird tourists sauntering toward Swanson's for breakfast. She went past the Methodist church at twenty miles over the limit. Eckhardt's therapy wasn't doing any good, none that she could see. If anything, Chris was getting worse. His personality seemed to be imploding, collapsing in on itself. He acted as if she, the girls, and the whole outside world had ceased to exist. He had become so self-absorbed that she would not have been surprised to see his eyes roll over in their sockets and turn their gaze inward.

She had phoned Eckhardt twice in the past two months to complain about the lack of results. He'd been patient with her first call, but had lost his temper the second time, when she'd shouted at him.

"Don't bully me, June," he'd answered back. "I'm a practicing professional, not some psychological private detective you've hired and who you think you can push around when he doesn't come up with any clues."

She'd deserved that rebuke, but dammit, she couldn't wait years for Dr. Eckhardt to discover the miracle vaccine or, to use his metaphor, to find the right clues and solve the mystery.

Clues, she thought, passing the sign that welcomed visitors to VIEUX DESERT, POP. 942, NATURE IN ABUNDANCE. An inspiration striking her, she touched the brakes and made a U-turn, heading back toward town. If Eckhardt did not want to play psychological private detective, she would.

At the intersection, where the light continued to cast its red at nonexistent traffic, she turned onto East Bay, then parked in front of the VFW Hall. I should have figured this out long ago, she said to herself, crossing the street to the war memorial, a large whitewashed boulder with a flag flying over it and four brass plaques bolted into its face, each inscribed with the names of the men from Raddison County who had fought in the two World Wars, Korea, and Vietnam. The names with stars after them were those who had, in the words of the legend, "sacrificed their lives in the service of their country." June, feeling she was on the threshold of a discovery, studied the Vietnam plaque like an archaeologist attempting to translate an ancient tablet. None of the names rang a bell, but then, why should they? Chris had never mentioned any of the men he'd served with, and maybe the names had nothing to do with his refusal to drive this street. Maybe the existence of the memorial alone was enough to make him panic. She read the list again. There were twelve names altogether, four punctuated with stars; but the only thing that drew her attention was that most of the surnames of the men who'd been to Vietnam matched those who'd fought in the other wars. Grandfathers, fathers, and sons—it was as if fighting in distant conflicts were a kind of legacy, passed from one generation to the next. That told her something about small-town patriotism, but nothing about what she wanted to know.

Frustrated, she debated whether or not to give Eckhardt another call. All right, it was worth a try. She cut across the street to the phone booth outside the post office.

Eckhardt wasn't in, either at the Center or at the office where he conducted his private practice. She got his home number from information and rang him there. The female voice on the other end surprised her; she didn't know he was married.

"Dr. Eckhardt, please," she said, avoiding the familiar "Jim."

"Who's calling?"

"Mrs. Starkmann. And tell him I'm sorry to call him at home, but it's important."

She waited, nestling into a corner of the booth and looking at the memorial, which resembled a giant stone that had been washed ashore. Herring gulls wheeled over the bay behind it—white, then dark, as they turned into and out of the sun.

"What is it?" Eckhardt asked. He did not sound pleased.

"Did your wife tell you I'm sorry—"

"That was my cleaning girl. My wife's in Pontiac with my kids."

"Sorry. I didn't realize you were divorced."

"Who isn't these days? What's so important?"

"This morning? Before daybreak? Chris was wandering outside with a rifle. Some kind of army rifle."

"Did he explain why?"

"He said the dog was barking and that he thought he heard a noise."

"Did you?"

"I was asleep."

"Did it ever occur to you," he said with overstrained forbearance, "that maybe he did hear something, and that, with you living out there miles from the nearest help, the rifle might have been intelligent precaution?"

"Don't talk to me like I'm an idiot. I know what I saw. Anyway, that's not the only reason I called. Do you remember my telling you how jumpy Chris got when I asked him to drive me down a street here in town? East Bay Road? That he told me he never went down that street? Drove miles out of his way to get to work?"

"Yes, vaguely."

"I think I've got an idea why."

"And what, June, has led you to this conclusion?"

Overlooking the sarcasm, she told him about the memorial. He was silent at first, but she sensed, as if telepathically, a piquing of his interest.

"Do you remember any of the names?"

"Some of them."

"Hang on. My notes are in my briefcase."

An empty logging truck, clattering down the street, almost drowned out Eckhardt when he came back on the line.

"Fishburn," June heard him say. "I don't suppose D.J. Fishburn was one of them."

"What did you say?"

"D.J. Fishburn. I don't suppose that was one of them."

"N-No," she answered, her throat catching.

"Didn't think so. Chris told me he was black, and there hasn't been a Negro up here in recorded history. How about Ramos and Hutchinson?"

"Were they friends of his?"

"Yes. They were killed over there."

"Killed? Christ."

"Are their names on the plaque?"

"No, no. Jim, he *talks* to them. My youngest daughter overheard him. I didn't tell you because all I had to go on was her word."

"I'm not following."

"He *talks* to those three guys like they're still alive. Christy heard him. D.J., Hutch, and Ramos. He talks to them, for God's sake!"

Eckhardt took a while to absorb this information, then told her not to overreact. "Believe it or not, that's not all that uncommon. I caught myself doing it a few years back."

"Talking to dead people isn't uncommon? That's normal?"

"Not exactly. It's hard to explain to someone who wasn't there. But sometimes your memories can be so vivid that, yes, it's like they're still alive."

"Whatever you say," she commented wearily. "Whatever. You're the doctor."

"I've got to run. Listen, June, do me a favor. Copy down those names if you can and either phone them in to me or drop them in the mail."

He hung up. June, watching the gulls fluttering over the smooth summer blue of the bay, reflected on this assurance: it's not that uncommon. Suppose Chris started to see his trio of dead buddies? Suppose he invited them over for dinner? What would Eckhardt have to say to that? Don't be alarmed, June—it's not that uncommon.

She jerked open the folding door and rummaged in her purse for a pen and a scrap of paper, questioning why she was going through all this trouble. I'm living with a man who'd rather talk to ghosts than to me, she thought as she copied the names: Allen, R.T. . . . Johnson, T.K.* . . . LeForge, P.G. . . . Mueller, J.L.* . . . St. Germaine, B.G.* . . . Swenson, O.R.

26

Starkmann is lying in the woods. The trees are very tall, their branches burned off, their trunks pointing toward the sky like blackened spears.

"He's still alive. Jesus Christ," someone says.

"Crow's Nest, Crow's Nest," another voice chants into a radio. "This is Ironhorse Bravo. Request emergency dust-off."

Soon the bird is circling overhead, its rotor-wash raising clouds of ash as it also fans the embers on the tree trunks into flame. The helicopter cannot land; it would impale itself on the fiery stakes. It hovers and lowers a sling attached to a steel cable. Starkmann is lifted off the ground, though he cannot feel the hands that hold him around the ankles and under the arms. He understands the reason for this lack of sensation: his skin has been burned off almost to the bone, his nerves clipped, like severed electrical wires.

Gently, gingerly, the hands strap him into the sling. The helicopter's winch turns, raising him off the seared earth. He ascends slowly past the tree trunks, studded with rubies of flame, past the smoke, the cable shining in pure light, the cool air a benediction upon his blistered face as he sways to and fro in the middle of the air. He is not afraid. He feels a peace and joy, which, though not yet complete, are fuller than any he has ever known before.

He looks up toward the helicopter. It is not green, as he'd expected, but white, with a scarlet crucifix painted on its fuselage. He is hoisted up to the hatch. The crew chief, a soldier wearing a flight helmet emblazoned with golden wings, pulls him on board. As the helicopter begins to rise, the crew chief raises his visor and he recognizes D.J., who smiles and gives him a thumbs-up.

The helicopter climbs, faster than he thinks is possible. It banks steeply, so that he can look below and see the cloud of smoke hanging over the trees. In seconds the pall diminishes to a black circle that is no larger than a flower—a dark orchid blooming in the woods. Then it shrinks to the size of a pencil point before vanishing altogether. The helicopter rises faster and faster, higher and higher, a fabulous bird winging beyond the clutch of gravity. He no longer hears the roar of the engine, only a wondrous silence. The sky deepens from pale-blue to indigo to plum to black, a black glittering with stars and constellations he has never seen before. Far below, the curve of the earth is haloed by the clearest light imaginable.

Hutch and Ramos are also aboard the magical aircraft. They are wearing the same kind of helmet as D.J.'s. Hutch kneels over Starkmann, replenishing his veins with plasma, renewing his flesh with aromatic ointments that smell like incense. In no time his body has been entirely restored, and he is able to sit up. A miracle! He now notices that two more men are on board, their faces hidden by the shadows at the rear of the helicopter. They rise from their seats, the one tall, the other of average height. Both are dressed in flight suits white as altar cloths, and are holding out their arms as if inviting him to embrace them. He still cannot identify the figures, but knows that as soon as their arms close around him, his joy and peace will be complete. He stands to go to them, and is shocked to find himself unable to move; it's as if his feet are bolted to the metal deck. He tries to free himself. It's of no use. He beckons to the figures to come to him, but they are as immobilized as he. They stand fixed, extending their arms across a space of less than ten feet that might as well be as wide as infinity. . . .

When Starkmann awoke, the sun was already high, its light paled by clouds that covered the sky like dirty gauze. The digital clock read ten in the morning, the latest he had slept in years. He lay staring at the slope of the ceiling, his mind on the puzzling dream. It had been as lifelike as his nightmare, but had obviously not been a voyage into the past, a "reexperience." Maybe it had been a trip into the future. Maybe, in his dreams, he could travel forward as well as backward in time. Whatever it had been, it had been pleasant, except for its ending; and he yearned now to recapture the serenity that had filled him as he rose in the sling, rocking back and forth in midair.

He got out of bed, showered with his usual thoroughness, and went downstairs to fry eggs for breakfast. Perhaps with a little food in his stomach he could think more clearly and make sense of the dream.

Although June had left for work two hours earlier, a sixth sense told him she was upset about something. The kitchen seemed to be charged with her bad humor. He soon discovered that this perception was accurate: a note fastened to the refrigerator informed him that the faucet in the girls' bathroom was leaking; next to that was another threatening letter from the bank. She'd put it there to prod him into looking for work, though he did not need any such reminders. He knew what was at stake. His unemployment benefits would not last forever. In recent days he'd skimmed the want ads, but his efforts at job hunting had so far not gone beyond that. He was afraid that a prospective employer would discover he was in therapy, think him crazy, and humiliate him.

He fried the eggs, sweating over the stove. Mid-August normally brought suggestions of autumn to the Upper Peninsula; however, today was unusually hot, the air so thick it seemed half water.

Starkmann ate slowly, musing on the dream. The tall figure could not have been anyone but his father, offering in death the forgiveness he had withheld in life. Had the dream been a kind of message from Lucius, a call from beyond the grave that he was ready to grant his absolution? If that was true, then who was the other man, and why had the dream concluded with the three of them standing stiff as posts, reaching out but unable to touch one another? What force had restrained them?

He sopped up the egg yolk with a slice of toast, then slid the dirty dish into the sink. He was a timber cruiser by trade, a man accustomed to scaling lumber, measuring densities, analyzing soil compositions; he had no talent for investigating the workings of his subconscious.

He decided to see what he could do about the faucet.

He went outside to the garage for his tool kit. Butternut did not greet him with her normal enthusiasm. She bristled with tension, as if aware of an approaching danger. The chipmunks hunkered down in the woodpile and ravens cawed in the woods while thunder growled far to the south. A mixture of irritability and apprehension overtook Starkmann as he crossed the yard. Christ, it was hot, the hum of mosquitoes like a violin string holding a single, strained note. Only Lisa was enjoying the peculiar weather. Dressed in a bikini, she was sunbathing on a blanket, basking in her last weeks of freedom before starting her sophomore year. She smelled of tanning lotion and insect repellant. It disturbed Starkmann to see the youthful firmness of her open thighs, her maturing breasts, curving into the flatness of her stomach, her unblemished skin glistening with sweat. What did she think she was doing, he snapped at her, lying around in that skimpy outfit? Getting a tan—what the heck else was she to do on a day like this, she replied in the curt, bitchy tone that honed June's voice when she went on the warpath.

Starkmann said nothing, and reentered the house to disassemble the faucet. The cause of the drip was easily found—the washers had worn out—but not so easily repaired. He had no new washers on hand, and with June gone, he did not have a car to go to Jensen's Hardware. There was nothing he could do. Overcome by a temporary inertia, he sat on the edge of the tub, sweating and staring at the holes in the wall where the spigot and handles had been. Lisa came into the bedroom. He saw her through the bathroom door and hoped she wasn't going to lie down for a nap. He didn't think he could bear the sight of her lying half-naked on a bed. But she'd only come in for her radio. In a moment it was blasting from out in the yard. What to do about the faucet? What to do about anything? He couldn't think with that radio playing at full volume—heavy metal, the kids called it, a music unlike the lyrical rock of the sixties, unlike the songs of Bruce Springsteen. This stuff had a beat in opposition to the rhythms of the heart; it was pure noise. The hell with the faucet. He would wait until June returned, then take her car to Jensen's. He left the hardware lying in the tub and went out to the yard to tell Lisa to turn down the radio. Without looking at him, sighing to communicate her perturbation with his imposition on her pleasure, she lowered the volume.

With nothing to do, he wandered around his forty acres, down the trails along the Firedog and the less-defined deer runs through the woods. Mosquitoes and black flies thrummed in the tamarack swamp. Attacked by the insects, he climbed the knoll and looked at the river and the blue spruce rising above the tag-alders, thick as mangroves. His mind was racing, its eye imprinted with the images of the dream: the trees shorn of branches, the white helicopter, the facelss figures with outstretched arms.

Not a branch stirred, and no birds flew, except for a raven that flapped low over the bog. The air reeked of ooze, of blooming plants and decaying wood. The heat and that peculiar stench of rot and renewal awakened his memories of the jungle. An ozone smell warned that the approaching storm would be violent; it reminded him of the odor that foretold the oncoming of the monsoons in Nam. Something was going to happen today. Starkmann could feel it coming, some awful inevitability that he could not yet identify. Everything—the weather, the strange dream—pointed to it.

When he heard Lisa calling him, an urgency in her voice, he

quickly recrossed the river and jogged across the meadow, where she stood, scratching her long, naked legs against the prickle of the shield ferns.

"What's wrong?"

"Nothing, Chris. It was a phone call. Some guy wants you to call him back. I left the message in the kitchen."

With Lisa alongside, a slimmer, younger reflection of June, June as she might have looked at fifteen, he returned to the house. The call had been from Eckhardt. As he dialed the number, Starkmann gazed out the kitchen window, watching his stepdaughter and Christine spraying each other with a hose and laughing beside the rows of the garden's tall corn.

Eckhardt told him that the time for tonight's session had been advanced two hours, to five-thirty. Could he make it? No, he couldn't; June usually didn't come home with the car until that time. Eckhardt, telling him that he had to be in Marquette on business earlier in the afternoon, offered to make a detour and pick him up on his way back to Iron Mountain.

"I'll try and borrow a car," Starkmann said and hung up.

Billy Treadwell was the only person in town he knew well enough to ask for the loan of a car, but he debated whether or not to call him. *Alert, alive.* The psychologist had sounded overly eager to get him to the session. Something definitely was up. What if today was the day that Eckhardt would attempt to lock him up in the hospital? There was only one way to find out, and if his suspicions proved valid, he would have to rely on his wits to avoid the trap. He phoned Treadwell.

After Billy showed up in his battered green Plymouth, Starkmann left instructions with Lisa to open the gate for her mother at five-thirty. Christy complained that she would be afraid, without Mommy or Daddy around. He told her not to worry; Mommy would be back very soon. Then he left, with his cassette player and Springsteen tapes. He was careful on the drive into Vieux Desert to conceal his apprehensiveness. He talked about the weather, the big rainbow he'd caught, and when Billy mentioned something about Lisa's figure—she sure didn't look like any fifteen-year-old in that bikini—Starkmann forced a smile and said jocularly, "That fifteen'll get you twenty years."

"I'll wait till she's old enough—say an hour or two," Treadwell quipped.

Starkmann manufactured a hearty, masculine laugh as they topped Hunter's Hill. In the distance, Superior was so flat and leaden it appeared as if a vast chunk of the sky had fallen to the earth.

He dropped Treadwell off at the Anchor Inn, then headed south, toward Iron Mountain, through the forests that advanced against both sides of the road. The oncoming storm inked a quarter of the sky above the horizon, creating a false night ablaze with lightning.

None of the regulars was at the center when he arrived, fifteen minutes early. Eckhardt asked him into his office and, as he'd done in their first interview, offered a cup of coffee. Starkmann scanned the place and, spotting no signs of danger, agreed.

He sat in the lounger, Eckhardt in his high-backed chair.

"If it's okay with you, I thought you and I might rap a little before the others get here."

"Yeah?" Starkmann's glance sidled toward the door to make sure it was still open.

"I don't know if you're aware of it, but June's called me a few times. The last time was a couple of weeks ago. I guess she's not happy with my performance. She doesn't think we're doing you much good."

"What do you think?"

"For one thing I'm getting fed up with listening to her complaints. As far as your progress goes, these things take time. Months and months." He removed a thick file or letter from one of his desk drawers. "But they can go a lot quicker when the volunteers cooperate."

Volunteers, the word the center used in place of *patients*. More linguistic camouflage.

"And we haven't been getting a lot from you. The object of a rap session is to rap. Talk. Converse. Lay your cards on the table. But I don't think you've said ten words a night in the time you've been coming here."

Again the showroom smile. Outside, thunder rolled long and rhythmically, and the first drops of rain began to fall.

"I figured you're a little shy about talking in front of a group, and that maybe I could crack the ice if we talked one-on-one."

Starkmann flashed a stiff grin. "But you figured I might not come in, so you gave me that bull about an early session."

Eckhardt's face reddened as he held up his hands in a plea of guilty. Starkmann had caught him; the ambusher had been ambushed. He was a match for this clever runt.

"It's not accepted practice, but sometimes you have to bend the rules. Look, if it bothers you, you can walk right on out, but I think it'd do a lot of good if we talked, just you and me."

"What about?"

"One of the things that upset your wife was that she found you, before dawn, wandering around your property with a rifle."

"Carbine."

"Carbine, then. I thought we might talk about that."

"My dog was barking at something. I went to check it out."

"Find anything?" Eckhardt rolled his desk chair backward and leaned against the wall, his towhead just beneath his gothic-scripted doctoral degree.

"No."

"Then let's try another topic. Like why you don't drive a certain street in town. East Bay Road, I think it's called."

"Where'd you hear that?"

"June."

"You and her must spend a lot of time talking together," Starkmann sneered, confident he had the upper hand. Driven by the wind, the rain was flailing the window now. "What have you two got going? You her back-door man?"

Eckhardt's smile faded, and with it the salesman's manner. For the first time, Starkmann saw the hard-nosed little marine he once had been. His eyes went as stony and level as a sniper's. The transformation was sudden and disconcerting, like watching a man you thought weaker than yourself peel off a baggy shirt to reveal a body roped with sinew and muscle.

"Knock off the bullshit, Starkmann," he barked. "The bullshit stops here. I don't mess around with married women, especially women married to men I'm working with."

Working with—more camouflage. He meant *treating*.

"Now that we've got the crap out of the way, maybe you can tell me why you never take that road."

"What's wrong about not taking a road? What's the big deal?"

"When you were working, you used to drive miles out of your way to avoid it. Doesn't that strike you as a little odd?"

"I liked the longer drive. I liked the scenery."

The small man, saying nothing, rose and walked across the room to stand between the potted ferns and stare out the window. At this time of year, sunset did not fall on the north woods until eight or nine o'clock; but the storm had pitched the early evening into midnight.

"Some squall," Eckhardt commented, his back to Starkmann. "When the weather gets like this, does it take you back there? It does me sometimes. Rain always reminds me of that goddamned place. Does that happen to you, Chris?"

"No. Other things take me back."

"What other things?"

"I wouldn't know."

Eckhardt returned to his desk, his eyes falling on the letter.

"Does the phrase *he saved me from the water, but I killed him with the fire* mean anything to you?"

Suddenly gaseous lumps formed under Starkmann's ribs.

"Chris? Did you ever say anything like that?"

Starkmann shook his head, his denial a half-truth. The words were slightly familiar, but he could not recall uttering them.

"In fact you did. The second time you were in the hospital, and you weren't in there with malaria."

Starkmann's legs twitched with an urge to bolt and run, but he restrained himself. Eckhardt could be trying to provoke him into such an action; possibly guards had been posted outside to capture him, drag him into an ambulance, and take him off to the hospital like Mike Flynn.

"You were in for acute depressive reaction," Eckhardt said. "The army shrinks couldn't get a word out of you at first. When they did, all you would say was: 'He saved me from the water, but I killed him with the fire.' What did you mean by that?"

Starkmann's attempts to meet the psychologist's dry squint failed. His own eyes ricocheted around the room, alighting finally on the ferns.

"How . . . How did you. . . ?"

"Find out? The V.A. helped me dig out your record at Army Headquarters in D.C. After June's last phone call, I figured I would have to do a little research if I was going to get anywhere with you. This letter is a summary of your service record, your medical record. And," he added, flipping the pages, "of a pretrial investigation into an incident that took place on September 21, 1969, near the Cambodian border."

Starkmann looked at the fern. It seemed to be changing form, its thin leaves widening, taking on the breadth of a banana or pineapple palm. He blinked to dispel this startling illusion—or hallucination. Outside, the rain drummed on the roof with a sound reminiscent of a monsoon against a shelter half-stretched taut over a foxhole.

"Hey, Chris, are you still with me? I didn't like digging into your past without your knowing it, and I don't like talking to you this way. I sound like a detective trying to squeeze a confession, but I don't know what the hell else to do."

Starkmann opened his mouth to speak, but his throat, squeezed by the swelling lumps in his ribs, had closed entirely, like a plastic tube pinched between a man's fingers.

"I've got an idea about you," Eckhardt went on. "You suffer from an overdeveloped conscience, and that causes as many problems as an underdeveloped one. Does that sound right to you, or like some shrink's theorizing?"

Starkmann gave no answer, either with voice or gesture. *Alert, alive.* Eyes open, mouth shut.

"All right. I'll give you another theory." Eckhardt turned to the letter. "Something happened on that date, September 21, 1969, something you found so repulsive to you that you've wiped it out of your memory. It was in the pretrial investigation. Your company commander, a Captain Hartwell, called in a tactical air strike on enemy rocket and mortar batteries that were shelling your position. The bombs fell short, a thousand meters short, almost on top of your company. Within a hundred meters. Do you remember any of that?"

"Dream," he managed to whisper. "I dream it, over and over."

"Well now. Maybe we're getting somewhere. What can you tell me about the dream? What happens in it?"

"Exactly what happened, like it's happening all over again."

"Exactly what *did* happen?"

Starkmann stared, transfixed by the fern. A strange drowsiness stole over him as if he were under a hypnotic spell. Had Eckhardt hypnotized him somehow? he wondered. Was that the reason, after all these years of keeping it secret, he had admitted to the dream?

"The letter doesn't tell me much, only that the bombs fell short, and that you made a statement to the investigating officer that you called in the coordinates for Hartwell because his radioman was dead and he was seriously wounded. Based on what you said, the investigation concluded that Hartwell read his map wrong, owing to his injuries. It recommended that no disciplinary action be taken, which was damned decent of the army because Hartwell died of his wounds in the hospital. That's right, isn't it?"

"Hartwell died."

"And the investigating officer flew out two days later, and sometime after that you . . ."

"Cracked up."

"The dream, Chris. Describe the dream to me."

He held his tongue, resisting with all his might the spell that urged him to speak, the spell cast upon him by Eckhardt's smooth, lulling voice.

"Chris, monologues don't work in this business." The psychologist moved again to the window, where he stood leaning against the sill, his short legs crossed at the ankles, his head only a few inches above the tops of the ferns.

"Hartwell didn't misread the coordinates, did he?"

Starkmann held on to the arms of the lounger, the drowsiness giving way to vertigo.

"You did."

Starkmann snapped his head back and forth.

"What do you mean? No, Hartwell did not read them wrong or yes, he did? My guess is, you did. It all happened a long time ago, and I'm not an investigating officer," the small man assured him. "I'm not trying to pin anything on you. But it adds up. If you didn't make the mistake, what else accounts for your cracking up, as you put it? Why else would you have said, 'I killed him with the fire?' Why?"

Why? Why? Just then, lightning cracked so close that it shook the building, its flash igniting the room with a pale-blue fire in which Eckhardt appeared as a figure in a photographic negative and the potted ferns became palm trees, the shadows of their wind-tossed fronds twitching on the walls. Starkmann realized he was traveling backward in time; wide awake, he was riding the temporal train into the past. Then, in the next fraction of a second, he returned to the present; he was once again in the office, where he saw Eckhardt, pacing the room and rubbing his eyes.

"Christ, that was close," the psychologist was saying. "Must've hit a tree."

He moved toward his desk, bowing his head to look at the letter.

"The investigation was called, Chris, because four men in your company were seriously burned by those bombs. They were in a listening post forward of your perimeter. Somehow or other, they'd kept themselves hidden from the North Vietnamese. One of them died while being evacuated to the hospital. He came from the same county you're now living in. His name's listed on a war memorial on that street you don't, or can't, drive on. But I figure you drove it at least once, saw what was there, and just couldn't face seeing it again."

His mouth dry, Starkmann clutched the arms of the lounger as the floor tipped to one side, then the other. His legs started to pump up and down uncontrollably, like a school kid who needed to go to the bathroom. He pushed his hands down on his knees, but could not stop the palsy.

"The guy had quite a name. Boniface George St. Germaine."

The sour lump expanded like a balloon, filling his chest, crushing his ribs, squashing his heart down to a nut.

"What can you tell me about him? All I know is that he came from the county you live in now."

Starkmann could not have spoken even if he'd wanted to.

"Do you remember that passage I read you from Homer? About Ulysses wishing he had died with his friends? Nowadays we call that

survivor guilt, and one of its symptoms is identification with the victim. Way down deep, so far down you probably aren't aware of it, you want to be this St. Germaine. That's what compelled your move to the same county he came from, only you didn't know why, not in the front of your mind."

Boniface George St. Germaine. Bonny George—the name he had not heard spoken in fourteen years, the name he had not dared utter or think, the name he had purged from his memory—now roared through his mind, louder than the thunder outside. Suddenly, Starkmann's eyes filled. An overwhelming emotion gushed from the center of his chest, opening his throat and forcing him to ask the question he'd wanted answered for years.

"Why?"

Eckhardt dropped into his chair. "It was an accident," he said softly.

"Why?"

"Chris, more than ten thousand men died in accidents over there. There is no *why* to it."

"You dumb fuck!" Now, his sorrow turning to a bitter rage, the words spilled out of his mouth, thick and foul, a verbal gall. "Why the fuck did it have to be him? You've got so many theories, you've got so many fucking answers—answer me that, answer-man. C'mon, *Doctor* fucking Eckhardt."

"Chance, Chris—"

"*Fuck you*. Chance. Why on top of him? A hundred yards to the right or left and he would have made it. Or a hundred yards long—"

"Or a hundred short," Eckhardt interrupted. "Then they would have fallen square on your company, and instead of feeling guilty about one death, you could have had a few dozen on your conscience. Hey, you could have really wallowed then, Starkmann. You would really have had a reason to punish yourself—if, that is, you weren't burned to a crisp yourself."

"Why, you midget turd? Four guys were hit, but only he died. Why him? Why?" He could feel the veins popping in his head as his knees drove against his restraining hands. "Give me an answer, answer-man!"

"I can't give you any answer except the one I just did." Eckhardt half-rose from his chair, palms flat on the desk. "Chance. One guy's number comes up, the other's doesn't, but it's nobody's fault. You didn't kill your friend. You're not a murderer."

"Give me an answer! Answer me!"

In another burst of lightning, Eckhardt once more assumed the form of an image in a negative, then dissolved completely. In his

place, another figure materialized, wearing a helmet and crossed canvas bandoliers, with leafy branches tied to his uniform as camouflage. His shadow was almost indistinguishable from the shadows of the wind-tossed trees; one of the bushpeople. The trembling in Starkmann's limbs spread throughout his body. A powerful force threw his head back over the top of the lounger as he shook, and a noise, half scream, half moan, shoved through his gritted teeth. An incoming rocket ripped the air and exploded. In its flash, he saw Eckhardt coming toward him, a bush with legs, one of the North Vietnamese, darting and dodging between the trees. Instantly Starkmann's tremors ceased. He leaped from the chair, seized Eckhardt by the arm and flung him across the room, into the palm trees, which, in another blaze of blue lightning, resumed the shape of potted ferns.

"Jesus Christ!" the smaller man exclaimed, rising from the floor. One of the plants lay on its side. "Starkmann!"

Eckhardt stumbled forward, groping for the phone. Christ, he was going to call an ambulance, maybe the cops. Starkmann saw then that he'd fallen into the trap, as Mike Flynn had done. He had to escape now. He shoved the small man aside and ripped the phone out of the wall in a single movement, then bolted outside and ran to Treadwell's car.

He drove fast through the slanting rain, under a sky the color of a bruise, his eyes flicking to the rearview mirror for the lights of a pursuing squad car. Elated by his escape, pumped up on adrenaline, Starkmann drove with only one hand on the wheel, the other tapping the dashboard as he covered the dark roads toward home and June, his whore, June.

June. June. June. He understood now what had happened. Thrown off balance by his question and unable to answer it, Eckhardt had resorted to hypnosis to regain the advantage. He'd hypnotized Starkmann, who, in the trance, had been tricked into believing the psychologist was one of the bushpeople so he would panic and do something crazy. It had been planned all along. That's what June and Eckhardt had been talking about in all those conversations—their plans to get him out of the way. The plot had almost worked. It had been a clever trap, but he'd escaped because he had been alert. *Alert, alive.*

Less than an hour later, he was splashing through the mud of the gravel road. The Big Firedog, rising from runoffs and the tropically dense rain, swirled under the log-and-plank bridge. As he rounded the bend beyond the bridge, he saw lights on all over the house, but

June's Wagoneer was missing. The rain was so heavy it drenched him during the short dash he made from the car to the back door.

Inside, Lisa and Christine ran down the stairs when they heard him enter.

"Daddy, you're home," Christine cried, throwing herself at him. "We were so scared. The thunder scared me—"

"Where's Mom? Where the hell is she? Where, Christy?"

"I don't know."

"Lisa?"

"She didn't phone. Maybe she got held up by the rain. Some guy called for her a little while ago."

"What guy? Who? Who, goddammit?"

"I don't know," Lisa said, her voice cracking. "I mean, I don't remember. Wait. It was Jim, Jim something, and he sounded worried. She was supposed to call him back."

"Jim Eckhardt? Was that it? Tell me!"

"I think that was it."

"Get up to your room, both of you. Move. *Move.*"

"Chris, what's wrong? What's the matter?"

"Get up there!" he shouted, water dripping into his eyes.

"Has Mom been in an accident?" Lisa wailed. "Oh, God, what if she went off the road in this?"

"Don't give me any lip. Get up there."

He raised his hand as if to strike her. The two girls, now doubly frightened, by the storm and him, ran upstairs.

Think, he commanded himself, shaking the water out of his hair with his fingers. Got to think. It was seven-thirty; she wasn't home, hadn't phoned. Jim had called. They were on a first-name basis, were they? She was waitiing to rendezvous with her back-door man, a lot of woman for that pipsqueak, but maybe he's got it all in the right places. Tonight was the night they'd planned to have him locked up so they could be together, like a married woman and her lover plotting to murder the husband.

Rain crackled against the side of the house. The sound of the wind through the trees was like the rumble of a fast train. Lock him up and put him away—that's what they'd been planning, only he'd stayed alert and escaped the trap, one step ahead of them. That bitch, she'd always been a whore. What else could he have expected from her? All those lies about wanting to help him, when what she'd wanted was the freedom to be with her sawed-off back-door man, the lying tramp.

Lightning fired into a tree not far from the house with a deafening crack.

"Daddy! Daddy!" Christy called from upstairs.

"Shut up!" he hollered.

Damned kids wouldn't let him think. The kids were messing with his head. *Think*. What would Eckhardt's next move be and how should he counter it? Search-and-destroy, but fight them on your own ground, at a time of your own choosing.

Here. Now.

That was it: Fight them here, tonight. Eckhardt must have called the police and an ambulance from the V.A. They were probably on the way right now, cops and paramedics, guns, handcuffs, hypodermics full of Thorazine. If it was war they wanted, war they would get; and if he had to die in it, better to die fighting on his ground than to be drugged and strapped down in a hospital bed.

He climbed the stairs two at a time, entered his bedroom closet, and lowered the trapdoor ladder that led into the attic, where his old uniforms, along with his medals, were stored in an olive-drab footlocker. He intended to dress for the occasion.

27

June was driving through the empty streets of Vieux Desert at that moment, squinting through the windshield. The headlights barely cut through what appeared to be a solid wall of rain. She'd been half mad to drive through this storm in her condition, woozy from the scotches she'd drunk at Vandy's with Erickson and Sandy. Erickson had offered to give her a ride home, but she'd insisted on making the drive herself, allowing him to take her to her car, no more than that, thanks very much Mr. State's Attorney.

At first the scotch had filled her with false courage and an exaggerated sense of confidence in her ability to drive in bad weather. She wasn't halfway home before its effects began to wear off, and frightened by the intensity of the storm, she'd slowed to twenty miles an hour. A couple of times she'd been unable to see much past the hood and thought she'd run off the road. If she hadn't been so conscience-stricken about staying late after work without calling the house, as well as about the wanton, impulsive thing she'd done to Erickson, she would have turned around and headed back into Marquette to wait for the rain to stop.

She could use the storm as a valid excuse for her tardiness, but she'd already determined not to make any excuses, to Chris or to the girls. She would apologize, but when they asked why she hadn't phoned, she would answer with the truth: She hadn't felt like it. She'd felt like doing exactly what she'd done, which was to take a brief vacation from her domestic responsibilities. She'd known Chris needed the car for his appointment in Ironwood, but, she'd thought, the hell with him and the hell with those sessions. They were useless anyway. The hell with him and his morose silences, his indifference and impotence. She'd also known the girls would be worried about her as well, but the hell with them, too—let them turn to Chris for comfort and a hot dinner. The hell with motherhood for a little while.

She'd been cast into this careless mood during her midafternoon coffee break, when she'd picked up a copy of the *Mining Journal* and saw the headline:

POLICE SEEK CLUES IN DOMESTIC KILLINGS

The story might have been printed in neon, the way it had blazed into her eyes:

> Law enforcement authorities are seeking clues and a possible motive in an apparent murder-suicide of four people in Paulding's Crossing, a remote settlement near Elkhorn, according to a spokesman from the Michigan State Police headquarters in Marquette.
>
> Dead of gunshot wounds are Edith Hermanson, 46, her estranged husband, Henry, 48, and two of the couple's three children, Henry Jr., 16, and Thomas, 13. Police are searching for the Hermansons' daughter, 17-year-old Freya, described as a teenage runaway.
>
> The tragedy was discovered yesterday afternoon by a rural mailman, who'd noticed a "strong odor" coming from the house as he delivered the Hermansons' mail. Paul Haanpaa told police he'd gone to the front door to investigate, discovered it unlocked, and found the four people lying in dried pools of blood in the living room of their isolated cabin.
>
> State police said preliminary evidence indicates that the elder Hermanson son shot the other members of his family with a high-powered rifle, then killed himself with the same weapon.
>
> "It looks like he stuck the rifle in his mouth and pulled the trigger," the spokesman explained, but cautioned that police have not ruled out the possibility that an outsider committed the crime, one of the grimmest slayings in recent times in the Upper Peninsula.

Disbelieving, June read the story a second time and a third; then, half-nauseated, choked on her coffee. She hurried back to her office thinking: I brought this on. It's my fault. She immediately called

Erickson for more details, but his secretary said he was in conference. She phoned the sheriff's police, the state police, and the *Journal*; none could, or would, tell her any more than what had already been printed. Nor could Erickson, when she was finally able to get through to him.

In no fit condition for work, she left her desk to spend the rest of the afternoon walking without direction through the muggy streets. As she passed the docks, where a ship was taking on ore, the L.S.&I. railroad cars lined up on a trestle far overhead, she remembered watching the freighters that slipped through the Sault Ste. Marie locks when she was a small girl, watching and yearning to be aboard one of them, sailing away across the shining lakes toward port cities agleam with lights and promise.

When she started to cry she didn't know if her tears were for the Hermansons or for herself, or for all the people in the world trapped by circumstances and their own ignorance. She walked through the park near the port, her head down, her hands in her skirt pockets. Now and then she glanced up at the Lombardy poplars that shaded picnickers in the park, or out at Presque Isle, or toward the tower of Marquette lighthouse, winking in the distance. Vacationers were lying on the beach. The heat had driven a few of the hardier ones to swim in the lake, a vast slate slab under the dull clouds. She could not comprehend how these people could be picnicking and swimming while the Hermanson family lay dead in their lonely cabin, how the men on the docks could go on opening and closing the chutes, the loads of ore spilling like dusty red waterfalls into the ship. She desired from the outside world an acknowledgment of the horror that had occurred fifty miles away, a moment of silence maybe, a brief stop to the idle play of the vacationers on the beach. She wanted to scream at them: "A young boy has murdered his family and killed himself because he couldn't find a way out, and if you don't feel sick about that and show it, then none of you are human and deserve any happiness." But when a sympathetic passerby, an elderly man walking his dog, noticed her crying and asked if anything was wrong, she merely shook her head and kept on walking until too hot and tired to go any farther.

She sat down on the grass to gaze out at the lake. Hank Junior couldn't find a way out—somehow June knew that the boy had acted out of despair. In that sense, Freya was better off; no matter where she'd gone or what she'd become, she'd escaped. Her thoughts turning briefly to her own life, June wondered if Freya might be better off than she: June had always seen the possibilities, going back to those days when she watched the freighters cruising through the locks.

What she'd lacked was the nerve to act on her visions of another life in another place. That was the distaff side of *sisu:* If you had the capacity to endure, you naturally tended to endure, even when endurance had no point or purpose. You endured for the sake of it, which, she supposed, explained why she hadn't ended her marriage.

She steered her mind away from that subject and tried to picture what had gone on in the Hermanson cabin. Like some Hollywood private eye attempting to reconstruct a crime from flimsy evidence, she imagined a number of scenarios: Henry Senior had come home to claim some personal belongings before returning to Texas and his oil-field sweetheart, had become abusive toward Edith, enraging his eldest son, who had snatched the rifle from the wall and shot him; then Edith, seeing her husband killed by her boy, had plunged into total hysteria, impelling Hank Junior to shoot her in a kind of mercy killing. Did young Tommy, at some point, try to wrest the gun from his brother and die in the struggle for the weapon? Did Hank Junior, awakening from his murderous rage, see what he had done and then take his own life?

Another possibility was that the elder Hermanson had gone to his "lodge" for some other purpose. Perhaps he'd discovered Edith's madness, a perfect reason for cutting her out of any property settlement, and had come to inform his sons that he was committing her to the hospital. To stop that at all costs, Hank Junior got the rifle, killed his mother first, then his father and brother, and, finally, himself.

Every possible scene was equally awful. It made June's insides turn over, imagining the gunshots, the screams and shouts, bloody passions loosed in a wilderness cabin, the crime witnessed only by the silent pines, the bodies rotting for a week before anyone found them. She gave up her detectivelike speculations, recognizing their uselessness. How it had happened wasn't really that important. The rifle with which she'd shot the bear had been used to wipe out a family, a fact that, irrationally, heightened her sense of complicity—and of failure. She'd tried to help, but had been no help whatever and had possibly made things worse. Could another have done more good than she, or wasn't there a thing anyone could have done? What difference did it make now? People were frolicking and picnicking on the beach while the big lake stretched away, still, gray, and cold.

From the park, she hiked two miles back to her car, intending to drive home; but when she passed Vandy's bar, the thought of returning to her depressing house and disturbed husband, to the kids and the routine of cooking and cleaning, revolted her. The hell with all of it. She was going to have a few drinks, maybe more than a few; maybe she'd close the place. She needed an anesthetic, and it might do Chris some good to get a taste of what life would be like without her.

Her mood lightened somewhat as soon as she walked into Vandy's, heard the music, and saw Sandy sitting at the bar as gracefully as if she were at a Junior League luncheon. Evidently Rick was on the high seas; Sandy had on her best makeup, heels, and stockings, as she surveyed the male customers for a halfway decent one-night stand. As it was still a little early for the after-work crowd, there were few candidates.

June sat next to her. By the time she'd finished her second scotch, she'd told her friend the story of the Hermanson family, and how their deaths had depressed her more than anything had in years. Sandy, who'd heard about the killing on the radio, offered the same counsel Erickson had, earlier, on the phone: She took these things too personally; there was nothing she could have done to prevent it, a bunch of screwball Finns living out in the boondocks—what could you expect?

"So let's toast to life in God's country." Sandy lifted her martini glass like a chalice. "Where the men are men, the women are women, and the sheep run scared, where it's too cold for blacks and too poor for Jews, but just right for drunken Finns who'd get the hell out of here if their brains were one-tenth the size of their livers."

June reminded her that she was half Finnish.

"You're the exception that proves the rule, although you haven't gotten the hell out of here. Not yet."

Her comment led June into a long complaint about all that was wrong in her life, an uncharacteristic confession for her; like most upper-midwesterners she was reluctant to discuss her personal problems, a restraint partly arising from the knowledge that one's triumphs and tragedies were reduced to irrelevance by the immensity of the forests and the eternity of the Great Lakes, those immense inland seas. Nevertheless, her loquaciousness fueled by the scotch, she talked on, even after Erickson joined them for an after-work cocktail. She felt a little ashamed of herself; it was one thing to gripe about your husband in front of a girlfriend, and another to do it in front of a man. Erickson seemed embarrassed for her, so she switched the subject, asking if there was anything new on the Hermanson case.

He shook his head. "It looks like the older kid did it. Christ knows why. What a mess. I saw the police photographs. . . ."

"And I don't want to hear about it," June slurred. "All right, Don? No gory details."

The storm broke a short while later. When June saw the rain whipping past the windows at a horizontal, she began to worry about the girls, but could not bring herself to call the house. Half an hour and another scotch later, her conscience was still needling her; Chris couldn't take care of himself, let alone two kids. She went to the pay phone to call and tell him she was on her way, but hung up before getting a ring. She couldn't bear to hear his dead, emotionless voice, not now, and decided to go home without checking in first. That's when the argument started with Sandy and Erickson about her ability to drive, followed by her acceptance of the lawyer's offer to drive her to her car.

From atop Ridge Avenue, looking down at the cabin lights of a freighter shining through the rain, she'd reminisced to Erickson about her girlhood fantasies of escaping the Upper Peninsula on a ship. The sight of one, with its high, proud bow and white superstructure, she'd said tipsily, still awakened her desire for flight.

"After what happened today, I felt like I could pack my bags and hitchhike out of here."

"This is some rain," Erickson said, his eyes on the street ahead. "You ought to let me drive you home."

"South. I'd hitchhike south, down to New Orleans maybe. No woods, no winter."

"I wish you'd stop talking like that."

"I'm not serious, for God's sake."

"I don't mean that."

"What do you mean?"

"I wish you'd stop talking about how badly you want out, and I wish you hadn't talked about Chris the way you did."

"Tacky, wasn't it? Tacky, tacky. I plead guilty to talking-tacky-while-intoxicated. T.T.W.I., talking-tacky-while-intoxicated."

"Guilty as charged. It's no excuse."

"What's it got to do with you anyway?"

He said nothing as he passed the courthouse, then turned, going by the ultramodern annex and sheriff's department, where globe lights glittered in the concrete courtyard, and entered the lot where the Wagoneer awaited her.

"Here you are. At least let me follow you home, June," he offered.

"So what's my talking-while-intoxicated got to do with you?"

"Do you want me to come right to the point?"

"Lawyers never come to the point except when they ask for their fees."

"You must know by now the way I feel about you. That's why I wish you'd watch the way you talk. It makes me think that . . ."

"I don't know how you feel about me," she interrupted, her pulse growing rapid. "Tell me, counselor. How do you feel?"

"Don't be coy. It's obvious."

"I thought you wanted to be pals."

"I thought so too."

"So how do you feel? You haven't come to the point, counselor."

"Well . . . Christ, this is stupid . . . I think you ought to divorce that guy. You're a helluva woman who deserves better. All right? Is that pointed enough for you?"

Excited by what he'd said, her inhibitions loosened by alcohol and a blind need for contact, she surrendered to an impulse to kiss him. It was no ladylike, tender kiss, but wild and wanton, with a suggestion of cruelty in it. Her mouth swallowed his, her teeth lightly bit his lip, her tongue flicked like a snake's as her hand slid between his legs. She had the odd experience, odd for a woman, of feeling a man struggle against *her* physical advances.

"Christ almighty, June," he said, pushing her away.

"What's wrong? Aren't aggressive females your type? Or are you too used to making the first move?"

"Not here, like this."

"I get it. The front seat of a car isn't your style, like a cheap motel, right? Okay, my place or yours?"

"What kind of a question is that?"

"I've got a better one. If I left Chris, what then?"

It almost made her laugh to see him temporarily speechless and disconcerted.

"We'd see . . . You could come down and join me for a while— Ann Arbor, I mean. I'm leaving in two weeks. We'd see, you know, how we get along, see what develops . . ."

"That's a beautiful proposal, Don, and a great offer." Now she wanted to slap him, almost as badly as she'd wanted to kiss him a moment ago. "I leave my husband to see what develops with you. Listen, I'm not the girl for you. I'm no lawyer's lady, or any kind of lady. Front seats of cars and cheap motels are *my* style. I'm a low-rent mama, always have been. I wouldn't be worth a damn, passing out canapés to the guests at the cocktail parties. So long, counselor."

She stepped out into the deluge, slamming the door behind her, and didn't look back to see the expression on his face as she jumped into her car and drove off.

Now, piloting her way down the county highway, she flushed with shame as she recalled the way she'd kissed him.

She turned into the entrance of the gravel road, hitting the brakes as her high-beams lit up the gate. That damned gate—she'd forgotten about it. To avoid getting out of the car, she tried to nudge it open with her bumper; but sure enough, Chris had left it barred. She honked the horn several times, waited ten minutes for him to come, then leaned on the horn, cursing him when he still failed to show up. Maybe he couldn't hear over the noise of the storm. Maybe he was drunk. Maybe this, maybe that—the screwball couldn't do this to her!

The barbed-wire fence ran off at angles from both corner posts, making it impossible to go around the gate; the only way she could open it would be to crawl under it, if she could: The gap between it and the road was less than a foot, and she wasn't about to snake under it and ruin her dress. She sat in the car, working up the courage to get out, and the longer she looked at the gate, the deeper grew her hatred of it and the madness it represented. If it were alive, she would have killed it. An alternative then occurred to her, one she would not have considered if she weren't a little high. What the hell, the Wagoneer was a rugged vehicle, built to take punishment. The Wagoneer had *sisu*. She backed up across the highway, shifted into first gear and took a deep breath. *Sisu*. With a mixture of prayers and obscenities on her lips, she floored the gas pedal and smashed through. The one-by-six bar cracked in half, its two pieces flying off into the trees alongside the road.

She had smashed the gate, struck a blow for her own freedom! But it seemed an act of vandalism as much as of rebellion, causing her to feel bold and guilty all at once as she raced the muddy quarter-mile to the house. Her mood changed to one of puzzlement when she saw the strange car parked in the driveway. Who could be visiting in this weather? Who ever visited them? Then she noticed the rivulets of water coursing through her garden, and her heart dropped; if this kept up, her tomato plants would be ruined, rotted to the roots. Well, there was nothing she could do about it now but hope for the storm to let up.

Inside, her resolve to be candid about her absence vanished when she found the girls locked in their room, scared to death. When they questioned why she'd been so late, she pled the excuse of the storm. As if to prove she was telling the truth, she wrung water from a length of her hair. Then, to change the subject, she asked whose car was outside.

"Bill Treadwell's," Lisa answered, glancing at the ceiling when something thumped in the attic. "Chris is up there, Mom. Some-thing's the matter with him. He's . . . He came home and . . . Something's just wrong."

June entered her bedroom closet, flicked on the light, and called to Chris from the bottom of the ladder. He didn't answer. She was about to climb up when he shoved his head through the opening above. The sight of his hideously painted face staring down at her made her jump backward into the bedroom. He clambered down, flung the trapdoor shut, and stood staring at her; if a demon instead of her husband had descended the ladder, June could not have been more terrified. He was dressed in a jungle uniform, with worn boots on his feet, a camouflage cloth tied as a sweatband across his forehead, and a row of military medals pinned above the pocket of his shirt. His hands and arms were blackened with shoe polish; black and green stripes, like an Indian's war paint, had been smeared thickly over his face; and his eyes, rimmed by painted dark circles, looked like ice cubes pressed into lumps of coal.

"Surprised, June Josette?"

He moved to the bedroom door, closed and locked it softly.

"Surprised, Jay-Jay? Surprised to find me here?"

His eyes took on a light like the iridescence of the bestial eyes she'd seen glowing in her headlights the night she'd driven Edith Hermanson to the hospital.

"You were expecting your back-door man, weren't you, you slut?"

Incapable of speech, she backed toward the window; she'd leap out the window if she had to—but no, she couldn't do that and leave the girls alone in the house with this . . . this *thing*.

"Here I am, June Josette." He spread his arms, a grin slicing across his tiger-striped cheeks. "But where were you tonight? Waiting for him?"

She started to edge toward the closet, wondering if she could draw one of the guns from its case before he could stop her. It was impossible; there was nothing she could do except try to escape through the door.

"You were balling Eckhardt tonight, weren't you, you whore?"

"I wasn't . . ." she managed to say. "Oh, Jesus, what's happened to you?"

"Weren't you? Let's hear it, slut!"

He took her by the arms, shoving her into the wall. All she could think about was the girls—she had to get the girls out of here.

"It was Eckhardt, wasn't it?" He slapped her. "Wasn't it?"

He struck her again, and the sting of the second blow both ignited her temper and expelled from her the supernatural terror aroused by the sight of him. He was only a man, after all. A madman, yes, but mere flesh, blood, and bone, her very own madman.

"It was Erickson," she hissed, in a half-deliberate provocation. "Want to slap me again? C'mon, slap me again."

"Who's Erickson? Who is he?" He shook her by the shoulders.

"What difference does that make? That's who I was with tonight, because you haven't touched me in months. We did it in the back seat of a car. You goddamned lunatic! Look at yourself. Go on to the mirror and look!"

She knew, in a corner of her mind, that the girls could hear every vile word being said; but a madness of her own had seized her. She wanted a catharsis, sought an end to her entrapment. She would compel him to do something awful enough to justify leaving him.

"We did it in a car, so c'mon, box my ears, beat the hell out of me." She mocked and challenged, thinking: Let him do whatever he wants. Let all the snakes twisting around in that twisted head come out. But the mental serpents she'd loosed with her rash lie turned out to be more monstrous than she'd counted on. He did not strike her again. Instead, he dug a thumb into a pressure point behind her ear, almost paralyzing her.

"I'm going to show you something, whore."

His one hand still holding her by the throat, the other tore at her dress.

"I'll show you what we did to whores."

Then, with all his strength, he bent her over the bed, ripped her underwear down around her thighs, and held her fast by the back of the neck.

"Please!" she screamed. "Not that, please!"

Spots flashed behind her eyes as he bored into her. Her insides burned. She managed to turn her face to the side to gasp for air and cried out. She could hear Lisa, pounding on the door and shouting, "Mom! Mom, what's wrong? Mom!" June couldn't answer for the scalding sensation that rushed from where he'd penetrated her, through her belly and into her throat. His hard thrusts made her black out for an instant, and in that momentary darkness, the hurt and revulsion she felt were as they'd been in the dream of the bear; the thing happening to her was like the defilement in the dream, an unspeakable violation.

After he burst into her, she lay still, choking. Downstairs, the phone was ringing. Lisa hammered on the door again.

"Mom? Mom!"

"It's all right." Her voice was a scratchy whisper. "I'm all right, baby."

The phone had stopped ringing. She crawled to the other side of the bed, stood unsteadily, and drew up her underwear, pulling the tatters of her dress over them. Chris remained on his knees, glancing up at her with a bewildered expression as if he had awakened from a nightmare of his own. The expulsion of his seed had exorcised, for the moment, whatever devil had possessed him; his eyes had lost their feverish light, his painted face its savage appearance. It now seemed more clownish than threatening. As she looked at him, a sick, pathetic brute kneeling before her, she almost felt sorry for him, a compassion partly arising from the knowledge that she'd incited his cruelty; but the pain scorching her insides blocked whatever pity she might have had for him.

"You animal! You filthy animal!"

Some kind of sound issued from his throat. It might have been a groan; it might have been her name or some other word—she didn't know and didn't care. The beast would have his forty acres of woods and swamp all to himself from now on. As she snatched her raincoat from the closet and belted it over her torn skirt, he rose to his feet and moved toward her.

"You animal!" she shrieked again. "Don't come near me!"

Her fingernails raked his face, drawing a trickle of blood. Then she ran down the hall, grabbed the girls, and rushed out to the car. They would spend the night at Sandy's. June wasn't sure what she would do tomorrow, but knew she would do something and survive. She always had.

When her car started and the headlights swept across the front of the house, Starkmann dashed down the stairs and out the door and ran after her, ran as he had long ago, sprinting downfield for the long pass, driving full-court for the layup. The Wagoneer was just ahead, bumping over the bridge. He lengthened his stride, slipped in the mud, recovered his balance, and continued his pursuit. She could not drive very fast in this weather on a dirt road; he had a chance of catching her before she reached the highway. He would beg her forgiveness, plead with her not to leave him.

He wasn't fast enough. The car was speeding down the blacktop when he reached the junction, where the sight of the wrecked gate caused his emotions to swing from remorse to fury. She had not smashed it just now. He would have heard the noise. She'd done it on her way in. Eckhardt must have called her with the news of his escape, so she'd destroyed the gate to open a breach in his defenses, an avenue of approach for the squad cars and ambulance that would soon be coming for him. Heedless of the rain plastering his clothes to his skin, he watched her taillights receding down the highway, growing smaller and smaller until they looked like two red eyes.

"June!" he shouted. "Don't leave, June!" Then, "Go ahead, leave, you bitch. You goddamned whore, leave!"

He stopped his ravings when the lights disappeared around a bend. The only sounds were the rain and the metallic rattle of the tin cans on the perimeter fence, rattling in the wind like bones. He looked at the gate again. There was nothing he could do about it now. No matter. Let them come, he thought as he sloshed back toward the house. Let them come. He would be ready for them. Butternut barked at his approach, as if his scent had changed and she, too, considered him a stranger.

"That's okay, girl," he said, going inside. "That's okay."

He sat on the couch in his wet uniform to formulate a plan of action. He sat for a long time. He started a fire and stared at the crackling logs, unable to think, his mind clogged by a sense that June and the girls had left invisible parts of themselves behind, presences that lingered like the scent of a woman's perfume after she's departed a room. He looked at the kitchen, half-expecting to see June there. He caught himself listening for the sound of Lisa's radio or the soft chime of Christy's voice; but all he heard was the thump of the generator outside and an occasional peal of thunder. He climbed the stairs to the girls' bedroom. Its silence was oppressive—the tranquillity of a crypt. The radio stood on Lisa's desk. A children's book lay open on Christine's mussed bed. June had spirited them off so quickly, he noticed, that she had not even taken their raincoats, which hung in the closet with the rest of their clothes. The dresses, blouses, and jeans, the shoes and sneakers arranged on the floor brought to him an ache of unrecoverable loss, as if the girls had died. He shut off the light, then entered his and June's room, where, hearing the echo of her cries, he was seized by a useless contrition. "June," he said to the walls. "June. June." She had betrayed him, but hadn't deserved what he'd done to her. God in heaven, what had he done to her, and to himself? He'd driven her out for good, and now he was as alone as any man could be. He could not stay another moment in this house. He was banished from it, as much as from his father's.

In this solitude, the outlines of a plan began to take shape. He went into the closet for his hunting poncho, military-looking with its pattern of brown, black, and russet spots, unsheathed his carbine, and locked the banana clip in the magazine well. After he'd darkened the room and the rooms downstairs, the generator coughing to a halt, the phone rang. It startled him at the same time that it stirred the hope that June was calling to say she'd forgiven him and wanted to come back. On the other hand, it could be Eckhardt, or Treadwell inquiring about his car. He let it ring several times before ripping the jack out of the wall. The hell with it. Radio silence from now on.

A drenching ten-minute walk brought him to the strong-point on the knoll above the river. He slithered on his back under the bottom strand of wire and entered the safe circle of the strong-point's perimeter. High ground. The storm had turned the foxholes into miniature wells. He jumped into the first one, arbored by the branches of the hemlock. The water came to his ankles. He bailed as much of it as he could and, after spreading a mat of boughs over the muck, rigged a hooch with his poncho.

He sat down, his knees drawn up, the carbine resting on his shoulder. The rain striking the hooch with a crackle as of spattering grease, the coldness of the carbine's barrel, the smell of the mud, the darkness illuminated by lightning—now flickering like shellfire, now flashing like a bursting flare—the thunder, whose long rolls mimicked the quarreling of guns: all these sensations enveloped him in a cloak of familiarity. He touched the sides of the foxhole, tracing the crevices made by his shovel. He felt at home in this muddy pit, beyond which there was no other sanctuary. Even if there had been, he would not have gone to it. He was sick of hiding, of concealing his past, of always looking over his shoulder for the retribution that had been stalking him ever since that September dawn when fire had fallen from the skies.

The wind mourned through the pines. *Wind-time, wolf-time.* On that foreign hill, where bombs had uprooted the trees and smoke had swallowed the sun and moon, he had been given a glimpse of how the world would end, and had learned that the world was not ordered, as he'd been taught and had once believed, but full of random violence, a chaos of which he was a part. And with that loss of faith, he had lost all hope of salvation. *Wind-time, wolf-time, 'ere the world falls, Axe-time, sword-time, ever shall brothers each other slay.* He had slain his brother, a fact he had kept secret even from himself until a few hours ago. He could no longer. It was as if Eckhardt, in a single stroke, had split his mind like a rock, uncovering the fossilized memory of what had happened.

Bonny George had been alive when they'd found him, his uniform in scorched tatters, his skin curling like shreds of burned newsprint, his dog tags so blackened no one could read his serial number when the pilot of the evacuation helicopter asked for it. He had been on the listening post; he could not possibly have known who had called in the mistaken map coordinates; yet there had been knowledge in his eyes as they stared up at Starkmann out of the mass of blood, pus, and charcoaled flesh that had once been his face, stared and cried out, *"I saved you from the water, but you killed me with the fire."*

It had been more than accusation; it had been a curse.

The helicopter had taken him up in a sling, then swooped off, the beat of its spinning wings fading to a soft *top-top-top.* Less than a minute after its departure, as Starkmann was filing back to the perimeter with D.J., Hutch, and Ramos, they heard the pilot's voice radioing a terse message to his base.

"Crow's Nest, this is Raven One. You can stand down on the emergency dust-off. Emergency dust-off is now routine. I say again, emergency is now routine."

After two or three seconds of silence, D.J. had said, "Shit."

Hutch said, "He's better off."

Ramos said, "Fuck it. It don't mean nothin'."

Starkmann, hearing a sharp crack inside his head, like an elastic band snapping, had not spoken a word; to him, it had meant everything.

The rain kept falling. The hooch sagged. He poked the bulge with his carbine, draining off the water. Now he had another charge against him. He had committed another sort of murder—the killing of love. He touched the scratches on his cheek, thinking of the last words June had spoken to him, their indictment as true as the one spoken by Bonny George's eyes. He was an animal, a beast from the jungle, and if he'd had the power, he would fly to the jungle this moment. But this wilderness would do. He was back where he belonged, a warrior in the bush, awaiting his enemy's approach. How to prepare for them? He didn't know, not yet.

His back against the side of the foxhole, he curled up in a ball, intending to catch a few minutes' sleep so his mind would be fresh and sharp when the patrol cars and ambulance came for him. *Alert, alive.* The earth lurched beneath him. His head spun. He opened his eyes, stopping the spell of vertigo. Closing them again, he felt the earth move once more; it heaved and opened up, and then he was plunging through blackness, like a parachutist free-falling through the skies of a moonless, starless night.

"Preacher."

The voice came from above. He looked up, but saw nothing, only the dripping walls of the foxhole.

"Preacher."

He stood and peered into the night. There were the silhouettes of the trees and the reflections of lightning in the river.

"Preacher."

"D.J.?"

"Yeah."

"Hutch, Ramos?"

"Yeah," Hutch answered. "What're you doing? Calling roll?"

If this is madness, Starkmann thought, then let it be. It had been waiting for him for years.

"I can't see you."

"You don't gotta see us," said D.J. "All you want to do is talk, right?"

"Yes."

"Talk, then."

He was silent. He didn't know what he wanted to talk about.

"We know," Hutch said, reading his mind. "They're coming and you can't afford to sit here, doing nothing and feeling sorry for yourself. You had best realize that this is what you've wanted all along."

"What?"

"To be alone, with nothing and no one. You *wanted* to mess up and you know it."

Starkmann imagined the medic's green eyes probing his skull like X-rays, exposing his innermost thoughts.

"Now you've got to get your head straight, so you do this right."

"Do what right?"

"The other thing you've wanted to do. You want to join us."

"No, Hutch. No."

"We're all you've got, Preacher," said D.J.

"No."

"Oh, yeah, Preach. Nothin' but us. That headshrinker was right. You shoulda gone with us. Now you can."

"The easy way would be to swallow that carbine," Hutch said. "The right way would be to take as many with you as you can. Make *them* pull the trigger for you, Chris. That's the right way for a soldier."

"There it is, Preach," Ramos said.

"You want to be with us. With us, your father, and Bonny George."

"No," Starkmann protested even as he recalled the haunting words Eckhardt had quoted: *Would God I, too, had died there . . . I should have had a soldier's burial.*

"You're going to have a small army invading this place pretty soon. They're all going to be here, everyone that wants to lock you up. It'll be perfect. One last firefight, and then you and me and D.J. and Ramos, we'll all be together."

Starkmann listened raptly, mesmerized by Hutch's disembodied voice. *I should have had a soldier's burial,* he thought. A soldier's burial, a soldier's death. *Would God I, too, had died there;* and it came to him, in a revelation like the burst of an illumination round, that he had been ashamed to be alive all these years. Now his brothers had shown him a way to end that shame and ransom the forgiveness that had been held from him. One last firefight. The idea seized him in a single stroke. A final firefight, a flaming climax to his life.

"Together, we'll all go down together," he said quietly.

"There it is, brother. You missed the first time because they stuck you in a hospital. Now you've got another chance, and they want to put you in one again. Don't blow it this time, Chris."

"How, Hutch? How do I do it? I need a plan—a good one, because I'm not taking anyone with me. Get that? No one else is going to die."

"However you want to do it. You'll think of something."

Then Hutch began to sing "Goodnight Saigon," the lyrics recalling those times when they'd dropped from the skies at a hundred miles an hour into tree lines where muzzle flashes twinkled like giant, lethal fireflies. "*We said we would all go down together, yes we would all go down together. C'mon, Chris, sing. Sing.*"

"*We said we would all go down together,*" Starkmann sang, adding his baritone to Hutch's tenor. "*Yes, we would all go down together.*"

D.J. and Ramos joined in. They remained invisible, yet Starkmann could smell their sweat, could feel the warmth of their closeness pressing tightly against him. All loneliness and isolation fled from his heart as their voices rose in a spectral chorus above the hiss of rain, the crack of thunder, and the wind's loud lament.

> *And it was dark*
> *So dark at night*
> *And we held on to each other*
> *Like brother to brother . . .*
> *And we would all go down together.*
> *We said we'd all go down together,*
> *Yes, we would all go down together.*

28

Butternut, her golden fur matted, greeted him with a plaintive whine as he crossed the yard. He should have brought her in; she was miserable, poor damn dog. He led her into the garage and filled her bowl with biscuits; she needed to be well fed and alert, to warn him if anyone started coming up the road. *Alert, alive.* He then got down to business, arranging the tools and equipment he would need on his workbench: electrical cord, copper wire, soldering iron, candle, matches, a five-pound bag of black powder, and an empty shotgun shell. He'd never felt happier than now, in the last hours of his life. His skin prickled with excitement as he unrolled lengths of cord from a spool, stripped the insulation from the ends, and twisted the bare wire to form stout legs for his makeshift blasting cap. He plugged in the soldering iron and lit the candle, then soldered a piece of copper to the legs. The ignition wire was dipped in paraffin. A shotgun shell would be the detonator. He put a hole in a plastic wad with a hammer and punch, placed the empty shell in his reloading machine, charged it with a magnum load of powder, then inserted the wad, tamping the charge with a pull of the reloader lever. The ignition wire went into the hole in the wad, snugged down against the powder and made secure, as secure as possible anyway, with more candle drippings. It was dangerous, working with flame and solder and explosive. He took great care as he held the candle over the shell; he intended to die from hostile fire, as a warrior should, not in an absurd accident. After the wax had dried, he jiggled the wire. It was solid. Now he had a homemade electrical blasting cap.

The bomb was easier to put together, but also more tedious. He took an empty half-quart paint can and punched a small hole in the cover, through which he snaked the wires of the blasting cap, then poured in a measure of powder, tamped it, added more powder, and tamped that. The can was a quarter full when Butternut started barking. Starkmann heard the rain beating a tattoo against the roof before he caught the sound of an approaching car. The retriever kept barking.

"Hush, girl, hush," he said, dousing the light and crouching behind the window. They could not be coming now, before he was ready. A pair of headlights swept up the road, illuminating the driveway. The car was unfamiliar, but Starkmann recognized Tread-well emerging from the passenger side in a yellow slicker. Billy ran up to the front door and knocked.

"Yo, Chris. You there? It's Treadwell." He rapped again. "Hey, Chris? You home? I need my keys."

Starkmann cursed himself. The keys were in his pocket. Why hadn't he thought of this and left them in the ignition? If Billy discovered him now, he would upset the entire plan, and Starkmann might have to shoot him. He did not want another death on his conscience, only his own.

"Doesn't look like anybody's home," said the man who'd given Treadwell a lift.

The interior light of the Plymouth winked on as Billy opened the door. "He didn't leave the key, either."

Starkmann eased a round into the chamber of the carbine. He would kill him if he had to, smash out the glass with the barrel and open up.

"It's an old car," the other man said. "It should be easy to hot-wire."

"That's okay, I've got a spare key in my wallet. I'd just like to know what the hell he's done with the other one."

"What do the cops want with him?"

"They didn't say. All they told me is that they found my car out here and that I'd better come get it. Thanks for the lift."

The cops! They'd already been here, probably when he'd been out at the strong-point. Starkmann whispered his thanks when Tread-well got into the Plymouth and drove away. Thank God he hadn't been forced to shoot Billy. He waited a good ten minutes before he switched on the light and resumed his work. The cops. He had to get this done quickly. The cops would be back.

The rain had slowed to a drizzle by the time he'd half-filled the can. He inserted the detonator—the shotgun shell—packing powder around and over it. His hands ached and his forehead was damp with sweat from the effort. The explosive had to be compressed as tightly as possible; a good deal of force would be needed to blow through the heavy-gauge metal of the propane tank. In another hour he'd crushed all the powder into the can, which was about half the size of the bag. He tapped the lid with a hammer, sealing it as tightly as it would go.

It was done at last. He coiled the wires, stuffed the electrical tape and a flashlight in his pocket, and carried the bomb outside, into the drizzle. Switching on his flashlight, he taped the bomb snugly to the fitting between the tank and the gas line, wedging the lid—the weakest part of the bomb container—against the tank to channel the explosion. The sky had begun to pale. He closed the garage light, which shut off the generator. His final step was to uncoil the electrical wires, run them the hundred-odd feet back to the garage, feed them under the door, and hook them to the light switch. He was finished. All he had to do now was wait.

He took up a position on the workbench, the carbine in his lap, his eyes on the side window, which faced the house and a part of the gravel road. Butternut dozed on the floor, her coat giving off a wet-dog smell. The sun rose through the ranks of clouds, its red light turning each drop of dew on the grass into a tiny flame, the puddles in June's garden into blood-colored pools.

Her garden had been ruined, the cornstalks knocked askew, the tomato plants drowned, the topsoil washed away. June, oh, June. Gone. Again, the pain of loss slashed his chest, its edge doubly sharp when he pictured Christy, with her coltish legs and pale-blond hair. The image of her, the thought of never seeing her again, sawed into his resolve. He could not lose his nerve now. To keep his mind from wandering, he ran through a mental rehearsal. Butternut would alert him to the approach of the ambulance and squad cars, if they came with their sirens off. He would wait, watching the road. When the vehicles appeared at the point where it curved into the woods, he would throw the light switch, which would start the generator, which would shoot 110 volts into the blasting cap, setting off the bomb and transforming the propane tank into a miniature napalm bomb. The explosion would probably blow the rear of the house down and set the rest afire. The noise and flames would throw the enemy into a temporary confusion, during which he would open up on them with the carbine. He would shoot out the tires of their vehicles if he could without risk of hitting any of the men; if not, he would fire a burst or two over their heads. In either case, they would be compelled to call for assistance, the more the better. Starkmann wanted to leave as little as possible to chance. He would keep the cops pinned down with well-aimed shots until the reinforcements arrived; then he would rush them single-handed, firing the last of his ammunition to force them to shoot back—pistols, rifles, riot-guns, a curtain of lead through which he could not possibly pass alive. It was a good, simple plan. It couldn't fail. The blazing demolition of the house especially appealed to him: scorched earth—leave nothing to the enemy. The loan officers threatening to foreclose on it could go ahead; they would repossess ashes.

Starkmann's only doubt was himself. Could he go through with it, or would he falter at the last minute, held back by the fear of death? He looked down at the medals pinned to his chest and, fondling his Purple Heart, reminded himself that he had faced death before, at an age when most young men had nothing more serious on their minds than getting some girl into bed or passing an exam. There was nothing to fear. If death was a journey into another world, then his soul would rise, cleansed, serene as smoke, and he would join his father and Bonny George, D.J., Hutch, and Ramos; if death was not a passage, then he would be cast into nonexistence. Whether transcendence or oblivion, death would bring an end to his nightmares, to all the pointless sufferings of this pointless life. His self-doubts began to fade, like the mists rising from the meadow behind the house, and he gazed with happy expectation at the fairness of the morning.

29

Like a lot of promiscuous women, Sandy Jackson had a low opinion of men. She would seize on the flimsiest evidence to support her conviction that they were contemptible creatures with few redeeming virtues. If ordinary masculine failings earned her scorn, male violence against women turned her into a Medea. Knowing what her reaction would be, and in no state of mind to listen to her rantings, June had not told her the truth when she'd appeared at her front door last night, her dress torn, two frightened children at her side. Instead, she'd fabricated a story that she and Chris had fallen into an argument over their financial problems, and that she'd somehow ripped her dress while running out of the house. It was the same lie she had given the girls, to spare them any more trauma than they were already going through. They did not believe her, and neither did Sandy.

"And how'd you get those marks on your face and neck?" she had asked skeptically. "Bumping into a door, I suppose?"

"We need some place to stay tonight. I don't know where else to go."

"You can stay as long as you need to. Rick's out of town the next two weeks."

Later, after Lisa and Christy had gone to sleep and Sandy had calmed her with a Valium, she admitted to what had actually gone on. Her version was somewhat sanitized, leaving out her provocative lie. She made the omission not because she wanted to gain more sympathy but because she did not fully understand her own motives in inciting him. Sandy did not offer much sympathy anyway; as June had expected, she offered a sword.

"That scum. You call the police and have him arrested. Right now. And first thing tomorrow, get hold of a lawyer and file for divorce."

"You make it sound so easy."

"Easy, no. Simple, yes."

"What do I tell the cops?"

"The same thing you told me."

"This is the Great White North, Sandy. It isn't California. They don't arrest men up here for raping their wives."

"He did more than just rape you." Sandy paced back and forth across the living room floor, a lean lioness. "We should call a doctor. You'll need a doctor's examination as evidence. Then you can nail the bastard to the cross."

"Oh, for God's sake."

"For God's sake what? What's the matter with you? Are you going to let him get away with this?"

"I'm not going to put myself through all that. If the cops do arrest him, the case would end up in court, then the papers." June hesitated. "And the fact is, I sort of egged him on."

"Egged him on, how?"

She told Sandy, who remained undeterred.

"Look. I don't care if you told him you'd taken on the whole Detroit Lions. It still doesn't justify what he did."

"It would come up in court, and I'm not going to put myself through that."

"Then what are you going to do?"

"I don't know."

Despite a second Valium, June had lain awake half the night, alternating between tears and curses, between hatred and pity, thirsting for revenge one moment, praying the next for the grace to forgive. Finally, listening to the rain rapping against the roof and windowpanes, she'd fallen asleep.

Now it was past one in the afternoon. The storm had ended. In a tranquilized haze, she shuffled from the spare bedroom to the kitchen to put on some coffee. A note from Sandy lay on the table:

Have taken Lisa and Christy clothes-shopping so they'll have something to wear till you can retrieve your things. Lisa knows your size. Will get you something also. Meantime you can wear Rick's shirt and jeans. They're laid out in my room. Should fit.

S.

P.S.: Lisa called you in sick.

*   *   *

June sat in one of the blue form-fitted chairs, impressed by Lisa's thoughtfulness and maturity. There's hope for that girl yet, she thought, pumping coffee into herself to counteract the Valium. She attempted to enjoy her new, if temporary, surroundings, but the note reminded her of the practical problem confronting her: somehow, she had to get her own and the girls' belongings out of the house. She sipped the coffee, prodding her drugged brain to find a solution to this logistical problem, which seemed absurdly trivial under the circumstances. There it was nevertheless: she couldn't afford a new wardrobe for the three of them. If Chris was still in the house, there was no telling how he'd react to her reappearance. There was no telling, for that matter, how she'd react. Whether or not he'd by now snapped out of the state he'd been in, she knew she could not look at him without seeing his frenzied eyes, without again feeling his thumb press into her nerve, numbing her limbs, and the sting of his slap and then *that*, that defilement of her womanhood. She didn't trust herself. She might just shoot him. Maybe she ought to call the police and have him dragged out of there in handcuffs. He belonged behind bars.

This thought caused her to resume her argument with herself. She could not deny her complicity. True, she had never imagined he would go as far as he had, but she'd opened the cage. Did she now have the moral right to call the law down on him because the beast had turned out to be more ferocious than she'd expected? Wait a minute. She hadn't let any beast out of any cage. It was already out when she'd returned home, and would have done something awful to her or to the girls regardless. Chris would not have listened if she'd pled her honest innocence instead of admitting to a false guilt. He had gone deaf to reason, to all voices save those within his head.

She had to act. She could not sit here all day, carrying on this debate. She picked up the phone and dialed the house. There was no ring. She tried a second and third time; still no ring. The lines must have gone down in the storm. Maybe that was for the best. What would she have said if he'd answered? Hello, darling, if you're sane today, I think we should have a talk?

After hanging up, she dressed, knotting the tails of Rick's shirt over the jeans, which, she was displeased to notice, were snug in the hips. Too broad in the beam to wear a man's pants. What a thing to worry about now. More to divert herself than to feed her empty stomach, she whipped up an omelet. A few forkfuls were all she could put down. She walked out onto the back deck, its faded planks drying in the sun. Out in front of her, the lake stretched away under a sky of broken clouds. The sun—how she loved the sun and this uncommonly warm weather. Crossing the patch of sand that was the Jacksons' backyard, she walked along the shore, skirting the snow-fences and ignoring the signs that warned: PRIVATE BEACH. NO TRESPASSING. She had stopped to watch a freighter easing toward the ore docks in the distance when, out of nowhere, the knowledge of what she had to do came to her. She turned and ran back to Sandy's, feeling a sickening anxiety.

No one answered at the V.A. Center. When she rang Eckhardt's private office, his secretary said he was with a patient and would call back if she left a number.

"Please tell him it's June Starkmann and that it's an emergency," she said, breathless from her run across the sand.

"Just a moment."

June did not expect him to answer. He would think she'd fallen into another fit of hysteria, but she had good cause for this call. *It is deemed more likely than not that in the near future the said person, Christian Starkmann, will inflict serious unjustified bodily harm on another person.* That was how the papers would read, and she could argue that the said person had already inflicted serious bodily harm. Waiting, she listened to the ridiculously cheerful piped-in music on the phone, nausea passing through her in waves.

"June, I've been trying to reach you since last night." Eckhardt sounded more urgent than usual. "I must have called four, five times."

She didn't ask him why, but immediately gave him an account of what had happened. She sounded in control at first, as if she were reporting the rape of another woman; but the emotions of the past twenty-four hours caught up with her; her voice faltered, then collapsed into sobs.

"You don't have to go on," Eckhardt said sympathetically. "I've heard enough. Do you know where he is now?"

"Still at the house, I suppose. I've got the car."

"The sheriff sent a patrol car out to your place last night, but didn't find anyone home. They're keeping a look-out for him."

"The sheriff?"

"I called him after I couldn't reach you. I'm required to do that if I think a patient might be a danger to someone else."

"Where could Chris have gone in that weather on foot?"

"I don't know. We had some problems with him at the center last night. That's why I called the sheriff."

"What problems?"

He told her.

"Why did he do a thing like that? Jim, what's happened to him?"

"I'd like to explain, but I can't right now. Give me a number where I can reach you. I'm in with a patient, an emergency case."

"So is this."

"I know. Christ, I'm sorry about what happened."

"It's a little late for *I'm sorries*."

"I had no idea he was going to, well, you know . . ."

"Sodomize me, Dr. Eckhardt. Forcibly sodomize me."

"I had no idea, and maybe he didn't either."

"Do you think I give a damn if it was premeditated or not? He isn't a criminal—he's a sick man. I think he should be put . . . Committed. I want him committed. Do you agree with that or what?"

"He needs hospitalization, yes."

"How long, do you think?"

"There's no way of telling. I've seen guys so far gone you'd think they'd be in the rest of their lives. Ten days, two weeks later, they go into spontaneous remission."

"And the others?"

"Some a few weeks, some a few months, some it takes years."

Years, she thought. *Years*. All right, if that's what has to be. "I'll sign the papers," she said.

"June, listen. I've had experience with this. The kind of episode Chris had is usually short-lived. If he's come out of it, it would be a lot better if he could be talked into committing himself before the police find him."

"We've got to find him first."

"If he spent the night in the rain, he might be at the house."

"Who's going to talk to him? Me? The resourceful woman?"

"No. You should stay clear. This will require a professional."

"Oh, a *professional*. Like you, I suppose."

"I'm the logical choice. I'll call the cops and tell them not to do anything without me there. They can go out with me to your place as a back up, if I need one. I should be ready in an hour, two at most. We'll work something out."

"An hour or two!"

"It's the best I can do."

"That isn't good enough! The hell with you and your professionalism. Some professional you've been. A lot of good you've done him."

"June—"

She slammed the phone back onto the receiver, then passed into the kitchen, searching the cabinets for something to calm her. She found a bottle of vodka and downed a shot in one gulp, Finnish style. An hour or two. She was supposed to wait around for a couple of hours until the cool professional was ready.

Committed—it sounded so irrevocable. A sheriff's deputy would take him into custody, accompanied, she supposed, by ambulance attendants who would be there with restraints in case Chris got out of hand. The picture of him being led off in a straitjacket while she sat in this apartment revolted her. Maybe Eckhardt would persuade him to go in of his own free will, but that picture wasn't a great deal more appealing. She would still be here, miles away while her husband went off to a mental ward. It seemed wrong somehow, although no one would reproach her for it. As she moved about the house, scratching her thumbnail with the nail of her forefinger, wondering what she ought to do, the feeling that she was being shadowed by her mother stole into her. She remembered the words her mother had spoken years ago, when June, aware of her father's philanderings and all-night drinking bouts and hating him for it, had asked why her mother didn't leave him. "Because I'm a married Christian woman," she had said. "I made a promise before God. As long as he lives under this roof, I'll be a wife to him, the same as I'm a mother to you." That was what she had been, until Paul Giroux walked out the door to find another roof for his head. Tammy Wynette would have loved Mom, June thought bitterly, but could not condemn her mother's foolish loyalty. She'd sworn an oath before God, without qualifications, reservations, or small-print exceptions. June knew what her mother would do in this crisis, and she could do no less. There are moments, she thought, when we are called upon to show what we say is in our hearts, and we must either live up to our best image of ourselves or fail it.

She drank another vodka both to settle and stiffen her nerves, then sat down and scrawled a note on the back of the one Sandy had left:

Dear Lisa and Christy,

    I've gone back home to talk to your father about something, if he'll listen. I didn't explain everything about last night, and I can't explain it now. I want you to understand that your father is not a bad man. He's sick in his mind. I can't leave him like this, just as I couldn't if he had heart trouble or cancer or some other disease. Please understand that. It's something I have to do.

                                      Love,
                                      Mom

She weighted the note with a saltshaker and went out to her car.

It was hot inside the garage, as stifling as a bunker in the height of the dry season. His legs stiff from sitting in the same position for hours, Starkmann looked through the window at the road and asked himself why they had not come. When would they come? This waiting in the heat was beginning to get to him. It was messing with his mind. It took him back to the times when he had lain in jungle ambush, praying for the enemy to fall into the trap so his tensions would be purged in the loud release of rifles, machine guns, and grenades. None of those ambushes had been sprung; the enemy had never shown up, and often, in the early-morning dark, Starkmann had fallen asleep.

He now felt the same desire for rest, his exhaustion weakening his resolve, diminishing the maniacal energies of the previous night. His sanity was creeping back into him, and his doubts had returned with it. Would he feel the impact of the bullets? Was death painful? Would his soul, purified by his self-sacrifice, live on, or pass into nothingness? He wished he could conjure up his brothers to answer these questions, but such a summoning required a dreamlike state of mind that was now beyond him.

He had to stop this sort of thinking, this niggling philosophizing. No one was going to put him in a hospital again. He would die a soldier's death and have a soldier's burial, and if he was lucky, his soul would go to a soldier's heaven, some blood-darkened Valhalla.

When would they come?

He pictured how it would look: the squad car in the lead, the ambulance following, lights flashing; then, with a flip of a switch—ha! a common, ordinary light switch—a tower of smoke, the blast of propane, chunks of burning wood tumbling from the sky like debris from a volcanic eruption. He heard the cops' panicked voices radioing for assistance after he shot out their tires. It was too bad the man in the maroon Plymouth would not be with them. The plan did not call for killing—killing innocents, that is. But if that bastard miraculously showed up, he would happily put a round through his chest. Bill King too. And Sam LaChance. Killing such men would not add another minute to the sentence pronounced upon him long ago. He wondered if Eckhardt would be riding with the ambulance. He would spare Eckhardt's life, but he would teach him something: When the bomb exploded, that smug psychologist who thought he had the answers would see in the burst the same message Starkmann had seen in the flash of napalm. That knowledge of senseless evil was all he had ever gotten out of the war. It was all he had now.

When would they come? It was the waiting that always unnerved you. Patience. That's what the other side had had over there, and that was why they'd won. Think about them, waiting for hours, for days—draw strength from their example. He rubbed the circulation back into his legs and flipped the carbine's safety off and on, off and on. *Snick. Click. Snick.* Come on. Let's get this done. C'mon, C'mon.

Monotonous and somber, the woods passed by the car window, no different from what they had been yesterday, or the day before, or, probably, than they would be a hundred years from now. Each tree in the endless parade of firs wore a watchful frown, as if guarding a secret no human being was meant to know. Not far ahead, the ridge above the Indian reservation gloomed through the sunlight. June turned off the highway onto the dirt road, which the storm had pummeled into mush. She shifted into four-wheel drive. The forests on either side were still wet, branches dripping and dark. Misgivings caused her to ease up on the gas pedal. She ought not to have started this venture without giving it a few minutes' consideration. She was at a loss as to what arguments she would advance, assuming Chris was capable of listening to them; what threats she could make, assuming he was any longer vulnerable to threats.

After crossing the bridge over the Firedog River, she braked to a stop, a belated fear rising in her. He had a small arsenal in the house, and her imagination wrote the headline: CRAZED VET KILLS WIFE, SELF. She tried to dismiss the idea as melodramatic nonsense, something out of a TV movie. Chris could not be so far gone as to turn a gun on her, for God's sake. Still, such horrors did occur; one had happened a couple of years ago not far from here in that town—what was its name? Wilson's Crossing. And who would have believed that the Hermanson boy was capable of massacring his family? A pair of bluejays squabbled in a pine branch while she sat weighing the risks and pondering whether or not she should take Eckhardt's advice and let him handle this mess.

Butternut barked up ahead. A moment later, the retriever came bounding down the road to prance at the side of the car, turning half-circles in its excitement.

"Hi, girl. Hi, sweetheart. Missed me, did you? Come on, hop in."

June opened the back door.

"Come on, girl. Come on."

Butternut leaped into the back seat, nuzzled her, and lapped her neck. She was as happy to see the dog as it was her. It restored her confidence, its normal behavior persuading her that she was not in any danger. She drove ahead. *Sisu.*

When he'd heard the squad cars coming up the road, Starkmann let Butternut out of the garage; her barking might have alerted the police to his hiding place before he was ready. Now he stood, watching the road, the carbine's butt jammed against his belt, its sling twisted over his forearm. The sound of the motors grew louder. Metal and glass glinted through the trees. Any second now. He reached behind him and, extending his arm its full length, rested his finger on the light switch. He wasn't frightened but elated, an intoxication that heightened rather than dulled his senses. He could distinguish every smell, and the woods beyond the house took on an intense shade of blue-green, the color of the big lake on a clear day. He was so convinced that a patrol car was going to emerge from the tree line that he thought it an hallucination when he saw June's Wagoneer instead.

The car was real enough, all right. His hand falling from the switch, he dropped into a squat, eye level to the windowsill. Goddammit! What was she doing here?

She parked and climbed out, and the mere sight of her—in a pair of faded jeans, black hair flowing over a checkered shirt knotted at the waist—arrested his heart, an emotion that surprised him as much as did her unexpected appearance. He watched her approach the front porch, thighs and hips switching under the snug jeans.

"Chris?" she called in a small, uncertain voice. "Chris? It's me."

Damn her, what could she want of him?

"Chris? Are you home? It's me."

A part of him wanted to answer, as if her voice, that voice he knew so well, were casting a charm on him, calling him away from his mission, luring him back to life. She was standing by the porch, one long leg bent at the knee, her foot on the bottom step. God, he swore he could smell her—a scent like a spring marsh, commingled odors of bog and laurel, a perfume sweet yet loathsome, the stench of life, of life.

"Chris, if you're around I'd like to talk."

The bitch! There was nothing he could do except what he had done last night when Treadwell had shown up: wait. Wait until she left. He sat down, his back to the wall, her voice echoing in his mind.

To deafen himself to its beckoning lilt, he summoned a memory of the battlefield's harsh meters, the long stanzas of machine guns, the precise, one-word sentence of a sniper's rifle. To stifle his longing to rush out and touch her once more, he fondled the carbine, its steel so cold and stern, and formed a mental blueprint of its inner parts: trigger, hammer, and bolt, rod-spring and sear, the engineering of death.

She called him once again, but sounded far away. He stood and froze when he saw the front door ajar. She'd unlocked it and gone inside. If she turned on a light . . . No. No.

"No!"

He flung open the garage door.

"June! No! Get out of the house!"

He saw her in the kitchen window, staring at him. He did not remember running across the yard. The next thing he knew, he was in the generator shed, pulling the wires loose. He covered the distance to the propane tank in three or four strides, ripped the tape from the bomb, and threw it toward the meadow. It tumbled through the air, the electrical cords streaming behind, and fell into the shield ferns. He stumbled toward the shed on legs as slack as a dazed fighter's, then dropped to his knees and looked dumbly at the bleached planks of the shed, at the meadow and the woods and the ridge beyond, rising into the wretched blue of the sky.

"Chris?"

She was behind him, her voice a whisper.

"Chris?" she asked again, as if she weren't sure of his identity. He did not answer, nor turn to look, but doubled over and wept because he had neither the wish to live nor the will to die.

After she'd gone into the house, June had been convinced that Chris had left. His materialization, his shouts, and the sight of him running across the yard in that outlandish outfit had been too sudden and surreal to frighten her. She was stunned in the same way she'd been when the bear had smashed Edith Hermanson's kitchen window. Now Chris was kneeling with his back to her, crying as she'd never heard anyone cry—a grief of such depth she knew she could never plumb it, or would ever wish to. She moved away from him, as one would leave a mourner to the privacy of his sorrow, and walked into the meadow to pick up the object he had thrown. Her senses registered disconnected impressions: paint can. Label says SHERMAN WILLIAMS EXTERIOR FLAT. Wires stuck in a hole in the lid. Can is heavy.

She carried it back into the yard. Chris had sat up, head bowed, hands locked around his upraised knees.

"What is this?" she asked quietly, sitting next to him.

He kept crying. She stroked his hair, the hair she had always loved, the color of sunlight on ice.

"You can understand me, can't you?"

His head moved—a nod, she guessed.

"What is this thing?"

When he made no response, she rose and went into the garage for a screwdriver to pry the can open. The army rifle was lying on the workbench. It was an evil-looking weapon, more evil-looking than his deer rifle and bird guns, a weapon whose very form said that it was designed for taking human life. After fiddling with it, she managed to detach the magazine, which, in a spasm of disgust, she threw into the weeds as she returned outside.

June opened the lid with the screwdriver and caught the smell of sulphur and saltpeter. When she tugged the wires, a shotgun shell popped out of the black powder like a toy out of a cereal box.

"Jesus Christ." Her fingers flew from the can as from a hot skillet. "What were you going to do with this? What, for God's sake?"

Chris's eyes were still wet, but he had regained possession of himself. He was staring at Butternut, nuzzling the woodpile.

"Tell me, damn you!" she shouted. This was no time for soothing words, for gentle stroking of his hair. "Look at me and tell me!" Cupping his cheeks in her hands, she wrenched his head so that his eyes, from which all light had departed, were looking into hers. "Tell me!"

"The tank."

"What about the tank?"

"Blow it," he said dully. "The house."

The story came out of him like that, in one- and two-word sentences, fragmentary phrases and mumblings. June listened as she might to an account of an atrocious crime, her emotions rocking from fascination to revulsion to disbelief. At one point she almost laughed, for there was something macabrely comic about his deranged fantasy. It was funny, that is, until she reflected on how close she had been to becoming its accidental victim. Blow up the house, shoot at the police, force them to kill him—an elaborate form of suicide, a ceremony of death, a ritual of self-destruction, the Yankee samurai committing hara-kiri. The whole scheme required a calculation that was beyond any truly insane person, but if he wasn't mad, then what torment could have driven him to such an extremity?

"Why? Why were you going to do a thing like that?"

He wasn't a monster, but there was one inside him, a lethal

parasite; and she wanted to see it, slithering up his throat, over his tongue, and out his mouth.

"Why? I asked you."

He swung his head back and forth, but she couldn't tell if he meant he did not know the answer or could not give it.

"What made you do this?"

He replied with another ambiguous shake of his head.

Distracted, she stood, walked toward her car, turned back toward him, then toward her car once again. Chris, sitting with his back to her, did not move. She was thinking about going upstairs to pack her clothes when one of his arms lifted, slowly and limply, as if in response to a hypnotic suggestion. This gesture perplexed her until she saw him reach behind his back, his open hand toward her. It was both a plea and a summons, and it wasn't in her to ignore it. She went to him and, standing over him, clasped his hand, feeling his fingers tighten around hers.

"There is something I want to hear from you, Chris," she said. There'd been a time when the pressure of his hand would have been statement enough, but she could suffer his muteness no longer. Words were actions too.

"I can't. I can't explain why."

"Not that. You can explain when you've figured out why. No, there's something else I have to hear, and it isn't that you love me."

"I'm sorry, June. God almighty, I'm sorry for what I did to you last night."

"And I don't need your apologies, either. I might have been killed if you hadn't called out. That should tell you something."

She waited for him to gather the strength to overcome whatever it was that blocked him from admitting to his feelings. The firs on the far side of the meadow stood as still as sentries in the windless afternoon, the lengthening shadow of the ridge turning their green to blue.

Chris released her hand and, without rising, buried his face in her thighs.

"I don't know what to say. I just don't know."

"Maybe it'll come to you later. Stand up. Come on, stand up."

She helped him to his feet and, looking up at him, felt a rill of hope despite his failure to speak the words she wanted to hear. For she saw the chance of recovery in his eyes, whose dullness was that of a man who has passed the crisis of a severe fever. Now she understood why Eckhardt had wanted Chris to make the decision. The act alone, that one step, would be half the cure. He would be committing himself, not to a hospital but to a different way of being; for his suffering was his own responsibility and it was up to him to free himself from its hold.

"There's something you have to hear from me. I came here to get my things and leave, or to ask you to . . ." She held back, fearing his response would force her into the choice she recoiled from making. "Anybody who would go as far as you have," she began again, "anybody who would do that has to go into . . . I don't mean forced into it, but of your own free will . . . I think you know what I mean."

"I think so." His face angled away, toward the ridge, whose shadow had begun to darken the meadow. "I'm not sure I can do that."

"What do you think? That you don't need help? That you're going to be just fine?" She laughed caustically. "I mean, take a look at yourself. Think about what you were going to do."

"I said I'm not sure."

"I've got the girls to worry about. Maybe you ought to give them a thought or two because what's wrong with you is that you're always thinking about yourself. I don't know how crazy you are, but I know you're selfish, Chris Starkmann. Your house. Your land." Her arm swept in an arc. "And *your* pain. You can't share it with anyone. I think you're hooked on it, like it's a drug or something. You want it all to yourself. You can't share anything with anyone—that's your trouble."

"I'm not sure because last night and today, all of it—it's like it didn't happen, like it was a dream."

"Well, guess what? It wasn't, and if you still can't see that you need help, then I guess there's no help for you. You don't need me or the girls, Chris. You don't need anyone but yourself."

Her last nickel of tolerance spent, she turned and walked away, chin tucked into her neck, arms tight to her sides, her palms slapping her legs. She went through the door and quickly climbed the stairs, giving herself no time for second thoughts. She should have known he'd refuse. She had been a fool to try this, acting out of loyalty and love, archaic emotions. She wasn't even sure any longer if love had been her motive. Possibly she'd made this attempt to save him, and her marriage, only because she was afraid of being alone. Her arm hooking into the girls' wardrobe, she pulled half the clothes from the rack in one swipe, carried the pile down to the car, opened the rear hatch, then tossed it inside. Chris, standing where she had left him, hovered in her peripheral vision. Without another look at him, she went back upstairs for the rest of the clothes, put them in the Wagoneer, and made a third climb for Lisa's and Christy's shoes.

I'll have to have the papers drawn up, she thought, stuffing sneakers, boots, and Lisa's first pair of heels into a plastic bag. It would be irresponsible not to. Chris had proved himself to be no quaint, harmless screwball. Though he'd recrossed the psychological frontier he'd passed beyond the night before, there was no assurance that he would remain on this side of the border. The guns—she would have to dispose of them, the props he would use if his impulses again moved him to stage Starkmann's Last Stand. She would sneak the firearms out of the house by concealing them in her coats when she gathered up her belongings. This could not be happening to her, but of course it was. That war, that filthy war. She wished the wives of dictators and prime ministers, of presidents and kings would experience for a single hour what she'd endured the past two years. Maybe then they would persuade their mighty husbands to think twice, three times, four times before sending young men to war, because they would know that wars don't end when the shooting stops and the treaties are signed. They go on and on in the wounded minds of those who did the fighting.

A mournfulness welled up in her. Sensing that this emotion would overwhelm her if she lingered another moment, she fled from the room. The stomp of Chris's boots on the front porch made her stop at the head of the stairs. Her breath held, she listened to him come into the house, then go out again. The sound of the station wagon's hatch slamming shut came a few seconds later, followed by more heavy footsteps. Cautioning herself against another rise of futile hope, she went down to the living room and saw a bundle of jeans and dresses draped over the couch. Chris passed through the door with a second batch in his arms.

"What's that?" he asked, casting a glance at the bag.

"Shoes. The girls' shoes."

"You might as well bring them back up."

"Do I have a reason to?"

Drawing a breath, he laid the clothes in his arms atop those on the sofa. "You said I didn't need you and Christy and Lisa, but I do. I need you more than anything. You're all I've got."

"How hard that was for you," she said after a moment's pause. "How hard to say such a simple thing."

"And I think—and I know this won't sound right because of what's happened—I think you need me. But not the way I've been. The way I used to be. No, better than that." He looked up at the ceiling and filled his lungs again. "And I'll do whatever I have to, to be that way." His lips drew into a tight, provisional smile as he reached down to pick up the clothes. "So you might as well bring the shoes back up. I'll take these."

"I'll get them. You go change and get cleaned up," she said, joy moving through her like a wind.

30

He had forgotten how quickly daylight faded in the Hurons. Although his watch told him it was two in the afternoon, the dimness in the forest belonged to a later hour. He had planned on getting off to an earlier start, but it had taken all morning to put together food, gear, and maps sufficient to last him in case he did not find the camp today, a possibility he refused to consider as anything more than remote.

Though his pack was light for fast traveling, nearly six weeks in a hospital had softened him. He grew short of breath as he climbed the granite-sided hill, one of the landmarks he remembered. Below was the Windigo River, its brandy color umbered by the shadows of the trees. It had been swollen with melted ice and snow the first time he'd seen it; now, because of a recent drought, it was in places as shallow as a brook. Otherwise it looked no different. And why should it? he thought, looking down on the same rocky ford Bonny George and he had crossed so many years before. That span of time, almost half the years he'd been alive, was but an instant in the life of the river, mothered into existence by the glaciers whose titanic recession had also created the mountains and the lakes.

He crossed the ford, hauled himself up a bluff, and looked for the logging trail that led to the old fur-trader's cabin, a major reference point on his search. It was marked as a small black dot on one of his survey maps. He could not find the trail, undergrowth having erased all traces of it, but the map led him to the cabin in ten minutes.

It, too, had not changed, which surprised him. He'd expected it to look more dilapidated, but there it stood, its flagpole still leaning out of the watchtower, its timbers sagging at the same angle, as if, having reached a certain stage of decay, some unknown preservative had kept it from further decomposition. He was tempted to crawl through the lower door and look for the carving of Edward Cadotte's name, tempted to linger and allow a tide of memories to wash over him; but he put the sun to his back and went on. He did not have the time for nostalgia, nor the emotional reserves to withstand the pain his memories would bring. Less than two days out of the hospital, he felt a postoperative fragility, a need to be careful with himself.

It was for that reason that Eckhardt, in their last conversation, had advised him against this attempt. He could not predict how Louis St. Germaine, assuming Starkmann found him, would react after all these years and how those reactions might affect Chris. Starkmann insisted, convinced that confronting Louis would do more to heal him than the hospital or Eckhardt's bookish therapy could.

Finding the old man's shack on the reservation had not been difficult, but it was locked and Louis's truck gone when he'd arrived, shortly after dawn this morning. The place did not appear abandoned, however, encouraging Starkmann's hopes that its owner was still living. He drove to a nearby store and asked his whereabouts from a plump Ojibwa woman who sat behind the counter with the hostile air of a watchdog.

"You say you got some information 'bout his grandson?" she answered. "Where'd you come from? Heaven? That boy got killed years ago . . . in the war."

"It's about that."

"All I can tell you is that if he ain't at his place, he's in the woods. Got him some sorta camp way back in there, but I don't know where it is. Nobody does." She hesitated, her eyes like two dull black slugs. "The old son of a bitch's gotten a little touched, y'know, hey. Don't know what cent'ry he's livin' in."

Now, maintaining his direction by the sun, Starkmann loped through stands of red pine, a climax forest which, free of underbrush, allowed him to set a fast pace. Three to four miles east of the trader's cabin: he remembered that much, and that the camp was pitched on a low ridge above a pond or small lake. Its name, if he'd ever known it, wouldn't come to him, and the map showed half a dozen small lakes and ponds in the direction in which he was headed. White Deer. Summit. Evergreen. Lost Lake. Pale-blue specks encompassed by a green that ran to the edges of the sheet. Even on a map, the Hurons looked forbidding. He pushed on, the red-pine plain dropping off into a washboard of hardwood ridges that slowed him down. Let's go, Starkmann barked out loud, playing drill sergeant to himself. Get your ass up the hill. Up the hill, down the hill, all day, every day. He sang "Jody" and other boot-camp marching songs to keep his spirits from flagging, his legs from tiring.

Finally he gained the treeless crest of the highest ridge, glanced anxiously at the sun, transiting westward, then scanned the forests for a wisp of campfire smoke. Two of the lakes glittered in the near distance, shores gilded by yellowing birch. The immensity of the woods dismayed him; he was looking for one man in a wilderness that could hide a thousand—a quixotic attempt, he supposed. But his conviction that it was the right, the only, thing to do drove him on. He clambered down the ridge, plunging again into dusk, and reached the first lake within half an hour. An otter dipped under a log as he skirted the edges in a search for tracks or other signs of human presence. Finding none, he followed a compass azimuth to the next body of water, more a marsh than a lake, uninhabited except for a family of mallards skimming through the cattail rushes.

By the time he came to White Deer Lake, the clouds that hung low on the horizon were taking on color from the falling sun. Starkmann booted a rock into the water and cursed. His need for order and symmetry would not be satisfied. He had wanted to speak to Louis on this anniversarial day, the first day of autumn, but he could not reach the next lake before nightfall. His hunt would have to be resumed in the morning; if that failed, he would return to the cabin and wait for the old man there.

A pine bluff overlooking a cove offered a suitable campsite. Dropping his pack, he smoothed out a space in the dry needles and covered it with boughs. A plastic tarp lashed between two trees made do as a shelter; a space-blanket—a lightweight foil sheet invented by NASA that had become a common item in sporting-goods stores— served as his sleeping bag. He then scoured about for firewood: birchbark for tinder, twigs from a deadfall for kindling, thicker pieces of mountain ash for heat. Soon he had a fire going, its warmth warding off the autumnal chill, its light holding back the fear that drilled through him when a pack of coyotes began to hymn. He took a tin of black bread and a packet of freeze-dried soup from his pack, then walked down to the shore with his cookpot to draw water. Rising fish wrinkled the surface of the cove, aflame in the sunset. The coyotes ended their evening vespers, the silence briefly filled up by a loon's hysterical trill. He returned to camp, hung the pot over the flames, boiled up some soup, and poured it into a canteen cup.

The day ended, Venus flickered in the twilight sky. Starkmann wrapped the blanket around his shoulders, holding the cup to his lips. A wolf celebrated nightfall with a long howl. He pulled the blanket tighter around his shoulders and drew closer to the fire, glad he'd brought a knife. If Bonny George could see him now, he would laugh as he had years ago. Starkmann was close to laughing at himself, a late-twentieth-century man wrapped in a product of space-age technology, trembling like a Paleolithic savage at the cries of wild beasts. Still, though his fears for his physical safety were ridiculous, coyotes and wolves posing no danger, his conviction in the rightness of this enterprise had begun to ebb. He felt as he had the day when he'd imagined—if he had imagined it—that a panther was stalking him. All these howlings seemed the voice of the wilderness, telling him that he was an unwanted stranger here.

He finished the soup, sopping up the last of it with slices of black bread and wishing he were back in his hospital room. It was clean, bright, and modern, and looked like a room in a budget motel, an Econo-Lodge or a Days Inn.

Though he'd committed himself, he was not at first given the priveleges of a voluntary patient. He was confined to a maximum security wing, and kept under observation. Later, when he proved he was in control of himself, he was assigned to the ward's open wing, which had none of the accessories of the maximum-security wing: the steel doors, the caged windows, the padded rooms, the stark corridors guarded by attendants who looked like ex-linemen. Maximum was for mental paraplegics, the open wing for the merely lame.

The hospital had turned out not to be the horror he had feared. Voluntary patients were allowed to sign themselves in and out with staff approval more or less any time they chose, as if they were guests in a hotel. For the first week, Starkmann had wandered about the corridors of maximum dazed as a shell-shock victim in the aftermath of his psychotic episode—Eckhardt's phrase for the delirium in which he had assaulted his wife and scripted his suicidal drama.

Afterward, emerging from his stupor, he fell into the open wing's relaxed routine of meals and television and card or checker games. Once a day, for an hour, he attended a session in the airless, windowless conference room where Eckhardt conducted in-patient interviews. Talk, talk, talk—that was all Eckhardt wanted him to do. The idea seemed to be that he could exorcise his devils if he could name them. Talk, talk, talk. Talk about whatever came into his head, about his father, his hallucinations of D.J., Hutch, and Ramos, the flashback in which the psychologist had assumed the form of the enemy in the blaze of blue lightning. It galled Starkmann to speak of these things, and the one he could not speak of at all was the one Eckhardt most wanted to hear about. Each time it came up, Starkmann's tongue turned to lead.

"Look," Eckhardt had said one day in frustration. "I know what happened on that hill. What's more, you know that I know. So why do you go into this mute act whenever I ask you about it?"

"It's not an act."

"Until you get through whatever's blocking you, you're going to be a prisoner of what happened, Chris. You could stay in here ten years, and you and I could go on talking in circles, and you'll remain a prisoner of it. Think about that."

He had plenty of time to think, too much time, but his thoughts, like the conversations with Eckhardt, went round and round, leading nowhere.

He read a lot to fill up the idle hours and to keep his mind off himself. The books were novels about the war. Some were little more than adventure stories, but others struck so close to his emotional center that he could not read them, the printed words transubstantiated into images of burning horizons and night skies alight with the silent alarms of flares.

The books were loaned to him by Dewey Miller, an ex-navy corpsman whose best friend, a marine rifleman, had been killed in the battle for Hill 881. That had not been the root cause of Miller's crackup: He was gay, a leprous stigma in the Upper Peninsula, land of iron miners and lumberjacks. He had managed to conceal his homo- sexuality for years, drinking a lot to relieve the pressure of living with his secret. A year ago, he'd gotten married in a doomed attempt to prove his manhood. Then, sick of lying and making excuses to his wife for his sexual failures, he held what he called his "coming-out party": He told her the truth. She responded by slapping him and spitting in his face, which caused him to explode. He turned their apartment into a shambles, knocked her unconscious, and was about to bash in her skull with a lamp when a neighbor intervened. Terri- fied of his own violence, Miller admitted himself to the hospital. His wife divorced him. He lost his job in an Iron Mountain record store, but he'd not lost his sense of humor.

"I can't blame the old lady," he'd said to Starkmann one after- noon. "Imagine you're a woman and your old man comes up to you one day and says, 'Dear, I've got something to say to you—I'm a cocksucker, literally.' "

Another patient on the ward was Peter LeBlanc, a thickset Canuck with whom Starkmann played checkers. He was nicknamed "Bone Spur" because he had a bone spur in his heel—"just like Joe DiMaggio," he'd said. LeBlanc had been a marine captain during the Korean War and had spent a year in a Chinese prison camp. He had entered the hospital to have the bone spur removed. He'd ended up on neuropsychiatric after the operation, when he'd told the doctors that the spur had been implanted by his captors, who were after him to torture him into divulging the classified information he'd refused to give them in the camp.

"But don't worry," he'd assured the surgeons. "I'll tell 'em now what I told 'em then. Name, rank, serial number, and nothing more. The Code of Conduct. I follow it to the letter."

LeBlanc was brilliant at checkers, the ward champion, with hopes of taking the all-hospital crown. Starkmann's game was careful and well thought out, but LeBlanc played with elan, relying on bold inspiration rather than planning. He defeated Starkmann consistently with his unpredictable moves, his daring triple jumps.

The oldest patient was another ex-marine, an octogenarian known as Gunny, which was Marine Corps slang for gunnery sergeant. That had been the ancient warrior's rank in the 1920's, when he'd served aboard a Yangtze River gunboat. In his lucid periods, which were few, he yarned about skirmishes with Chinese warlords and opium bandits, battles that had taken place so long ago it seemed impossible to Starkmann that anyone now living had fought in them. Gunny was a living relic who, when he wasn't telling tales of his adventures in old China, talked about the coffee served aboard his ship. "You shoulda tasted it, black as a lump of engine-room coal—and just as hard," he would say, squinting to see if his listener appreciated the simile. He would then describe the coffee in detail, its bitter taste, the stains it left in the crew's tin cups, and on and on in an agate voice that implied that anyone who hadn't drunk this brew should hold his manhood cheap. Everyone on the wing had heard the story of the gunboat coffee at least a dozen times, but Gunny was unaware of his repetitiousness. He had Alzheimer's disease. He also suffered from emphysema, the result of a lifetime of smoking unfiltered Camels. Often, in the midst of one of his rambling stories, he would fall into a wheezing fit, his throat rattling like a New Year's noisemaker, and would then clamp his gums over the mouthpiece of the oxygen tank beside his bed, sucking in air until his faded old eyes bulged.

A senescent eighty-year-old, a homosexual corpsman, a paranoid ex-prisoner-of-war—these were Starkmann's companions, along with a former chaplain who sometimes heard God speaking to him in TV commercials, and three Vietnam veterans, one of whom, an auto mechanic, had committed himself after he'd beaten a co-worker with a wrench in an argument over who should go on lunch break. In the early part of his stay, Starkmann held himself aloof from his wardmates. He did not like to think of himself as having anything in common with such psychological cripples, though, obviously, he did. He preferred to look upon the hospital as an asylum in the oldest sense of the term, a refuge where he hoped to find the answer to the only question that mattered: how to live. When he had seen June carrying his daughters' belongings out of the house, he had realized he wanted to live. But how? How to live with the legacies of the war, with his loss of faith, his guilt and nightmares?

He did not discover the answer in the long hours spent thinking in his room, or in the sessions with Eckhardt. Part of it began to come to him in the course of day-to-day life in the hospital.

Whether they had come in voluntarily or had been forcibly committed, the patients shared a common life as intense and inescapable as life in a barracks or on a perimeter in Nam. It denied Starkmann his solitude. He resented the intrusion on his privacy until The Loneliness began to assault him, usually in the late hours when, looking out the window at the town, he would imagine the everyday people sleeping in the darkened houses and envy them their ordinary lives and untroubled slumbers. Then he would find his own company inadequate and yearn for the simple warmth of human companionship. He ached for June and the girls, but their visits, though frequent, were brief and awkward. June would fidget in the visitors' lounge, obviously embarrassed to see her husband in a mental ward, even though it had been her idea. Lisa and Christy would look at him silently and studiously, as if trying to figure out who he was. And so, in an attempt to recapture at least a facsimile of the brotherhood he'd known in the war, Starkmann began to seek out the company of his wardmates, his comrades in a battle against madnesses born of inescapable memories. Almost willy-nilly he found himself doing things for them, as he had for D.J., Hutch, Ramos, Bonny George, and all the others with whom he'd faced an easier, external foe.

One morning, well before dawn, LeBlanc entered his room, startling him awake with shouts of "LeBlanc, Peter! Captain! Four one zero six seven four! That's all you get! Code of Conduct!"

"Pete, it's me, Chris," Starkmann whispered. "Keep your voice down, or they'll—"

"Don't give me any of that cock-and-bull. I'm onto your tricks, you Chink son of a bitch. LeBlanc, Peter! Captain! Four one zero six seven four!"

Knowing that if LeBlanc kept on he would be taken to the security wing, Starkmann led him to his room and slowly talked him back to reality. He'd recognized that the former captain had been traveling backward in time, and only needed to be spoken to in order to return to the present.

Another time, passing by Gunny's room, he heard the old man gasping more loudly than usual. Starkmann peeked in and saw him, rolled over onto his stomach, his bony fingers groping for the mouth-piece, which had fallen to the floor. Gunny was too weak to reach it from his elevated bed. Starkmann picked it up, cleaned it with a tissue, and inserted it in Gunny's mouth, staying at his side until he was breathing normally again. The old man gave him a curt nod of gratitude as he left.

One drizzling night, the dream paid another call. Unable to go back to sleep, Starkmann paced the corridors, trying to tire himself. He found Dewey Miller alone in the day room, crying and staring at the test pattern on the TV screen.

"Miller, what's up? What're you doing here? It's four in the morning."

"What're *you* doing here?" Dewey asked, drying his eyes with the back of his hand.

"Couldn't sleep."

"I couldn't neither. It's the rain. The rain made me think of him. He died in the rain. Siddown, Chris. Talk to me."

He sat beside the ex-corpsman, who confessed that the marine who had died in his arms had been considerably more than his best friend.

"When the battalion got liberty in Hue, and all the other guys went to the bars and whorehouses, me and Tim—that was his name, Tim McNulty—we'd rent a room in the back of this opium den run by this old papa-san. We'd get a room, and we'd, you know, Tim and me, we'd love each other. I suppose that disgusts you."

Although, in fact, it did, Starkmann shook his head.

"Bullshit, Chris, it disgusts you, and I don't give a damn, neither. Was it wrong for me and Tim to do that? He was a smart guy, you know, read a lot, and he told me that in ancient Greece and Rome the legionaires weren't just buddies but lovers. They loved each other. Was that so wrong?"

"I don't know anything about ancient Greece and Rome."

"I don't give a damn. Those other guys, they'd go to the whores and didn't care if those bitches lived or died, same as the whores didn't care if they lived or died. It was just money. It was business. That's what was disgusting to me. But me and Tim loved each other. In the middle of all that *shit* over there, all that mud and filth and the whoring and the dying, we loved each other. What was so wrong about that?"

"What the hell do you want me to say, Miller?"

"Then we went up Hill Eight-eighty-one," Miller went on.

"Our company got pinned down. The skipper called in artillery. He called in gunships. He called in fighters. Those guns kept firing, like you couldn't have blown them out with an atom bomb, they were dug in so deep. The skipper says, 'We gotta get those guns,' and Tim says, 'Hell, Captain, that's my specialty.' See, he'd got a Silver Star a few months before, knocking out machine guns. That's why he said that. Everybody thinks faggots are chicken, but Tim was a brave guy. He was beautiful and brave, and he went up that hill all by himself throwing grenades and knocked out the guns. Then we heard him screaming." Miller paused, his eyes filling again. "I ran up after him, slipping and sliding. It was raining, like I said. They'd hit his femur artery. I tried to stop the bleeding, but you can't do that when a femur's hit. The blood came out of him like out of a bathtub faucet, and then he . . . Then I saw his eyes go wide, and he . . . the rain falling on him the whole time. Aw, goddammit, Chris, goddammit to hell, goddammit all."

Miller, bawling like a child, curled up like one, his face falling on Starkmann's chest. Starkmann recoiled from the other man's touch for an instant; then, his restraints breaking as they had done long before, when Bonny George had rescued him from the river, he clasped his arms around Miller and rocked him gently.

"It's all right. There was nothing wrong about it. Be easy, brother."

Flesh to flesh, Miller's tears dampening his shirt, Starkmann forgot about his nightmare and his own misery. A strange happiness flowed through him, the pleasure of giving himself to another without expectation of receiving anything in return. He saw that no matter how much he tried to distance himself from the Millers and the LeBlancs, he was one of them after all, another casualty.

Though his sharing in the anguish of others eased his own pain, he had gained enough self-insight to know that it alone could not unlock the cage that made him a captive of his past, that barred him from finding a way to live.

Then, on Saturday—just three days before this trip—June had come on a visit, this time without the children. She was carrying a file folder, her mien both serious and nervous. He soon found out why: She'd found serious buyers for the property, a group of Chicago sportsmen who wanted to convert it into a private hunting and fishing retreat. She reached into the folder and pulled out a completed sales contract, with her signature already affixed to it. Now she needed his.

"They're offering less than it's worth, but we'll still clear a little under five thousand."

They were in Starkmann's room, sitting in the molded Fiberglas chairs. He said nothing as he stared out the window, down at the grounds shaded by maple. The leaves had begun to turn.

"You got me in here. Now you want to sell our place. What's next? Donating a pint of blood every week?"

"Honey, we're about broke. If we don't take this now, the place will go into foreclosure and sell for taxes."

All of it gone, he thought, watching a groundskeeper ride a mower across the lawn. Gone. He pictured the house, the meadow where the woodcocks sang, the Firedog flowing darkly under the tamaracks, and felt a sickness in his stomach.

"They don't plan to come up till the spring and said we could rent it from them till then. We'll have plenty of time to find something else."

"So I don't have much choice."

"You don't have any choice."

He said nothing, continuing to look out the window. Maybe he'd been wrong about the place from the start. Maybe it had never been a sanctuary, but only a hideout.

"Okay. Give me the pen."

"I know that must have been hard for you," she said after he'd signed. "Real hard. I love you, Chris."

She gave him a matrimonial peck. He took her face in both his hands, kissing her full on the mouth, his tongue searching.

"I didn't expect that kind of reaction." She smiled.

He kissed her again, his hands falling to her hips. He needed to hold her, to feel in her embrace the sense of place and belonging that had gone out of him when he signed the paper.

"Chris! Not here."

"Why not? It looks like a motel room."

"That would be . . ." She stifled herself. "I guess that isn't the word to use around here."

"Well, I am officially crazy."

"Oh, for God's sake." She wriggled free of his arms. "I mean what would we call it if we did it here? Love among the loons?"

He let out a brief, sharp laugh and went to kiss her once more when he was stopped short by the shocked expression on her face.

"What's wrong?"

Her long hair whispered as her head moved from side to side.

"What's the matter, June?"

"Didn't you hear yourself just now?"

"Hear what?"

"You laughed." Now it was she who took him in her arms. "That's the first time, baby. The first time I've ever heard you laugh."

It had delighted him to see her pleased with him for a change, but he had not felt much like laughing later, when the reaction set in. He stalked about the ward, an anger welling in him, the sort of helpless anger that, he imagined, must have come over a defeated chief who had signed away his tribal lands. It seemed to him he had capitulated too quickly, too easily, probably out of a need to make up for what he had done to June. That he owed her a great deal of compensation was without question, but as a guilt-tax the house and land had been an overpayment. By midafternoon he sensed dangerous pressures building in him and knew he had to talk to Eckhardt before he started punching holes in walls.

He got approval to sign himself out for the afternoon, then phoned to see if the psychologist was home for the weekend. Eckhardt was, and said he would be right down as soon as he showered and changed; he'd been practicing his archery for opening day of bow season.

"Don't bother," Starkmann said. "I've signed out. I need to get the hell out of here for a while. And I need a drink."

"What'd you have in mind?"

"Maybe we could talk at your place."

"I don't do that as a rule."

"Then break the rule."

"Just what's up, Chris?"

"I don't know. I feel like talking. You're always wanting me to talk. All right. I feel like talking, but not here."

"Okay. I can pick you up."

"I'll take a cab."

Eckhardt's house, on an acre of land at the edge of town, was built in the eclectic style considered in good architectural taste by successful small-town merchants at the turn of the century. Starkmann, as he stood on the sidewalk looking at the house, with its Queen Anne turret and gothic gables and curving veranda, maple trees shading the front lawn, thought of Booth Tarkington's Middle West, a quieter, saner age than the present one, a time when families gathered on porches to sip lemonade on leisured summer Sundays.

Eckhardt, in jeans and checkered shirt, greeted him at the front door, then led him through the dim, high-ceilinged hall to the backyard, its mown green rambling two hundred feet to the skirts of a pine woods. Straw bales, to which a silhouette target of a bear was attached, were stacked against the garage wall. A bow and quiver, like a leather vase filled with bristling flowers, were propped against the lawn table.

"Nice place," Starkmann said. "Must be nice to have a place like this."

"Sure. If you like faulty wiring, bad plumbing, and a leaky roof. My wife and I were going to restore it before the divorce, but now . . ." He shrugged.

"Why do you hang on to it, then? It's a lot of house for one guy."

"What'd you come to talk about? Real estate?"

"Maybe. What've you got to drink?"

"Name it."

"Bourbon. Ice. No water."

While Eckhardt was inside, Starkmann sat at the table, taunted by images of big-city hunters carousing in the house that was no longer his, lugging their out-of-shape bodies across what had once been his meadow, ambushing the deer that watered in the still pockets of the Firedog River; and his anger dissolved into a deep sadness, as if someone had died.

"Here you go," the psychologist said, returning outside with a bottle of Jack Daniel's and two ice-filled glasses. "Normally I'm a sun-over-the-yardarm drinker, but like the old saying goes, the sun's over the yardarm somewhere."

"You're breaking all kinds of rules today."

"I've broken worse ones. What's on your mind?"

He told him about the sale. Predictably, Eckhardt asked how he felt about that, and Starkmann answered that he'd been relieved at first, then bitter, and now felt as if he'd come from a funeral.

The small man, wiping the rim of his glass, squinted up at the painfully bright sun.

"In a way you have, Chris. Come back from a funeral."

"What kind of riddle is that?"

"Maybe you needed to get rid of that place, even if you don't think so. It's one way of making a break with who you used to be. You're burying the old Chris."

"Now you're a mortician."

"Listen, Starkmann, I usually don't interview patients at my house, and I goddamn well don't let them come here to insult me."

"You listen. Maybe I don't want to bury the old Chris." Starkmann finished half his drink in a single gulp, the whiskey peppering his throat after weeks of abstinence. "I went through something over there, Eckhardt—something out of the ordinary."

"All of us did. For all of us, what was out of the ordinary became ordinary."

"I mean I saw things over there, learned things I don't want to forget. I don't think I should forget them. All I want is to figure out how to live with them."

The small man leaned forward, chin on his folded hands. "That's a lot of progress right there. A few weeks ago you were doing your damnedest to figure out how to die with them."

"You still don't get me," Starkmann said, half-rising and gripping the edge of the table. "I've got the feeling that you and June want me to forget. Some kind of lobotomy. Iron out all of Chris Starkmann's wrinkles and kinks. She got me to sell the place, and I suppose the next thing she'll want is to put me behind a picket fence where I'll cut the lawn once a week and make sure I take my vitamins and see that my tires are rotated regularly."

"Put the paranoia in the drawer, Starkmann."

"Are you following me? My kinks and wrinkles are *mine*. I don't want to get rid of them. I'm not interested in forgetting, and I don't care how crazy that makes me."

"Don't worry about that. Don't worry about becoming domesticated," Eckhardt said with a faint, almost sad smile. "Whatever kinks and wrinkles you picked up over there are going to be with you the rest of your life. And so will your memories."

"Then what am I doing in a hospital? What the hell is the point of all this talking?"

"Ever tried this?" the psychologist asked, pointing to the bow.

"No. What's that got to do with anything?"

Without answering, Eckhardt pulled a leather armguard from a pocket in the quiver and strapped it to his left forearm. "Concentration is the key. There's a little Zen in it. Most of the time, I know where the arrow is going to hit before it's released. Like I've willed it to hit where I want it to." He got up and, notching one of the barbless arrows, took a stance a hundred feet from the target. Drawing in a sure, fluid movement, he bent the bow, the string forming a triangle with the apex at the corner of his mouth, the arrow bisecting the triangle, a deadly geometry. A barely visible relaxation of his fingers released the shaft. The string cracked against the armguard almost at the same instant that the arrow buried itself in the bear's shoulder.

"Pretty good, Eckhardt. But guns are more efficient."

"That's the trouble with them. No challenge. The trick is to do what I just did after you've sat in a tree-stand for five, six hours, and then have a real bear in front of you, not some paper outline. Care to give it a try?"

It was less a question and more a dare. Starkmann took the bow and tugged with all his strength, amazed that he, twice the other man's size, could not pull to full draw. The arrowhead and two or three inches of the shaft protruded beyond the edge of the rest.

"It's got an eighty-five-pound pull," Eckhardt said from the side. "It's no amusement park toy. It kills bears."

Starkmann let the arrow go just to relieve the strain on his muscles. It did not fly with the straight authority of Eckhardt's, but wobbled in a low arc, striking the straw backstop below the bottom of the target.

"In a real situation, that might have hit his foot and just pissed him off."

"I didn't come here to play Robin Hood," Starkmann said, setting the weapon down. "Let's hear an answer to my question. What's been the point of all this talking?"

"It's not to make you forget what happened. It's to get you to forgive yourself so you don't try to kill yourself again. Sound reasonable?"

Starkmann flopped into the chair and watched the way the light was falling through the trees at the border between lawn and woods. Forgive himself. Yes, that was what he had to do, but how did a man grant self-absolution without its being granted by another? And who was there to forgive him?

"Make you a bet, Starkmann."

"What's that?"

"Give me ten minutes and I'll have you pulling that bow to full draw."

"What're the stakes?"

"That you tell me what happened on that hill."

"I've tried. You know that."

"Maybe not hard enough. You just won't let it go, will you?"

"It won't let me go."

"Like it has a will of its own? Bullshit. Was what happened so awful that it's actually got a grip on you? So awful that you can't say a word about it? Just how awful was it really?"

"You read that report."

"Right. One guy got killed in an accident. He was your best buddy, but still one guy. It wasn't the apocalypse, was it?"

"What the hell do you know? You weren't there."

Eckhardt tilted back his chair, his short legs lifting off the ground.

"You don't like me talking about it that way, do you? Making your traumatic experience sound a little less traumatic than you'd like it to be. Trivializing it or, better yet, putting it into perspective."

"I don't get you."

"Our experiences end up being what we make of them. Another guy could have gone through the same thing you did and seen it for what it was, an understandable mistake, an unavoidable accident. But you've turned it into something else. I assume there's a reason for that."

"And what's that, answer-man?"

"I don't have any answers, but I don't get the impression that you can't talk about what happened because you're afraid you'll fall to pieces if you do. It's not like you're guarding some deep dark guilty secret. It's like you're guarding a treasure."

"A treasure!" Starkmann scoffed. "Maybe you need a stay in the hospital."

"And I think maybe you cherish whatever went on, on that hill. You don't want to let it go, for reasons we'll discover one of these days. I can give you a few hints."

"Don't bother," Starkmann replied, squeezing his glass in both hands, feeling he could crush it into crystalline dust.

Eckhardt rose and ambled across the lawn to the target, where he picked up the spent arrows.

"Why did you enlist?" he asked, dropping them back into the quiver.

"I told you weeks ago," Starkmann answered, confused by the abrupt change in subject.

"Tell me again."

"He was drafted. He had to go. I didn't. It didn't seem right."

"I smell bullshit. The same bullshit as when some guy tells me he joined up to fight for the flag, Mom, and apple pie."

"I'm getting sick of your calling everything I say bullshit."

"I figure you had other reasons for enlisting."

"We've been through that too."

"More bullshit, although the smell's not as strong. Fact is, I almost bought it a while ago. Religious son of militant pacifist minister joins up in rebellion against father's values. Blames self for death of best friend. Returns home burdened with guilt, which eventually drives him to self-destructive behavior. Case closed. It's a nice neat story, but there's something wrong with it."

"Another one of your riddles, Eckhardt."

"And you're the only one who can solve it."

The small man picked up his bow and strung another arrow.

"I'll show you a couple of things you did wrong. First, you profile to the target—you don't stand facing it head-on. Second, don't hold the grip like a club. Wedge it in the webbing between your thumb and forefinger. Keep the rest of your fingers loose."

He demonstrated these techniques, confident and relaxed, then sent the arrow hissing through the air. It spiked itself just below the bear's shoulder.

"Heart shot. Bye-bye, bruin. How about giving it another try?"

"Forget it."

"I can show you. I can show you how to draw this bow, Starkmann."

"Some other time."

"Give what I said some thought when you go back."

He did, after returning to the hospital, where he lay awake half the night, replaying the conversation over and over. He was inclined to reject the idea that he cherished the memory of his best friend's absurd and violent death; to do so would not be evidence of madness but of a moral sickness. Nevertheless, the idea intrigued him, and as he pondered it, he felt within inches of grasping a crucial truth about himself. He could almost see it, suspended in the air above his bed; but each time he reached for it, it slipped away, elusive as mercury. Worn out by his mental efforts, he fell asleep, dozed fitfully for an hour or two, and woke up with his mind still going around and around, a whirling that produced a vertiginous sensation. He went into the bathroom and rinsed his face and head in cold water; that was when, out of the disorder of his thoughts, the inspiration to seek out Louis came to him. It was not a notion or fancy, but a compulsion, one so powerful that he had an urge to sign out immediately, though it was three in the morning. He saw that a need, unacknowledged until this moment, to unburden himself to Louis had been the imperative that had first drawn him to these northern woods and impelled him to settle on the border of the reservation. If the story of Bonny George's death was indeed a treasure he'd been guarding, he'd been guarding it all these years for Louis, who had rightful claim to it. And the heretofore hidden desire to tell it first to him accounted for his inability to breathe a word of it to Eckhardt or anyone else. Louis. It was Louis to whom he had to confess, Louis whose forgiveness had to be granted before he could absolve himself. Starkmann stayed awake till dawn, too excited to sleep.

The next morning, he called Eckhardt to say he was going to sign himself out and search for Louis, a plan about which the psychologist was more than skeptical.

"I don't want to play mother hen," he said. "Talking to that old man, if he's still alive, is probably a good idea. But I think you ought to put it off for a while."

"I've been putting it off for years. I'm not waiting anymore. For the first time in a long time, I know what I have to do."

"Go ahead. I can't stop you. But I hope you know what you're doing. I hope you realize it might turn out all wrong."

"I do."

"He might not give you what you're asking for. Even if he does, it won't make much difference, because you've got to give it to yourself first."

The wolf had stopped baying. Now he heard only the crickets and the splash of a fish. The moon rose, full and brilliant, a stalker's moon. Not yet tired enough to sleep, Starkmann decided to brew an after-dinner tea. The bags were rolled up in his uniform, which he'd brought along as vestments for a private ceremony he planned to hold after speaking to Louis. If, of course, he ever found him.

After tossing another ash log on the fire, he again went down to the cove to draw water. A big fish, probably a lunker pike, smacked its tail. Starkmann saw the rings of the splash in the white stripe the moon painted across the cove, its surface rippled by a puff of breeze. The breeze carried the aroma of his fire, and he breathed it in, a fragrance as of burning cedar—cedar and something else, a strong, incenselike odor. He'd never known ash to smell like that. It suddenly occurred to him that the scent could not be coming from his fire—the wind was blowing not from behind him but down the length of the cove from the open lake beyond. He sniffed the air to make sure he wasn't imagining things. Yes. Cedar. He set down the pot and, following his nose, picked his way along the rocky shore to the point of land that jutted out into the mouth of the cove. The lake, not much larger than the cove, spread out before him, a piney island in its middle. The island struck a note in his memory. There had been an island in the lake where Louis pitched his camp, but he could not recall its size or shape. His eyes traced the contour of the shore, sweeping around until they caught a flash of orange showing through the trees on the lake's near side, a hundred, maybe two hundred yards away. It could be anyone: a trapper, campers, or, more dangerous, poachers out to bag a preseason buck. He would never find out just standing here. The moonlight showed him a well-worn game trail that girdled the lake. He started toward the campfire, his heart beating like a bird's wing.

31

Starkmann thrashed through a clump of thimbleberries, hailing the camp to give plenty of warning and establish his friendly intentions. If it was a poacher's camp, he did not want to be mistaken for an animal or a game warden, both fair game to bush outlaws. He came out of the thicket. The fire flickered not far ahead, but neither tents nor people were visible through the trees, only the glimmer of the flames. The smoke continued to give off the incenselike odor, and now he caught the smell of cooking fish. Before going on, he called out another hello. No one answered.

"Louis? Is that you? Louis St. Germaine?"

Wawiekumig did not stir from his seat on the log, nor did he give answer. He had heard the sounds of the man's approach—he would have had to be deaf not to. But who was this stranger, addressing him by his other name? Who could know he was here?

"Louis? Is that you?"

Forgetting himself, Wawiekumig called out in the old language; then, remembering, asked in English, "Who's there? Come on out of there where I can see you."

Starkmann recognized the voice immediately. He entered the camp, passing out of the darkness of the woods into the ring of light, trembling inside when he saw the familiar face with its bent nose and thin lips, its skin as brown and creased as an old wallet. Louis's hair had grown whiter, as white as Starkmann's father's had been, but the eyes were as penetrating as ever, though they did not appear to recognize him.

"Louis? Do you remember who I am?"

Starkmann stepped forward, squatting to bring his face into the light.

Wawiekumig scrutinized the tall young man for several moments, and was startled when he identified him, too startled and too exhausted by his long ordeal to answer with anything but a nod.

"Chris. I'm Chris Starkmann," the young man said, shaking his hand firmly.

"Chris Starkmann."

"Do you remember who I am?"

"You were my grandson's friend. You and him used to fish together."

The voice was as empty of emotion as the face was blank of expression. Starkmann was both puzzled and disappointed; he'd expected some sort of response, shock if nothing else.

"You must be wondering what I'm doing here. How I found you way out here."

Wawiekumig made no answer. He was not interested in how the young man had found him, and his purpose in coming was of less importance than the Creator's purpose in sending him here to his sacred place, on this special day.

Starkmann, discomforted by the old man's silence, wondered what to do next, how to lead into the difficult thing he had to say.

"I tried to find you at your cabin this morning. The woman at the store said you were probably out here. I sort of remembered where this was, but I couldn't recall which lake it was on exactly. I guess it was just luck that I found you. It's important—important to me, I mean—to talk to you today."

Starkmann waited to be asked why; instead, the old man invited him to take a seat.

"You look tired. You've come a long way."

"It's been longer than you think, Louis."

He sat down, apologizing for disturbing Louis's dinner when he noticed the plate of fish.

"I've finished. That's extra. You can have some if you want." He passed the pie tin to the young man. The English was coming more easily now; he was beginning to think in it. "Maybe you'd like some coffee to wash it down."

"I'd like that, yes."

"I'll get some fresh water."

"I can do that."

"That's okay. You take it easy."

While Starkmann sat eating, grateful for the extra few minutes to gather his courage and plan what he would say, Louis shuffled down to the lake shore, the coffee pot swinging in his hand. He, too, wanted a reprieve, a moment or two alone to think about this astonishing visit. That the young man had been sent was without question, but for what reason—that, a mystery. He was accustomed to surprise encounters, but only in visions. Kneeling to fill the pot, he looked at the birches, trunks whiter in the moonlight than in the sun, and briefly considered the possibility that he was experiencing another vision. Perhaps he was speaking to his grandson, whose spirit had entered another body, someone he would recognize. The possibility appealed to him, but his inner voice told him it wasn't true. There is some other reason for this happening, he thought, climbing the trail back to camp. I'll talk to him and listen to him, and let him declare his purpose. Let the mystery reveal itself, and if it doesn't, then let it remain a mystery.

He hung the pot over the fire and, pouring coffee from a cloth sack into the strainer, carefully observed the young man's manner and appearance. He had not changed greatly, the difference between man and boy a subtle one: the same pale skin, the same bright-yellow hair, the same blue eyes. The eyes were wary, like a deer's when it senses danger. Maybe they had been that way before. Louis could not recall. His memories of the young man were indistinct.

"Guess you ain't hungry," he said, glancing at the fish, hardly touched.

"I'm camped just down the lake. Had something to eat before I saw your fire."

He sat on the log, facing the young man, who was sitting on the ground with folded legs, hands in his lap. A memory coming to him, Louis mentioned that the young man bore a resemblance to his father, the tall preacher, whom Louis had liked.

"Yeah, I've been told I look a lot like him."

"How is he?"

"He died last spring." Starkmann paused, giving Louis time to offer his sympathies; but the old man said nothing, stirring the coals with a stick.

"A stroke killed him. He was in the hospital a few days, in a coma, before he died."

"Well, we all come to it. I ain't far from it myself."

It was not what Louis had wanted to say. He'd heard the sadness in the young man's voice; but he had lived alone for so long and it had been so long since he'd spoken English at length that he'd been unable to hunt down the words to express compassion properly.

"I guess we do, but I didn't come all this way to talk about my father."

An agitation came over Starkmann, who stood and walked to the edge of the camp as if he were going to leave, then turned around and walked back, remaining on his feet.

"I told you it was important to me that I talk to you today. I suppose you've guessed why."

"I try not to guess things. I try to know things."

"Didn't George ever write and tell you that we were together overseas?"

"I'm not sure he did."

"I would have thought he'd told you."

"Maybe he did and I forgot," Louis answered, too proud to admit he hadn't been able to read his grandson's letters—five, six of them. They had been read to him, but he couldn't recall any mention that the young man had been with Boniface.

"Did anyone ever tell you what happened? How he died?"

"You were with him then?"

"Yes."

There was an odd, stale taste in Starkmann's mouth.

"A soldier told me. He came to the train station in Marquette with Boniface's body. Had some sort of letter with him from the army. He told me Boniface got killed in an accident. Somethin' about bombs fallin' in the wrong place."

"That's all?"

"That was about it. There's more to it?"

"Well, yes. It's what I've come to tell you about. I should have told you a long time ago, I . . . "

Louis watched him walk once more to where the circle of firelight bordered the forest's blackness, then turn again and stand, speaking to him across the distance.

"I've been living up here almost since I got out of the army. I should have seen you, but . . . well, there were a lot of reasons why I didn't. They're not important now."

Louis listened, puzzled by the young man's disturbed manner, aware of a disturbance within himself. He felt that he was dividing into two persons, each with its own name; there was Louis, conversing in English with the young man, and Wawiekumig, thinking in the old tongue, pursuing the meaning of the mystery—why on this day when he had attempted to make contact with his grandson, there should appear out of nowhere his grandson's friend. Boniface's spirit did not occupy the young man's body, but perhaps Boniface was attempting to speak *through* him. Let him talk, the inner voice that spoke to Wawiekumig said. You listen, but listen carefully.

He summoned the young man to join him in a cup of coffee.

Starkmann moved back to the fire and, perplexed by Louis's apparent impassiveness, waited while he filled two metal mugs with a quivering hand. The old man's skin was like earth that had suffered drought.

"It was important for me to talk to you today because he died today," Starkmann said, under the impression that the old man might be failing and in need of a reminder. "Fourteen years ago today."

"I know that. The soldier told me the day. That's how come I'm out here. I come out here every year this day of the month."

"I don't think I understand," Starkmann said, recalling what Bonny George had told him long ago about his grandfather's dual personality. And indeed, Louis seemed very different tonight from the man Starkmann remembered. He was opaque, enigmatic, somehow more "Indian."

"And you wouldn't understand if I told you. What is it you've got to say?"

"Are you interested in hearing it?" Starkmann asked, using Louis's seeming lack of curiosity as an excuse to stall.

"He was my grandson. My grandson and my son both."

A vibration started in Starkmann's chest: Grandson and son; it was as if he were responsible for two deaths.

"The soldier, did he mention anything about a mistake?"

"He said somethin' about these bombs fallin' in the wrong place."

"They did. It was a mistake." Starkmann, the vibration now a hammering, forced himself to look directly into Louis's eyes. They were as dark as gun barrels. "It was a mistake I made. The accident was my fault. That's what I've come to tell you."

Without taking a breath, afraid he would go mute if he paused for a fraction of a second, the story he'd secreted for so long rushed out of him, a torrent of words, his voice stumbling occasionally, his eyes darting, his fists opening and closing as if squeezing invisible rubber balls. As he spoke, he looked for a change in Louis's face, but it remained as immobile as a carving. Nor did the old man make a sound or gesture when he'd finished, and this indifference or stoicism, whatever it was, caused a shroud of depression to drop over Starkmann. Louis's eerie calm in the face of what he'd just been told blocked the feeling of relief he'd hoped his confession would bring. He might as well have unburdened himself to the lake, to the woods, or to the cold dead moon.

Possibly he had not made himself clear. His story had been full of military jargon—air strikes, map coordinates, medevacs—terms with which the old man would be unfamiliar. This prompted him to ask if Louis had understood everything.

"Most of it."

It was Wawiekumig's Louis-half that spoke aloud. The inner voice of his other half spoke silently, telling him that more important than understanding the story was the perception that the one telling it was out of harmony with himself. The inner voice and experience told him this. In the past, he had healed too many uncentered people not to recognize the outpouring of words, the flitting eyes, the nervous gestures of the hands as signs of an affliction spiritual in nature. So a new puzzle to contemplate: what was the cause of his disharmony? If the young man were one of his own, Wawiekumig would know the cause to be sorcery, or perhaps a trickster that had entered the young man and tampered with his balance. But the young man was white, and while whites had their own diseases of the soul, they were not subject to the influence of sorcerers or tricksters.

"What parts didn't you understand?" he heard the young man ask.

"A few things. They ain't important. I got the important parts."

"I blamed myself for what happened. I still do," Starkmann said, resentful that he had to explain the obvious. "I haven't been able to forgive myself, and I think I haven't because I needed to hear it from you."

Wawiekumig made no reply. He knew the word, but the concept was alien to him.

"Louis, do you know how hard this is for me? I'm asking for . . . Why are you making it harder by making me spell everything out?"

"You know, we never had that word. *Forgive.*"

"What do you mean?"

"We never had that word in our language."

"What're you saying? That you people never forgave anybody?"

"No, I'm not exactly saying that."

"Then what are you saying?"

"I'm saying that we never had that word because we never needed it. Just like we didn't have jails and policemen because we didn't need them." His mind ran through the country of unfamiliar language, chasing the right words, but, unable to find them, he fell silent, aware of how much better he could have explained this in his own tongue.

"That doesn't make any sense to me," Starkmann said, a resentment rising in him. "You know, I'm not sure you've heard a word I've said. I haven't forgotten what happened. I can't forget. I've dreamed about it. I see that happening over and over again. Do you know what that's been like?"

He stood up and paced off a short way, determined to force some kind of reaction out of the old man. He hadn't gone through all this effort just to receive a lesson in native folk wisdom.

"I've blamed myself. I wonder if you've got any idea what that's been like. It's driven me . . . I was in a hospital before I came here. Did you know that? No. How could you? All right. Now you do. A mental hospital. Do you know what that is, or do I have to spell that out too?"

"I know what it is," Wawiekumig replied calmly, recognizing the young man's outburst as another sign of imbalance.

"Does that make any difference to you? Has anything I've said made any difference to you? Why are you just sitting there? Do you care about the way he died?"

"For a long time I was . . ." His tongue stopped for a moment; he could not think of the English for *mourning.* "For a long time I was sad about what happened, if that's what you mean. A lot sadder than you could be. He was my grandson and my son."

"And he was more than just a friend to me. I loved him."

"A son and grandson to me, a friend and a brother to you."

"And I loved him," Starkmann said, his eyes filling from both sorrow and frustration. "Can you understand *that*? I loved him."

Yes, Wawiekumig thought, I understand your love, as I understand your tears to be like mine, blood of a wound not healed. I understand also that you hold yourself responsible. Possibly this self-reproach, joining with your sadness, has put you out of harmony.

He stirred the fire, rolling over one of the logs so that the flame entrapped beneath spurted up. As its heat touched his face, *ahmunisoowin* showed him the Creator's purpose in sending this young man, his grandson's brother-friend. The revelation came in a single instant, flaring up like the flame hidden under the log, a revelation that solved one mystery and created another. The young man had been sent here to his sacred place to be healed; but how could he, Wawiekumig, cure him? His medicine was his religion, his religion his medicine; it would not work if the afflicted did not believe it could. How to instill such faith in one not born into it, in one who, like Madeline and Clement, would probably mock his medicine as superstition? Nevertheless, he had to try something. A suffering human being had been sent to him, and he, a *Mide* brother, could not turn his back.

"Sit down," he said to the young man, who, drying his eyes, did not move.

"Sit down. I want to talk."

Starkmann scuffed the ground, embarrassed by his tears.

"I'll talk. You listen. Sit down and calm down."

The strength in the voice took Starkmann unawares. It possessed his father's authority but lacked his father's cold peremptoriness, compelling without commanding.

"Talk about what?" he asked, composing himself.

"There's a couple things you said I don't understand. You said you blame yourself. I don't understand that. Come on and sit down."

Starkmann, recalling what the woman in the store had said about Louis, took his seat in front of the fire.

"I just got through explaining all that. I panicked and he got killed. For no damned reason."

"Nothin' happens without a reason."

"Well, that did. I've tried to think of one. Goddammit, I've tried."

"He got killed because of somethin' I done."

"*What?*"

"My grandson got killed because of somethin' I done. It wasn't no accident. You might say it was somethin' that had to happen."

Starkmann gazed at the face, its creases like painted black lines in the fluttering light.

"Louis, how old are you?"

The old man's expression changed for the first time, his lips bending into a thin smile that formed wrinkles like cat's whiskers at the corner of his mouth.

"I'm all right up here, if that's what you mean," he answered, pointing to his temple.

"No, no. I didn't mean that. I . . ." Starkmann flushed. That was precisely what he'd meant. "I was trying to say that you were here, ten thousand miles away. What could you have done?"

"It was somethin' I done a long time ago. So if anybody's to blame, I am. You might think you are, but I know I am."

"You know it?" Starkmann asked, humoring Louis as he'd humored Gunny in the hospital.

"There's things you know that I don't and things I know that you don't. I might sound like some ignorant old blanket-ass to you, but I ain't."

Starkmann blushed again. "I didn't say that, Louis. You must see why what you're telling me doesn't make any sense."

"You ain't ready to understand, that's why. There's things I'd have to teach you first."

"All right. Why don't you start?"

"You ain't even ready to be taught yet. So for right now, you just got to take my word for it. You ain't the one to blame. I am."

Wawiekumig ceased talking for a moment to listen to his inner voice. *You are not reaching him. You cannot reach him. He sits within an arm's length of you, but there is a barrier between you that cannot be broken through or climbed over, the barrier that has always divided your people from his, your way of understanding the world is as strange to him as his way is to you. You have the medicine, but you don't have the language.*

Starkmann was also silent, too bemused to say anything. He felt cheated and a little ridiculous. The dramatic meeting he'd hoped for had turned into a farce; he had tramped all day through a wilderness only to find a deluded, senile old man. The difference between expectation and reality reminded him of his first assault, when, terrified yet in some way looking forward to the crisis of battle, he had leaped off the helicopter, yelling and firing his rifle at—nothing. No enemy, no fiery combat, only empty, silent jungle, while the veterans in the platoon laughed at his theatrical charge.

He looked into the fire and tried to think of some logical explanation for Louis's absurd assertion. He kept coming back to senescence, even though the old man showed none of the usual symptoms, the rambling speech, the vacant stare. He thought and thought, until an old memory spontaneously bobbed to the surface of his mind, a memory that made him jump up in excitement.

"My God," he said, smiling into the seamed face of the Indian, who, he now realized, was anything but senile.

"What is it?"

"I just remembered something. Why did you think I wouldn't understand?"

"What was it you remembered?"

"When George was drafted he wrote to me that he was thinking about going to Canada."

"That's right. He wanted to go to Canada."

"He told me he talked to you about it. He wasn't sure what to do, so he talked to you. That's what I just remembered."

Wawiekumig gave a nod, an inner light flooding him, his divided selves coming together: Louis, who understood the white way of thinking, giving Wawiekumig the language with which he could break through the barrier.

"And you told him not to," the young man said.

"That's right. I did. That was the advice I gave him. That was the thing I done a long time ago."

"Why didn't you think I'd understand that?"

"Because there was more to it than that, things you wouldn't understand. They ain't important right now."

Wawiekumig leaned forward, as Red Sky used to do when he had something especially significant to say. "What's important is that you see that he'd still be alive, up in Canada, if it wasn't for me. You got nothin' to blame yourself for. Nothin' at all."

Starkmann sat down and leaned back, palms flat on the earth. At last he'd heard, in somewhat different words than expected, the pardon he'd been seeking; but he did not feel pardoned, and he knew why. Louis appeared to have found the secret. What accounted for his serenity? Was it a mask, or genuine? Was it the apathy of old age, or the self-possessed calm of a man who had learned to come to terms with his fatal mistakes?

"A little while ago," Starkmann said, "you told me there are things you know that I don't."

"A lot more'n you realize."

"You sound like you've forgiven yourself. How?"

"I told you we never had that word."

"Christ. You just told me he'd be alive if it hadn't been for you. He was your grandson. How the hell have you been able to live with yourself? That's one thing I'd like to know."

Wawiekumig perceived the true meaning of this question, but he did not answer quickly, taking time to stalk the right words.

"No," he replied when he thought he had trapped them. "That isn't what you want to know."

"Yes . . . yes, it is."

"What you want to know is how to live with yourself."

Starkmann could only stare, more than impressed by the old man's perceptiveness.

"How to live with yourself. How to live, period. That's what everybody wants to know."

Yes, Starkmann thought, yes. All my questions distill into that one, yes. "For a long time I . . . because of what happened . . . I was ashamed. I know this sounds a little crazy, but for a long time I was ashamed—to—be—alive."

Wawiekumig did think it sounded crazy, but a madness of the spirit, not the mind.

"Listen and I'll tell you one of the things I know." Wawiekumig leaned forward again, his face above the glowing coals. "I know that life is a gift. I know that life should be a song and a prayer. I was taught that. It's nothin' to be ashamed of, and you got nothin' to be ashamed of. There's only one reason why you should be, and that's because you want to be. And the only reason I can think of for a man to do that is because there's somethin' makin' him want to."

"What? What? If you know so much, tell me what."

"Well, we've got our way of lookin' at things." Louis gave a gap-toothed grin. "Tricksters, we call them. Spirits that get into a man and fool around with his reasoning. I don't expect you'd believe that. Superstition, you'd call it. There were people in my own family called it that."

That was, in fact, Starkmann's opinion, though he thought that Louis, superstitious or not, had proved no less insightful than Eckhardt. The observation that he held himself responsible because he wanted to was the same as the one the psychologist had made the other day in somewhat different language. It sounded more profound on the old man's untutored lips, bearing the weight of a wisdom learned through hard experience, rather than the glibness of something plucked out of a textbook. But it wasn't in reality any more profound.

It struck Starkmann then that he had come full circle, by an odd path. Whether speaking to a Ph.D. or an unlettered Indian, he sought the answer to the same question and was in both instances forced to look into himself, the only source of answers, and of forgiveness.

32

They slept in the wigwam, Starkmann accepting Louis's invitation to spend the night. Reed mats covered the dirt floor, and the musty darkness smelled of woodsmoke and unwashed wool blankets; but, tired from his long walk, emotionally drained, he slept one of the soundest sleeps of his life.

Wawiekumig dreamed.

In the dream, magizi clutched him and the young man in its talons, its mighty wings carrying them beyond the crack between night and day to a far place neither man recognized, a beautiful forest of towering cedars. There, Wawiekumig built a small fire, and the smoke of the cedar wreathed the young man, his grandson's brother-friend. He brushed his head with an eagle feather four times, singing a healing song. He sang in the ancient tongue, but the young man understood every word. He understood everything: the significance of the purifying cedar, of the eagle feather, each strand representing what was beautiful in the world, migizi's feather, the instrument for curing diseases of mind and spirit. The young man understood this; there were no barriers of language or concept in the beautiful forest. When his song was done, Wawiekumig took his pindgigossan and shot a megis shell into the young man, who fell. While he lay as one dead, Wawiekumig offered a prayer to the manitos: *I have cleansed him with the eagle feather and with cedar. Let him sleep nights and no longer reproach himself. Let him come back to himself, let him come home. Show him how to get through life as a man. It is I, Wawiekumig, who asks this, asks this.* Then he raised his pindgigossan and shot the young man with life-restoring power. The young man sprang to his feet, in outward appearance the same, but not as he had been before. Then migizi took them in its talons once again, and they soared down the winds of heaven back to earth.

So vivid was this dream that Wawiekumig, upon awakening from it well before dawn, knew it had not been a dream of sleep but a medicine vision. It had actually happened, the event occurring in the world of manitos. In sleep their spirits had been taken there, and there Wawiekumig had once again, perhaps for the last time in his life, practiced his ancient arts and healed human suffering. For that he was grateful, and whispered a thanksgiving. Then he wrapped himself tightly in his blanket and fell back asleep, happier than he could remember.

Starkmann was up before sunrise, groggy but refreshed by his deathlike sleep. Outside, the predawn gray was intensified by the dense mists rising off the lake and the wet earth. He emptied the dregs of the coffeepot and went down to the shore to draw fresh water. The fog was so thick that he found the lake by stepping into it. The island, with its straight pines, showed through the mist as a ghost sailing-ship. An invisible loon giggled. *Christ's cross has saved us from the pagan circle*—the phrase from Saint Augustine came back to him as he returned to camp and stoked the fire. But on this shrouded morning in the unpeopled Hurons, with firs and birches looming eerily in the smoky woods, he felt the pagan circle closing around the Christian cross, so that the idea that trickster-spirits had entered him, compelling him to condemn himself unreasonably, did not seem like so much absurd folklore.

He lay down, resting against the log as he waited for the water to boil. The peacefulness of the camp slipped into him, the peacefulness he remembered feeling the last time he had been here, years ago. The rounded wigwam and sweat-lodge, the well-swept circle of cleared ground, and the meticulously stacked firewood imparted a sense of order without an unnatural rigidity. This place was separate from the woods, yet as much a part of it as the trees. It was imbued with Louis's tranquillity—or was he with its? Either way, Starkmann felt at home, which was not so strange; he and Louis, for all their other differences, had a bond, one beyond their shared loss. Louis, like all his people, had been made a stranger in his own country, and something similar had happened to Starkmann. He saw himself as a kind of halfbreed: his hair and skin were pale, but the war had made him an outsider in the land of his birth. The war had reddened his heart.

But now the time for bitterness had ended. Life was a gift, a song, a prayer. He thrilled to those words, Louis's gift to him, one that Eckhardt, with all his learning, could not have bestowed. *Life*.

The smell of brewing coffee stirred his appetite. Not wishing to disturb Louis by rummaging for his food stores, if he kept any in the wigwam, Starkmann inched his way along the cloaked trail toward his own camp. Halfway there, he startled a buck and a doe, watering in the lake. Rather, they startled him. He must have been moving very quietly because he almost bumped into the male before he saw it raise its head, antlers like lightning bolts. It whoofed, then sprang off with the doe, vanishing in two quick leaps. *Life*. June had called him back to it; she had returned the gift he'd been on the verge of casting away—no, exchanging. He'd thought, in his madness, his life had to be bartered for forgiveness. But forgiveness was also a gift and he was the giver. Full circle again. How did you do it? Through what ceremonies and rituals did you achieve self-absolution? How do you live? Full circle.

At his camp, he gave his mind a rest, busying himself with remaking his pack. He left out a packet of soup, with which he would make breakfast for Louis and himself. He owed the old man some small gesture of thanks for his hospitality, his ear, and for the present of those beautiful words.

When he returned, he found the Indian squatting before the fire, shawled in a blanket, a steaming mug in his hands.

"There you are," he said. "Where'd you go off to? You could get lost in a fog like this."

"I got my gear together." Starkmann dropped his pack. "Thought I'd make a little soup for breakfast."

"Out of what? That?" Louis asked, pointing to the foil packet.

"It tastes like the real thing. Freeze-dried stuff."

"I've hardly eaten in four days. Need more'n soup. How does grouse sound to you?"

"Fine. Where do we get the grouse? This doesn't look like bird country."

"There's a thorn-apple meadow not far from here. Grouse'll be there dryin' themselves soon as this fog lifts."

"I'll get them for you," Starkmann volunteered. "The gun inside?"

"Don't need a gun. Go on out and cut me five, six birch sticks. Three feet long, four maybe."

"You're going to catch grouse with sticks?"

"Go cut 'em now."

As he listened to the young man hacking at the branches, Wawiekumig savored coffee and the effect his medicine had brought about. The young man's physical appearance no different, but spiritual change was manifest to those with the vision to see it.

He rose and brought his rucksack and medicine-bundle out from the wigwam, taking from the first several lengths of basswood twine, from the second some tobacco and powdered aster. He tied the twine into nooses, and tamped the aster and tobacco into his pipe.

"What's that?" the young man asked, returning with the sticks.

"A pipe."

"No. That fur bag."

"It's called a pindgigossan," Wawiekumig replied, knotting the nooses to the sticks.

"Pind . . . ?"

"Pindgigossan. Pind-gig-o-ssan. It means medicine-bundle in English. It's my religion."

He stood, the snares in one hand, the pipe with the game-attracting mixture in the other, and walked off, leaving Starkmann to wonder how an animal hide could be a religion.

The fog had risen like a stage curtain and the sun was glinting off the lake when Louis returned, walking with a bowlegged, old man's gait, a brace of grouse dangling from his belt.

"I'll be damned," Starkmann said admiringly. "How'd you pull that off?"

"Might show you some time."

They fell to gutting and skinning the birds, then spit and roasted them. Starkmann ate like a wolf. He had not realized how hungry he was until he'd smelled the meat.

Wawiekumig observed with pleasure the way the young man feasted, spiritual cure now manifesting itself in a physical manner. He had thought about his dream while lying in the meadow, his reflections opening the door to a new perception, one that pleased him greatly. He'd seen that the Creator had sent the young man for two reasons, but could he make the young man see this also?

After they'd finished eating, they sat in the sun, washing down the meal with more coffee. Wawiekumig decided to approach the subject of his insight indirectly.

"What do you think you'll do now?" he asked.

"There's a spot on the Windigo River, a big rapids downstream of a beaver dam. Do you know it?"

"Sure. Big rainbows there in the spring."

"I'd like to go there, but I'm not sure I can find it."

"It's a four-, five-hour walk from here. Head a little west of north. In four, five hours, you'll come to a ridge—"

"With white pine on it," Starkmann cut in, remembering. "Big trees."

"The last of 'em. Go on up that ridge, hey, then head down the west side, and you'll see it. The rapids come through a gorge."

"That's it."

"When do you suppose you'll be goin'?"

"This morning."

"And after that? You don't mind my askin'.."

Starkmann glanced at Louis, hair as white as a gull's wing, then looked off toward the lake, blue under an amethyst autumn sky. He hadn't given much consideration to what he would do.

"I don't know exactly. See my wife and kids, I suppose."

"You got a family?"

"Yes. You're getting at something, Louis. What is it—you don't mind *my* asking?"

"Remember when you and Boniface was kids, and we used to fish together? You and him, me and your father?"

"Sure. Those were good times."

"Better'n the ones that come after." He cracked a grouse bone with his fingers and sucked out the marrow. "I thought maybe you and me might try that again. Salmon should be startin' up some of the rivers any day now."

"Just the two of us, you mean?" Starkmann asked, beginning to catch the old man's drift.

"That's right. You and me, nobody else. Anytime you want."

Now Starkmann understood fully, a quiet thrill passing through him.

"I know some good places. There's a lot of things I know you don't," the old man repeated.

"Like how to snare grouse."

"Things like that."

"Like life is a gift."

"Things like that too. Well, you know where my place is. You can stop by anytime you want, as many times as you want. What do you think of that idea?"

"A lot, Louis," Starkmann said, feeling something moving through him, an emotion he could not name, powerful and resistless, like a river. He clasped the old man's hand. "I think a lot of it."

*   *   *

He climbed through the white pines, their high branches, quilled like giant arrows, slivering the sun. He climbed steadily, with sure steps, his feet moving quietly in rhythm with the forest's timeless music, a music unheard by the ear. When he reached the top, he stopped to catch his breath, sitting on one of the lichen-covered granite slabs that looked like bloodstained altars. Far below, to the west, a bend of the Windigo showed through the trees. Northward, the hills rose and fell toward Superior, the reddening hardwoods on the pine ridges like islands of fire in green seas, the pines on the hardwood ridges like green islands in seas of fire, and the big lake away off, its cold eye staring skyward out of the face of the wilderness.

There was no need to chase memories. They were here, waiting for him, imbedded in the rocks, the earth, the trees. They brought him no grief, only a mild melancholy, a kind of nostalgia that was easy to bear. Rather than sad, he was grateful for having found Louis, and the new gift of Louis's kinship. They'd adopted each other, each finding in the other what each had lost.

He reshouldered his pack and headed down the ridge to the rapids. When he reached them, he found them a trickle compared to the way they had been when he'd first seen them, crashing with irresistible force. The Windigo here was as low as it was downstream, its old depth marked by a line six feet up the sides of the gorge. The wind-fallen hemlock from which Bonny George had leaped to his rescue was gone, probably swept away in a spring flood. Otherwise, nothing had changed. The turtle-backed beaver lodges still stood above the rapids, and the same birch woods whitened the far side of the river.

Starkmann stripped and cautiously stepped into the chill water. He waited a few moments, splashing his arms and chest to lessen the shock he would feel when he dove in. Then he waded out, past his knees, up to his hips. The channel, considerably shallowed but still over his head, was a few feet farther out. He inched toward it, skin tightening, testicles shriveling. The pebbly bottom crumbled beneath him. He rose on tiptoe and launched himself into the current, allowing it to carry him downstream. He floated calmly, submitting himself to the river, not fighting it, the river buoying him up in exchange for his surrender. He had planned this immersion days ago, without completely understanding why. Now he did.

He dove, opening his eyes to the amber swirl of sand, the water at the channel's bottom clamping over his temples, a painful but mind-clearing cold. He surfaced with a quick kick, dove again, his body arching, and surfaced once more, feeling as within his element as an otter or beaver. Turning, he swam upstream, then let himself go into an eddy, which carried him into the shallows. He got to his feet, waded to the shore, and climbed the bank into the birch woods where, more than fourteen years before, he'd made the decision that had changed his life.

He stood looking at his reflection in the smooth backwater. and saw that the decision had not been made purely out of love and loyalty for his friend, but also out of hatred for his father. That insight was as plain as his own image, glimmering in the water, though he was mystified by how he had obtained it. Logic had had nothing to do with it.

Hatred, yes, that was apparent. His enlistment had been more than a liberating apostasy; it had been an act of vengeance as well, a form of bridge-burning. He'd gone to war seeking an experience so awful there could be no coming back from it, one that would cut him off entirely from Lucius. He'd wanted to return, a creature incapable of loving him or being loved by him, a creature beyond forgiving and forgiveness, scorched and scarred by war. And so he had, in his own mind. He'd came back a stranger and an exile, but his banishment had been largely self-imposed.

Insight leading to insight, he saw, too, that the war had denied him the experience he'd sought up until that morning he'd watched napalm boiling like a solar storm while men burning to death screamed in the jungle, Bonny George's screams among that infernal chorus. And he'd enjoyed it, for it is always gratifying to find what you've been looking for; he'd enjoyed it deep, deep within himself, so deep he'd not been aware of his pleasure. But his conscience had been aware, and the secret delight in the horror that had taken his friend's life had been the source of the guilt that had racked him with nightmares and had almost led him to take his own life.

That was what Eckhardt had meant by saying our experiences are what we make of them: His own hidden desire had transformed what had been, after all, a common misfortune of war into an apocalyptic vision of chaos, and himself into a murderer.

If he could do that to himself, then surely he could forgive himself. No rites or ceremonies had been necessary for the one; neither were they necessary for the other. He kneeled down and, gazing at his reflection, said out loud:

"I forgive you."

His clemency extending outward, he shut his eyes, picturing Lucius, and repeated:

"I forgive you."

That was how you did it. It was that absurdly simple. You forgave by forgiving.

He waded back into the river and swam to the other side, where he removed his uniform from his pack and filled the pockets with stones. The tarnished Purple Heart and campaign decorations were still pinned to the shirt. This would not be easy, for those badges had no small value to him, but this was one ceremony he had to perform. He stood by the bank and tossed the uniform into the deepest part of the channel. The shirt, its back billowing and arms spreading, briefly assumed the appearance of a drowned man's torso. Starkmann watched it float briefly, then twirl in an eddy and sink, his weightless heart rising.

Never had the air smelled so good, nor seemed so clear, and the trees appeared to be holding out their arms in welcome. He looked at the world around him as if it had just been created, though he knew it was old and worn, full of death and pain; yet it appeared new to him because he saw it through new eyes, and so it was also full of life, renewal, and hope.

"I forgive you," he repeated, as unashamed of his nakedness as he was of his joy in the life he was just beginning. Then he shouted the dispensation at the top of his lungs, the forests picking up his jubilant cry and carrying it through their blue depths, as if they, too, celebrated his repatriation.

When the echoes died away, he dressed, hoisted his pack, and started walking, though not toward home; he was already there, returned to himself. Home, the place he had not seen or been these many years. *Home.*